"I'M GOING TO PURSUE YOU, VIVECA LANCASTER, IN WAYS YOU'VE NEVER BEEN PURSUED BEFORE . . . "

Vivid blinked. "Why?"

"Because each and every time I'm around you, the only thing I want to do is take you somewhere and make love to you until they hear you screaming in Kalamazoo."

She swayed, slightly dizzy from his confession. "I need time to think about this."

"I'll give you time and I'll go slow. However, I mean to have you, Lancaster, and whenever I find you alone, I'm going to do my best to help you make up your mind."

"What exactly does that mean?"

"Exactly this . . . "

Nate bent his head and brushed his lips across hers, and Vivid didn't even try to resist. She wanted his kisses . . .

FRIENDS of
The Santa Maria

Public Library
Funded by the Friends of the Santa Maria Public Library

Other **AVON ROMANCES**

CONQUER THE NIGHT *by Selina MacPherson*
THE HEART AND THE ROSE *by Nancy Richards-Akers*
HEART'S HONOR *by Susan Weldon*
LAKOTA PRINCESS *by Karen Kay*
MIDNIGHT LORD *by Marlene Suson*
REBELLIOUS BRIDE *by Adrienne Day*
TAKEN BY STORM *by Danelle Harmon*

Coming Soon

COURTING REBECCA *by Susan Sawyer*
DANCING AT MIDNIGHT *by Julia Quinn*

And Don't Miss These
ROMANTIC TREASURES
from Avon Books

LADY OF SUMMER *by Emma Merritt*
MY RUNAWAY HEART *by Miriam Minger*
RUNAWAY TIME *by Deborah Gordon*

Vivid

BEVERLY JENKINS

iUniverse.com, Inc.

San Jose New York Lincoln Shanghai

Vivid

Published by iUniverse.com, Inc.

For information address:
iUniverse.com, Inc.
5220 S 16th, Ste. 200
Lincoln, NE 68512
www.iuniverse.com

ISBN: 0-595-16202-9

Printed in the United States of America

Acknowledgments

These people are to be thanked for their help in bringing *Vivid* to life.

First, as always, my agent, Vivian Stephens; Christine Zika, my editor at Avon Books; Paul Beadle and Sami Buisson-Daniel at the Pennsylvania Education Association; Ann Kirschmann in Boston; a very special thanks to Ms. Theresa Taylor, Associate Archivist in the Archives and Special Collections on Women in Medicine at the Medical College of Pennsylvania. Her assistance in providing background information on the coursework and alumnae of the Woman's Medical College of Pennsylvania proved invaluable.

Thanks, too, to the Canton Public Library for providing me access to its excellent collection and for its hardworking librarians in Inter-Library Loan; Michelle Montour is also owed thanks for the word "trabrasera"; last but not least, thanks to the children who call me Mama, my parents, and Alex, for his continued love and support.

Prologue

Grayson Grove, Michigan
August 1865

Nate Grayson stood before the big bay window in his large, book-lined study watching the rain. By all rights, he should have been more concerned with the business being conducted across the room by his barrister and his wife, Cecile, but Nate preferred the rain. As he stood there, his thoughts drifted to last evening when he'd stood in much this same way . . .

He'd been in the doorway of the upstairs bedroom, indifferently watching Cecile pack. He'd not been allowed to share the room or her bed since his return from the war in June, and he'd not much cared.

When she had spotted him, she'd tossed a rose silk gown atop the bed and haughtily said, "At least try not to hate me, Nathaniel."

He responded with a bitter chuckle. "It's a bit late for that."

She strode over to the polished cherrywood wardrobe that once belonged to his grandmother Dorcas and took down another armload of gowns, which she tossed alongside the others. As she held each gown up for critical inspection, she glanced back at him and said, "Were you more worldly, you'd not hate me. Marriages end

1

everyday. At least we're not being hypocrites by pretending otherwise.''

More wordly. He'd heard her throw out that phrase so many times to describe his shortcomings, he swore the words echoed in his head while he slept. More wordly. Had he been more worldly maybe he wouldn't have cared that she came to their marriage secretly carrying another man's child. Had he been more wordly maybe he wouldn't have been bothered by the gossips whispering that she preferred other men to her husband in bed. He admittedly knew nothing about living in this more worldly world she described.

As she continued her packing, he realized he had never loved her, not really. And he never should have married her. He'd been an eighteen-year-old Michigan farmboy, and she the pampered only daughter of one of Philadelphia's best known abolitionist ministers. They'd grown up in entirely different worlds; worlds that would ultimately pit his beliefs and values against hers. Unfortunately, at the time he hadn't known that. When he first met Cecile Gould on a visit to Philadelphia in the spring of 1862, he thought a more beautiful and accomplished woman had never been born. He fell in love with the way she moved, the way she laughed, the way she smelled. She was a brightly gowned butterfly compared to the practical, everyday women he'd grown up around, and he'd been blinded. Despite having known Cecile only seven days, he'd proposed marriage rather than return to Michigan without her, and she'd accepted with tears in her beautiful brown eyes. Only later did he learn that her tears sprang from relief, not joy. She'd married him to give a name to her lover's child, and when she lost that child a few months after their marriage, she began taking new lovers.

She paused packing to ask, ''Is there a reason you're here? I'd prefer to do this without you hovering over my shoulder.''

"A simple question, Cecile. Did you ever love me?"

She had the decency to avoid his eyes as she answered, "Truthfully, Nathaniel? No. I never did."

The answer did not surprise him, nor did it cause new pain. Any feelings he'd ever had for her had turned to ash long ago.

Then she raised her beautiful eyes to his and said, "Nathaniel, you're a decent, handsome man, but you need a woman more like yourself. I detest this place. I detest the mosquitoes. I detest the mud. I detest living in the middle of nowhere without anything to do or anyplace to go. I need the theater, and dinner parties, and gaiety. Not chickens and trees."

He didn't bother to reply. She'd never understood how much this land meant to the people here. To her way of thinking, land had no value if it didn't sit beneath a fancy house. During the first months of their marriage, he'd hoped she would one day come to appreciate the raw vitality and potential of Michigan, but that was not to be.

"So you only married me for what, my name?"

"Frankly? Yes. I was desperate, and at the time you were my salvation, but I don't need saving anymore."

"What will you tell your father?" he asked her then. The Reverend Gould would demand an explanation when he saw the decree dissolving the marriage.

"That you changed after the war and we no longer suited."

Nate supposed the lie was close enough to the truth— the war had changed him. The haunting sounds of men screaming as they died still echoed inside him, especially at night. If he closed his eyes, he could see the dark clouds of cannon fire, smell the gagging stench of burned flesh and powder in the air. The horrifying memories of Fort Pillow had come home with him, and he could not shake them. "And your lovers, what will you tell your father about them?"

She stopped packing, unable to mask the surprise on her face. The Nate Grayson who'd marched off to fight for Mr. Lincoln in 1863 would never have broached such a subject. Even when confronted with her adulterous behavior, he had blindly set aside his doubts, knowing that of all the men Cecile could have married, she'd said yes only to him, Nate Grayson, an eighteen-year-old farmboy.

But he was older now, in age and in spirit.

Nate asked her again about her father and her lovers.

"There is no need for my father to know anything other than what I tell him," Cecile remarked sharply. She swept all the tiny bottles holding her perfumes and cosmetics atop the dressing table into a large leather valise. "If the country can start anew, Nathaniel, so can I."

"I wouldn't dream of stopping you," he replied, his eyes cold.

She paused and stared as if that, too, had been unexpected. "Surely, Cecile, you didn't think I would care that you're leaving, not after all you've done?"

She laughed, a forced, fake sound. "No, Nathaniel. Although I wasn't really certain you'd actually agree to the decree, considering how provincial you farm people are about things like this."

"Every man expects his wife to be faithful, Cecile, provincial or not."

"Well, next time, choose a nice provincial girl. Maybe she'll be more appreciative of that long drawn-out rutting you seem to enjoy."

The barb hurt, just as she'd intended. He bore it, though, because she would be out of his life soon, taking the hurt with her.

He left the room, and Cecile, intent upon packing her many pairs of shoes, didn't even look up.

*   *   *

The soft voice of Nate's barrister interrupted his musings and brought him back to the matters at hand.

"Nate, I need your signature. I've worked up some figures, if you'd care to review them."

Nate didn't move. "Give her whatever she wants, as long as it doesn't involve Grayson land or property."

"I'll still need your signature," the barrister, John Freeman, replied.

Nate walked over to the desk and took the documents from Freeman's hand. "Where do I sign?"

Freeman cautioned, "You should review the figures, Nate—"

Nate looked down at the man and repeated, "Where do I sign, Freeman?"

Freeman pointed to the spaces with a finger.

Nate affixed his name in the three places indicated, then tossed the papers onto the desk. He turned his eyes on his faithless wife, "You'll be leaving soon, I hope?"

"Not soon enough, Nathaniel. I can't wait to put this backwater behind me," she replied coolly.

Nate wondered again how in the world he could have ever been in love with her.

Freeman looked between the two of them, then hastily gathered up his papers to leave. "I'll file the decree as soon as possible. Good luck to you, Mrs. Grayson. Nate. I'll see myself out."

Freeman's exit left the two of them alone, a risky situation considering Nate's strong urge to choke her. He'd never put his hands on a woman in anger, and to keep himself from temptation, he went back over to the window and concentrated on the drizzle rolling down the pane like tears. A few moments later, he heard her rise and leave the room. He didn't move.

She left his life two hours later.

Watching the buggy drive her away, Nate swore he'd never love again.

Chapter 1

Ogallala, Nebraska
May 1876

Dr. Viveca Lancaster, affectionately called Vivid by family and friends, glanced up from the medical journal she had been reading, when the blue-coated conductor entered the car. His appearance drew a passing interest from the other nine passengers, who quickly drifted back to their books and conversations as he came down the aisle. But Vivid continued to watch him. He probably wasn't much of a poker player, she noted offhandedly. His nervous eyes and the uncertainty sketched on his face told her what he was about. She almost felt sorry for him—almost. After all, he'd been polite since her boarding. However, there would be nothing polite about the insult he'd come to deliver.

"Uh, ma'am?"

Vivid put aside the *Lancet* medical journal and looked up into his young face. "Yes."

"Um, I'm going to have to escort you to another car. There's been complaints."

Vivid assumed the complaint had been lodged by the man across the aisle. Ever since he'd gotten on at Cheyenne, he'd been unable to mask his displeasure at the sight of her seated in the car. She glanced his way now, and he flashed her a superior smile of triumph. Vivid looked away. A majority of the passengers had boarded the Central Pacific as she had at the station in her hometown of San Franciso. At the Great Salt Lake they'd all switched to the eastbound Union Pacific. None of them had been overly polite, but none had gone so far as to take issue with her presence.

The young conductor appeared relieved now that he'd given his speech, but there was nothing for her to say in reply. She was en route to Michigan to open a practice and had journeyed as far as Nebraska without any such complaints, so in some ways she counted herself lucky. Jim Crow was a plague creeping across the nation. Many trains both local and transcontinental were refusing to seat Blacks on some runs. Vivid wanted to rail at the man across the aisle about this injustice; after all, she'd purchased her ticket just as he had, but she held back her words. She had no desire to share the same fate as the woman she'd recently read about who, after being Jim Crowed from an Iowa train, spent the night alone on the plains, snapping and unsnapping her umbrella to keep away the predators. Vivid could also hear her mother's advice in her head, reminding her to pick her battles, and this was not one Vivid could win, so instead she gathered up her bag and books from the unoccupied seat at her side.

She paid scant attention to the covert glances from the other riders or the low-toned buzz her banishing evoked. With the dignity of an ancestry that spanned three continents, she held her head high, stepped into the aisle of the moving train, and followed the conductor from the car.

He led her to a small unoccupied boxcar at the train's rear. The noise was deafening. The windows were unsecured against the elements, and as a result the smoke and cinders from the train's stack poured in freely to foul the air and cover the floor and walls with a thick coat of coal dust and black ash. There was only a narrow wooden bench built into one wall where she could sit, and she had to share that with a mound of soot.

The conductor stayed no longer than necessary. He mumbled something that sounded like "Have a pleasant trip," then hurried back to resume his duties. She watched his departure silently.

Alone now, Vivid walked over to the bench. She extracted a petticoat from her small traveling bag and blackened the snow-white garment by wiping the dust from the seat. As she sat on the hard wood with her handkerchief to her face to filter the thick smoke billowing in, she wondered how her great-great grandfather Esteban would have dealt with such treatment. He'd been of Moorish descent and had sailed with the Spanish on one of the early expeditions to the land now called California. He'd settled there and married her great-great grandmother Maria, a Spanish slave of Ethiopian ancestry. Together, they and twenty-four others with African blood were among the forty-four people from eleven families who founded the Spanish settlement of Los Angeles.

But Vivid's illustrious ancestry mattered not at all in 1876. Today she'd been bitten by Jim Crow, and even though she was one of a small but growing cadre of women able to declare themselves certified physicians, society forced her to travel under conditions even oxen would find appalling.

As the sunlight waned and shadows filled the car, Vivid began to wonder where in the ashes she could sleep. The bench she sat on was barely wide enough to hold her hips, let alone her whole body if she were to lie prone. Frustrated, she took a deep breath, refusing to give in to the tears of anger and loneliness threatening to roll down her cheeks. She was dashing away any telltale moisture when she was startled by the door opening. The conductor, looking even more uncomfortable than before, stood in the opening, and after some hesitation finally spoke. "Miss, I feel real bad about putting you back here, especially with night coming on. Why don't you come with me?"

She wondered briefly where he planned on taking her now, but didn't ask. She gathered her belongings and followed him out.

He led her to the crowded and very noisy smoking car. Inside were men seated around tables playing poker, men on the floor circled around a dice game, and others lounging on the upholstered seats with bottles of liquor and gaudily dressed fancy girls. The smoke from the cigars and pipes thickened the air. Vivid looked the room over, then smiled. For the first time since leaving San Francisco, she felt at home.

All activity and conversations stopped at their entrance. The conductor mumbled his standard "Have a comfortable trip," and backed out of the door.

"And you are?" one of the card players asked in regal tones.

Vivid saw that the high-toned voice belonged to a very well-dressed, dark-skinned man. He looked close to her father's age. His face had been ritually scarred. The exotic scarification coupled with his great height made him appear quite imposing. "I'm Dr. Viveca Lancaster," she replied.

He bowed at the waist, saying, "We are graced by your presence."

In a voice loud enough to be heard clearly by everyone in the car, he then stated, "The lady doctor is under my protection. Approach her with anything other than respect and you will die. Is that understood?"

The men were a spectrum of race and class. Not a one said a word, so Vivid assumed the gambler had been understood.

The activities resumed as he beckoned her over to his table. "Welcome, Dr. Lancaster." He then commanded,

"Someone get this young woman something to eat. Let her have a seat, boys."

At her approach, every man at the table instantly stood and offered her his chair. She smiled politely at them, then took the seat nearest her newfound protector. The man whose chair she'd taken retrieved another for himself from a table nearby and rejoined the group.

As if by magic, a plate appeared on the table before her, piled high with ham, chicken, yams, and bread. She smiled, and everyone seemed pleased as she picked up the silverware and ate.

For the balance of the evening Viveca found herself charmed by the men who'd taken her under their wing. They all went out of their way to be polite in their manner and speech, and not once did the scarred man who introduced himself as Ned Johnson find it necessary to kill anyone. He'd spent quite a few years in Michigan, Vivid found out as the talk flowed and the card game resumed. He'd escaped from his Missouri slave owner in 1846, and followed the North Star to the edge of Michigan's northern peninsula. As fate would have it, he discovered a large deposit of copper on the land he had purchased and sold the mineral-rich lode to a group of Boston capitalists for more money than he would ever need.

"So what is your life's work?" Vivid asked during a break in the poker game.

"This is my life," Ned said, smiling. The matching scars on either side of his face creased like dimples. "There is seldom Jim Crow at the poker table. Gamblers tend to judge you on your honesty, not on the color of your skin."

Vivid saw some of the other men at the table nod in agreement. One man, whose dark skin bore the true hue of his African ancestry, added, "Gamblers don't care who your daddy was as long as he didn't teach you to deal from the bottom of the deck."

That brought a round of laughs and more nods of approval. The game continued, and when Vivid asked to be dealt in, a quiet settled over their small group. "I can play," Vivid assured the men around the table, all eyeing her skeptically. "Not as well as I play billiards," she confessed, "but I won't embarrass myself or you."

Their eyes widened. Vivid, familiar with the shocked stares, assumed they would not let her join in. To convince them, she added, "Gentlemen, I have played in hell houses all over San Francisco, surely you'll give me a—"

"You play poker *and* billiards?" Ned asked, grinning. "Yes."

Ned looked to the other faces at the table, then surveyed Vivid. Finally he said, "Gentlemen, deal the lady doctor in."

They agreed to play for matchsticks out of respect for Vivid.

Ned explained, "We make our livings at cards, Dr. Lancaster. We don't wish to take advantage of you."

"I do appreciate that, Mr. Johnson," Vivid replied genuinely, then proceeded to win the next two pots.

As Vivid scraped up the cards for her turn as dealer, she smiled as Ned proclaimed with awe, "You can indeed play."

Vivid held them all spellbound as she shuffled the deck with an expertise born of long practice. That done, she slapped the deck down on the tabletop for the mandatory cut and replied, "Yes, Mr. Johnson, I can indeed."

For the remainder of the journey to Omaha, and then from Omaha to Chicago, Vivid played poker with her new gambler friends, read her medical journals, and slept as best she could on one of the lounges in the car.

When the train pulled into the Chicago station, the games and talk ended. Her small cadre of protectors had been more than kind, yet when she attempted to express her gratitude for their outstanding company, they waved it off. "You're traveling alone," one of the men said in explanation.

Another offered, "You remind me of my sister. I'd want somebody making sure she arrived safely."

The men nodded, smiling.

"It has been our privilege to serve you, madam," Ned intoned as he bent over her hand. Then added, "I don't say this to offend you, but were I thirty years younger—"

Vivid grinned. "I know all about you gamblers. A woman is secondary in your lives. Your first love will always be the cards."

Ned bowed his head as if accepting her statement, "You are as astute as you are lovely, Dr. Lancaster."

Ned and his friends escorted Vivid to the baggage car and graciously saw to the removal of her many crates. They then helped the porters transfer them all to the train bound for Michigan. When everything had been put aboard, Vivid turned to them and and once again expressed her sincere thanks.

Ned shook her hand one final time, saying, "Some of my companions will be traveling east also. I will leave you in their charge. Good luck, Dr. Lancaster."

Ned and the men who were heading for the train to St. Louis and other points south left as one. The three gamblers taking the same eastbound train as Vivid made certain she boarded safely. They left her in the care of one of the kindly porters, then removed themselves to the pleasures awaiting them in the smoking car.

The new train proved to be far more crowded than the previous one, but the mutton-chopped conductor sat people fairly and not according to race. With that worry out of the way, at least for now, Vivid removed her hat, leaned her head back on the seat, and fell asleep.

Chapter 2

Niles, Michigan
May 1876

Vivid sighed with relief when the train roared to a stop and the conductor loudly announced they had arrived in Niles, Michigan. She gathered up her bags from the seat beside her and stepped into the aisle to disembark. The thick black smoke from the train's stack billowed in through one of the car's open windows, making Vivid cough and quicken her pace to escape the foul air. Once she stepped onto the platform, she wanted to put a fair amount of distance between herself and the train; she was only slightly rumpled after the long journey from Chicago and had no desire to have her appearance destroyed by the coal dust and burning embers belching like brimstone from the stack. She'd already had to sacrifice a favorite jacket to cinder holes at the depot in Virginia City.

Vivid spent the next few moments supervising the porters unloading her crates and trunks; she had them stack everything against the weathered wood wall of the depot. When they were done, she fished in her handbag for a tip, but the older of the two men declined.

"Put your money away, Dr. Lancaster. Having your smiling face on the ride from Chicago is tip enough."

Vivid smiled her thanks and put the coin back into her bag. She'd spent most of her life among people who

provided service for others, and she knew a genuine refusal when she heard one. She thanked the porters again
and watched them hurry away.

The train blew a shrill warning to announce its im-
minent departure. She heard someone calling her name
over the roar and turned to see some of the gamblers
smiling and waving from the smoking car. A grinning
Vivid waved enthusiastically and then offered a curtsy
in humble thanks.

The train departed, leaving behind a roaring shower
of cinders and smoke. When things settled, she looked
around and saw that the depot was nothing more than
an open-faced wooden shelter in a clearing, surrounded
by more trees than she'd ever seen. There weren't many
people around, either, a marked contrast to the hustle
and bustle of the depots she'd seen in San Francisco,
Denver, and Chicago. Here there were no vendors loudly
hawking their wares over the cacophony of foreign and
native voices so prevalent in San Francisco. The only
person selling anything appeared to be the lone Black
woman offering dippers of water from a barrel for two
cents. Vivid knew she should be trying to locate Abigail
Grayson, who was supposed to meet her, but at the moment her parched and dust-filled throat craved refresh-
ment.

"You here visiting?" the woman asked Vivid after
accepting her money. Vivid had politely declined to
drink from the offered dipper and instead had the woman
dip into the barrel with the small tin cup Vivid always
carried in her bag. Only after Vivid had drunk deeply
did she answer.

"I'm here to be the new doctor at Grayson Grove."

The woman smiled, pleasant surprise showing on her
face. "You really a doctor?"

"Yes, ma'am, and I'm supposed to meet Abigail
Grayson. Do you know her?"

"Everybody knows Miss Gail. Haven't seen her to-

day, but her nephew Nate's here. Saw him just a while
ago. Your people must be real proud."

Vivid smiled, thinking about her parents, and replied,
"Yes, they are."

"And they should be. Little bitty thing like you, a
doctor. That's something. Wait until I get home and tell
folks I met you." The woman looked around the depot.
"I don't see Nate right this minute, but he's around here
somewhere. Can't miss him, biggest man in the depot,
handsomest, too. What's your name?"

"Viveca Lancaster."

"Well, it's been a pleasure meeting you, Dr. Viveca
Lancaster. My name's Kate Pierce; I have a boy down
at Wilberforce."

"Pleased to meet you also, Kate Pierce."

They spent a few moments discussing Kate's son and
then Kate shooed her on. "If Nate's supposed to meet
you, he'll be mad at me for keeping you. The next time
you're in Niles, you have someplace to sleep if you need
it."

Vivid thanked the woman, then went off in search of
this Nate Grayson.

There were only a few people still waiting on the platform. Most of those who'd disembarked with her had
since departed with friends and family, or bartered the
price of a fare with the drivers of one of the three horse-
drawn hacks waiting beside the tracks.

She heard someone hailing, "Dr. V. Lancaster."

She spotted him on the far side of the depot and from
Kate Pierce's description knew that this was probably
Nate Grayson.

His height dominated the premises. His wide shoulders and muscular chest were prominent beneath the
plain brown shirt. His sleeves had been rolled back in
deference to the humid day, revealing strong mahogany
arms. Vivid raised her eyes to his face. Kate Pierce had
not erred in that description, either. He had a smooth,

shaven face which appeared to have been chiseled from dark marble. The nose was prominent, the jaw strong. He wore a weather-beaten hat atop his head, and a pair of oval wire-framed spectacles in front of a set of arresting, smoky-black eyes. The spectacles were necessary, she decided. Without them to deflect the masculine beauty of his face, women would undoubtedly swoon in his wake.

Smiling, Vivid approached him and held out her hand, "I'm Dr. V. Lancaster. Pleased to meet you." Up close, his chiseled good looks were even more devastating.

He did not take her offered hand. Instead he smiled down politely, and said, "I'm looking for a real doctor, miss, not someone to play doctor with."

He strode off then, again calling for Dr. V. Lancaster.

Vivid stood there, stunned. "Play doctor with," indeed! On any other day, Vivid would have pointed out the error of his ways; however, she was far too tired from her transcontinental trip to chase him all over the depot trying to convince him of her identity. So, taking a cue from her mother, Francesca, who always exuded calm in a situation like this, Vivid decided to take a seat on the bench near her belongings and relax. He'd be back.

Nate glanced around the nearly deserted depot and wondered if the damned doctor had confused the arrival date. Nate's Aunt Abigail had done all the corresponding with the physician. She hadn't accompanied him this morning because she'd gone to Kalamazoo to sit with a sick friend, but she'd specifically said that the doctor would be on today's early train. So far no one had answered his call except the fashionably dressed young woman who'd sidled up to him earlier. He'd seen her get off the train, and her beauty had drawn every male eye on the platform. When she introduced herself, he hadn't put much stock in her words because he'd seen

her waving goodbye to a group of men just before the
train pulled off. No decent woman would put on such a
display.

He could see her now seated on the depot's lone
bench across the way. Beside her were enough stacked
valises, trunks, and crates to outfit a small Egyptian ex-
pedition. Nate wondered whom she'd really come to
meet in Niles. He'd always been partial to the darker
roses of the race, and she was indeed a beauty: clear,
chocolate skin, gleaming black hair coiled below a pert
little feather-tipped green hat, jet-brown eyes. If she was
a fancy girl, she dressed far more grandly than any he'd
ever met. Her emerald-green traveling suit with its snow-
white blouse appeared to be of good quality and very
expensive. The fit of the buttoned-front jacket emphasized the swell of her small bosom and the trimness of
her figure. She glanced up as if sensing his perusal, held
his gaze a moment, then coolly looked away. Hell hath
no fury like a woman scorned, Nate thought with amusement before turning his attention back to discovering the
whereabouts of the missing Dr. Lancaster. He decided
to go over and ask Kate Pierce if she could shed some
light on the mystery. Kate oftimes knew more than the
depot's agent about the comings and goings on the platform.

Vivid watched Grayson walk over and begin talking
to Kate. When the water woman turned and pointed to
where Vivid sat, Vivid quickly looked away lest he catch
her watching him. Secure in the knowledge that he'd be
begging her pardon very soon, Vivid resumed her con-
templation of the landscape.

To her surprise, he came over and sat down on the
end of the bench. He didn't speak, just sat silent, arms
crossed. Vivid sat silent also, noting his long legs
sprawled out before him and the dirty scuffed boots on
his feet. Since she was still simmering from his earlier
"play doctor with" remark, she waited for him to open

the conversation. She didn't have to wait long.

"Name's Nate Grayson," he stated in a low voice. "Kate says you told her you were a doctor, too. She believes you."

"She struck me as being an intelligent woman," Vivid replied in the same neutral voice, her attention still focused straight ahead. "I am who I say I am."

He turned, briefly met her eyes with his startling gray ones, then looked away. "You don't look like any sawbones I've ever seen."

"We female physicians are still fairly rare," she admitted.

Vivid opened her mouth to ask after his aunt but closed it when he stated evenly, "I'd feel a whole lot better if you were really an actress my aunt hired to impersonate Dr. Lancaster."

Vivid kept her vision forward and her voice low. "An actress?"

"An actress."

"Why would my being an actress make you feel better?"

"Because then I'd simply pay you to leave and my life would continue on an even keel."

Vivid wondered if he were deranged, but decided Kate would have mentioned that little fact. "Why would your aunt hire an actress?"

"To bedevil me."

"To bedevil you?" Vivid echoed.

"It's her calling."

Vivid answered, "I see," although she really didn't. "Well, I'm sorry to disappoint you, but I am not an actress."

His eyes journeyed slowly over the features of her face. "Pity."

Vivid looked down at her gloved hands. "Mr. Grayson, I assumed I would be met by your aunt today."

When she glanced up again, he had returned his attention to the countryside.

"She's in Kalamazoo," he replied, seemingly distracted.

"Kalamazoo?" Vivid repeated slowly, wrapping her tongue around the unfamiliar word.

"It's a city north of here. Kalamazoo is the Indian word for the river. It means, 'where the water boils in the pot.' "

"And does the water boil?"

"No," he offered. Then added, "A logical conclusion to draw, though."

She was grateful he hadn't made an issue of her ignorance. "So when will she be returning?"

"She said this evening." Then he added in a lighter tone, "You know, until I came here today, I couldn't figure out why she'd been so antsy all week, or why I knew nothing about this sick friend until I caught my aunt sneaking out of the house, with her bags packed, very early in the morning. She claimed she forgot to mention the friend, but I know Aunt Gail to have the memory of a griot."

A very confused Vivid asked, "And all this means?"

"It means there is probably no sick friend. In fact, I'd be willing to bet Aunt Gail never even left town. She knew you were coming today but made herself conveniently absent."

"Why?"

"So she wouldn't have to face the music." He paused a moment to survey her features once again. "Though I must admit, you are her best maneuver to date."

Vivid had had enough of this back-and-forth. She'd just completed an exhausting journey; surely it wouldn't be rude of her to demand he get on with it. "Mr. Grayson, I have gone along with this cryptic game quite willingly up until now, but I'm beginning to lose patience. Please explain to me what this is all about."

Still maintaining his arms-crossed position, he said, "I came to the depot today expecting to meet a man."

"What man?"

"Dr. V. Lancaster."

Vivid shrugged. "Well, everyone makes mistakes now and again, Mr. Grayson. As I said, female physicians are still rare."

"You're missing my meaning. You're *supposed* to be a man."

For a moment Vivid didn't understand, then warning bells went off in her head. She turned to him and stared, forcing herself to remain calm and keep her voice even as she asked, "You believe I should be a man?"

"Frankly, yes. Doctoring's a man's job."

"I see. Well, I certainly wish someone had explained that to me before I finished my training. I would have taken the money spent on my education and used it to become an *actress*!"

Silence.

Vivid took a deep calming breath. At least he was honest, she told herself, but Vivid had fought this battle so many times over the past year and a half, she'd grown quite weary of hearing the frank opinions of honest men. "Mr. Grayson, when your aunt hired me, she said nothing about my having to alter my gender."

To her surprise, he chuckled softly. "You do have a way with words."

"Honed by years of debating men who speak their minds, Mr. Grayson."

"Touché, mademoiselle."

Vivid could still feel him observing her when he said, "I wonder how Aunt Gail figured to get past me on this."

More cryptic speech. "Mr. Grayson, believe me, I haven't any idea what you are talking about. Your aunt and I have been corresponding for the past seven or eight months. She made no mention of my gender being a problem to anyone."

"Well, she should have," he pointed out as he looked back out over the trees.

Vivid wondered why her gender suddenly mattered. If her memory served her correctly, Nate Grayson had affixed his signature to the contract she'd received from his aunt. Why would he now pretend no knowledge of what the V in V. Lancaster represented? "Mr. Grayson, what is your role in the community?"

"My grandfather settled the Grove. Like him, I own the land, the general store, and the bank. I'm the sheriff and also the mayor."

"That's quite a bit of responsibility."

"Sometimes."

"Given that, I fail to see why this issue is even being debated now. You must have been aware of my gender when you signed my contract."

He turned as if startled. "What contract?"

Vivid sighed. She very calmly reached into her reticule and withdrew the packet of papers she'd wrapped in oilskin for protection and handed them to him.

A highly skeptical Nate unwrapped the documents and slowly perused the wording. The papers were a contract between one Dr. Viveca Lancaster and the Black community of Grayson Grove, Michigan. The agreement hired the doctor for one calendar year, subject to renewal, and bore the signature of one Abigail Grayson and one Nathaniel Grayson! Nate studied the signature. He determined immediately that it was his signature, but he didn't understand how Aunt Gail had managed to obtain it without his awareness.

Nate handed the papers back and the doctor, rigidly sitting there, took them from his hand, rewrapped them, and placed the packet back into her handbag.

"So," Vivid said, "I suppose now you'll claim your signature's been forged?'

"No, I just don't remember signing it."

"Ah, amnesia—an exotic form indigenous only to
Michigan, no doubt.''

Nate could only shake his head and chuckle softly.
The last thing he needed in life was another overly educated female to add to the Grove's population. Aunt
Gail and her troops were more than the town could handle already.

"Let me be frank," Nate said. "When I agreed to
offer the position, I assumed Aunt Gail had hired a
man.''

Vivid's face mirrored her confusion. "When *you*
agreed to offer the position? I assumed your aunt had
the authority—'' She looked over at him and began to
get a very bad feeling. "Mr. Grayson, surely you are
not telling me that I have traveled all the way from San
Francisco to take a position that is not in reality mine
because I happen to be a woman."

"Possibly.''

"I hope you are jesting with me," she said softly.
Vivid searched his face for some hint of humor, but
found none. The implications were so staggering that for
the first time in her life she almost fainted dead away.
She took a deep steadying breath in an effort to regain
her composure. She'd been so elated at this chance to
practice. Now she found herself precariously close to the
same situation that had forced her to come all these
many miles in the first place. After completion of her
studies at the Woman's Medical College in Philadelphia,
she'd written letters until her hands ached, but could find
no physician willing to take her on, not even as an ap-
prentice. She'd queried doctors and institutions all over
the country, but most hadn't even bothered to reply. Re-
ceiving a positive offer from Abigail Grayson had been
an answer to her prayers. Did this man know how many
miles she'd traveled, or the expenses she and her parents had incurred? "I really must speak with your

aunt," Vivid stated, still shaken by the startling turn of events. "When will she be returning?"

"Later this evening, but it's I who'll have the final say in this matter."

Vivid's dark eyes locked with his. She wondered if he really planned on denying her the position for such an unfair reason. "You said 'possibly' the position isn't mine. Can I assume there's also the possibility that it can be?"

He shrugged his wide shoulders. "I'm all but convinced your gender makes you unsuitable, but I may be wrong."

"Mr. Grayson, your community needs a physician. My gender shouldn't matter."

"If it hadn't mattered, my aunt would have mentioned it early on. She knew what she was about, believe me."

"She knew you were prejudiced against women doctors," Vivid said.

Nate smiled. She'd asked the barbed question so innocently, he hadn't even felt the sting of the shiv until it slid between his ribs. "Let's just say she knew you weren't the type of physician I had in mind."

"You had a man in mind, since doctoring is a man's profession."

"I had in mind someone less beautiful."

Vivid blinked. "So now my features make me unsuitable?"

"For town doctor, yes," he said.

"Why do you believe a man would be more suitable?"

"The weather, for one. Winters here are hard. Ever try to pull a wagon and team out of a six-foot drift?"

Admittedly, Vivid had not. She shook her head.

"Then there's the traveling involved," he added. "The Grove's spread out over quite a few miles."

"Surely there are maps—"

"More importantly, I'm not certain how people will

react, especially the men. You plan on treating them also, I assume?''

''Yes, and I agree, some men may be put off by me at first. I'm even willing to concede some won't let me near them. However, I'm confident most will come to see me for what I am—a trained and qualified physician.''

Nate wondered if she was really that naive. ''Men are going to see you as trained and qualified for marriage, so the sooner your husband arrives, the better it will be.''

''I have no husband, Mr. Grayson.''

That statement seemed to increase his woes because he removed his spectacles and rubbed his eyes as if he were very weary. ''No husband,'' he stated softly. ''Good Lord.''

''I take it you consider that to be a problem as well?'' Silence.

He stood and looked out over the land, then cast a glance at the gray sky. By his estimation, it would be storming later and the sooner he headed back, the better. ''Look, Miss Lancaster—''

''Dr. Lancaster,'' she corrected.

''Dr. Lancaster,'' he repeated with an apologetic inclination of his head. ''It's going to storm later today. I can't just leave you here, so I'm going to take you back to the Grove. You can stay a few days and see for yourself why it isn't the place for a woman to practice.''

''Your aunt didn't think that would be the case.''

''Well, when you meet Abigail, you'll understand. In her mind, women are capable of handling anything and everything.''

''Then she is an intelligent woman.''

''Sometimes.''

Vivid said, ''Well, since I've no desire to reside in the Niles depot, I'll accept your invitation, Mr. Grayson, but only if you give me a fair opportunity to try to alter your opinion.''

"I very rarely change my mind," he told her truthfully.

Vivid looked him straight in the eye and stated, "Then it's only right to warn you—I seldom take no for an answer."

"Somehow I already knew that," he answered. "These your things?"

Vivid looked to where he indicated. "Yes."

"All this?"

Vivid nodded.

She watched him run his gaze over her possessions. She was about to explain that most of the crates held books and medical supplies when he asked, "Where do you keep the tame animals?"

Vivid stared back, confused.

"There's enough stuff here for a circus," he explained.

Vivid was insulted, but upon taking an objective look at all the items she had stacked against the depot wall, she realized she did resemble a traveling show. She smiled sheepishly. "The animals arrive tomorrow."

He simply shook his head. "I have to fetch the buggy. Wait here."

Vivid watched him walk away.

Moments later, he returned driving a small horse-drawn buggy. He jumped down and walked across the tracks and gravel to where she stood waiting on the edge of the platform.

"Are you ready?"

Tall as he was, he loomed over her like a city building and she could only hope all Michigan men weren't as tall. "Mr. Grayson, I don't believe your buggy's going to be large enough to haul my circus."

"I've made arrangements with the depot agent. He'll store the majority." Then, looking down at her, he added, "*If* you can convince me to let you stay on, you can send for the rest later."

Vivid ignored his verbal challenge for now. She hadn't counted on being separated from her things. She'd shepherded her circus cross-country without losing even one piece, and now she was being asked to abandon it to a stranger. Suppose it did rain later? She had medical supplies in some of her crates, and they had to stay dry.

Nate must have sensed her worries because he said, "The agent is a good man. You really don't need to be concerned."

"He must make certain nothing gets dampened."

"Everything will be taken care of."

Vivid didn't want to leave her belongings behind, but she could see no other way out of her dilemma. With a small sigh, she began to search through the stacked luggage.

"Bring whatever you think is essential," he told her.

Vivid looked until she found the big brown valise that held some of her clothing and toiletries. She also picked out a slim black case that held another essential. She passed it to him.

"And this is?" he asked.

"My rifle."

"Your what?"

"Rifle," Vivid stated succinctly. "My mother doesn't let me or my sisters travel without one. Here, take this also."

He took a small green case from her hand and asked, "What's in here, your bullets?"

"No. Billiard stick."

The answer rendered him speechless, Vivid noted with a small smile. Good. "I'm ready to depart now, Mr. Grayson."

Vivid thought he had the oddest look on his face. It was a familiar odd look. She'd seen it on the faces of her teachers and professors back in San Francisco. She'd seen it many times on the faces of the men she beat at billiards, especially those who wagered and then lost large sums of money after playing with her. Her mother called it the look of a man meeting an unconventional woman. To break him out of his stupor, she handed him her brown valise, saying, "You wanted to beat the rain, remember?"

He shook his head as if to clear it, then, staring at her with a shocked expression on his face, replied, "Yes, you're right. This way."

Vivid grabbed her black medical bag and followed him back across the tracks.

He placed her essentials behind the seat, then held out his hand to help her step into the buggy. Vivid placed her gloved hand into his palm, swept up her green skirts, and let herself be assisted aboard.

He climbed in. Vivid hazarded a look his way and found him observing her very intently. She thought he might speak but he did not. He studied her a few moments longer, shook his head again, and turned his attention to his horses. He slapped the reins across their rumps, and the buggy lurched into motion.

It was a humid day, and less than an hour later Vivid could feel the sweat beginning to stick to the blouse inside her jacket. The weather had been rainy when the train left Chicago last night and her suit had been just right for the temperature, but on this side of the lake the air was thick and cloying. If Vivid were traveling with a more cosmopolitan companion, she would have thought nothing of removing her jacket and letting the little breeze cool her, but she knew the men of the Midwest were far more conservative than those at home, and since she was still trying to make a good impression, she sweltered in silence.

She still couldn't believe his attitude. She thought she'd left such narrow-minded people behind, but here one of them sat beside her, grim-faced as if he were the injured party. Had he really not been aware of signing the contract? Vivid thought not. Nate Grayson did not impress her as a gullible man.

As they continued riding, Vivid refused to speak unless he spoke first, but after a while she couldn't keep silent because, frankly, Vivid enjoyed conversing. She also reasoned that if they talked, maybe they could learn a bit more about each other, and he might come to see that she was indeed suited to be the doctor here. "Is the weather always this warm in May?"

"Sometimes."

He said nothing more.

Vivid tried another topic. "How long before we reach our destination?"

"Two hours."

Two hours! She wondered how on earth she'd pass the time if he refused to answer with more than two words. But even though she had to travel with a man who thought her unqualified simply because she wore skirts, she was determined to be pleasant. She'd always had an open, outgoing personality, and very few people remained distant in her presence. However, Nate Grayson seemed to be one of those immune to her natural charm. In the end she gave up trying to be polite.

Nate decided to avoid conversation because he needed to think. He admitted to himself that he was impressed by the lady doctor despite his opinions. That she'd made the cross-country journey unaccompanied spoke of her fearlessness. In the face of the rampant progression of Jim Crow and the frightening newspaper reports of the increasing violence perpetrated against members of the race by White Leaguers, Kluxers, and the like, she'd been undeterred. Furthermore, to be a doctor in this day and age, she needed to be a woman of strength. He looked up from the road to where she sat next to him watching the trees and scenery roll by in pace with the wagon. He saw her soft smile as her eyes followed a brown hawk soaring languidly above. She seemed to take pleasure in the surroundings, which he found surprising. Yet she still looked as if she'd spend more time shopping than doctoring. And the Grove desperately needed a doctor. When Doc Miner died last year, Nate had to ask Wadsworth Hayes, a traveling doctor, to add the Grove to his circuit. Hayes was an ancient man, nearly blind, yet he was the only physician available to treat the Grove's Black population. Nate and his Aunt Abigail harbored concerns over the man's methods of bleeding his patients to restore health and questioned some of his other remedies, too. But they had no other medical expertise to call upon. If Grayson Grove were not such a small and isolated community, they would not have such a frustrating time finding a physician. But the Black men graduating from medical schools like Howard and the closer University of Michigan in Ann Arbor were seeking to establish practices in larger cities such as Boston, Philadelphia, and Richmond. Nate had written many letters, but it seemed no one wanted to practice in a place like the Grove where payment for services was more likely to be rendered in chickens and vegetables than in coin. There were also no big city amusements available unless one counted the gambling and whores at Maddie's Liberty Emporium outside town. There were no theaters, no tea houses. Only occasionally was the Grove treated to a traveling troupe of Black actors or singers. The lack of cultural offerings had been one of his ex-wife Cecile's main complaints. Dr. Lancaster reminded him of Cecile in some ways. Both women were fashionable, intelligent, and dark-hued. He supposed the memories of his traitorous ex-wife played some role in his thinking. Cecile's departure had left him with a bitter taste for city women, and decidedly wary of the doctor's commitment to stay in a place such as the Grove.

While Nate concentrated on the dilemma the doctor presented, Vivid concentrated on the countryside. Every-

where she looked she saw green. California was green,
too, but not like this. Here in Michigan the variety of
shades was dazzling to behold. Even under the cloudy
sky of the humid day the majesty of nature could not be
denied. Along the sides of the packed-earth road were
large hardy trees whose full leafy tops kissed the sky.
The foliage beneath the trees was thick with ferns and
tall grasses. She spotted wildflowers of many hues and
heard the calls of birds and the low hum of insects
against the wild silence.

"This is beautiful country," she remarked before she
remembered she wasn't speaking to him. And for the
first time since they'd left the depot he looked at her,
really looked at her. Vivid felt a strange sensation course
through her under his silent scrutiny. As he turned back
to the road, she let out a breath she didn't realize she
was holding.

A large patch of black-eyed susans caught her eye.
She wanted to ask him to stop because the flowers were
one of her favorites, but she didn't want him to think
her just another frivolous female. So she fought to keep
the longing from her face as the wagon passed them by.

He surprised her by saying, "That's a beautiful stand
of susans back there."

"Yes," Vivid answered. "Quite beautiful."

Their eyes held a moment, then his went back to the
road. "Where did you get your training?" he asked.

"In Philadelphia at the Woman's Medical College."

"They teach only women there?"

"Yes, since 1850."

Vivid felt it time to let this man know where she
stood. "Mr. Grayson, do you really believe only men
can be physicians?"

"Until I'm convinced otherwise, yes."

"But you've admitted you've never seen a female
doctor."

"Nope, I haven't, and neither has anyone else around here."

"But that's hardly a reason to be so rigid in your thinking. You don't believe I could live here as a member of your community?"

"Not as a doctor, no."

"Why?"

"As long as you don't mind a truthful answer, I'll tell you."

She nodded that she understood.

"You have two marks against you, the main one being you're a city woman."

"Why is that a problem?"

"Because women like you are useless out here. You're more concerned with the price of gowns than the price of seed."

Vivid thought that a very prejudiced and harsh statement. "I beg to differ."

"Beg all you like," he offered easily, "but I've yet to meet a city woman able to do anything besides complain about the lack of shops and how cold it gets here around the new year."

Vivid thought about what he'd said for a moment and then responded. "Granted, I can certainly envision a city-born person being unhappy here, after all, where we are headed does seem a bit off the beaten track. However, one must adapt to life. If one makes the effort, happiness can be found anywhere. And besides, I've spent winters in Philadelphia; surely your winters aren't any worse."

Nate thought she displayed quite a bit of naivete in comparing the winters in Pennsylvania to the frigid wasteland that Michigan turns into from late November to late April, but he ignored it because he was more interested in her opinions on happiness. He turned to her and asked. "Is that what you believe, Doctor, that happiness can be found anywhere?"

"Yes, Mr. Grayson, I do."

"Interesting philosophy. Naive, but interesting."

"If you embrace life, Mr. Grayson, happiness will follow. And if you believe I'm naive, so be it," she added with a shrug. "It won't alter my outlook."

He asked then, "What do your parents do?"

"My father's a caterer and my mother oversees our home."

"Do they approve of your occupation?"

"They raised me and my two sisters to make our own choices, so yes, my parents approve."

Nate could see the perspiration beading around her hairline. "You're going to die in this heat with all those clothes on, Lancaster," he noted.

"You won't mind if I remove this jacket?"

He shook his head.

Relieved, Vivid removed her gloves, stuffed them into her handbag, and undid the buttons of her jacket. As she went to remove it, she looked over at Nate and found him intently watching her. Ignoring him as best she could, she removed the jacket and placed it on the seat beside her. There was hardly any breeze but she felt much cooler. "Thank you for your consideration. I'll put the jacket on when we reach our destination."

"It's not a problem. Folks know it's hot. Nobody expects you to be bundled up like it's November."

Vivid wanted to undo the top buttons of her high-necked blouse, but she doubted folks would be that understanding.

"Can you really use that rifle?" he then asked.

"Mr. Grayson, why would I bring a rifle cross-country if I couldn't use it? Don't the women here shoot?"

"Yes, they do, but you don't look the type who would know how."

"Mr. Grayson, every woman needs to be able to protect herself, or are you one of those men who believe the best protection for a woman is a man?"

Nate smiled. "You said that so innocently, Lancaster. Do you always ask questions that bite?"

"I'm a doctor and I carry a rifle, what do you think?" she asked, smiling.

"I think you don't suffer fools real well," he replied.

"I think you might be right," Vivid answered.

"Why didn't you try practicing in San Francisco?"

"I did, for about a year. But our community already has two male doctors who are well-respected. I couldn't drum up enough patients to keep my doors open. When I read your aunt's notice in the local San Francisco paper advertising for a doctor, it seemed the answer to my prayers."

Then she remembered that he'd said there were two marks against her, and so far they'd discussed only one. "You haven't explained what my second shortcoming is."

"I don't believe you'll stay," he said seriously. His eyes held hers. "The first time a man proposes marriage to you, you'll leave—doctoring in the Grove will be the furthest thing from your mind."

"You're wrong, you know. I'm here to be a physician. I'm not looking for a husband."

"Sometimes a man doesn't care what a woman is looking for, especially if he wants her for his own."

"I don't need a husband."

"Every woman needs a man."

"Only a man would say that."

He chuckled. "Ah, Dr. Lancaster, you and I are going to butt heads often, I see."

"Does that mean you will give me a chance and let me stay?"

"I think I've pretty much made up my mind," he said, looking her way.

Pleased, Vivid returned her attention to the landscape. He finally brought the horses to a stop before a cluster of small buildings erected in a clearing surrounded by trees. The largest was a log cabin with a sign across the front which read GRAYSON GROVE GENERAL STORE. Next to the store were a few other clapboard and log buildings with signs that read GRAYSON LIVERY, VERNON THE BARBER, and BATES UNDERTAKING. Next to the undertaking establishment stood a newly built cabin with a large painted sign above the door announcing the *Gazette*. She was pleased to see the town had its own newspaper. She counted nine buildings of varying age and construction. Up the dirt road stood some type of mill in front of which men sat atop large wagons filled with cut trees. She guessed that this was the end of the journey, but Grayson gave her no indication either way. He simply got out, tied up the horses, and walked into the store. As his broad back disappeared inside, she prayed to the saints above to give her strength.

Vivid put on her jacket, stepped out of the buggy and followed Nate. She entered the store just as someone inside asked, "Where's the new doc, Nate?"

At her entrance the place grew silent. Nate looked back over his shoulder at her and said, "She says she is."

Vivid's eyes narrowed at his mocking tone and assessing eyes, but she stood silent as the small group of people in the store craned to get a good look at her.

"Why, she's a woman," a man said with a gasp.

"I'm Dr. Viveca Lancaster," she said in introduction. Silence followed—a reaction she'd become accustomed to whenever she announced her profession, but this time she was unnerved because she couldn't determine if the men and women watching her approved or disapproved of her.

One of the men in the back finally asked, "She staying, Nate?"

"Nope," he replied easily.

Vivid's eyes widened at that announcement. "I beg your pardon?"

"You're not staying. Next train back to Chicago is due in a couple of days. You'll be on it."

"But I thought you—why?"

He didn't respond. Instead he spoke to one of the women behind the counter. "Edna, she can stay with you until then, just send me a bill."

He gave Vivid a brief nod as he passed her on his way out the door.

Dazed from this sudden turn of events, Vivid turned to Edna and asked, "Does he really have the authority to send me back without his aunt's say-so?"

Edna nodded. "I'm afraid he does, dear."

Vivid let fly a very distinct curse and went after him. She hoped the saints noted how patient she'd been because she'd had just about enough. She thought an agreement had been worked out between them, so why had he suddenly changed his mind? He'd vowed to give her a chance!

She looked left, then right until she spotted him. She quickened her pace, snatching open buttons on her jacket as she went. She felt betrayed. She was hot, tired, and frustrated. If he planned on sending her home, she'd go, but she wouldn't go quietly.

She paid absolutely no attention to the people who'd trailed her from the store or to the farmers who stopped and stared curiously.

"Are you that pig-headed and prejudiced that you would deny people a doctor?!" Vivid shouted at his back.

He stopped and turned.

"Yes, I'm talking to you," Vivid yelled. "Who in Jessy do you think you are?" She ran down the wooden walk until she was close enough to confront him face to face.

Nate couldn't believe his eyes or his ears. He was

being accosted in the middle of the street, in his own town, by a black-eyed little susan who obviously had no idea what she was about.

"Mr. Grayson, you promised me the time to convince you."

"Don't need the time. You won't do."

"But that is not fair."

"Lancaster, I have the health of three hundred people to take into consideration and I've made up my mind."

Nate had thought this through and he was not convinced that this woman was right for his town. She was a female for one, and a young female to boot. He simply did not believe she would stay longer than a few months and he didn't want to have the people come to rely on her and then have her walk out on them.

"Mr. Grayson, I insist we talk about this," Vivid stated, trying to keep up with his long-legged stride.

He didn't slow his pace or look at her as he answered, "No. Now go on back to the store, and Edna will show you where you can stay until the next train comes through."

Vivid stopped, totally outdone. What had happened to change his mind? she asked herself. She wondered if maybe he was suffering from some sort of mind derangement. It was as if the invitation he'd extended back at the depot had never been given. "Mr. Grayson!"

He continued walking away from her.

"Mister Grayson!" Vivid yelled again. When he ignored her again and again, Vivid put away all sense of good manners. She looked around for something, anything to make him stop and talk to her. She spied a farmer tying up his team-drawn wagon to a post near where she stood. On the seat of the big wagon lay a rifle. Vivid walked over to the man and demanded, "I need to borrow your rifle, sir."

The farmer seemed so surprised by her authoritative manner he handed it over without a word. Vivid quickly checked the shells, closed the chamber, sighted, and fired.

The first shot blew her target's hat off his head and sent it flying into the dust. She handed the wide-eyed farmer back his weapon, smiled politely, and waited for Nate to come to her.

She didn't have to wait long.

He very gently but firmly grabbed her by the upper arm, turned to the small gaping crowd, growled a very polite "Excuse us" to them, and escorted Vivid across the street and into a low-roofed log building. Once inside, he released her and closed the door. Then in a soft voice belying his anger he said, "You're not a doctor, you're a menace."

Vivid realized her actions had been a trifle extreme but she'd had no other choice. "If I had a white flag, I'd raise it," she offered.

His expression didn't change.

"I'm sorry about your hat, but if you hadn't lied to me I wouldn't have lost my temper."

Nate had no idea what to do with this woman. "Do you do that often?" he asked.

"Lose my temper?"

"No, shoot at people."

Vivid looked down at her shoes a moment, then back up to his stormy eyes. "No."

"Well, that's something," he stated. Nate noted that her suddenly meek manner reminded him very much of his nine-year old daughter, Majestic. Magic, as she was usually called, was forever in trouble of one sort or another, and when chastised she also played apologetic and meek. However, Majestic didn't have a meek bone anywhere in her body and Nate didn't believe this hat-shooting Dr. Viveca Lancaster had one, either.

"You really do owe me an explanation, Mr. Grayson," Vivid said, wondering meantime if he planned on taking her back to the depot immediately or first thing tomorrow morning.

"I *owe* you?" Nate replied in disbelief. "You shot my hat off in the middle of the damned street, woman."

"I will pay for the hat, Mr. Grayson. But you impress me as being an intelligent man; why won't you give me a chance? And don't tell me any manure about it being because I don't have buttons down the front of my drawers like a man."

Nate eyed her. Impressed by her challenging manner he shook his head in wonder. "Are you always so forceful?"

"It's a necessary trait for someone like me."

Before Nate could speak further the black-garbed Widow Moss came charging into his office towing his daughter, Majestic.

Chapter 3

He sighed. "Hello, Widow Moss. Is there a problem?"

He knew that was an asinine question; neither his
daughter nor the widow looked pleased. The widow's
face had been set in a permanent frown since the day
he'd hired her to be Magic's governess. Nate thought
that the woman would be able to offer the child badly
needed lessons in deportment. However, Magic, oper-
ating under no such misconception, had disliked the
widow woman on sight. And the situation had not mel-
lowed over time.

"Who's she, Pa?" the girl asked, gazing at Vivid.

Nate wanted to reply, "She's a menace posing as a
doctor," but said instead, "She's a doctor. Dr. Viveca
Lancaster, my daughter, Majestic Grayson. Dr. Lancaster, the Widow Moss."

All three females nodded politely to one another, then
Nate turned his attention back to the matter at hand and
asked, "What's happened?"

As usual, Magic opened her mouth to tell her side
first, but one glance from her father's dark eyes and she
closed it.

The black-dressed widow gave Magic a smug look,
then spoke. "Mr. Grayson, I have tried and tried to exercise some influence over this child's behavior but I
cannot any longer. She absolutely refuses to cooperate."

"Pa, I hate sewing."

The widow leaned down to look the young girl straight in the eye and related sharply, "You liked it well enough last night when you sewed my drawers together!"

Nate hid his laugh with a faked coughing fit.

Vivid was not so fortunate. The widow's statement caught her so off-guard the laugh bubbled out before she could choke it back. The breach of manners garnered her a stern look from Widow Moss and one of surprise from the child. When the widow turned back to Nate, Vivid took the opportunity to wink at the little girl, who responded with a beaming smile.

The sour-faced widow continued, "I won't be working for you any longer, Mr. Grayson. This child has put snakes in my bed and rotten eggs in my bonnets, and I refuse to even think about that nasty incident with my shoes and the cow manure."

Nate didn't want to think about that, either. One morning about a month ago, Widow Moss had stepped into her shoes only to discover them already occupied. He'd given Magic a good old-fashioned licking for that prank and she hadn't been able to sit for a week. Only after she'd gone to bed did he laugh until tears ran down his cheeks. Truthfully, he didn't like the widow any more than his daughter did.

Vivid didn't know the prune-faced old crone well enough to form an accurate opinion, but she did like the little girl. Cow manure in the woman's shoes! Outstanding. Vivid wished she'd had that type of nerve at that age, although she did remember standing on the ornate balcony of her great aunt's house in Mexico City and surreptiously dropping small spiders down onto the heads of the dinner guests below. She could still feel the sting of that whipping to this day. Had Majestic suffered a similar fate? Vivid guessed she probably had, but that would only deter her until the next time. Vivid's partner-in-crime had been her late grandmother Maria, founder of the Female Plotting Rebelling Society. Grandmother Maria believed that all females, regardless of age, race, or circumstances, should always be plotting rebellion to better the state of women. Vivid had been raised as a practicing coconspirator. And the little girl at the center of attention here looked to be a prime recruit.

"Magic, what do you have to say for yourself?" Nate asked after hearing the litany of sins from the Widow Moss.

"She can eat her old bonnet. I don't want to be a lady."

"Do you see, Mr. Grayson? No manners, no politeness, and no desire to be any better."

"Apologize, Magic. Now."

The girl did, grudgingly.

The Widow Moss did not appear mollified. "Mr. Grayson, no amount of washing or deportment lessons will rid her of her bastard beginnings. She would try Christ himself."

Vivid watched the youngster's shoulders tense under the slur and waited for Grayson to respond. "Widow, I'd advise you to keep such thoughts to yourself. Magic had no say in her birth."

"Excuse me, ma'am," Vivid interrupted frostily. "Are you a Christian woman?"

The black-bonneted head turned and nodded. From the look on the widow's face, she obviously had not forgiven Vivid for laughing earlier. "Of course. I attend church every Sunday."

"Then maybe you can help me. There's a passage from the Bible that begins, let's see, I think it reads, 'Suffer the little children to come unto me . . .' I can't seem to remember the rest. Are you familiar with that passage?"

Vivid watched the woman's whole body tighten as if it had been dipped in alum. The widow obviously knew the rest of the verse. "So," Vivid continued, "in light

of that, do you really believe the good Lord would turn
His back on this child?''

The widow had no place to hide from Vivid's icy
calm. "No," she finally answered.

"Spoken like a true Christian. I'm a regular church-
goer myself. What time are Sunday services?''

"Eleven."

"Thank you. I hope to see you there."

To Nate, the Widow Moss looked as if she hoped no
such thing. He also didn't believe he'd be able to convince her to stay on in his employ. After the cow manure
surprise, only Magic's sincere promise that the pranks
would stop, and an increase in pay, kept the widow from
quitting on the spot. Now, after the chastisement from
Lancaster, there was not enough money in Michigan that
would make the woman stay.

Vivid realized she'd probably made an enemy of the
widow but she didn't care. She walked over to Grayson's daughter and asked in a soft voice, "Majestic,
since I'm new here, may I count on you to be my first
friend?''

"Oh, yes!''

Vivid smiled. "Good. When I get settled maybe your
father will let you come visit me?''

Nate hated to see these two get together as he had no
doubts his daughter's behavior would only deteriorate
under the influence of the unconventional Viveca Lancaster, so he said instead, "We'll see, Magic. We still
have to settle this matter with Widow Moss.''

"I've already settled the matter, Mr. Grayson," the
old woman countered. "You will have to find someone
else to take over as governess. I refuse to do it any
longer.''

Nate sighed. "Well, I'm sure there's nothing I can
say to convince you otherwise, so I thank you for your
help. Send my the bill for your . . . drawers, and stop by

the bank and tell Joshua to give you a month's extra
pay.''

"Thank you, Mr. Grayson."

She turned, blessed both Vivid and Magic with acer-
bic looks, and walked out.

"What happened to your hat, Pa?" Magic asked,
picking it up from where he'd tossed it on the desk. She
stuck two small brown fingers through the hole and wig-
gled them. "Looks like it's been shot to death."

"Accident," her father explained. He took the hat
from her, saying, "Why don't you go over to the store
and see if there're any new newspapers? Aunt Gail
should be back by the time we get home, and she'll be
glad if we bring her one."

"Okay, Pa." The beautiful little girl with her pigtails
and topaz eyes then turned to Vivid. "I'll come visit
when Pa says I can, okay?"

"That'll be fine," Vivid replied.

Magic ran out.

"Walk!" her father called belatedly.

"You have a lovely daughter, Mr. Grayson."

"Thank you, but she's a tornado sometimes."

Vivid watched him walk to the desk and lean over to
retrieve some papers. "Would you approve of *her* being
the doctor here?" she asked.

Nate looked her in the eye, surveyed her a moment,
then replied, "My daughter grew up here. She won't run
the first time we get a half-foot of snow."

"And I will?"

"I believe so, yes."

Vivid shook her head at his stubbornness. "How does
your wife feel about female doctors?"

"I don't have a wife. It's just me, Abigail, and my
daughter."

Vivid wondered if he was a widower.

Her eyes settled on his hat. "I'll pay for the hat," she
offered again.

"Save your money. You'll need it for the ticket home."

"Mr. Grayson, I am not going home. I have a signed contract."

"Since I don't remember signing it, how much legitimacy can it have?"

"The papers, which you signed, were drawn up by my cousin Alejandro, who can stand before the bar not only in these United States but in Mexico and Spain as well. He gets very offended when someone questions the integrity of his documents."

"So?"

"And so, unless you wish me to bring legal charges against you, I expect you to honor the contract *you* signed."

Nate looked at the sparkling challenge in her eyes. "You *are* going back, Lancaster."

"Not quietly I won't."

"No?" he asked.

"No."

Nate sighed and walked over to the window. A glance outside showed him that a small crowd had gathered, peering in to observe the proceedings. He pulled the curtains closed.

"Okay. Since you are so hell-bent on having this job, it's yours."

Vivid smiled in triumph.

He walked back to the desk, "Don't look so pleased; this is only a trial—"

Vivid protested, "The contract states—"

"I read it. But if I conclude you're really not qualified, you're out on your bustle, contract or not. I'll take my chances with your cousin Alejandro and the courts. Things being the way they are for the race these days, we'd be lucky to get inside a courthouse."

She knew he was right, but since Vivid also knew she was the best damned doctor these people had ever seen, she

saw no problem in accepting the modified agreement.
"Fair enough, but why did you change your mind?"

He leaned back on the edge of the desk, folded his
arms across his chest, and replied in a pleased tone,
"Because this way I can win the war without firing a
shot."

Her eyes narrowed in confusion. "I don't understand."

"My aunt and her very formidable minions would
hound my backside to the grave if I simply sent you
home without giving you a chance. But if I sit back and
wait for you to fall flat on that perfect little . . . face of
yours, I can say 'I told you so.' "

"Your support is duly noted," Vivid drawled and
then added, "Do you prefer your crow hot or cold, because when I serve it, I'll need to know."

He smiled.

Further discussion was set aside when Magic returned
with a strange man, about the same age as Nate. He
nodded politely to Vivid, and she smiled.

"Well, Nate, everybody wants to know, she staying?"

Nate looked over her way. "Yes, Vernon, she's staying."

Vivid smiled triumphantly in return, then heard Nate
tell the man, "When you go to the depot tomorrow,
Vernon, pick up her trunks."

The man nodded, then asked Vivid, "Where do you
want us to take them when we get back, Doc?"

Vivid didn't have the slightest idea and she looked to
Grayson for an answer. Magic spoke first, as usual.
"Shouldn't she live where Doc Miner lived, Pa?"

"Where did Doc Miner live, Magic?" Vivid asked.

"In the little house behind ours."

"I see. Well, Mr. Grayson, where should the man take
my trunks?"

"Take them over to the house, Vernon. Thanks."

Vernon turned to leave but Vivid called him back. "Mr. Vernon?"

He gave Vivid a smile. "Name's Stevenson, Doc. Vernon's my given name."

"I'm sorry. Mr. Stevenson—"

"Call me Vernon."

She shook her head and smiled. "Thank you, Vernon. I just want to say, most of those trunks contain medical supplies and books; please be careful with them."

"I'll treat them like they're made of gold."

Vivid nodded her thanks.

"Have Nate bring you by to meet my missus when you get settled," Vernon said. "That fine with you, Nate?"

Nate thought about having this unconventional woman in his own backyard and it gave him a headache. He took his spectacles off, set them on the desk, and rubbed his weary eyes. It was still early in the day, yet he felt as if it were way past dark. "Fine with me, Vernon."

Vivid turned to Magic then and said, "Well, Magic, looks like you and I are going to be neighbors."

While Magic clapped with glee, Vivid looked over at Nate. Their eyes held and Vivid smiled.

Nate saw Vernon out to the wooden walk, then took a moment to shoo the small but curious crowd away from his door and window. Everyone wanted to know about the lady doctor, and all had questions. He promised their questions would be answered at the next council meeting and they reluctantly dispersed.

When he reentered the office, Magic was seated in the chair behind his desk, and the doctor was drawing something on a piece of paper. At his approach Magic looked up and said, "Pa, Dr. Lancaster is real smart. She just showed me how to beat Wendell in marbles tomorrow."

"Oh, really?"

"Yes, she said it's just a matter of geometry."

Nate peered over his daughter's shoulder at the diagram. He could see the small circles he assumed were marbles. A series of angled lines and arrows had also been drawn, showing the paths the marbles could take.

Nate looked over his daughter's head and into the dark eyes of the doctor. "You play marbles, Doctor?"

"All my life."

"And you studied geometry?"

"Yes."

Before Nate could absorb that information, Magic said to her father, "Dr. Lancaster wanted to know if we had a hospital, I told her no."

Nate confirmed his daughter's statement, adding, "We have to go to the hospital up in Kalamazoo."

"Have you ever considered building one here? It wouldn't have to be a large facility."

"No," Nate replied, though he found the idea intriguing.

"Well, after I complete this trial to your satisfaction, maybe we can discuss it."

"You're awfully confident, Lancaster."

"Part of my nature. Will you agree to a discussion of the idea?"

"Finish the trial and we'll discuss it."

Vivid was pleased he'd agreed without a battle. "I'd like to see Dr. Miner's office if I may."

"He practiced out of the cabin you'll be living in."

"He didn't have an office in town?"

"No. When he first came to the Grove in '56, the only building in this clearing was the old trading post that stood where the general store is now."

Vivid thought about that a moment. Since she was from a large city she had just assumed the doctor would be located in town. "How large is his cabin?"

"Not very."

Does the cabin have any type of ward?"

"No."

Vivid knew that would never do. Even in a town as slow paced as this one seemed to be, accidents and epidemics occurred. There needed to be a place for her to house patients who might need extended care or quarantine. "Where did Dr. Miner house his patients overnight?" she asked.

"Sometimes on the small cot in the front room, but he rarely had folks stay over."

"Then what did he do in an emergency, say if three or four people were injured or ill at the same time?"

"If they weren't contagious we'd put them up at our place. If they were, Doc treated them at home."

Vivid decided that would never do either; the Graysons shouldn't have to house patients. "Is there a space in town I might lease to use as an office?"

"There is the old seamstress shop. She pulled up stakes last fall."

"May I see it?"

"Now?"

"The sooner I open for business, the sooner I can see to the health of your people, Mr. Grayson."

He gestured her to the door and followed her out.

Unbelievably, the day had gotten even more humid. The thick air had a heaviness reminiscent of the fog back home in San Francisco, except the Michigan air held not a degree of coolness. Vivid thought she was going to melt.

Beside her, Nate could see she was suffering from the heat. "You know, Doc, heat like this can make a person sick."

"I'm fine." If she fainted from the heat, he'd ship her home first thing tomorrow.

Nate smiled knowingly.

The empty cabin that had once been a seamstress shop stood only a short distance down the street from Nate's office. Vivid didn't know if she wanted him to be so close by. She imagined daily arguments and his peering over her shoulder all the time, but if this was the only space available, it would have to do.

Nate extracted a ring of keys from his shirt pocket and stuck one of the keys into the padlock fastened to the wooden bolt on the front door. When he opened the door he went in first, followed by Vivid and Magic.

It was like stepping into a furnace; the hot air made it hard to breathe. The room was gloomy due to a lack of light, and the single window frame had been boarded shut. Enough light entered through the open front door and the cracks between the logs to show the dirt-packed floor and the dimensions of the room.

Nate said, "The seamstress displayed her goods out here and lived in one of the two small rooms in the back."

"Why did she leave?" Vivid asked, waving away a pesky insect.

"Couldn't take the winter."

Vivid didn't rise to his bait. Instead, she walked into the deep shadows, barely able to make out the interiors of the two back rooms. She peered around in the dark, then rejoined Magic and her father.

"It's in better shape than I imagined," Nate said. "There's field mice in here somewhere." He used his foot to indicate a small nest in the corner. "Won't take much to clean it up, though."

Vivid asked, "Has the window ever held glass?"

"Yes, but after the seamstress left we put the pane in the window of the store. Didn't make sense to let the glass go to waste."

Vivid doubted the glass would be returned now, so she would order more. She also needed to have a proper floor installed. After that, she would take care of the dozens of other necessary improvements in time.

Nate waited, arms folded.

Vivid looked over at him standing in the dim light and asked, "How much?"

He quoted a reasonable price, adding "And I'll arrange for the cleaning."

Vivid looked around once more. "And there's no other place available?"

"No."

"Then I will take it."

Nate ushered them out and relocked the door. He turned to his daughter and said, "Magic, run over to the store and bring back some pastries and something cool for the doctor to drink. Meet us back at my office."

"Sure, Pa."

After a short repast of the pastries and the sweetest, coldest water Vivid had ever drunk, she and Nate drew up the papers for the lease. When everything had been signed, he suggested they leave for the Grayson home. Vivid agreed. She wanted to inspect the house she would be occupying. Although she'd vowed to be content with whatever the fates bestowed, Vivid dearly hoped the living accommodations were in better condition than the store she'd leased for her office.

Chapter 4

The wagon bearing Vivid and the Graysons rattled along on the pocked and rutted road. For a half hour, Magic sat between the two adults trying to convince her father to build her a tree house. Vivid, sitting quietly on the end of the seat, listened with a smile as Nate recited all the fatherly reasons why a nine-year-old girl should not have such a place—safety being his main concern. Vivid understood his anxiety, but since she herself had had a tree house, she silently sided with Magic. However, she didn't offer any opinions because she had no place in the discussion between father and daughter, so instead she reviewed all that had happened. When she left California, she'd imagined that coming to Michigan involved nothing more than a simple introduction to Abigail Grayson and an immediate opening of a practice in Grayson Grove. She'd not planned on Nate Grayson being the joker in the deck. He impressed her as a stubborn, opinionated man, who'd become well accustomed to having his own way. In all truth, she guessed he probably found her cut from a similar cloth, but Vivid believed such traits were necessary for females in a male-dominated world; in a man they were simply irritating.

Her musings were interrupted by the constant bounce of the wagon against the unleveled road, lifting her up and bringing her down. Hard. After enduring the transcontinental train ride and the jolting two-hour ride to

Grayson Grove, her backside was decidedly unhappy.
She would surely be unable to sit on anything for at least
a month if this kept up much longer.

"How much farther?" she asked.

"About a mile," Grayson answered.

While Magic continued to plead her case for the tree
house with all the fervor of a nine-year-old, Vivid returned her attention to the view. Michigan was so unlike
home. Here one could hear the songs of birds, the wind
whispering secrets from the endless stand of trees. There
were no mountains, but up ahead the land dipped and
then rose. For as far as she could see, there were trees,
trees, and more trees. Here and there small patches of
cleared plots anchored by little houses and farms dotted
the landscape, but mostly the land exuded newness and
raw vitality.

"Rain ahead, Pa," Magic pointed out.

"I see it. Get the slickers. They're in the bed."

While Magic climbed into the back of the wagon with
the quick agility inherent in most children, Vivid wor-
riedly scanned the dark clouds filling the sky ahead. The
trees she'd viewed earlier as just examples of pastoral
beauty began to respond with a distinct restlessness. The
wind picked up and was now blowing against her face.

Once again in her seat, Magic handed a patched and
well-used slicker to her father and another to Vivid, who
donned it immediately while Magic shrugged into the
last one, smiling. "I love storms."

Vivid wondered if the child had suddenly become de-
lirious. Magic watched the road ahead with unbridled
glee as she said, "There was a real bad one last year.
Took Widow Moss's pigpen all the way to the river."

The first boom of thunder rumbled into hearing. The
trees were louder now, the tops bowing to the superior
force of the increasing winds. Vivid had been caught
outside in a few showers back home, but she doubted
this would be anything near those mild affairs. The light-

ning dancing ominously ahead didn't seem to dampen Magic's mood one bit. "Count, Dr. Lancaster!"

Count? Vivid had no idea what the girl meant, but she could see Magic's lips moving as she counted silently. Then she heard a boom of thunder.

"Nine, Pa," Magic reported as she sharp crackling died.

"Thanks, keep me posted."

Magic turned to Vivid. "It's how to tell where the storm's going. You have to watch for the lightning. When you see it flash, count until you hear the thunder. Then you watch again and count. If the number is smaller than the first time, the storm is closer. If the number gets bigger, it's moving away."

Vivid had never heard of such a thing.

"The See-Pees taught it to Ol' Pa Grayson when he first settled the Grove, and he taught it to Grandpa. Grandpa taught it to my pa, and Pa taught it to me," Magic explained proudly.

"You counting or talking, Majestic?" her father asked.

"Sorry, pa."

Vivid was about to ask who or what See-Pees were when the rain began: fat, wet pellets the size of dollars. Vivid's hat, a fashionable confection on the streets of San Francisco, offered no protection against the deluge of Michigan wind and water.

"Six, Pa!"

He nodded, then bent and kept one eye on the reins as he reached beneath the seat to bring out two weather-beaten hats. He wordlessly passed one to Magic and tossed the other onto Vivid's lap. She hastily removed her hatpin and hat. The wind tried to take her lovely green hat, but she fought off the gust and pinned the soggy felt between her knees while she pulled on the other hat, grateful for its large size and wide brim.

The sky above had gone from slate-gray to a tumultuous black in a matter of minutes. Rain blew across Vivid's face with a strength that made it hard to see and breathe. She could only pray Grayson knew where he and the horses were headed. The smaller trees were now prostrate in obeisance and the older ones were bowing at the waist. The angry, deep bass sound of thunder rumbled louder and louder.

"Four and a piece, Pa!"

"We'll hole up at the old Reynolds place!" he shouted over another crack of thunder, loud as cannon fire.

How he found the small rut that led from the main road to the burned-out hulk of the old Reynolds place, Vivid did not know. She'd never been so grateful to see shelter. She and Magic scrambled down quickly while Grayson unhitched the horses. Humans and animal sought refuge within.

"Over here, Dr. Lancaster," Magic said, grabbing Vivid's hand. "Southeast corner, always."

Vivid went quietly, all the while marveling. Did all Michigan people know about counting lightning and the safest corner inside a house? When Magic sat down on the dirt floor, so did Vivid. She had no idea if sitting was part of the drill, but sitting on something that didn't bounce against her tender backside felt wonderful.

The storm did not qualify as wonderful. Outside, the rain and wind screamed. Inside, the partially standing walls and what remained of the roof cut some of the fury but not enough to keep them from experiencing the wrath of the wind, the ground-shaking cracks of lightning strikes, and the malevolent echoes of the accompanying thunder.

"Are storms always this way, Magic?" Vivid yelled above the noise.

"Oh, this is a big one, but wait till it gets hot in the summer. Then you'll see some big storms."

Vivid shook her head, still unable to comprehend the

child's fascination. Vivid liked storms also, but she'd never experienced such violent weather. But if she planned on being the doctor here, she'd have to accustom herself to such episodes. Not all medical emergencies happened on bright, sunny days.

She looked up to see Grayson watching her. Their eyes held. Vivid felt something touch her from within the distant gaze, then he turned away.

A few moments later, the storm passed as swiftly as it had appeared, leaving behind a soft rain and a cool breeze.

The wagon was stuck in the mud. Grayson jumped down from the seat and called to his daughter standing next to Vivid in the doorway of the shack. "Majestic, come take the reins."

Magic ran through the mud out to the wagon and scrambled aboard. Her father went around to the back to push. Vivid was smiling as she watched him slog through the slop until he turned her way and said, "Doctor, you either help push or walk. Your choice."

Vivid wondered how he'd feel about having *two* bullet holes in that old beat-up hat of his instead of one. She had absolutely no desire to traverse that mud, but rather than be judged unfit, she started toward the wagon. She gasped as the cold mud swallowed her shoes. Her stricken face met his amused eyes. She slogged through the mud just as he had, although she was certain he hadn't mourned the loss of an expensive pair of shoes during the journey. She did her best to hold her skirts up from the muck but the going was slow at best.

"Now while Magic reins the team, we'll push," he told her.

In tandem with Grayson, Vivid gave it all she had. It took three tries to free the wheels enough for the horses to gain leverage. When the wheels finally came free, the sudden movement made Vivid lose her balance and land facefirst in the mud. Grayson's uproarious laughter gave her a sense of how she must look. She stood up, wiped the mud from her eyes, and looked down at her beautiful ruined dress. The snow-white blouse with its hand-done lace and mother-of-pearl buttons looked as if it had been doused in gravy. The traveling dress her aunt had sent her from Mexico would never be emerald-green again. Grayson was still laughing, and so was Magic, the traitor.

"If we're finished, may we go now?" she asked haughtily.

"Sure," Nate told her, but he couldn't stop laughing. Vivid gave him a blistering look and climbed into the wagon.

Some time later a shocked Abigail Grayson met them at the door. "Oh, my dear Dr. Lancaster, look at you. What happened?"

Magic piped up, "She fell in the mud, Aunt Gail. I thought Pa was going to bust a gut laughing so hard."

"Nathaniel!" his aunt said scoldingly.

"Don't 'Nathaniel' me, Abigail I'm-gone-to-Kalamazoo Grayson. You have some explaining to do."

Had Vivid not been so wet and chilled she'd have laughed at the look of feigned innocence on Abigail's face as she replied, "Why, I've no idea what you mean."

"I'll bet you don't," Nate said, smiling.

Abigail smiled back, then said, "Dr. Lancaster, come on in here where we can get you dry. Nate, bring in some water for her. Magic, change out of those wet things and set the table."

Abigail Grayson was nearly as tall as her nephew and had the same smoke-black eyes. She leaned on a cane and moved as proudly as if she were royal-born. She steered Vivid through the well-furnished front room of the very large house and back to the kitchen.

"There's biscuits in the oven. I'm sure they won't mind you stealing a little of their heat."

A shivering Vivid warmed her hands near the warm metal.

Moments later, Nate reentered from the back of the house carrying a huge cauldron of water. From beneath her lashes Vivid watched his arms strain with the weight as he set it atop the stove, the corded muscles as beautifully detailed as an anatomy drawing. Vivid forced her attention back to Abigail, "I'm sorry, Mrs. Grayson, what did you say?"

"It's Miss Grayson, Dr., and I asked if you wanted some tea."

"Oh, yes, please. Anything to cut these shivers."

Abigail handed her a cup. The warmth against Vivid's hands made her smile and purr, "Thank you."

"You're welcome, and once you finish I'll show you where you can wash up and change. Then you can tell me about the fit Nate threw when he found out you weren't a man."

Shocked, Vivid turned to Nate, who said, "Told you I knew nothing about that contract. But later my beloved aunt is going to tell me how she accomplished that not-so-small feat."

"Nathaniel, if I tell you, it won't work the next time."

His eyes narrowed.

Abigail said, "Oh, all right, maybe there won't be a next time."

Vivid smiled. Yes, she liked the Grayson women.

Nate looked from aunt to doctor, shook his head, and said, "I'm going to wash up and change."

Dinner that night was glorious. Vivid sat at the table in a fresh clean skirt and blouse and knew that her mother would have been appalled at the amount of food she had just consumed. Her mother believed that a lady never ate more than a nibble of this and a dabble of that, but Vivid had always had a healthy appetite, and as long as one didn't display the table manners of a cretin, she didn't feel it necessary to apologize for enjoying well-prepared food. Besides, she'd been eating train and coach meals for what seemed like months. She was close to starving.

"There's more turkey, Dr. Lancaster."

"I can't eat another bite, Abigail. Thank you."

Vivid could feel Nate Grayson watching her so she turned to him. "Yes?"

"Just wondering where you put all that food, Lancaster."

Vivid felt embarrassment stroke her cheeks.

Abigail smiled over her teacup and said, "Behave," to her nephew.

Vivid made it a point to ignore Grayson for the remainder of dinner. He seemed content to let her be, though on more than one occasion Vivid looked up to find herself under his speculative scrutiny.

When the conversation dwindled to a close, Vivid could not hide the large yawn that escaped her. She was tired, but the excitement of this new adventure made her want the day to continue. Abigail had other ideas. "Nate, take her over to the doc's place and make sure she gets settled in. Magic, you go on, too, and help the doctor unpack what she needs for the night."

"That really isn't necessary," Vivid offered. "If you point me in the right direction, I can find it."

"Nope. Nate, go with her. Take Magic. I'll be over after I clean up here."

Abigail steadfastly refused Vivid's offer to help with the dishes. "Young woman, you can barely stand. Get on over to the house before you fall asleep on your feet and Nate has to carry you."

That got Vivid moving.

The little house she would be occupying was set in

back of the main house. The land surrounding it had been cleared for acres around. She could only imagine how long it must have taken the Grayson ancestors to carve out this small paradise.

"How long has your family been here, Mr. Grayson?"

"Since '37," Magic answered for him. "Ol' Pa Grayson got freed and came here all the way from Carolina."

"Did he come alone?" Vivid asked her.

"No, there were thirty-four people. They came here and founded Grayson Grove. Do you have a family, Dr. Lancaster?"

"Yes, I have parents and two older sisters. Jessica and Alicea."

They stepped onto the wooden porch and Grayson opened the door and held it aside for the ladies to enter. The front room was small, consisting of a blanket-covered cot against one wall and a small desk and chair against another.

"This is where Doc saw his patients till he got drunk and fell off the roof of the Emporium and died," Magic volunteered.

Vivid stared. Grayson offered nothing but a stern look in his daughter's direction.

In the back there were three more rooms: a bedroom, a kitchen, and a room equipped for surgery.

"How many people are in your community?"

"Almost three hundred if you also count the Black folks in Casapolis and Calvin Center."

"Spread out over how many miles?"

"Most are within a few, some as far away as ten, twenty. Why?"

"Because I need to meet everyone, get their names, ages, medical histories."

She saw the odd look on Grayson's face and asked, "Is something wrong, Mr. Grayson?"

"Doc never did that."

"I'm not Doc," she said with a smile. She then turned to his daughter. "Magic, why don't you help me unpack?"

Since the bulk of Vivid's belongings were still at the station, it only took Vivid and Magic a few moments to transfer the clothing and toiletries into a big Saratoga trunk sent over by Abigail. When the job was done, Magic headed back to the house, leaving Vivid alone with Nate Grayson.

"I still believe you'll leave before the worst of the winter," he said, his powerful-looking arms folded across his chest.

"I do enjoy a challenge, so I'm determined to prove you wrong."

"What else do you enjoy?"

The tone of his voice made Vivid hesitate. He seemed to want to know something more than just her leisure activities. "I enjoy poker, playing billiards—"

"Billiards," he echoed skeptically. He looked over at the case that held her stick.

"Yes. You're familiar with the game? You lean over a big table that has holes in the corners—"

"I know how to play, Lancaster," he said in exasperated amusement. "But what's a woman like you doing playing billiards? What did your parents think about this pastime of yours?"

"My father taught it to me when I was seven or eight. He says I have a gift."

"A gift?"

"Yes, Mr. Grayson. Women can be gifted in other things besides hat choosing."

"Wait," he said, holding up his hands. "Let me get a seat. I want to hear all of this." He pulled out the chair, turned it around, and settled his big body in it. "Now, you say you have a gift for billiards, according

to your father. What about your mother? Does she think
you're gifted, too?''

He was laughing at her, and Vivid narrowed her eyes
at his tone. Would this man ever take her seriously?
''No, my mother thought my gifts were limited to getting into trouble. She nicknamed me 'Trabrasera.' ''

''Which means?''

''Trouble.''

''So that's what's wrong with my Magic. She's
gifted.''

''She does remind me a lot of myself at her age.''

''Lord help us,'' he whispered. ''Go on. Where did
you play billiards? Because no self-respecting woman I
know would even walk past an establishment of that
type, let alone go inside one.''

Vivid ignored his intimation that she was not respect-
able. ''I played wherever there was a table. My father
is one of the best chefs and caterers in San Francisco,
but when he was younger he cooked in all types of
places—brothels, men's clubs, mansions. Sometimes my
sisters and I had to go along when Mama had to help
him in the kitchen. Most of those places had billiard
tables. While my parents and the rest of the staff people
were in the kitchen setting up before the evening's activities, my sisters and I were encouraged to play, mostly
so we'd stay out of the workers' hair. At night we
weren't allowed near the places, but by the time I
reached adolescence, a lot of the gamblers and club owners knew of my penchant for playing, and I became like
a favorite pet. A woman playing billiards was and is
quite an oddity.''

''Your sisters play billiards, too?''

''Not as well as I, but yes, they play.''

''And your father encouraged this?''

''He never believed in keeping us from anything we
enjoyed, and he saw no harm in it.'' She paused for a
moment and then said, ''You know, men can be such

fools sometimes. They see a woman with a cue in her hand and for some reason believe she must be using it to take pots off a stove. Men would bet me outrageous amounts of money and stand agape when they realized I could play. My mother threatened to send me to a Mexican convent when she found out how much money I had accumulated.''

Dumfounded, Nate could only stare.

"You look so stunned, Mr. Grayson.''

"And that is also how you learned to play poker, too, I take it.''

"Yes. I'm not as good at cards as I am with a cue, but I play a decent hand.''

"What other vices do you practice?''

"Well, let's see. I've thrown dice and darts. I play faro and keno. I was a pickpocket for about an hour when I was ten.''

"A pickpocket!''

"Yes. When I was young I would go to go to wharf every day during the summers with my father to buy fresh vegetables. There were some street children who frequented the wharf. They had no families and they would steal watches and coin purses, and the vegetables and fish from the vendors' stalls. One day the constables were chasing the band through the market and I remember thinking how exciting it must be to live that way.''

"Go on,'' Nate said.

"Well, a few days after the constable incident I slipped away from my father at the wharf and went off in search of the children. I found them living in an old shack not far from the market and I asked if I could join. They were suspicious of course, but I gave the leader the gold crucifix I had around my neck and I was allowed in. Of course, I was caught the first time I tried to cut a purse, and what made matters even worse, the pocket I'd tried to pick belonged to the sexton at my church. He marched me right over to my father, who had been frantically searching the wharf for me.''

"What did your father do?''

"After he kissed me for being alive, he listened to the sexton's story and took me home.''

"And?''

"And gave me over to my mother. He told me later he was too angry to punish me the way he thought I deserved, and he didn't want to injure me.''

"In other words he wanted to whip the tar out of you?''

"Exactly. So my mother did it instead. I'd done some dangerous and stupid things in my short life until then, but that was the topper. My mother lectured me for weeks afterward on responsibility and perceptions and being an example for the race. But it was my father's disappointment that hurt me more than anything else, and I never did anything even remotely similar again.''

"Do your people call you Viveca?''

"No, they call me Vivid.''

"Why?''

"Viveca was hard for my sisters to pronounce when we were all small. Closest my sister Jess could come was Vivid. My father says Vivid also defines my personality. My mother prefers Viveca, however.'' Vivid looked over at Nate Grayson and wondered if maybe she'd said too much. He could certainly use the information she'd just volunteered against her even though he had promised her the job on a trial basis. Her mother often faulted her for being so open about personal matters. As she'd gotten older Vivid had curbed the practice to some extent, but it was a habit she still found hard to break completely.

"Anything else I should know?''

"Whether you believe it or not, I'm accustomed to hard work.

He appeared skeptical. "And what do you consider hard work?"

"I've put up fences, cleared brush."

"Cleared brush?"

Vivid nodded. "Yes, my *abuela*—"

"*Abuela*?"

"My grandmother has a large ranch down by the Mexican border. My sisters and I would visit her in the summers sometimes. We'd help her and her vaqueros clear brush, repair fences. We even helped at round up one year, and each of us took a turn at branding cattle."

"You've branded cattle?"

"Only once. The vaqueros swore to me the cattle didn't feel the brand, but after I smelled the burned hide and saw the terror in the poor animal's eyes, I didn't believe them and I never did it again."

Nate found her tales so amazing he didn't know whether to believe them or not. Women branding cattle, and what in the hell was a *vaquero?* If all she said was true, he realized he was only beginning to understand just how vivid this woman truly was. However, he was still convinced she would not stay.

"Mr. Grayson, I admit I am not conventional by anyone's definition, but if you judge me on the kind of medicine I practice, the rest shouldn't matter. And who knows, we may even become friends."

"Anything is possible."

"Yes, it is."

He stood then and pushed the chair under the desk. "I should be getting back."

"I thank you for affording me the opportunity to stay, especially when you don't believe in my ability."

Nate looked into her eyes. There was no guile in this female. She laid her cards right on the table. "You always this straightforward?"

"A good physician goes to the heart of the matter," she replied. "And I've learned men respect frankness, even when they don't respect me as a physician or a woman.''

"Touché,'' he said.

"You misunderstood me. I wasn't being catty, Mr. Grayson, simply truthful.''

Nate had to admit there was more to the doctor than he first imagined. He walked to the screened door.

Her voice stopped him just as he pushed it open. ''Mr. Grayson?''

Nate turned back.

Their eyes met and held.

"Thank you,'' she said quietly.

He surveyed her a moment, then nodded. ''You're welcome.''

And he was gone.

That night, Nate lay in bed in the big attic bedroom. He'd been thinking about the doctor most of the evening. How would folks react? He assumed she'd receive staunch support from the women, especially from his aunt and Miss Edna over at the store; although the Quilt Ladies could be a problem if they decided the doctor didn't match their old-fashioned image of womanhood. But it was the men of the Grove who would be hardest to bring around. Hell, if Nate himself had such little faith in her, he could imagine the grief she'd receive from some of his male neighbors. In fact, the debates had probably already begun with the news of her arrival. He would have to remain neutral in order to be fair to both sides. Even though he had his opinion, it would not be right for him to influence the others.

Nate still held fast to his belief that she would be gone before the first winter snow. She was from San Francisco, for heaven's sake. However, if her success here depended on sheer will and determination, she'd win hands down. He truly believed most females would not have had the gumption to confront him as she'd done in town today, and none would have gone so far as to shoot a hole in his hat. He dearly hoped Magic would not become too attached to the good doctor, because the two of them together would only bring trouble. More importantly, he didn't want Magic to be heartbroken when the doctor pulled up stakes and high-tailed it back to San Francisco.

Chapter 5

Very early the next morning, a pounding on the door awakened Vivid from a sound sleep. Stumbling from the cot, she stuck her arms into her robe and crossed the plank floor to the door. She expected to find someone in need of medical assistance or maybe Nate Grayson; what she found was a brawl in full-swing in the yard. Men were everywhere; punching one another, violently wrestling in the grass, standing nose to nose and arguing at the tops of their lungs.

There were other men in the yard, too, all dressed in their Sunday best and lined up as if waiting to purchase theater tickets. In their hands were bunches of wildflowers, squawking chickens, hams, and even animal pelts. Others were accompanied by goats or sad-faced children, and one man held the lead to a spotted milk cow. Vivid could only stare, amazed.

"Quite a sight, isn't it?"

The question came from a man standing on the porch. He smiled kindly at her with a sparkle of mischief in his smoke-black eyes. His handsomeness rivaled Nate Grayson's—in fact, the two men looked enough alike to be brothers. "I'm Eli Grayson," he said. "Abigail's son and Nate's cousin. You must be the new doc."

"Yes, I am. Dr. Viveca Lancaster."

He shook her outstretched hand. "I heard Nate threw a fit when you arrived. I also heard you shot his hat off his head."

"Yes, he did. And yes, I did. But tell me, what is all this?" she asked, indicating the chaos in her yard.

"They're deciding who gets to see you first."

"What?"

"Where are you from, Dr. Lancaster?"

"California."

"Ah. Well, I don't know what this is called in California, but here it's called courting."

Vivid stared. "Courting?"

"You're unmarried, or at least that's the story going around. They think you'd make a good wife."

Vivid looked over the men, some standing triumphantly over opponents knocked out cold and prone. She couldn't decide whether to be flattered or appalled. "Mr. Grayson—"

"Call me Eli."

"Eli, I didn't come here for a husband," she explained with a hint of exasperation. "I'm here to be a physician."

To her surprise, he pulled out a small sheaf of papers and a pencil. "Can I quote you on that? I run the newspaper."

Before she could answer, the drama in the yard took on new proportions as a rifle went off. In the resulting silence, not even the birds dared sing.

Rifle in hand, Nate Grayson, dressed in his trousers and without a shirt, turned a malevolent look on the crowd and shouted, "What the hell's going on here?"

Eli stepped down from the porch and said, "They're all here to see Dr. Lancaster, Nate. Can't say as I blame them. Look at her. I'm thinking about stepping in a bear trap myself."

The gaze Nate turned on Vivid would have sent any other woman running back into the cabin. She knew he would consider this display a prime example of why she was unsuitable, but Vivid was not responsible in any way and refused to allow him to blame her.

Vivid stepped into the yard. Ignoring Nate Grayson, she said in a loud voice, "Gentlemen, I am only going to say this once. I am here to be your doctor. I am not seeking a husband. Do not court me. Now, anyone needing medical assistance may stay. The rest of you, go back to your homes."

There was a bit of grumbling and a few disgruntled faces, but they complied. After she took care of the few men with cuts and bruises, she was ready to contend with the Grayson cousins.

Vivid turned to Eli and said, "I would appreciate it if you would not write about this in your paper."

"You're news, Dr. Lancaster. The size of the crowd alone attests to that."

"I didn't come here for a husband, Mr. Grayson, just to practice medicine."

"Then practice it wearing something other than your nightgown, Lancaster," Nate snapped, stepping up on the porch. His worse fears had come true. Once word got around about her beauty and lack of husband, men and lumber beasts from as far away as Saginaw and Muskegon would descend on the Grove in droves to court her.

Vivid looked down at herself. She'd forgotten her state of dress when all this began, but her gown was not a revealing one. She sensed part of his temper could be traced to the melee in the yard, but she vowed to keep her retorts to herself. Grayson held her future in his hands. It would not do to have herself dismissed and escorted to the train station over an issue she considered trivial. With him, she would have to pick her battles. "You're correct, Mr. Grayson. The next time someone comes pounding at my door, I will make certain I am dressed properly. I only hope a seriously wounded patient won't mind bleeding to death while waiting for me to comply with your wishes."

Eli chuckled, "Dr. Lancaster, the Grove's going to enjoy having you here."

Nate turned to his cousin and asked coolly, "When did you get back?"

"Last night. And don't worry, I won't be here long. I'll be heading for the Centennial in Philadelphia in a few weeks."

"Good. Stay out of my way."

Vivid could almost touch the tension between the two cousins as they glared at each other. She'd no idea what lay between them, but she had had enough brawling for one morning, so she told them, "If you two cocks are going to fight, do it elsewhere, please."

Eli spoke first, "Nate's the one spoiling for a fight, aren't you, cousin?"

"You keep printing that hogwash in that rag you call a paper and there's going to be more than spoiling."

Nate turned angrily and took off across the grass.

"You'll have to forgive his manners, Dr. Lancaster," Eli said. "He and I are having a political disagreement of sorts. He's always right and I'm always wrong."

Vivid silently watched Nate until he disappeared through the line of trees that separated the cabin from the main house. "What do you mean?"

"I'm a registered Democrat."

Vivid turned to him and stared. "A Democrat! You are jesting with me?"

"No."

Vivid, thinking about the terror in the South, said quietly, "Some folks would say your cousin has a right to be angry."

"I agree, but the Republicans have done nothing but betray us."

Vivid knew about the debate raging nationwide over which political party deserved the Black vote in the upcoming presidential election. But to be a Democrat?

"How do you justify all that's happening in the South and Washington?"

"How does Grant justify what he hasn't done to protect the people who elected him?" Eli asked.

Therein lay the debate. Black Republicans were becoming increasingly disenchanted with the country's do-nothing policy concerning the South. Many Black men had lost their lives to Democratic forces while trying to vote in the election in 1874, yet representative Blacks such as Douglass and Pinchback were calling on Blacks to consider voting Democratic this time around to keep the Republicans from taking the Black vote for granted. As far as Vivid knew, few Blacks had crossed over.

"Have dinner with me and I'll explain my position."

"And what will your cousin say?"

"Nothing I can print."

Were it not for Nate, Vivid would have probably agreed. She seriously doubted Eli's ability to convert her, for she and her family were staunch Republicans. However, she always enjoyed stimulating conversation.

"So will you have dinner with me?"

"I'll have to speak with your cousin first. I really don't know if I'm allowed to keep company."

"You're going to ask Nate if I can take you to dinner?"

"He is my employer, after all. I've no desire to be dismissed because I may have transgressed some rule."

Eli held her eyes a moment. "Well, I'll be real interested in what Nate has to say, so let me know. In the meantime, I'd like to do a story on you for the *Gazette*. May I stop in next week after you're settled?"

"That would be fine." Vivid doubted she would need permission for an interview.

He walked back to the road where he had left his buggy, got in, and with a departing wave, headed his rig toward town.

Vivid reentered her cabin wanting to go back to sleep,

but with all she had to do today, she washed and dressed instead. She longed to put on a pair of her trousers, but they were still with the crates at the depot, so she settled for a shirtwaist and skirt instead. Her first order of business was finding food. There was none in the cabin and she didn't have utensils, either. She wondered if she'd be allowed to enlarge the kitchen, as the space now was totally inadequate for the daughter of one of San Francisco's premier caterers. Vivid enjoyed a good meal and, thanks to her father, knew how to prepare one.

In the end she sat down and composed a list of things she needed, which she planned on showing to Abigail. The woman would certainly be able to advise her on how best to make her purchases.

A knock at the door broke her concentration. She opened it to find Nate Grayson on the other side and wondered if he was still angry about that morning.

"May I come in?" he asked.

She stepped back to let him enter.

"Aunt Gail says you're welcome up at the house if you're hungry."

"That's very nice of her." Vivid replied.

Silence fell between them and Vivid mused on how best to bring up this morning's incident. Finally, she asked, "Mr. Grayson, are you holding me responsible for this morning?"

Nate surveyed her a moment. "No," he replied, though he did wonder if she realized the dangerous potential of the situation. Those men could have easily stormed the little cabin and harmed her. Her safety had been Nate's first concern when he awakened to the shouts and yells of the mob. He'd rushed to his bedroom window, and upon surveying the scene, jumped into his trousers and grabbed his rifle. To come out and find her standing on the porch in her nightclothes, prim though they may have been, made him wonder why on earth he'd bothered to come to her rescue. His mood

had turned even grimmer when he noticed his handsome cousin Eli smiling down at her.

He'd calmed down after he got back to the house once
he realized he had no rational reason to be angry with
her.

"Did my cousin ask you to dinner?" he asked. Nate
knew Eli would try and be among the first to court her,
and for some reason the knowledge struck in his craw
like a fishbone.

"Yes, he did."

"I thought you weren't looking for a man."

"Your cousin invited me to have dinner, Mr. Grayson, not his children. Besides, I told him I had to ask
you first."

"And he said?"

"That you'd say no."

Nate chuckled, "He knows me well."

"I've no desire to be a pawn in whatever feud you
two are embroiled in. If my accepting his invitation will
fan the flames, or get me tossed out on my bustle, please
tell me now and I'll decline."

"Just like that."

"Just like that."

Nate held her gaze. "Tell him it isn't allowed."

Vivid nodded.

Her immediate acceptance surprised him. "You aren't
going to argue with me."

"Nope."

"Why not?"

"You're my employer."

"And what will you tell my cousin?"

"That you said no, just as he predicted."

Usually when Nate and Eli weren't embroiled in an
argument, they were competing against each other.
They'd been at it since they were boys, each trying to
best the other in everything from fishing, to lacrosse, to
women. Nate had effectively delivered a checkmate by

refusing to let the doctor dine with him, but somehow the victory rang hollow—maybe because of the quiet censure in Lancaster's eyes. "You won't argue, but I can tell by your eyes you don't agree."

Vivid shrugged. "It's not for me to agree or disagree. You don't want me to have dinner with your cousin. So be it."

"And you don't mind?" he asked skeptically.

"Of course I mind, Mr. Grayson. I found your cousin quite nice, but his invitation isn't worth arguing over. You and I will find many more substantive issues to fight about before I serve you your crow, so I'm picking my battles."

He gave her a brief smile. "You see this as a series of battles?"

"I view this as a campaign of sorts, yes."

"Don't tell me you've studied military strategies also?"

"No. Hannibal."

"Hannibal?"

"Yes, the great general who took the elephants over the Alps—"

"I know who Hannibal is, Lancaster, but . . ." Nate found her so absolutely amazing he didn't even know what to ask next.

"My mother has devoted her life to studying him."

"Your mother?"

"Yes. My sisters and I grew up on the tales of General Hannibal's bravery. Did you know it is said he tossed cauldrons of snakes onto the decks of opponents' ships during one of his naval battles?"

He didn't; in fact, Nate had no idea Hannibal had ever fought on water.

"Do you want to come up to the house?"

His abruptness caught her offguard. "I'm sorry, Mr. Grayson, I didn't mean to bore you—"

"You weren't boring me. You just leave me speechless at times is all."

Vivid looked up and fought to keep her smile hidden.
"Is that good or bad?"

"I'm not sure," he replied, looking down into her
extraordinarily lovely eyes. "But I'll let you know."

The room suddenly became very warm, or at least it
felt that way to Vivid. She took a step back and said,
"Um, just let me get my list and I'll come have breakfast."

"What list?"

"Things I need to purchase. Food supplies, that sort
of thing. Is there a place nearby where I might purchase
a horse and wagon or buggy?"

She seemed flustered, and Nate wondered if it was his
imagination or not. "Miss Edna over at the store can
probably order you one, but I'll also check around and
see if anyone has one for sale."

"That would be fine."

After breakfast and a discussion with Abigail, Vivid
rode into town with Nate. The trek to town seemed
shorter than it had yesterday when they were delayed by
the pouring rain. Today's sky was much brighter. And
with the rain gone the mugginess had disappeared also.
There was a nice breeze, and it felt good on her face.

Once in town, Nate let her off at the store and told
her he'd be back to fetch her after he conducted his
business at the mill. Vivid nodded and went inside.

"Well, hello, Dr. Lancaster," called the woman from
behind the store's counter.

Vivid smiled in reply. She remembered her from yesterday. "Good morning, Miss Edna."

Edna appeared to be a contemporary of Abigail's. She
had thick chestnut and gray hair coiled in braids around
her head. The beauty of her youth still showed strongly
in her ivory-skinned face. "I heard you had a few visitors this morning."

Remembering, Vivid shook her head in amazement. "Yes, and it was quite the scene. Mr. Grayson finally cleared everyone out. I didn't know whether to be flattered or appalled.'

"Well, it's for certain that won't be the end. You, young woman, were put on the drum yesterday. Men as far north as Grand Traverse Bay will be hearing about you by the end of the week. Women are scarce out here. Perhaps not as scarce as they were when I came to Michigan in '58, but scarce just the same. They'll hear about you and come. Some, simply because they've never seen a female do doctoring before. Others will come because they'll have heard how beautiful you are. I even had a few of the Napowesipe come in this morning and ask about you."

Edna must have read the confusion on Vivid's face because she explained, "The Napowesipe are the native people. At one time they owned all the land in this region. Most were forced out by the government many years ago, but a few still live nearby."

"Magic mentioned something about See-Pees yesterday; are these the people she meant?"

"Yes. Some of the children call them See-Pees; some of the adults, too, I'm sorry to say. Nate prefers they be called Napowesipe or Neshnabek which are their tribal names. I do, too. Shortening their names to See-Pees is as shameful as having our ancestors' beautiful names changed to things like Toby."

Vivid saw the rightness in Edna's thinking and made a mental note to keep her words in mind. She was about to ask whether the Napowesipe had a doctor when Edna excused herself to help a customer who'd just entered. Vivid nodded a greeting to the newcomer, and slowly strolled through the store while waiting for Edna to return.

For such an isolated place, the Grayson Grove General Store had quite a selection of goods. Vivid saw flour and spices, bolts of material, saddles, boots, building supplies, and a shelf that held a few out-of-town newspapers both Black and White. There were barrels of pickles and crackers, and on another shelf cans of Mr. Van Camp's beans in tomato sauce. "You have a well-stocked place here, Miss Edna," Vivid remarked after the customer exited.

"Well, Nate makes sure we have everything we need here," Edna replied proudly.

Vivid noted that the mail order catalogs were well thumbed and nestled next to the newspapers and the penny peppermint jar atop the counter. Above the papers Vivid spied the bottled and packaged nostrums that claimed to cure everything from baldness to lovesickness to the flushing away of an unwanted child. The store had quite a few varieties of the pretty bottled potions. Vivid hoped the quantities stocked did not indicate that the "cures" were widely purchased in the Grove. If they were, she anticipated a hard fight weaning her new patients away from them. Most of the powders and syrups were harmless; some, like the packaged calomel, were dangerous. She began to take the jars down from the shelves. Taken in large quantities, it could harm rather than heal.

"Miss Edna, I want you to stop selling calomel."

The woman looked at the bottles Vivid placed on the counter and asked, "But why? Folks have been using calomel for years."

"It's dangerous."

"Dangerous how, Dr. Lancaster?"

"Do you know anyone who uses this regularly?"

Edna thought for a moment. "Well, let's see. There was old man Crane who used to own the mill. He died last year. He used calomel every three or four days for as long as I knew him, said it kept him cleaned out, if you know what I mean."

Vivid understood. "Now, Edna, think about this. Do

you remember what condition his teeth were in when he died?''

"I don't even have to think on that one. He had none. Most of them fell out years ago."

"It was the calomel. When you use it for long periods, it destroys the gums and teeth."

"Really?"

"Really."

Edna looked at the bottles again with renewed interest. "This is one of the things they taught you in school?"

"Yes, ma'am."

Vivid could see Edna evaluating the information. Their eyes met, and Vivid could sense the older woman was not quite convinced. "Dr. Lancaster, I believe what you're saying is true, but what do I tell my customers?"

"Tell them I said they can benefit more from eating the fruits on their trees and the vegetables in their gardens."

Edna remained skeptical, so Vivid opened her handbag and began searching inside for her coin purse. "How's this for a solution? I will purchase your entire stock of calomel, that way you can tell your customers you're out of it and it won't be a lie."

"They'll want me to order it the next time the salesman comes through."

Vivid put the money atop the counter. "I'll buy the next shipment also, and I'll talk to Mr. Grayson about my concerns."

"Fine with me. If Nate says to stop selling it, I will." Edna took the money and placed it in her cash box.

For the rest of the morning Vivid and Miss Edna worked on Vivid's list of items. Miss Edna had to excuse herself a couple of times to help other customers, but Vivid used the opportunity to introduce herself to those willing to shake her hand. Some greeted her enthusiastically, while others were a bit more reserved. A few of the farmers entered to buy necessities, then sat around watching Vivid and drinking Miss Edna's coffee.

"You the new doc?" one of the men asked.

Vivid walked over and introduced herself. "Yes, sir, I am. I'm Viveca Lancaster, and you are?"

"I'm Abraham Patterson, this here is my brother Aaron."

Vivid looked at the two middle-aged men and realized they were mirror images of each other. "You're twins."

Abraham looked over to his brother and said, "See, Aaron, told you she'd figure it out. She might be female, but she ain't a blind female."

Vivid couldn't decide whether they were pulling her leg. "Why didn't you think I'd be able to tell you were twins, Mr. Patterson?"

"Females ain't known to be real bright."

"I see," Vivid replied. "Well, would you be amenable to me taking your histories?"

"Why?" asked the skeptical Aaron.

"So I'll know what diseases you've had, how much you weigh, how old you are—that sort of thing."

She waited. She could see Miss Edna watching intently.

Aaron said, "Got nothing to say to a female."

Vivid looked around at the seven or eight other men in the store. "Is this how you all feel?"

Silence.

"I see," she said.

Miss Edna's voice broke the quiet. "Every last one of you should be ashamed of yourself. This girl came here to be your doctor when nobody else would, and you're all treating her like a Democrat. Avery Jackson, you had to go clear to Battle Creek last year when you fell off your roof. At the council meeting you were the one yelling the loudest about Nate finding us a doctor. And Aaron Patterson, I have apple trees with more sense than you. How dare you question her intelligence?"

Her comments were met with furious mumbles, then someone in the back said, "I still say a woman's got no right being a doctor."

"And you have mutton for brains, Peter Templeton," Edna said.

Vivid did not want to start an argument. "Please. I'm sorry that some of you feel the way you do. All I ask is that you save judgment until you know me better."

Silence.

Vivid sighed. This was going to be harder than she'd imagined.

She turned to go back to the counter but stopped. Nate Grayson stood in the doorway watching, and she wondered how much he'd heard.

"I'll be ready as soon as I take care of my purchases."

He nodded.

He assumed the mountain of supplies stacked beside her were her goods. He knew that fine chefs were paid top wages in big cities, but it appeared she spent money easily. His ex-wife, Cecile, had been that way. Accustomed to her minister father's pocketbook, she seemed bent upon shopping her husband and his family into the poor house during the first few months of their marriage, until he put a stop to it. But Lancaster seemed to have purchased other items beside hats and scented soaps. She had rain slickers and wide-brimmed hats, sturdy boots and cooking pots. He also spotted candles, a washboard, and two pairs of denim trousers. Lord knew what else lay beneath the mound on the counter, but it appeared she'd made sound use of her funds.

Vivid watched Nate out of the corner of her eye while she finished up with Miss Edna. She could see him evaluating her goods and she couldn't help but notice how grudgingly impressed he appeared. She supposed he'd assumed she'd come here to purchase hats or some other female fripperies.

She wondered how long it would be before he began judging her as a person and not against some antiquated notion of female behavior? She thanked Miss Edna for her help.

Miss Edna replied kindly, "Don't let those men rile you, Dr. Lancaster. Most of them have good hearts. We'll bring then into the nineteenth century, whether they like it or not. Don't you worry."

Vivid smiled, grateful for the support.

"Are you ready to go back or is there something else you need to do while we're here?" Nate asked, coming up to the counter.

"I believe I have everything. Miss Edna will let me know when the other things I've ordered come in."

"Sure will," Edna promised. "Treat her nice, Nate. She's one to keep."

Nate began carrying Vivid's goods out to the wagon.

"So," Nate asked while he was loading the wagon, "still believe it's going to be a hoedown getting folks to accept you?"

"I told you yesterday at the depot, I fully expect opposition, at first. They'll come around."

"Uh-huh," he replied skeptically.

Once they both climbed onto the bench he picked up the reins and said, "This is only the beginning."

As promised, Vernon had dropped off Vivid's crates at the Grayson house. They were there waiting in front of her cabin when she and Nate returned from Miss Edna's.

Nate helped her put everything inside. When they were done, he left without even waiting for a thank you or a goodbye. He got back atop his big wagon and rumbled away.

Vivid began to unpack, then realized she had absolutely no place to put anything. She had no wardrobe to hang her clothes in, no bureau with drawers, not even a shelf for her many books. At the store today, she'd been so intent on ordering her stove and purchasing needed supplies, her lack of furniture hadn't even crossed her mind. Where in the world was she going to put all her possessions?

"Hello, Dr. Lancaster, may I come in?"

Vivid turned to see Magic standing in the doorway.

"Why certainly, dear. Is school dismissed already?"

"Yes, on account of the bucket of hornets Becky Carpenter's brother Simon hid beneath old man Phillips's desk."

"Hornets?" Vivid asked, looking up from one of the crates. "Was anyone stung?"

"Old man Phillips, but not too badly. Becky says Simon's going to be stung too once her pa finds out."

"Do you think Mr. Phillips needs a doctor?"

"No, I don't think so."

"Why in the world did he bring hornets to school?"

"To upset old man Phillips."

Magic looked at all the crates piled up everywhere, her eyes wide with amazement. "Goodness. Is all this stuff yours, Dr. Lancaster?"

Vivid smiled, remembering that Nate had said much the same thing. "Yes, it is. Only I'm afraid there isn't a place for any of it."

There were so many crates and boxes clogging the floor that it was necessary to turn sideways to walk through them.

"Maybe Aunt Gail will let you borrow some of the old furniture in the attic."

"No, Magic. I don't want to impose upon your family any more than I have already. Your aunt is feeding me; that's burden enough."

For the next hour or so, Magic helped Vivid unearth the items Vivid absolutely needed for her practice. She found her microscope, which Magic oohed and ahhed over; bedding; bandages; and her precious bottles of Mr. Lister's carbolic solution.

"What's this for?" Magic asked as Vivid checked each of the bottles to make certain none had been cracked or damaged during her long journey. "I use it to keep wounds, and dressings, and my instruments clean."

"You can't just use water?"

"I could, but this makes everything extra clean."

Vivid set the bottles against a wall and when she looked back Magic was gone. Perplexed, Vivid called the girl, thinking she might have gone into one of the back rooms for a moment, but no one answered. She pondered the abrupt disappearance for a moment, then, shrugging, went back to her inventory.

Around mid-afternoon, Vivid heard a wagon pulling up outside and she stepped onto the porch. Atop the wagon sat Eli, Abigail, and Magic, and behind them in the bed were large pieces of dark wood furniture.

Vivid stepped down to meet them. "Majestic Grayson, I thought I told you not to bother your family about my needs."

Magic bowed her head and said, "I'm sorry, Dr. Lancaster, I forgot."

Vivid didn't believe her for a minute, and by the looks on the faces of Abigail and Eli, she guessed they didn't, either.

It took a while to get everything unloaded and when they were done, Vivid's small bedroom sported a bed, vanity, bureau, and wardrobe. The matching writing table wouldn't fit, so Vivid had Eli set it in the front room.

Soon after, Abigail went back to the house, while Magic and Eli remained to help Vivid unpack. Vivid discovered Eli to be intelligent, witty, and very much a flirt. She was glad Magic was there to keep him in line, but not even the young girl's presence could stop him from flashing his flirtatious smile her way. By the time

Abigail came back to announce that the afternoon meal was ready, most of their tasks had been completed. Magic had managed to fit a good portion of Vivid's clothing into the drawers and the wardrobe, while Eli and Vivid had nailed up the slat shelves. Her many books were now well displayed, and the instruments and supplies in the surgery were all in place and ready for use.

"You got these two lazybones to really work, didn't you, Viveca?" Abigail said, impressed. "It looks like a home now, doesn't it, Eli?"

"I must say, it doesn't look like Doc's place anymore," Eli confessed, smiling at Vivid. "Who did these paintings?" he asked, indicating the framed sketches and watercolors they'd hung on the walls.

Vivid smiled. "My sister Jessica."

"She's very talented," Abigail replied.

"Pa paints sometimes," Magic added.

Vivid found that surprising.

"Not as much as he did before the war," Abigail noted with a bit of sadness in her tone. Then she turned to her son and asked, "Are you going to eat lunch with us?"

He shook his head no. "It's Nate's house, Mother. He and I would only argue."

Abigail shook her head, "Eli, the two of you need to settle this."

"You need two people to settle a disagreement. When's he willing to listen, I'm willing to talk," Eli replied.

Eli then looked over at Vivid. "I'm going up to Kalamazoo for a few days. Do you need me to purchase anything for you?"

"No, Eli, thank you."

"Mother?"

"Yes, bring back to brains—one for you and one for your cousin. Come, Magic, let's set the table."

The Grayson women exited, leaving Vivid and Eli alone. "I should be going, Dr. Lancaster," he said, heading to the door.

"Please call me Viveca."

He smiled. "Whatever you say, Viveca. When I return, will you have dinner with me?"

"I can't."

"He said no, didn't he?"

Vivid nodded.

"I knew he would. My cousin may be stubborn but he's not dumb." Seeing the confused look on Vivid's face, he continued, "When the time comes, he's not going to want competition, especially from me."

"Competition? For what?"

"You, my dear doctor."

Vivid stared at him a moment, then began to laugh. "For me? You can't be serious. He'd rather boil me in oil."

"I'm not jesting, Viveca. You're a very beautiful and spirited woman. If I may be frank, I find you very attractive."

Vivid could feel her embarrassment spreading on her face.

"And if I find you attractive, Nate will, too, believe me. He and I are more alike than we care to admit, present politics aside, of course."

Vivid shook her head. "Eli, you've been in the sun too long. Your cousin and I spit like cats every time we come near each other. He's opinionated, arrogant, and too accustomed to having his own way, and this I've learned in less than twenty-four hours."

Eli grinned. "Well, don't say I didn't warn you."

Vivid waked to the porch with him.

"I'll see you when I return from Kalamazoo," he said. With a polite inclination of his head, he was gone.

Vivid didn't spend much time mulling over Eli's startling revelation. She knew how Nate Grayson felt about her, and she had no doubt Eli was wrong in his assumption.

Chapter 6

After dinner that evening, Vivid helped Abigail with the dishes, then crossed the grassy field back to her cabin. Once inside she looked around her new home proudly. The furniture had improved the overall look of the small place, as had the addition of Jess's paintings. Vivid thought about her sisters as she bent over a full crate she'd been saving to unpack last. She searched through the special odds and ends and unearthed the small square item she'd been after. She drew back the protective flannel cloth and stared into the smiling eyes of her sisters positioned on either side of her in the small pewter-framed portrait. Vivid had been eight years old when her mother had the portrait commissioned. Alicea, the eldest, had been twelve, and Jessica, ten. They were all dressed in their Sunday best, and to this day Vivid remembered how hard it had been for her to stand still for the initial sketch rendering. Alicea had tried to appear solemn, while Jess, who'd always looked the most like Mama, posed as regally as a queen. Between them stood Vivid, smiling. This portrait had been one of the many on Vivid's nightstand at home and now she set it on the dresser in her small room. As she went back to unpack her other keepsakes and mementos, she vowed to write to Alicea in Boston and Jess in Liberia as soon as she could. She and her sisters were very close and although they'd nicknamed her La Brat Trabrasera when they were younger, and sometimes even now addressed their letters to that moniker, she missed their loving teasing very much.

Nate turned the wagon into the tree-lined drive leading to the back of the Grayson house. He could see light glowing through Lancaster's screened front door. On any other night, he'd go straight to the barn after coming home so late, but tonight he wanted to stop and see her first.

As he'd expected, word about the morning brawl in her front yard had already spread through the Grove. Everywhere he'd gone today, men stopped him to ask if she was really as beautiful as reported. He'd tried to avoid answering, saying each man would have to form his own opinion, but they refused to be put off. He finally had to admit that, yes, her dark beauty was unrivaled. He didn't tell them she was also opinionated, arrogant, and far too accustomed to having her way; he figured they'd find out soon enough on their own. He did inform them of her staunch refusal to be courted, but they simply laughed and accused Nate of trying to keep her for himself.

Nate stopped the wagon, walked to her door, and knocked.

Vivid set aside her broom and wiped her dusty hands on the apron tied at her waist as she went to the door. Her actions slowed when she saw Nate Grayson standing on the porch against the night.

"May I come in?" he asked.

Vivid pushed the door open. "Of course, Mr. Grayson."

He eased by her and stepped inside.

Vivid closed the door. He appeared pleasantly surprised by the furnished interior and spent a few moments glancing around. He walked over to view some of Jess's watercolors hanging on the beams above the small desk and asked, "Is this you?"

Vivid went to stand at his side. "Yes, that is me, at

nine summers. My sister Jess is the artist.''

"Your sister painted this?"

"Yes."

Nate took down the picture and looked at the smiling young Lancaster clad in a pair of patched knickers, standing atop a crate. She held in her small hand an upright billiard stick. She stood like a child posed with a fishing pole. Her sister had caught the playfulness and humor in Lancaster's dark eyes. Viveca Lancaster had been beautiful even as a child. "Your sister is quite talented," he said, handing the painting back.

"Yes, she is. She painted this while studying in Spain. She's married and lives in Liberia now. I miss her dearly."

Vivid hung the picture back in its spot. "Magic says you paint also?"

"Yes, but I haven't in many years. You spoke of having two sisters. Is the other one in California with your parents?"

"No, Alicea lives in Boston. She's the eldest."

His response to her inquiry about his painting was so abrupt, she sensed it was not a subject open to discussion.

He stood looking at the books on her shelf when he said, "The Quilt Ladies want you to come to tea tomorrow. Two o'clock, at their place." He took down a volume and leafed through the pages.

"Who are the Quilt Ladies?"

"They do charity work in the area. They also consider themselves the town's moral society."

"And they'd like me over for tea?" Vivid swallowed. "For what purpose?"

"To see if you're up to snuff, I would imagine." He replaced the book.

"Are they an influence here?"

"They think they are."

Vivid didn't have to think long about this decision. If

members of the community wanted to meet her, she had no recourse but to go. "Then I suppose I'll be having tea at two. You didn't tell them I play billiards, did you?"

"No," he replied with a small chuckle.

"That's probably best for now."

"Probably," he said. "I doubt they share your love of the game."

Vivid chose to ignore the quip and asked instead if he had been able to find an animal to transport her about town.

"Vernon's going to see about it later in the week; his uncle up in Calvin Center has one for sale."

"Thank you."

Nate wondered if she'd been paid any other unseemly visits. "Any of the men from this morning come back?"

"No. Miss Edna doubts I've seen the last of them, however."

"She's probably right."

"Well, I hope you're both wrong. Doesn't anyone realize that if I wanted a husband, I could have stayed in San Francisco?"

"Did you have a beau back there?"

She shook her head no. Beaus were a sore point with Vivid. "I don't do well with beaus."

"Why not?"

"I simply don't," she said, shrugging. "They disapproved of my billiard playing, or my tendency to say what I believe, or my choice of profession. In some cases all three."

He held her eyes. "You are a mite overpowering," he stated, looking down at her, his arms across his chest. "For some."

"Some—most—it doesn't matter. I have trouble being the docile woman they want me to be."

"So you're planning on going through life without a mate?"

"Medicine is my mate."

He smiled; an amused dark-skinned archangel.

"You find that idea funny?" she asked.

"It isn't the idea, it's you, Lancaster."

"Ah, that's right. You believe every woman needs a man."

"I do."

"Well, so far I have done very well without one," she stated.

"Have you now?" he asked in a skeptical voice, his eyes holding hers.

"Yes, I have," she replied proudly. "I don't need a man dictating what I may or may not do."

"A man shouldn't have to dictate. His woman should want to please him."

Vivid surveyed him a moment, not quite sure if he was teasing her or if he was serious. "And when will the man please the woman?"

"Whenever she asks, and if he does it properly, she should have no complaints."

Vivid blinked. His words made her heart race and she looked away, flustered. "I believe we're discussing different subjects, Mr. Grayson."

"Weren't you speaking of a man pleasing a woman?"

"Yes, but on a more . . . intellectual level."

"Ah, I thought you were speaking about passion."

Vivid's cheeks flooded with heat. "No."

"I didn't mean to embarrass you, Lancaster."

"I'm not embarrassed, Mr. Grayson. I am a physician, after all. A simple discussion of physical functions will not send me running to the hills."

Nate eyed her. Despite her claim to the contrary, she appeared as ruffled as a schoolgirl. He found this facet of the vivid Dr. Lancaster unexpected and quite interesting. "So no beaus and no desire for a husband."

"No."

Nate didn't believe her at all. Most of the young

women he knew were forever angling for a man. And he was certain a woman as beautiful as she would have her pick of bachelors. "So you've never been in love?"

He'd dredged up another sore point. She simply shook her head, unwilling to confide her despair of ever finding a man who'd truly value her enough to share her dreams. "And have you?" she finally asked.

"I thought I was at one time, but I was wrong."

She sensed by the sadness in his tone that Nate Grayson had been hurt very badly in the past and wondered when and by whom. "Do you still believe in love?"

"Despite my own failure, I do. My mother died when I was nine, but I distinctly remember my parents loving each other very much. I'd hoped to share that with someone one day."

"Do you continue to hold that hope?"

"No."

Nate had never discussed such things with a woman before and he felt odd and a bit out of his realm.

"My parents are deeply bound to each other also," she said. "My father likes to say he had as much business courting my mother as a goat had going to school."

Nate met her smile with one of his own. "What did he mean by that?"

"He was a runaway working on the San Francisco docks. My mother was the only daughter of one of the wealthiest men in California."

"I see what your father meant. Society says he wasn't even supposed to look at a woman of her class. How did they meet?"

"He was on the docks one evening when Mama and my grandparents were leaving a ship. He said at the time she was the most beautiful woman he'd ever seen, slave or free. And he didn't let his station in life deter him. He wooed her and eventually married her. She gave up her inheritance to be his wife."

"Would you give up a fortune to be a wife?"

Vivid looked up into his eyes. "A fortune, possibly. My medicine, no."

He chuckled. "Lancaster, I hope I'm around to see you eat Coyote's black currants one day."

"Coyote's black currants?"

"It's an old Native tale about a young maiden who enjoys working so much, she refuses to marry any of the braves in the village. Coyote makes her fall in love with him by bringing her black currants. I'll tell you the rest some other time."

"So in other words, you wish to see me struck by Cupid's arrow?"

"Something like that, yes."

"Oh ye of little faith. Not every female is rendered mindless just because a man brings her flowers or writes her sonnets in which moon always rhymes with June. The women of today are looking toward the next century. There are issues to confront, a race to move forward, and we are not content to make a man's home our sole reason for being."

"Traveling life's road alone breeds loneliness. Believe me, I speak from experience."

It was not the rejoinder Vivid had expected. She sensed a depth in him she'd not felt before that moment. He was far more complex than she'd originally thought him to be, and whether or not she cared to admit it, she found him intriguing. Vivid shook herself out of her reverie. How on earth had she gotten on this track in the first place? She decided to change topics, as the course they had begun could only prove dangerous. "So I should hear from Vernon soon about his uncle's animal?"

"Yes."

Nate had no name for what had just passed between them, but something had changed. He was certain she'd felt it, too. He picked up his hat and started toward the door. "I'll be escorting you to the ladies' tea tomorrow."

Vivid was surprised. Why hadn't he mentioned that early on? she wondered. She also didn't think his escorting her was a good idea. She and Nate Grayson would undoubtedly end up disagreeing over something on the ride there, and she'd be angry and frustrated when she was introduced to the Quilt Ladies. And she'd hardly be able to charm them if she was angry and frustrated. "Mr. Grayson, I'm certain you are much too busy to spend an afternoon having tea, so if there's a buggy and a map I may borrow, I'm certain I can get there on my own."

"They requested my presence, also."

"Oh."

Hat in hand, his big body filling her doorway, he gazed over at her and said, "If I didn't know better, I'd say you were trying to avoid my company, Lancaster."

"Truthfully, I am."

"Why?"

"Because when we are together we argue, and I don't wish to meet these Quilt Ladies while I'm in a snit."

"I hadn't thought of that," he said. "Well, if you promise to be on your best behavior and not provoke me, I believe we'll do fine."

"Me?" she croaked.

"Yes, you."

"Mr. Grayson—"

"Good night, Lancaster." He tipped his hat politely and stepped back out into the night. She swore she heard him laughing as the wagon rolled away.

The next morning Nate had already left for town and Magic for school by the time Vivid went over to the Graysons for breakfast. She found Miss Edna seated at the big dining table and they shared a few pleasant moments of conversation while Vivid devoured a plate of stacked oatcakes swimming in maple syrup. Afterward the women talked about the Quilt Ladies.

"They're a nest of hypocrites masquerading as Southern belles," Abigail stated frankly.

"Gail," Miss Edna said warningly. "Now, you promised not to influence the doctor. She has to form her own opinions."

"Ed, Viveca is not blind. She's going to see them for what they are—a bunch of busybodies who think they're saints."

Viveca interrupted. "Your nephew led me to believe these women had a strong influence here in the Grove."

"Oh, they do if you happen to be the one they're hissing at in church, or the person they're spreading gossip about. They know how to make your life miserable. That's the type of influence they wield."

"They do good works, too, Abigail."

"Sometimes," Abigail admitted grudgingly.

"Why are they called Quilt Ladies?" Vivid asked.

Miss Edna answered, "They've been making the best-looking quilts this side of the state for two decades."

Abigail nodded. "Now that I agree with. They can wield their needles."

Vivid smiled. "Do either of you have any suggestions as to how I should go about making a good impression?"

"Bloodlines," Miss Edna stated over her coffee cup.

"Bloodlines?" Vivid repeated.

"Bloodlines," Abigail said in agreement. "Caroline Ross heads their little group, and she mistakenly believes that the miscegenation in her ancestry makes her somehow better than the rest of us."

"Caroline can be quite obnoxius at times," Edna admitted. "Viveca, Abigail says your people have Spanish blood?"

"Yes."

"Well, make sure you share that information during

the interrogation this afternoon. Once Caroline learns of your ancestry, you'll have no problem gaining her approval and support.''

Vivid wanted to gain their support because of what she stood for, not for who her ancestors had been. ''Are you certain it's the only way?''

''Do you want their approval, or do you want them hissing at you in church?''

''Their approval.''

''Then play up your bloodlines.''

After breakfast, Vivid returned to her cabin and spent an inordinate amount of time trying to decide what to wear. She didn't want to appear too prosperous, nor did she want to appear poverty-stricken. In the end, she decided on a very tasteful white lawn blouse, an emerald skirt with a thin line of black velvet piping at the bottom, and a matching jacket. She'd already pulled her thick black hair into a chignon and wore her grandmother's small emerald stud earrings.

She peered critically at herself in the glass hanging near her small cot and wondered if she'd pass inspection. A knock at her door startled her. It was Nate Grayson.

Nate watched her disappear into the bedroom and return a few heartbeats later wearing a hat similar to the one drenched in the rain. It was also emerald, but piped in black. She was a stunning woman.

''You're staring, Mr. Grayson,'' Vivid said, pulling on her gloves. ''Is my appearance that unacceptable?'' She wondered if she had time to change clothes.

He cleared his throat. ''No. You look fine.''

''That's relieving. You had me concerned. Are we ready?''

He nodded and let her precede him out the door.

On the ride, they kept the conversation on simple topics such as the sunny May weather and the landscape. Neither wanted to be the cause of any altercation.

Finally, Nate halted outside a fence surrounding a

very large house set back from the road. Vivid stepped down and nervously patted her hat. She checked to make certain her skirt hadn't become overly wrinkled on the ride, then adjusted the sleeves of her jacket. When she glanced at Nate, she saw him watching her with that same amused look he'd worn last evening. "Is something wrong?" she asked.

"Nope. Just watching you."

"And?"

"You're nervous."

"I want to make a good impression," she confessed.

"Nothing wrong with that."

Their eyes held for a moment before Vivid said, "Shall we go in?"

"Probably. Caroline has been standing behind the curtains since we drove up."

Vivid's eyes widened. "Why didn't you say so?" she said as she hurried up the walk.

Nate smiled and slowly followed in her wake.

"Please come into the parlor, we're all anxious to meet you," invited Caroline Ross. The beautiful older woman met them at the door dressed as if she were hostessing a Southern ball instead of an afternoon tea. Vivid couldn't remember the last time she'd seen anyone wear hoops in her skirt, but the woman moved as if she'd worn the swaying weight all her life.

A glance around the sun-filled room revealed crocheted doilies, lace curtains, and four ivory-skinned women who appeared to be the same age as Caroline. They were seated around the parlor with a regal air about them reminiscent of her Spanish aunts. Vivid nodded to each of the women as Caroline named them in turn: Brenna, who stared at Vivid with distant, violet eyes; Effie, who wore a faded yellow prewar hooped dress and had fixed her graying hair in elaborate ringlets; Felicity, whose disdainful glance made Vivid feel like a servant;

and Poppy, who met Vivid's eyes with a smile. Vivid wondered if they all lived here together.

"Thank you for escorting her, Nathaniel," Caroline said brightly. "Please be seated."

Vivid sat on one of the elegant but old embroidered-back chairs. She sat with all the poise of a queen, her back erect, her chin raised. The ladies would find no cracks in her manners.

Nate sat in a large, overstuffed chair on the opposite side of the room postioned far away enough for him to maintain his neutrality but close enough so that he could watch the show.

"Ladies, I see the service is set out. May I pour?" Vivid said.

The ladies looked at one another, and Caroline, obviously the voice of the group, replied, "Why, most certainly."

Vivid knew how to pour tea. She and her sisters had begun serving tea as soon as they were able to heft the pot and pour safely. She remembered many afternoons when she poured tea for her mother and the older female relatives to show that she could do the job properly. Slopping tea on one of the Spanish aunts or, Lord forbid, one of the guests, meant polishing silver for a week as penance. Back then, Vivid looked upon this task as just another one of those tedious chores her mother insisted she and her sisters learn. She'd had no idea it would be a talent she'd one day need to help sell herself as a doctor.

Vivid lifted the ornate silver tray holding the filled cups and served everyone, then she took her seat. All the women seemed impressed.

"Where did you learn to pour so elegantly, my dear?" Caroline asked.

"From my *abuela* in Mexico."

"Your *a-buela*?"

"It's Spanish for grandmother."

"I see," Caroline replied, staring at Vivid strangely. "Your people are Spanish?"

"Mama's side of the family came over with the conquistadors. Papa's came in the hull of a slaver."

Caroline appeared to be speechless for a moment. Vivid politely raised her cup and sipped daintily.

Poppy laughed. "Well, Caroline, now that she's established herself as having the best bloodlines in town, do you have another question?"

The violet-eyed Brenna gave Poppy a withering look and said, "Poppy, if you are not going to take this seriously, I suggest you leave."

Poppy turned and replied, "My dear Brenna, must I remind you again under whose roof you are living?"

Brenna's vellum face reddened and she looked away, evidently not in need of a reminder. Vivid was fascinated by the exchange.

"Do you plan on treating men, Dr. Lancaster?"

"I have been trained to heal both, so yes," Vivid replied in answer to Felicity's question.

"You're aware the idea is considered unseemly in most places?" Effie pointed out.

"Yes, ma'am, I am aware of that. However, I can hardly be a true physician if I'm allowed to administer to only half the population."

To her surprise, Effie nodded her head as if agreeing.

Vivid spent the next hour answering questions from Caroline and the others concerning everything from her educational background, to her family, to her charity work. Vivid had done charity work in San Francisco, and also during and after her medical training in Philadelphia. This started a discussion of the tradition of Black women helping the less fortunate members of the race. As early as 1793 the Female Benevolent Society of St. Thomas, organized by free Black women in Philadelphia, aided fatherless children and widows. In 1809 the free Black women of Newport, Rhode Island, came together as the

African Female Benevolent Society. In 1821 the Daughters of Africa, whose members were the washerwomen and domestics of Philadelphia, combined their extra pennies and paid out sick and death benefits for those in the community. In 1840 New York City had the second largest Black population in the segregated free North, but by 1827, the Black women had already seen a need and formed the African Dorcas Association. They met weekly in sewing meetings to provide clothing for the needy children in the city's Free African Schools. Even in the slave city of Washington D.C., in 1828, free Black women took it upon themselves to help their own under the auspices of the Coloured Female Roman Catholic Benefit Society.

The Black women in Vivid's part of the country were also actively involved in helping others. Vivid, in addition to relating to the ladies her own experiences in the charity wards of San Francisco and Philadelphia, also told them of Biddie Mason. Mrs. Mason, a former slave, had become one of California's largest landowners. Her generous purse helped establish schools, churches, and homes for the aged and infirm.

The conversation then turned to other topics and Vivid gave the ladies her opinions on women and work, and her stance on women and the vote.

Afterward they requested she play them something on the gleaming piano on the far side of the parlor. Vivid hadn't played in many years, and that became quite evident once she began. However, she finished before anyone could go running from the room so she considered the impromptu recital a success.

Vivid retook her seat, purposely avoiding Nate Grayson's eyes.

"Well, Doctor," Caroline said. "I know I speak for everyone when I say we find you most impressive. Having you in our community will be a true coup. We have one request before we bestow our blessings."

"And that is?"

"In order to protect your reputation, would you be agreeable to having a male present in your establishment when you're with male patients?

Vivid was nonplussed; she'd never considered such an arrangement. "Do you feel that is necessary?"

"I do believe that would allay any gossip, especially during your initial stay here. Gossip can truly ruin a woman such as yourself. Wouldn't you agree, ladies?"

The ladies all nodded in agreement.

Vivid did not need a man to guard her reputation, she had a rifle for that, but she forced herself to remember where she was. Grayson Grove was neither San Francisco nor Philadelphia. Grayson Grove was a small, backwoods town in Michigan. These women considered themselves keepers of the town's morals, and she had to live by their rules if she wanted to live here peacefully.

But a man in her office?

"What about Nathaniel?" Poppy asked.

Vivid's eyes widened.

Nate sat up straight in his chair when he heard his name.

"Poppy, that is a splendid idea," Caroline replied enthusiastically. "No one would dare make unseemly remarks or exhibit ungallant behavior in his presence."

They all began to chatter back and forth like excited hens. Vivid held up her hands. "Excuse me, please. Am I to understand that you are recommending Nate Grayson as my chaperone?"

Nate considered slipping out of the room before anyone noticed, but he knew they'd find him. He had absolutely no intention of playing nursemaid to the doctor, but lately his intentions hadn't much mattered. First Abigail and her damned contract, and now this. Arguing that he was too busy or had commitments elsewhere would not be a deterrent to them; once the Quilt Ladies took something by the bit you had to join them or be run down.

But he had to try. "Ladies, you know how busy the Grove keeps me. I doubt I will have—"

"Nathaniel Grayson, are you saying you are too busy to be concerned about this young woman's reputation?" Caroline asked.

"No, Caroline, that's not what I'm saying. I—"

"Good," said Poppy. "We knew you'd agree."

Vivid hadn't agreed, however. "I still don't believe all this is necessary."

"Dear, a woman without a reputation is no woman at all," Caroline pointed out sternly.

Vivid felt as if she'd been chastised by one of her great aunts. "But—"

"So are we all agreed?" Caroline asked.

They were.

Vivid sighed in surrender.

"Welcome to Grayson Grove, Dr. Lancaster."

On the ride home, Nate swore he could feel the steam wafting off her small body. He didn't think she could get any angrier than she'd been when she shot his hat off, but apparently he'd been wrong. She'd gone absolutely stone-still when the ladies suggested installing a man in her office. Her face registered shock, then surprise, then outrage in less than a blink. At the time, he'd almost laughed but thought better of it once she showed him the fire in her eyes. After all, she'd already taken a rifle to him once that week; he didn't want to find out the shot through his hat had been one of luck and not skill.

"You stepped into a real bear trap back there, Lancaster."

"I'm not speaking to you," she said.

He couldn't mask his humor. "No?" he asked, peering over at her and that saucy little hat.

"No," she repeated.

"May I ask why?"

"Because this is all your fault. If you had stood up to them, we wouldn't be in this ridiculous situation."

"I tried. You heard me."

"I heard you surrendering. I do not need a man in my office to protect my honor."

He glanced over at her angry face. "Do you want to shoot me?"

"The thought had crossed my mind. Maybe later."

He shook his head again. Lord, what a woman. He'd almost felt sorry for her back there. He knew how controlling Caroline could be and Lancaster hadn't known she'd stepped into a trap until the jaws snapped shut. She'd been a lamb among wolves.

Initially, Nate had been angry, too, at the ladies' decision, mainly because he'd stepped into the same trap. These manipulative episodes were becoming a bit too commonplace for his liking. First his Aunt Gail and Miss Edna and now the Quilt Ladies had turned against him to try to force his hand regarding the doctor. The women were a cross men of the Grove seemed destined to bear. Their small community had been blessed, or cursed, depending upon the point of view, with women who were not only intelligent but educated. When the Grove was founded, his grandmother Dorcas made it the law that every child, male and female, must learn to read. As a result, some of the women who'd married men from outside their community could think circles around their husbands, a situation many of these men found outrageous. But what could Nate do? He certainly couldn't threaten to lock them away unless they began to mimic the docile, barely literate women of other communities, as suggested by one husband during last month's Men's Association meeting. Who knew the ramifications that might bring? The women owned many of the businesses, oftimes they voted as a bloc on Grove affairs, and generally they had their way when they wanted it. According to legend, during his grandfather's day the men once tried to rein in their wives. It resulted in a disaster so cataclysmic that even today Nate could not get any of the elder men to discuss what had transpired. The women won, that was all Nate and his contemporaries knew.

Yet while he hadn't been pleased by this afternoon's outcome, once he calmed down he realized how much he enjoyed having Lancaster beside him, mad as hell at this unexpected turn of events, and that made him smile.

Vivid kept telling herself this was a small town, reputations meant everything, especially to a woman practicing medicine. It didn't help. She continued to believe that Nate could have done something to bring about a more rational outcome, regardless of his protestations. Wasn't he supposed to be the authority in this town? She'd just resigned herself to having her new office only a few doors from his own, and now the Crazy Quilt Ladies had made the man a member of her staff. She glanced over and saw him smiling. "I fail to see the humor in this, Mr. Grayson."

"Depends on your point of view," he replied.

Admittedly, Vivid had only one point of view. "You should have told them you were unable to comply."

"I tried. We already had this conversation, remember?"

"You should have been more forceful."

He grinned. "Your piano playing was forceful enough, Miss Bach."

Vivid stiffened and whirled to face him.

Her outrage would have warned off a less confident man, but Nate looked into her flashing eyes and stated, "The next time you're invited to play, before you begin, give me a moment to tiptoe out of the room first. Okay?"

Vivid knew she was supposed to be angry with him. She knew that for that remark he deserved a blistering lecture on his duty as a gentleman, but she remembered

pounding away at that piano and succumbed to the sparkle in his eyes. "It was a pretty atrocious display, wasn't
it?"

"Nothing pretty about it at all," Nate replied. "And
you said you took lessons?"

"Yes," Vivid stated with mock pride. "Believe me
or not, I did, every Wednesday afternoon following
school. The teacher's name was Madam Henry, and if
you struck a wrong note, she'd smack you across the
knuckles with a baton. I wished her to perdition many
times. So if I play badly, it is Madam's fault, not mine."

"Glad to see you can laugh at yourself. Many people
can't."

Vivid held his gaze a moment, then looked away, her
confidence suddenly overcome by the odd sensations she
was feeling.

Nate enjoyed seeing nervous shyness take hold of her
because it afforded him a glimpse of the woman she kept
locked away. She'd given him a fascinating peek at that
facet of herself last night during their conversation in
her cabin about a man pleasing a woman. She'd stammered like a virgin bride in response to his words and
it was not the reaction he'd expected.

However, she'd conducted herself well this afternoon.
The ladies were a major hurdle. Everyone knew they
could be as touchy as a nest of hornets, and there were
no guarantees they'd continue to offer the doctor their
support, but she'd passed their tests with flying colors.
Her manners were stellar. Nate noticed that even Brenna
had begun to imitate the way Lancaster held her head
and the way she raised her cup to her lips. Watching her
conduct herself with such decorum and grace made him
wonder once again how someone so elegant expected to
survive in such a place as this. "If it will make you feel
any better, you probably won't be needing me at your
office."

"Oh, splendid, you're going to ignore their edict. Mr. Grayson, thank you so—"

He looked into her dark eyes. "Hold on a minute. Don't get me wrong, I will be abiding by the ladies' decision because I don't want them camped in my doorway until I do. You won't be needing me because the men won't be seeking you out."

Vivid searched his face. "I don't understand."

"They're going to wait for the circuit doctor to handle their complaints."

Vivid stared. "And this is supposed to make me feel better? Why won't they come to me?"

She didn't really need the answer. She knew. She sat back against the bench and for a moment couldn't speak. Finally, she asked, "Will they keep their wives and children away also?"

"Some will."

"How do you know this?"

"From listening to the talk down at the mill and out on the farms. You're a female; some see nothing else."

"And you, is that all you see?"

Nate sighed. Another one of her pointed questions. "You've only been here three days, Lancaster."

"Yet three days is all the men around here need to keep their wives and children from seeking trained care."

Nate didn't respond.

"I suppose it would be silly of me to believe you've stayed neutral in all this?"

"Now there you're wrong," Nate countered, looking her way. "I've made it my business to let folks decide on their own."

Vivid held his eyes. "Then I apologize."

"Apology accepted."

He thought it only fair she know which way the wind blew. As he'd predicted, folks were already choosing sides. Unfortunately, the lines were being drawn mainly by gender. Women on one side, men on the other. Adam Crowley, a boyhood friend of Nate's late father and the man Aunt Gail deemed the bane of her exsistence, wanted Gail to be censured. He said she'd overstepped her bounds by bringing in an untrained young female without council approval. Abigail had been charged to search for a doctor, and while no one denied her judgment, no one had expected a female, either.

Yet here she sat, and Nate had given her permission to stay, albeit temporarily.

"When will my office be ready?" she asked, refusing to let him see how devastating his revelation had been to her spirit. A big part of her wanted to run home to California and wail in her mama's arms. Didn't these men know anything about dreams?

"I really don't know. I'm having trouble finding someone to take the job since everybody's planting." Nate could see that she was upset by the men's plans and was surprised by how disturbed he felt. For the past three days she'd had enough inner fire to fuel a train's engine, but it appeared as if the flame had been suddenly extinguished. She stared out over the roadside with distant eyes.

"Would it be agreeable for me to do the work myself?"

He looked over at her, and before he could open his mouth, she warned softly, "If you say anything about my ability to clean I will shoot you right now, not later."

He inclined his head politely. "Pax, madam. I will give you the keys whenever it is convenient."

"Thank you, I'd like to begin first thing in the morning."

Later that evening, as Vivid sat in the chair in her front room watching the shadows chase away the last bit of day, she fought off the feelings of melancholy. She'd known coming to this place and proving herself would be a challenge and she'd anticipated some resistance, but she'd never envisioned anyone mounting a campaign against her. Had she really been as naive as Nate Grayson accused on the day they met? Had she taken it for granted folks would be so grateful for good sound medical treatment that they wouldn't care what she looked like beneath her clothes?

Maybe she had, but she still didn't want it to be true. The race needed women like herself stretching the lines of both gender and race, especially now when the country seemed bent upon moving back and not forward. These were frightening times and even more horror lay ahead if the political climate continued to play true. Every advance the race made was necessary if it was to survive. More women like Maria W. Stewart were needed, not fewer. In 1832 Miss Stewart, a Black woman, became the first American woman of any race to lecture to public audiences. And there was Mary Shadd, who in 1853 grew tired of being vilified in Henry Bibb's Black abolitionist weekly, *The Voice of the Fugitive*, and so founded *The Provincial Freeman* in response. By doing so she became one of the first women, and the first Black woman on the North American continent, to edit and publish a newspaper. Vivid herself owed a tremendous debt to another pioneering Black woman, Miss Rebecca Lee. Fifteen years after Elizabeth Blackwell became the first American woman to gain a degree in medicine, Rebecca Lee received hers from the New England Medical College. Had Miss Lee not pursued her dream, Vivid might not have been afforded the opportunity to succeed on her own.

Those women and many thousands like them had uplifted not only the race but the country as well, and just like Vivid they had to defend themselves from small minds and the rocks thrown at them by opposers in order to carve out their niche. When Mary Shadd published her first edition, she thought it best her name not be placed on the masthead of her own newspaper for fear the men in the abolitionist movement would not take her editorials seriously. Poor Maria Stewart caused such an uproar with her ringing antislavery speeches, she was driven from her home city of Boston. Yet these women did not give up.

"Dr. Lancaster, are you at home?"

Vivid's musings were abruptly interrupted by Abigail calling her through the screened door.

Vivid greeted her, then pushed the door aside so she could enter.

Abigail held her ebony cane in one hand and a covered plate in the other, which she handed to Vivid. "This is for you, dear. You missed supper."

Vivid thanked her, then set the offering on the table. Vivid hadn't gone up to the house that evening because she hadn't had much of an appetite.

Abigail walked over and sat in one of the stuffed chairs. While Vivid ate from the plate filled with green beans, potatoes, and ham, Abigail seemed content to sit quietly in the deepening shadows. Dusk had given way to the first clear black of night.

Vivid ate in silence and when she finished everything on her plate, she realized how hungry she really had been. "Thank you, Miss Grayson. You seem to know more about what I needed than I did."

"You're welcome. I expect you at our table every evening from now on, young lady, and call me Abigail or Gail."

Vivid nodded with a smile.

"So how did you fare with Caroline and the coven? I've spoken to Nate, but I'd like to hear your view."

Vivid told her about the afternoon tea and even confessed the details of her awful piano performance. She finished by saying, "So whenever a male patient is in the office, your nephew must be in attendance also."

"You and he aren't getting along very well yet, are
you?"

"Yet?" Vivid chuckled sarcastically. "Ever seems to
be more the word. I lay this whole mess directly at his
door."

"Nate said as much."

"No disrespect intended, Abigail, but your nephew is
a very trying man."

Abigail sounded amused as she said, "That is the
truth, but we love him in spite of that fault. You will,
too, eventually."

Vivid stared, "Excuse me?"

"Oh, dear, I mean that in a neighborly sense. My
nephew, for all his faults, is a splendidly caring man.
He wouldn't be heading this town if he weren't."

Fortunately for Vivid, the darkness shrouded her skeptical expression. "Did he also tell you about the men
refusing to see me, and maybe keeping away their wives
and children?"

"It's all over town. It's probably fortunate Caroline
gave her approval, otherwise she might have lined up
on the side of the men. But don't worry, it's mainly the
men we always have problems pleasing, the men born
outside the Grove. Nate hasn't declared one way or the
other. Adam Crowley, damn his wooden head, is raising
a stink also, but only because I'm involved. He's an
influence here and should know better."

Vivid wondered when she'd meet this Adam Crowley.

"So, Viveca, in the face of all that has happened today and all that will undoubtedly happen before things
become normal, what do you plan to do?"

"This afternoon I had serious doubts about myself and
where my dreams might be headed; however, the longer I
sat here and thought about all the women who've come
before me, the more I realized that they succeeded because
they refused to give up. This community needs a doctor. I

am that person. I'm here to stay and I will fight to practice.''

Abigail applauded. ''Bravo, my dear. I told Edna you wouldn't run. One day I'd like to meet your mother. She must be an extraordinary individual to raise such an outstanding young woman. Bravo!''

Vivid grinned under the ringing endorsement. ''Do you have any suggestions as to how I might bring these men over to my side?''

''I wouldn't worry about them for now. If the situation becomes serious, we'll implement a plan, but until then you just go on about the business of settling in and introducing yourself. Most folks are smart enough to see the light.''

They then discussed Vivid's plans for the office. Abigail offered to assist any way she could and also suggested that Vivid take Magic along to help with the cleaning. She even promised Magic's mouser, Cleopatra, to deal with any vermin.

Vivid thought the idea a splendid one. She enjoyed Magic's company and decided it might be an opportunity for the two of them to become better acquainted.

Abigail stood with the assistance of her cane and strode to the door. ''I will leave you now, Dr. Lancaster—''

''Please call me Viveca.''

''Thank you, I'd like that. And Viveca, don't worry. Next year this time, you'll have proven yourself, and everyone will be trying to remember what the fuss was all about.''

''Thank you, Abigail.''

''You're welcome. Get some rest now.''

''Abigail?''

''Yes.''

''Why didn't you tell your nephew I was female?''

Abigail chuckled softly. ''Because, dear, although my nephew is one of the most intelligent men I know, he's still a man. He would have given me all the silly reasons why a female would be unsuitable. I am the only Grayson female in many generations and I'm accustomed to having my way. We needed a doctor. I reviewed your credentials and found you qualified. I've also learned it is far better to beg forgiveness than to seek permission in some situations, and you were one of those situtations. Does that answer your question?''

Vivid grinned. ''Yes.''

''Then again, good night.''

Vivid watched her walk across the grass until she disappeared into the night.

Chapter 7

The predawn chill in the cabin gave Vivid goose-flesh as she left the warmth of her bed. It had been hot as blazes for the past few days, but this morning felt like San Francisco in January.

The wood floor was cold and Vivid made a mental note to buy rugs soon. She hastened into her robe and pulled on her boots. Then she picked up the bucket and headed outside to the Graysons' pump.

A brisk wind greeted her the moment she stepped onto the porch, whipping at her clothes so unexpectedly, only her quick hand kept them from flying up around her thighs. Laughing, she held her clothing as best she could then went about her business.

The breeze felt fresh, invigorating, so much so that she set down the bucket and turned her face to the wind. It rushed over her, filling her with its sounds and vitality, and evoking fond memories of being young. She and her sisters had always been very imaginative, and for the longest time Jess had Vivid believing that if she closed her eyes, stretched out her arms, and concentrated, the wind would make her fly. Vivid hadn't flown in many years. She took a quick glance around and, fairly confident she wouldn't be seen at such an early hour, she released her hold on her robe, then slowly extended her arms.

"What the hell is she doing?" Nate whispered in amazement as he stared down at Viveca Lancaster from

112

his bedroom window. She stood with her arms stretched out, slowly twirling in the wind. Then she stopped, held her robe wide, and let it unfurl around her, becoming a sail in the breeze. The thin, loose-fitting gown she wore alternately clung to her then fluttered outward. The capricious breeze blew the hem to her knees, then undulated it higher, affording him a startling look at her dark, slender legs in a pair of black Western-cut boots just before her hand clamped the gown down again.

His arousal was immediate.

If he had any sense he'd move away from the window and forget what he'd seen, but she called to him like a siren, and he'd already become ensnared.

He watched as she resumed her slow twirls. Her hands held the robe wide again and it blossomed. She dipped it, then lifted it, making it ripple high, then low. She had all the enchantment of a wind sprite come out to play, and as Nate watched the breeze mold the gown tautly against her breasts and thighs, he discovered yet another facet to this dark jewel. This innocently sensual display proved a woman did dwell within the no-nonsense, serious doctor. Only a woman with a deep well of passion would be out taking pleasure from the kisses of the wind.

Vivid knew she should pump her water, but the wind felt so invigorating and so glorious she let herself enjoy it a few moments longer. Truth be told, she wished at the moment to be on a deserted island where she could safely shed every stitch of clothing and feel the wind as nature had intended, on her bare back, her arms, her legs, her thighs. Decidedly unladylike thoughts, but Vivid didn't care. She felt free.

"Good morning, Dr. Lancaster."

Vivid spun at the sound of Nate Grayson's voice. Fighting the wind for possession of her clothing, she stared aghast. Where on earth had he come from? More importantly, what had he seen? Judging by those smiling smoke-dark eyes, plenty. "Um, good morning, Mr. Grayson. I . . . came out for some water."

"So I see."

At least he hadn't been able to read her last scandalous thoughts. Or had he?

He reached down, picked up the bucket, and without a word strode over to the pump.

Dismayed, Vivid followed.

He set the bucket below the spout. She tried not to stare as he undid the buttons of his cuffs and rolled the sleeves up past his elbows, but her eyes were instantly drawn to the beautiful structure of his arms. Watching the ebb and flow of the sculpted mahogany muscles as he pumped the handle made her begin a mental recitation of muscle names and tendon groups just as if he were a model in her anatomy class. Her fascination gave way to contemplating the muscles in his back and shoulders, and she wondered if they were as finely molded as the rest.

Shocked by her thoughts, she tore her eyes away. Definitely unladylike. When she glanced back she found him watching her with a gaze that made her throat suddenly go dry.

"Do you often play in the wind?" he asked.

Vivid swallowed. She no longer felt the wind or heard the rustle in the trees. There was only his gaze and her own pounding heart. "Uh, no, not usually, at least not since I've been grown." She sensed she was babbling so she stopped talking. She also realized that she was developing an attraction to this man, and that startled her.

"Do you need me to carry this back for you?" he asked, pointing to the full bucket.

"No," she said, shaking her head. "That won't be necessary, thank you."

She took the bucket from his outstretched hand. "I . . . should be going."

He nodded.

Vivid headed back to the safety of her cabin feeling his eyes following her every step of the way.

After washing up and getting dressed, Vivid coiled her hair into a knot and secured it low on her neck. She tried not to think about Nate Grayson and this morning's incident. "He probably assumes you've lost your mind," she told her reflection in the glass hanging on the wall. Her behavior hardly fit a woman wanting to be taken seriously, and she knew he would take great pleasure in pointing that out as soon as the opportunity arose. That she found him attractive was not an admission she took pride in. Nate Grayson had proven to be stubborn and opinionated. He had openly voiced a disbelief in her abilities. Such attributes hardly qualified him as a "catch" in a mama's book of eligibles, but here she stood attracted to a man she had as much business being drawn to as a goat had going to school, to quote her father.

Yet by the time Vivid left her cabin and walked across the yard for breakfast with the Graysons, she'd convinced herself that her attraction could be directly attributed to the residual weariness of her cross-country journey. She was tired. Were she properly rested, she would not be contemplating the deltoids and pectorals of a man she'd known less than five days, not even one as strikingly handsome as Nate Grayson; either that or she'd contracted the ague.

Vivid had breakfast with Abigail and Magic. Nate had already departed for town. He'd left instructions that she could retrieve the keys to her new place from him at his office.

After the meal, they all headed into town along with Cleopatra.

When they arrived, Vivid tied the buggy to the post outside her new office while Abigail and Magic went off to Miss Edna's store to enlist her help with the cleaning.

Vivid then strode to Grayson's office. She walked in and found him standing near a black-bellied stove pouring a cup of coffee from a battered pot. He looked up at her entrance. "Mr. Grayson, I've come for—"

Those were the last words Nate heard. As she stepped further into the office he took in her full attire and lost all his senses. He stared, speechless, at the denim trousers encasing the lower half of her body. He'd seen other women in such male attire but he'd never been so affected. The trousers displayed the lean, lush line of her hips, tempted him with the enticing structure of her legs, and evoked the memory of seeing them bared by that morning's wind. On her feet were the boots he'd seen beneath her gown. He gave them, and the long-sleeved, red plaid shirt she wore, barely a glance other than to note the shirt appeared to be a few sizes too large, because his eyes kept returning to her denim-shrouded legs. In fact, the sight held him so absolutely riveted he didn't realize he was still pouring coffee until the hot liquid spilled over the cup and onto his hand. With a loud curse he quickly set down both pot and cup and shook his injured fingers.

Vivid rushed to him, her face filled with concern. "Are you all right? What on earth were you thinking?"

Her hands were warm and firm as she checked his hand for damage. She looked up at him, then quickly around the office. "Is there a towel or—never mind, here—"

She proceeded to dry his wet hand on the front of her shirt. He knew she'd acted strictly out of reflex but his arousal was immediate, just as it had been that morning.

He looked down at her shiny hair as she peered at his hand. "It doesn't appear as if you've scalded yourself. You might want to run it under cool water just to be safe. Does it sting?"

She released his hand. He flexed it. "No."

"Good. If it begins to, let me know. And you really

should be more careful in the future, Mr. Grayson."

"I will," he replied, but the sight of her continued to tempt him mightily. He wondered how long he'd be able to keep his hands off her. Since this morning, he'd thought of nothing else, a galling admission considering the circumstances. Her attire did not help matters. He decided it best he go sit behind his desk. Truth be told, she made him as hard as railroad iron, and in a few more moments his condition would be impossible to conceal.

He heard her ask, "Are you certain you're all right?"

"Certain, Lancaster. Let me get you your key."

He walked as if he were in pain and Vivid remembered that the men would take their ailments to the circuit doctor. Had he really injured himself but refused to believe her competent enough to treat a scalded hand? Vivid sighed with disappointment, then said quietly, "I am capable of treating a simple burn, Mr. Grayson. You needn't wait for the circuit doctor if you're in pain."

Seated safely behind his desk now, Nate tried not to smile. She obviously had no idea what he needed to salve his real pain. "My hand's fine, Dr. Lancaster. Truly."

Vivid didn't believe him. "May I have the key, please?"

Nate extended the key to her and she took it from his hand with a curt "Thank you."

As she sauntered out, Nate forced himself to concentrate on some papers atop his desk, hoping they would distract him, but his will was weak. He looked up and watched those denim-clad hips until they disappeared from view.

After Vivid removed the padlock, Magic gently tossed Cleopatra inside and closed the door. Twenty minutes later, they opened it again. The cat strolled out with a small brown field mouse in her teeth. She laid the dead rodent at Magic's feet, then strode back inside. All in all, she made five trips. When she sat down after the last one and regally licked her paws, Magic proudly declared the job done and they could all go safely inside.

The wood boarding up the window front kept light from entering. Vivid stepped back outside to assess how the wood had been attached to the window frame and she determined that a good stiff crowbar would do to remove the boards.

"Well, hello, Viveca."

Vivid turned to see Eli Grayson coming up the wood walk.

She smiled. "Hello, Eli. Welcome back."

"Thank you. Quite a blustery morning, wouldn't you say?"

"Yes, it is. What happened to the warm weather?" The temperature had risen since the early morning hours, but still hovered at least twenty degrees below the warmth of the past few days.

"This is Michigan. We have a saying, 'If you don't care for the weather, just wait a few moments and it will change.' "

She smiled. "Is it really that temperamental?

"Would a newspaperman lie?"

Vivid ignored that barb and asked instead, "How was Kalamazoo?" She still found the name strange and decided that after things quieted a bit she would have to travel there.

"Still standing. Nate didn't marry you while I was gone, did he?"

"Of course not," she responded with a laugh.

"Good, then there's still hope for me."

Vivid shook her head, amused by his teasing.

"So what are you doing here?" he asked, gesturing at the shop.

Vivid explained it to him as she took him back inside. After he greeted his mother and Miss Edna, and surprised Magic with some new marbles, he offered to lend a hand in the effort.

With the aid of two crowbars, Vivid and Eli made short work of the wood covering the window. If Eli found it strange to be engaged in such activity beside a woman, he didn't let on. Vivid silently blessed him for being one of the few men she'd encountered here who seemed intent upon helping rather than hindering her quest. She did notice that he spent quite an inordinate time staring at her trousers and smiling, but she ignored it. She wore trousers most of the time; he and the rest of the men would simply have to become accustomed to the sight.

Once the wood was removed, the light streamed in and the crew could better determine what they were up against. Dust and dirt mostly. There were a few dress forms tossed like cadavers in one corner and some dust-covered bolts of cloth in another, but other than those things, the front room appeared to be easy to clean up.

The two small back rooms had to be lit by the lanterns to be seen fully. They would require much more work. Spiders had taken over the space, and there were sticky dust-filled cobs throughout. The mice had also taken up residence in an abandoned mattress; their droppings and pieces of the mattress's cotton batting littered the floor, along with what appeared to be hundreds of acorn shells and other seed husks.

"Squirrels," Miss Edna remarked.

"There must be a fairly decent-sized hole in the walls somewhere," Eli said.

"How long has this shop been empty?" Vivid asked.

"Nearly a year now," Abigail said, leaning on her cane. "Reba, that was the seamstress's name, left last August."

"I was told she left because she didn't like the winter."

"Partially," Eli said, smiling at her as handsomely as his cousin. "Partially."

Then Magic piped up and said, "Becky Carpenter

said she left because Pa wouldn't marry her.''

Silence.

Abigail cleared her throat and said, ''Majestic, dear, why don't you begin taking those dress forms over to the store and place them in Miss Edna's cellar.''

''Sure, Aunt Gail.''

She departed happily and they all began to work.

Vivid thought about Magic's revelation as she and Miss Edna swept up the debris from the dirt floor. Had the town's former seamstress really left because of unrequited love? Vivid remembered the night she and Nate Grayson discussed how he had lost all hope of finding a woman to share what his parents had shared. Had that hope died because of this Reba? Vivid finally decided it made no sense to wrestle with questions for which she had no answers. Besides, why worry over a man who didn't even believe her competent enough to treat a small burn?

Vivid and her small contingent worked full bore until a bit past the noon hour, at which point Abigail declared a luncheon break. Abigail, who'd spent the morning supervising everyone, left to retrieve the basket of food from the buggy. Magic tagged along to help, and when they returned, Magic told her great-aunt, ''I promised Pa me and Cleopatra would have our lunch with him today. May I be excused?''

''Why certainly, dear.''

Vivid watched Magic exit with a run.

''Walk!'' her great aunt warned, too late as always.

After lunch, Vivid and her helpers went back to work. By mid-afternoon, though, she was alone. Miss Edna had to return to her store, and Eli left to take the tired Abigail and Magic back home and then head off to tend to business at the *Gazette*. Vivid thanked him and promised to treat him free of cost should the need ever arise. Eli asked her to have dinner with him instead and departed with a smile.

Vivid spent the balance of the afternoon sweeping acorns and hauling the debris to a growing pile in back of the shop. She returned from yet another trip to find one of the Patterson twins inside the shop.

"May I help you?" she asked. Vivid remembered their names as being Abraham and Aaron but she had no idea which of the two stood before her now.

"You know which one I am?" he asked challengingly.

By his manner, she assumed him to be the more cantankerous of the two. "Aaron."

He didn't answer. She noticed then that he kept rubbing his right jaw and wincing. "Something paining your jaw, Aaron?"

"No," he replied almost too quickly.

"Are you certain?"

"Not letting a female doctor on me."

"That's your choice, Mr. Patterson. Why are you here, then?"

"Heard you were moving in. Just came over to get a look is all."

Again he held his jaw, but he quickly dropped his arm and said, "Reba Winston used to own this place."

"Yes, I've heard that."

"Good-looking woman, Reba."

Vivid hadn't heard that.

"Yep," Aaron said. "Right good-looking woman."

Vivid waited to see where this strange encounter was heading. He looked around once more, then added, "Well, just wanted to take a look."

"I'm pleased you showed an interest. Stop back anytime, Mr. Patterson."

He grumbled something that sounded like thank you, then left. Curious, Vivid walked to the doorway and saw him clutching his jaw as he headed up the walk. He was obviously in pain from something. Vivid stepped back inside, shaking her head at his stubbornness, and the stubbornness of one other man in particular.

As the afternoon waned into evening, Vivid decided she could do no more today. The front of the shop appeared infinitely cleaner, but it would be several days before the back rooms were usable. She stretched to relieve her muscles of the tightness and aches. She'd worked hard today. After dinner she planned on taking a hot bath and going straight to bed. Tomorrow was Sunday, and Sunday meant church.

After closing the door and throwing the bolt, she took the short walk to Nate's office to ask if he wanted the key returned.

Nate had convinced himself that his reaction to Lancaster that morning had occurred simply because he'd been caught unawares. He had not seen many women in trousers. He doubted he'd be so bowled over by her a second time. Yet when he looked up and saw her at the door, he was thankful he was already seated. "Evening, Dr. Lancaster. Are you ladies still working?"

"No. Your aunt and daughter left a few hours ago."

"How's it coming?"

"Not too badly. The back rooms are a mess, but nothing that can't be remedied. I came to ask if I may keep the key."

"You might as well. The shop's yours now."

Vivid nodded and slipped the key into her breast pocket.

Nate tried not to be interested in the way her shirt brushed against her nipple as she buttoned the pocket flap, but he was finding it extremely difficult. "Do you need a ride?"

"No, Abigail left me the buggy. Your cousin Eli came by and took them home.

Silence.

Vivid felt compelled to explain. "He stopped in and remained to lend a hand."

"Always helpful, my cousin. How long did he hang around?"

"He didn't just hang around. He worked very hard and stayed past lunch. When your aunt tired, he drove them home." Vivid wondered if the tension between the two men was rooted in more than a difference in politics.

He asked, "Are you going to be able to get back alone?"

Vivid hadn't really thought much about the return trip. She'd made the ride into town only a few times but felt fairly confident she could drive back home without losing her way.

"How's your sense of direction?"

"I've no idea."

"No idea?" he repeated.

She shrugged. "I've never had to test it, so I can't say whether it is good or bad."

"Do you at least know west from north?"

Vivid didn't lie. "No, but I will learn."

Nate shook his head.

Vivid felt the need to defend herself, "Mr. Grayson, we established your perceptions of my shortcomings the day we met. Surely not even you expect me to become a trailblazer overnight."

He looked over at her standing before him, dirty and disheveled from all the work she'd done that day, and replied, "No, you're right.

She smiled. "Are you actually agreeing with me?"

Nate wondered if there was a man on the planet able to resist her smile. "It seems I am. I don't plan on making it a habit, though."

Vivid didn't take offense. "Hannibal didn't cross the Alps in a day, Mr. Grayson."

"True, but how many times did he get lost?"

When Vivid turned and stalked out, they were both smiling.

*   *   *

Vivid was lost. She pulled back on the reins and sat a moment looking around. The surroundings didn't appear even vaguely familiar. She should have taken that left fork about a quarter of a mile back. She emitted a soft oath, then picked up the reins and headed the buggy back the way she'd come.

As luck would have it, she reached the fork just as Nate Grayson, atop a big black stallion, rode up. He pulled back on the reins and waited for her to drive out of the brush and back onto the road. Hiding his amusement, he asked, "Admiring the scenery?"

"As a matter of fact, yes," she replied, chin up. "I wanted to see where the fork went, is all."

"Uh-huh."

She watched him dismount, then lead the horse around to the back of the buggy. "What are you doing?" she asked.

"Just move over," he replied.

"Excuse me?"

He tied the horse's reins to the buggy and came back around. "Move over, I'm driving."

"You most certainly are not," Vivid stated.

He looked up at her and wondered if every encounter with her would be akin to pulling teeth.

"Dr. Lancaster, you are going to be the main attraction at church tomorrow and no one will be pleased if you don't make an appearance because you couldn't find your way home."

"Mr. Grayson, I will admit that your directions may be needed, but I am perfectly capable of handling a one-horse buggy. If you choose to come along, I drive."

Nate sighed with frustration. He could count on one hand the number of times he'd been driven anywhere by a female.

Vivid looked down at him and said, "I assume driving is a man's job, too?"

He didn't reply, but the answer was evident.

She shook her head. "Mr. Grayson, if I could concoct a cure for misguided male thinking, I would be a very wealthy woman indeed. Are you coming or not?"

He smiled inwardly, went around to the passenger side, and climbed in.

Vivid gently slapped the reins, and they were off.

"So," she said, "I know now to take the left fork instead of the right. What else should I know?"

He began to point out landmarks. Unlike the big cities where markers were usually shops or streets or buildings, here they were distinctively shaped trees, flowing streams, or the lay of the land.

He asked her at one point, "Do you see that big willow over there?"

Vivid eased the buggy to a halt, then looked where he pointed. The tree seemed to be miles away, across the rolling clearing, yet its hanging branches made it distinctly visible.

"That's Adam Crowley's land. The fork you took back there leads to his place. He's about three miles from us. If you're ever out admiring the scenery again on that portion of the Grove, that willow should be your beacon."

She ignored his sarcastic allusion, but filed the willow information into her memory.

She started the buggy again and Nate admired the way she handled it. "Your driving is not bad."

Vivid turned to him and asked, "Is that a compliment, Mr. Grayson?"

"I believe it is."

"Two pleasantries in one day. Will my constitution be able to handle such shock?"

He had to glance away or fall prey to her sparkling eyes. "Just drive, Lancaster."

Chapter 8

In her dreams Vivid felt someone shaking her roughly. She didn't want to be roused but the jostling by the strong hand was insistent enough to make her grudgingly open her eyes and realize she wasn't dreaming at all. She was startled by a man looming over her in the darkness. He was bearded and as big as a bear with the rifle in his hand glistening in the moonlight bathing her room. She sat up slowly as she heard him ask, "Are you the lady doctor?"

"Yes," Vivid answered nervously.

"My pa says I'm to bring you—at gunpoint if necessary."

"That won't be necessary," she told him, eyeing the long-nosed weapon. "If someone's been hurt, just let me get dressed and we can go."

He eased his rifle down and Vivid cautiously slid off the bed and asked him to wait outside, hoping the man would be reasonable.

He nodded, then added, "No tricks now. Hate to have to truss you up."

"No tricks," Vivid assured him. "It would help to know who needs my help and why."

"It's our Jewel, she's real sick. We can't wake her up." He stepped out of the bedroom and closed the door, leaving Vivid the privacy she needed to dress and gather her medical supplies.

When they were ready to depart, her escort mounted

a big gray stallion, then pulled her up behind. "Put your arms around my waist and hold on tight, Doctor. Don't want you falling off."

Under the eerie illumination of the night's full moon, they galloped away. Vivid glanced toward the dark Grayson house as they raced past. It came to her that maybe she should have left a note about her whereabouts but it was too late, and besides, she had no idea of her destination.

The giant's advice to hold on tight proved sound indeed. He took her on one of the wildest rides of her life. For the first few moments she tried to peer around his big frame to survey the terrain ahead, but the trees and branches were rushing by so perilously close, she pulled back and swallowed her fears. The horse beneath her seemed surefooted and strong, the man controlling the reins competent. She had no choice but to hang on and pray that they arrived without mishap.

The mad flight through the night ended a few miles away from Vivid's cabin, and she sighed with relief when the giant helped her dismount. She followed him to a beautiful house even larger than the Graysons', with gables and cornices and trellises.

However, the stench inside was arresting, gagging. Instinctively, Vivid brought a hand up to shield her nose.

"No one's cleaned the place since Jewel took sick," her escort explained. "We've become accustomed to the smell, I guess."

He led Vivid through a kitchen that hadn't been cleaned in quite some time. China, cutlery, and cooking pots were stacked almost to the ceiling on a large table in the room's center. A smaller stack occupied the top of the cooking stove. In one corner a churn had been knocked over and the contents left spread across the wooden floor. Vivid stepped cautiously over the putrid puddle and kept her eyes focused on his back to avoid seeing any more of the kitchen's wondrous sights.

The hallway off the kitchen led into a parlor. There, amid the beautiful framed paintings of animals and birds gracing the walls, dirty laundry reigned. Articles of clothing, enough to stock an army regiment, lay in piles everywhere. Trousers, union suits, shirts, and socks hid what appeared to be fine furniture.

"Jewel usually takes care of the washing, too," the man said as they crossed the parlor and headed up a flight of stairs, but Vivid was only half-listening. She couldn't decide which part of herself, the doctor or the woman, was more appalled at the house's state. The place was as filthy as a sty.

Upstairs, conditions were no better. It was a wonder that every person in the household hadn't succumbed to some sort of sickness, Vivid thought, feeling the beginnings of anger take hold. Her escort was a big strong man; why in the world hadn't he bothered to clean the place instead of waiting for poor Jewel to get better?

In the hallway they walked through she had to sidestep piles of sheets, pillow slips, coverlets, and blankets stacked against the walls in mounds as high as Vivid's waist. The farther she walked, the more determined she became to hold her tongue until after she'd seen the patient. After she took care of Jewel, she would blister this man's hide for living in such squalor.

He opened a door at the end of the hall and Vivid followed him in. Five men were positioned protectively around a bed upon which a woman lay.

The five were as big as the man at Vivid's side, and all were similar enough in appearance for her to assume they were related to one another. An older man stepped forward; he was even larger than the others because age had added to his girth. He critically assessed Vivid for a moment, then stated, "This is the new doctor? Why, she's no older than our Jewel."

"I know, sir, but I got her here as soon as I could."

"You did fine, son."

The older man then turned his attention to Vivid. "Young woman, I am Adam Crowley, and these are my sons, Noah, Abraham, Ezekial, and Jeremiah, and you met Paul."

The men, all of various ages, greeted her politely, and Vivid nodded in turn.

Mr. Crowley continued, "As you've probably heard, I'm against you being here. The wilds of Michigan are no place for a cotillion girl."

Vivid raised an eyebrow at that tart remark, but remained silent.

"However, since you are the only physician available, you will have to do."

Vivid wondered if he was always this brusque. She found Abigail's description of Mr. Crowley as having a wooden head to be very apt indeed. "How may I assist you, Mr. Crowley?"

"It's my daughter, Jewel. Can you tell us what's ailing her?"

The brothers parted like a fortress gate to let her near the bed. Jewel was a beautiful, cinnamon-skinned young woman but terribly, terribly thin. "How long has she been ill?" Vivid asked as she bent close to Jewel and gently opened the lids of the sleeping woman's eyes.

"On and off for nearly a month now, but she wasn't laid low like this until yesterday," Jewel's father answered.

Vivid was pleased to see that Jewel's eyes were clear. She ran her hands lightly over Jewel's jawbones in search of unnatural swelling. There was a bit, but not enough to signal any major inflammation. Her forehead felt warm beneath her practiced hands but not unnaturally so. The woman coughed in her sleep, filling the otherwise silent room. "Mr. Crowley, I'd like to examine her if that's agreeable."

"That would be fine."

He did not bother to mask his concern for his daughter, nor did his sons. All of them appeared genuinely distressed, so much so that although Vivid waited patiently for them to leave, they all remained standing there. "Gentlemen, may we have some privacy?" Vivid asked gently.

Quickly, they all began mumbling apologies and headed for the door, but Vivid could tell by the way they kept looking back at the bed that they were departing with great reluctance.

Once alone with her patient, Vivid conducted a preliminary examination and surmised that the young woman had a slight inflammation of the lungs. However, the inflammation did not account for the gaunt face, dull skin, or overall thinness. According to the men, Jewel had not been ill long enough to have lost so much flesh. Vivid immediately ruled out lack of nutrition as the cause because the giant brothers looked healthy and well-fed. Curious, Vivid picked up the woman's lifeless hands and peered at them closely. Vivid found her answer. Satisfied, she covered Jewel and went out to join the men.

Adam Crowley confronted her immediately. "What's your diagnosis, Dr. Lancaster? I tell you now, I will not have her bled."

"Don't worry, Mr. Crowley I don't believe in bleeding my patients. Your daughter is not in serious danger."

"That's good news," he said with a sigh of relief.

"She has a slight inflammation of her lungs. A recoverable illness given the proper rest."

"Is that why she won't wake up?" Noah asked.

"No. That has to do with something else. I'll explain, but tell me, what does Jewel do on a typical day?"

Vivid watched the brothers look at one another, then Paul spoke. "Well, she gets the eggs first thing, then cooks our breakfast and does the milking."

"After breakfast," Ezekial chimed in, "she starts the

bread for the evening meal, then does the washing.
About midday we all come in to eat. After that, if it's
not too hot, she does the gardening."

"She feeds the chickens and slops the hogs," added
Noah.

"Is this every day?" Vivid asked amazed.

"Just about," said Jeremiah.

Vivid looked around at the able-bodied men and then
said, "All of you need a buggy whip taken to your back-
sides! What do all of you do all day long?"

"Hunt, fish, trap, why?"

"Because that girl is exhausted, that's why she won't
wake up! I'll bet my certificate she keeps this house
spotless, doesn't she?"

"Why, sure. How'd you know?"

"Because her hands and fingers are cracked and red
raw from soap and lye." Vivid looked around at the
giant men and then thought back on the woman lying
silently in bed. "All of you should be ashamed!"

"Now hold on a minute, young woman!" Mr. Crowley spoke sharply.

One of the brothers interrupted his father to say, "Dr.
Lancaster, we would help if she'd let us, but she doesn't
like us in the house when she's working."

"She says we take up all the air," another pointed
out sadly.

Vivid could understand why Jewel would feel that
way. Having all of them in the room was a bit overpowering, but Vivid saw that as only as an excuse. She
asked, "So have any of you ever offered to help with
the chores?"

"Sure, she lets us chop wood—and slaughter the
hogs."

"Sometimes," one brother noted sarcastically.

"But mostly we stay out of her way. She says she
can do in ten minutes what takes us an hour, so she does
mostly everything herself. Dr. Lancaster, we love our

sister very much. We'd help if she'd let us.''

The men seemed sincere, Vivid noted as she surveyed them. Vivid looked into Mr. Crowley's eyes and felt humbled. Now would be the best time to remove her foot from her mouth. "Mr. Crowley, I owe you and your sons an apology. I made a wrong assumption.

"Yes, you did, young woman, but I'm going to forgive you because you took what you thought was Jewel's side. I like that."

"Feisty little thing, ain't she, Pa?''

"She sure is," Mr. Crowley said, smiling for the first time. "Which one of my sons you want to marry up with?''

Vivid grinned in return. "I'm here for doctoring, Mr. Crowley, not marrying."

"Pity. You remind me of my Margaret when she was young, all spirit and determination."

"Then I'll take that as a compliment."

"When will she wake up, Doctor?''

"When her body's ready."

Vivid spent the night at the Crowley home, and in the morning everyone pitched in to help clean the place.

"Jewel's not going to like us doing this, Dr. Lancaster," one of the brothers said.

"I'll handle Jewel, you get that laundry started."

Vivid took over cleaning the kitchen. It required the better part of the morning for her to make the kitchen usable again, and once done, she went out to help with the laundry. She learned that, despite their giant frames, the Crowley sons were as fun-loving and playful as a batch of puppies. They spent as much time wrestling around and teasing one another as they did doing the chores. The work went smoothly. However, all of them, Mr. Crowley included, were too scared of Jewel's wrath to go anywhere near the garden, so Vivid spent the afternoon on her knees weeding and planting the spring vegetables.

During the course of the day's activities, she looked up more than once to find Adam Crowley watching her from afar. He never said anything, so she didn't, either. Upstairs, Jewel slept.

Briefly, she regretted missing church. She had been looking forward to acquainting herself with the congregation. Well, maybe next Sunday, she thought with a sigh.

Vivid was washing her hands at the pump when Adam Crowley walked up and asked, "Young woman?"

"Yes, Mr. Crowley."

"I've been watching you all day, and you're not a cotillion girl, are you?"

"No, Mr. Crowley, I'm not."

"That's good. Cotillion girls don't fare well here." Then he added, "If you doctor half as good as you worked here today, you'll be a fine addition to the Grove."

Vivid looked up at him and asked, "You're not saying that just because you want me to marry one of your sons, are you, Mr. Crowley?"

He laughed heartily. "A sense of humor, too. I like that. No, I'm not, though it would be nice if you consider it; they eat like a regiment."

"I am not here to marry," she said, laughing.

"Pity," he said. "So tell me all about yourself."

Vivid did. Over the course of the evening she found that Adam Crowley didn't actually have a wooden head at all. He was intelligent, well-read, and blunt about his opinions.

"Frederick Douglass represents only Frederick Douglass," came Mr. Crowley's response to Vivid's inquiry about whom he would designate as the true spokesman of the race. "Oh, Fred's a great orator, probably one of the best the race has ever seen, but he always waits for someone else to test the water first. He was one of the last on the wagon for taking up arms to end slavery.

Never much respected his opinion after that, and his private life is a mess.''

The five sons eventually drifted out to the porch. Vivid sat talking to the Crowley men until way past candlelight. Finally, Adam Crowley asked, ''Should I have one of the boys take you back?''

Vivid shook her head no. ''I believe tomorrow will be soon enough. I really would prefer Jewel be awake before I leave.''

''Fair enough. Well, you can bed down in her room again tonight. The boys and I will see you in the morning.''

Jewel awakened the next day. Vivid, who had come in to check on her, smiled when the young woman's dark eyes met hers.

''Who are you?'' Jewel asked in a weak voice.

''I'm Dr. Lancaster, Jewel. How do you feel?''

''Like I've been asleep for a hundred years.''

Vivid smiled and placed her hand on her patient's forehead. ''It's been more like three days. Does anything hurt or ache?''

''My chest hurts a bit, probably from all the coughing I was doing. And my head feels like it's full of moss. Did my father and brothers bring you here?''

''Yes, they were very concerned. What was the last thing you remember?''

''Well, I'd been sick for about a week. I was too weak to do my chores, I remember that. Then—'' She seemed to take a moment to think back. ''Oh, yes, I remember not wanting to put the washing off any longer. It was starting to pile up. So even though Zekial told me not to, I was carrying water in and I started to feel real queerlike—''

She looked at Vivid, who nodded for her to continue.

''Then I dropped the buckets and that's the last I know.''

''How old are you, Jewel?''

"It'll be my nineteenth summer come July. Doctor, you don't look any older than me, and you're a doctor?"

"Yes."

"Why?"

"Why am I a physician?"

Jewel nodded.

"I always wanted to be a doctor. What do you want to be, Jewel?"

"Oh, I don't know. I can't really think about it until my brothers marry."

Vivid, puzzled by that remark, asked, "Why not?"

"I promised my mother."

"I see," Vivid said, although she didn't really see at all. However, now was not the time to pursue the matter. Instead, she asked, "Do you want anything to eat or drink?"

"Maybe a drink of water."

Vivid poured some from the pitcher on the stand beside the bed, then handed her the cup. "Drink slowly now," Vivid cautioned.

Jewel took a few swallows. "I think I want to sleep some more. Can you hold off my pa and brothers for just a tad longer?"

"Certainly," Vivid replied, smiling. "At the moment they're out fishing for supper, so you can enjoy your solitude for as long as you require."

"Thank you, Dr. Lancaster. And welcome to the Grove."

"Thank you," Vivid replied genuinely. "Get some rest. I'll be back to check on you later."

Jewel was once again asleep before Vivid left the room.

The men returned later in the afternoon, their poles and baskets fat with fish. They greeted the news of Jewel's recovery with wide smiles and would have run pell-mell up the stairs to her room had Vivid not cautioned them to let her rest a bit longer. They all appeared disappointed as they cleaned the fish for the evening's meal.

Jeremiah had taken over in the kitchen and proved to be a surprisingly good cook. The meal-dusted fish he fried was tender enough to melt in the mouth. Vivid had just begun to tell him that her father would pay excellent wages to a man with Jeremiah's abilities, but she was interrupted by Noah, who was standing by the window. "Nate Grayson's riding up, Pa. He looks mad."

A couple of the brothers went to the window and echoed Noah's observation. "He's mad about something."

Mr. Crowley went to the door to greet the visitor. "Nate, how are you this evening, son?"

"Fine, Adam," Nate answered. "Have you seen the damned doctor in the last couple days? I seem to have lost her."

Adam stepped aside to let Nate enter.

The "damned doctor" in question stood in the center of the front room, hands on hips. "I'm right here, Mr. Grayson," Vivid said.

She thought she saw relief fill his eyes, but that expression quickly vanished when he asked quietly, "Where the hell have you been?"

"Here. Mr. Crowley's daughter has been ill."

"Do you know I have been searching the Grove for two whole days? I didn't know if you'd been shanghaied by a lumber beast or were lying dead in a ditch somewhere."

Vivid was touched by his concern. "What is a lumber beast?" she asked gently, hiding her smile.

One of the Crowley sons supplied the explanation. "You probably know them as lumberjacks, Dr. Lancaster. Here, some folks call them beasts because of the way they carry on when they come into town with their pay."

She turned back to Nate. "I didn't mean to worry you, Mr. Grayson."

"Next time leave a note."

Adam Crowley spoke up then. "It was my fault, Nate. I was so worried about Jewel, I had one of the boys fetch Dr. Lancaster in the middle of the night."

Nate continued to stare into Vivid's eyes as he asked Adam Crowley, "How's Jewel doing?"

Vivid held his gaze.

"The doctor says she'll be fine with a little rest," Mr. Crowley replied. Then Vivid heard him say, "I'm hoping the doc's going to marry up with one of my sons."

Nate smiled, saying, "But Dr. Lancaster isn't going to marry anyone, are you, Viveca?"

Hearing him address her by her given name for the first time sent her senses spinning.

"No, I'm not marrying anyone," she answered in a voice far softer than she'd intended. She tore away from the undertow in Nate Grayson's eyes. "I . . . should go check on my patient," she said and quickly headed for the stairs.

Nate's voice made her stop. "Viveca?"

She turned.

"When you're done, I'll take you home."

She nodded nervously and fled.

Upstairs, Vivid found Jewel up and dressed and gathering laundry in the hallway.

"What in Jessy are you doing, Jewel Crowley?" Vivid asked. Up close Vivid could see the perspiration beaded on the young girl's brow. "Back to bed. Now."

"But—"

"Now, miss, or I'll call your father."

They had a standoff for a moment, then Jewel dropped the sheets, trudged back to her room, and climbed under the sheets. "Now I expect you to spend the next few days in bed. You need rest if you are to recover."

"There's too much to do."

"Then let your father and brothers help."

"And spend all the day undoing what they've done? It's easier to do it myself."

Vivid said softly, "They are a lot more competent than you know, Jewel, and believe me, they were very worried about you when you fell ill. Let them help so this doesn't happen again."

"You don't understand," Jewel replied sadly. "I promised my mother."

"Promised her what?"

"On her deathbed she made me promise I would take care of Pa and the boys."

"How old were you?"

"Almost twelve summers."

Vivid thought back to when she was twelve and how devastated she would have been had her mother died. "Did you love your mother, Jewel?"

In answer, Jewel turned her head on the pillow, and Vivid could see the sadness in her eyes. "Very much. I still miss her."

"Then think about this. Would she have wanted you to work yourself to death? When she made you promise to take care of your father and brothers, I don't believe she meant to the detriment of your health. There are six strong men in this house. Please let them show you how much they love you by letting them help out."

Jewel lay with her head on the pillow, looking at the ceiling. Vivid asked her, "Will you at least consider it?"

After several silent moments passed, Jewel finally gave a small nod of affirmation.

"Good," Vivid said, smiling.

"But what if they make a mess?"

"Then show them how to do what you want without making a mess. They'll listen, I promise. Every one of them is scared to death of raising your ire. They'll behave."

Jewel appeared to mull over the suggestions, then said, "Well, I suppose it won't hurt to give it a try."

For the first time Vivid saw her smile. Beneath all the thinness and exhaustion, Jewel was a very beautiful young woman.

"Good," Vivid replied genuinely.

"Thank you, Dr. Lancaster."

Vivid smiled. "You're welcome. And now that you're on the road to recovery, I need to get on the road home."

Jewel turned her head on the pillow and asked, "Was that Nate's voice I heard downstairs?"

"Yes."

"Are you in love with him, yet?"

"Jewel Crowley!" Vivid said with a laugh.

"I'm only asking because every woman in town has been sweet on him at one time or another. The girls in the choir can hardly sing sometimes for looking at him sitting in the front pew. Then there was Miss Edna's daughter who came up from South Bend, last August first. And Maddie's been in love with Nate since they were Magic's age. Have you met Maddie yet?"

"No."

"Some folks don't like her because of the type of place she used to run, but she grew up here. Nate and Eli never let anybody talk mean about her when she comes to town."

Vivid wondered if this woman was the same Maddie who ran the Emporium, the brothel she had heard about.

A knock on Jewel's door interrupted Vivid's thoughts.

"How's my baby girl?" Adam Crowley asked as he walked in.

"Come on in and see for yourself," Vivid said.

As father and daughter smiled at each other, Vivid slipped out, leaving them alone.

Downstairs, the brothers surrounded her for news of Jewel. When Vivid related their sister's promise to accept their help, they threw their hats to the ceiling and filled the house with sounds of joy.

The sun had begun to set when Nate and Vivid started

for home. Beside him on the seat, Vivid sat silently,
thinking about the way he'd addressed by her Christian
name earlier. The shock of the moment had been akin
to touching a hot stove. She'd tried not to dwell on her
reaction but her efforts were futile. She glanced over at
him and thought he'd become more handsome in the
days she'd spent with the Crowleys. She hastily looked
away and chastised herself for her thoughts. It must be
fatigue again, she rationalized. After all, she'd worked
hard the past few days, even Adam Crowley had attested
to that fact, so it was only natural that she would be a
bit more vulnerable to Nate Grayson's overpowering
masculinity.

However, the attraction she'd admitted to harboring
the other day had surfaced like an emerging spring bulb.
Despite the complications sure to arise, the shoots continued to grow. Vivid could see no other alternative but
to hope for a good hard frost.

The sky-high trees growing on both sides of the road
sheltered their passage beneath a canopy of green. The
beauty of a brilliant Michigan sunset filled Vivid's
senses and served to uplift her pensive mood.

Marveling at the trees and the beautiful splashes of
color provided by the wildflowers, she asked, "Will I
ever become accustomed to this?" without realizing she
had spoken out loud.

"I never have, and I've been here most of my life,"
Nate replied. "Wait until autumn, now that's spectacular."

Vivid had seen autumn in the East, but her studies
had been so tiring and all-consuming that she'd had little
time to enjoy the metamorphoses of the seasons. "I can
see why your grandfather decided to settle here. Is the
rest of this state as beautiful?"

"Pretty much. The lumber beasts are clearing a lot of
the forests north and east of here, though. They brag
about cutting down every tree on both peninsulas."

"That's not possible, is it?"

"If the lumber barons smell profit, anything is possible."

Suddenly, a white-tailed deer darted across the road. Nate pulled hard on the reins to avoid a collision, then fought to keep the buggy upright. The abruptness tossed Vivid across the seat and almost into Nate's lap. A blink of an eye later, calm returned and she found herself staring up into his too close features. "Are you all right?" he asked.

She was near enough to feel the heat coming off his chest and see the rise and fall of his measured breathing. "Yes, I believe so," she said, but she seemed unable to move back to her spot across the seat.

He reached out and for a long, drawn-out moment, lightly traced the surface of her bottom lip. "I worried when I couldn't find you, Viveca . . ."

He lowered his mouth to hers, and Vivid shuddered. The sweet intensity proved far more wonderful than she would ever have imagined. He put his hands on her arms and pulled her close, then closer still. Under the passionate coaxing of his mouth, she forgot everything— her name, her profession, the fact that they were on opposing sides. When he brushed his mouth across her lips, then slowly nibbled the parted corners, Vivid melted like wax.

He left her mouth tingling and slowly moved down to explore the skin beneath her jaw, then the sensitive shell of her ear. Vivid reeled from the heated trails he blazed, and from the lingering, passionate way in which his mouth reclaimed hers.

He let her go finally, reluctantly, and she sat with eyes closed, swaying. When she opened her eyes, he was watching her, his face unreadable.

"Let's get you back," he said.

Vivid reclaimed her seat beside him, feeling hazy from his kiss.

He picked up the reins and their journey resumed.

*   *   *

From his bedroom window later that night, Nate looked down on Vivid's cabin. He'd never meant to kiss her. One moment he'd been dodging the white-tailed deer and the next . . . The next moment she was in his arms and he hadn't wanted to let her go. Her virgin's mouth had been just that, virginal, ripe. Even now, hours later, he could still feel the taste of her on his lips. Women rarely affected him in such a manner. Since Cecile he'd limited himself to playful dalliances with a lusty widow or two, but he'd never let himself be so moved by a woman that he wanted to take her right there on the seat of the buggy, as he had with Lancaster. He could offer no rational explanation. He'd been frantic when he couldn't find her Sunday morning. Abigail assured him there was no need to worry, especially since her medical bag couldn't be located either, but anxiety had consumed him for the balance of the day. His concerns multiplied when she didn't return the next night, so he'd gone out to search. Finding her at Adam's had filled him with such relief, he'd almost pulled her into his arms then and there.

Nate moved away from the window and stretched out on his big bed, trying to make sense of his growing attraction to Viveca Lancaster. Considering the potential for battle whenever they came near each other, he couldn't understand what made him muse over the warmth of her throat beneath his kisses, the feel of her hips against his palms, the scents she wore between her breasts. By all rights, he shouldn't be thinking about her at all unless it related to how long she'd stay before she headed off to a place more in line with her upbringing. And she would leave, he was certain. With that in mind, he'd be better off devising a plan for a replacement physician instead of remembering how passionately she responded to his embrace.

But as Nate drifted off to sleep, his last thoughts were of her lips.

Chapter 9

B y the following Sunday, Vivid was in terrible need of a Sabbath rest because of all the sweeping, hauling, and scrubbing she'd been doing to get her office ready. With Eli and Vernon's help, the holes in the foundation and roof had been patched and tarred, and the Crowley sons had begun installing her new truncheon floor. The cobwebs were finally banished from the back room via the flames of a torch. On Thursday, an older man of Adam Crowley's age and stature entered the office. He introduced himself as Hiram Farley and announced that he'd come to encircle the base of the outside foundation with a screening wire.

Vivid followed him outside, puzzled by this announcement. She'd never heard of such a thing.

He was unrolling the wire mesh like a bolt of fabric as he explained what he'd come to do. "Edna says the squirrels got in."

"Yes, sir, they did."

"Well, after we nail this around the foundation they won't be able to gnaw through. Rodents like familiar places and they're probably gonna want to bed down in your place next winter, but this'll tell them their boardinghouse is closed."

Vivid smiled. "How much do I owe you, Mr. Farley?"

"Not a cent, little girl. This is me and Adam Crow-

143

ley's way of saying welcome to the Grove, Dr. Lancaster."

Vivid stilled. Had her visit to Adam Crowley turned him into a supporter?

Hiram chuckled. "You impressed that old lumber beast."

She was surprised by that bit of information. "Mr. Crowley is a lumberjack?"

"In his youth he cut trees from here to Superior. He didn't tell you, I take it?"

Vivid shook her head no as he took out some tin snips and tools from the belt around his waist and knelt near the rolled-out wire.

Hiram stated, "Adam spent the whole time quizzing you, I'll bet."

Vivid grinned. "As a matter of fact, he did."

Farley nodded and smiled. "Well, you go on back and do what you were doing and let an old man get to work."

Vivid smiled and complied.

In addition to Mr. Farley, Vivid had other visitors during the week. The Quilt Ladies stopped in, as did Miss Edna, curious farmers on their way to and from the mill, and the Patterson twins. Vivid noticed that Aaron Patterson's jaw continued to plague him, but he refused to let Vivid examine him.

The only person Vivid did not see was Nate Grayson. He'd gone up to Kalamazoo for some business, Abigail informed her the morning after Vivid returned from the Crowleys.

She didn't see Nate again until Sunday morning. She stepped onto her porch and noticed him seated atop the buggy ready to take them all to church. She shouldn't have expected any more than the impersonal nod of greeting he gave her, but she was upset by his cool manner nonetheless. Obviously, the kiss they'd shared had meant very little to him. In retaliation, Vivid remained quiet and impassive all the way to church.

"Our church started out as a tent," Abigail explained to Vivid as they toured the interior of the stone and wood structure before the service began. Unlike the two large A.M.E. churches Vivid and her father attended, this church was small. However, Vivid had never seen a more beautifully carved choir box. Every beam, railing, and pew in the sanctuary gleamed from the care it obviously received.

"This is where we hold all our meetings." Abigail gestured as Vivid followed her into a fairly large room down the hall. Vivid looked around and smiled at the children's Sunday school pictures proudly nailed up on a portion of the wall. There were shelves of books and in one corner a lectern made of dark wood. A plaque near the doorway listed the scheduled dates and times for a book reading group, a historical society, the Men's Association, the Women's Club, the Quilt Ladies, and the Bible class, which met every Wednesday at seven. "I never thought there would be so many gatherings here," Vivid said, impressed.

"We're small but we try and keep up with the rest of the country. Between my son's newspaper and my historical society, there isn't a lot we miss."

"You head the historical society?" Vivid asked, surprised.

"Yes, I'm compiling a history of the race. I'll show you my work sometime."

"I'd be honored."

On the way out Vivid stopped to look at the items displayed on the shelves of a doorless highboy. There were various plaques honoring past and current reverends and a large, beautifully patterned quilt.

Abigail came up next to her and explained, "The Quilt Ladies took first place at last year's fair with that quilt."

"It's beautiful," Vivid noted, running her eyes over

the delicate stitching and patterns. "But what in the world are those?" she asked, picking up the odd-looking items. They appeared to be small balls fashioned out of burned wood.

"Lacrosse balls."

Before Abigail could explain further, organ music filled the air. Vivid placed the balls back on the shelf. The service was about to begin.

Vivid took her seat next to Abigail in the Grayson pew at the front of the church. Nate and Magic were already seated. His eyes held hers for a brief moment as she passed by, but they were the same distant eyes he'd turned on her that morning, so she decided to put him and his kisses out of her mind. As the choir came in, she concentrated on singing the processional hymn instead.

Vivid's mother, Francesca, had been raised in the Catholic faith, but Vivid and her sisters were, like their father, members of the A.M.E., or African Methodist Episcopal faith. One of the first Sunday school lessons she and her sisters learned had been the story of how the A.M.E. church came into existence.

Prior to the mid-eighteenth century, most free Blacks in the North worshipped in White Christian churches. Mainstream denominations such as the Baptists, Methodists, and Episcopalians welcomed Blacks into their flocks but rarely allowed them to pray with the main congregation. Instead, Blacks were relegated to uncomfortable benches placed in the back of the church marked B.M., for "Black Members," or forced to sit in balconies and galleries that bore such names as "African Corner" or the more denigrating "Nigger Heaven." Even the Quakers, who until 1830 stood at the forefront of the abolitionist movement, did not allow its Black and White members to pray side by side.

In 1794, two Black men sought an alternative to this

practice and forever changed the way America worshipped.

Richard Allen had been born a slave in Philadelphia. When his lawyer-owner sold the Allen family to a planter in Delaware, Richard Allen became a devout Methodist. His convictions were so strong he converted the planter, who in turn allowed Richard and his brother to buy their freedom in 1777.

In the years that followed, the freed Allen continued his religious work and eventually resettled in Philadelphia where on off hours he was allowed to preach to the Black congregation of the city's St. George Methodist Episcopal Church.

For years the church had allowed its Black worshippers to sit and pray with the rest of the congregation in the comfortable seats on the main floor. This Christian policy drew so many free Blacks that the trustees decreed Blacks were no longer allowed on the main floor.

One cold November morning in 1787, Reverend Allen and an associate, Reverend Absalom Jones, entered St. George for the regular Sunday service. Aware of the change in seating, the Reverends Allen and Jones journeyed to the balcony which overlooked the seats they'd occupied before Jim Crow. The two men knelt to pray. Moments later, Allen heard a scuffle and raised his head to see a church trustee trying to raise Reverend Jones from his knees. It seemed the seating policy had undergone yet another change. That Sunday morning Blacks were allowed to worship only in the *back* of the balcony. Reverend Jones and Allen were kneeling in the front.

"You must get up," the trustee hissed at Reverend Jones, pulling at his arms. "You must not kneel here."

The Reverend Jones asked that he be at least allowed to finish his prayer, but the trustee refused and threatened to have Jones forcibly removed. Faced with such a Christian attitude Allen and Jones left St. George.

To deal with the very real need for separate Black

churches where Blacks could pray free of Jim Crow Christianity, the two began to raise funds for a church site. To help with this cause they enlisted prominent Whites such as Benjamin Franklin, Thomas Jefferson, Benjamin Rush, and the nation's first president, George Washington.

The money was raised, but because Allen and Jones could not agree on the new church's affiliation, each man formed his own church: Jones an Episcopalian one and Allen a Methodist one.

In July 1794 Philadelphia witnessed an historic event, the dedication of the Reverend Jones's St. Thomas African Episcopal Church, and the Reverend Richard Allen's Bethel African Methodist Episcopal Church. Both Black churches were the first of their kind.

As a result of the groundwork laid by Allen and Jones, the independent Black church movement spread. In 1808, the Jim Crow services at the First Baptist Church of New York led to the formation of the all-Black Abyssinia Baptist Church, and in 1809, Reverend Thomas Paul started several independent Black churches in major cities in the East.

The oldest Black church in Michigan, the Chain of Lakes Baptist Church, had been established in 1837 not too far from the Grove in another Black township called Calvin Center. All these churches served as anchors of their surrounding communities, and the Bethel A.M.E. in Grayson Grove was no exception.

After church, courtesy of the Quilt Ladies and the Women's Club, a gathering had been arranged to welcome Dr. Lancaster. Vivid had known nothing about the event until the reverend announced it before giving his sermon. She'd stared at Abigail, who'd kindly patted Vivid's hand, then leaned over and whispered, "The sooner they find out you don't have two heads, the sooner you can get on with your work here."

So now Vivid stood with Abigail beneath a bower of

trees and watched the people she hoped would be her patients set up tables and chairs in the cleared field behind the church. She fought off her nervousness and hoped they would accept her.

The friendliness of the people warmed her heart. There was music provided by the small but mighty Grayson Grove band. They could only play hymns however, since it was Sunday, but they played with lively spirit. The food stretched from one end of the long trestle table to the other.

As Abigail and Miss Edna introduced her around, Vivid took a few extra minutes getting to know the families in attendance and introducing herself to their children. She made it a point to observe the physical appearance of the little ones. Although they were all thin, she was pleased to see that most were bright-eyed and healthy. One family did concern her, though. The three children, two boys and a little girl, were terribly thin and their eyes bore the same haunted look she'd seen in the eyes of children back in the charity wards of Philadelphia where she'd done her last year of training. Their father, a small, thin man, was a farmer who rented land from Nate but was barely making ends meet. His name was Garret Turner and he'd lost his wife three years ago. Everyone in the area had offered to help with either the farm or the children, but Turner was a proud man and he wouldn't accept help from his neighbors. Vivid walked over and introduced herself. When she stuck out her hand, Mr. Turner looked at her face with confusion. Vivid concealed her smile. He didn't shake her hand but Vivid didn't mind. Every time she introduced herself in this manner men seemed taken aback.

"I'm Garret Turner," he said, assessing her, "and these are my three children, Missy, Josh, and Garret the second."

Vivid sensed the father's wariness so she tried to set him at ease. "I just came over to say I'll be visiting all the Grove families over the course of the summer in order to get to know everyone better and write down medical histories. I want to make sure I have your permission before I venture out your way.''

Garret the second piped up, "I didn't know they let girls be doctors, Pa.'' The boy appeared to be about Magic's age.

Turner looked down at his son with a smile that left no doubt as to how much he loved these children, and replied, "Your ma used to say girls can do anything, Garret, so I guess she was right.''

Vivid smiled at his reply, but her smile faded when he told her that he wouldn't be needing her care.

Vivid looked at his waiflike children and longed to disagree but she kept her silence instead. She had plenty of time to make them more comfortable with her presence. Hannibal didn't cross the Alps in a day, she reminded herself. "I'll respect your decision, Mr. Turner, but please, if the children ever need me, send someone and I'll come.''

He nodded, but whether it was a nod of affirmation or dismissal Vivid couldn't tell. She said goodbye to the children and went to join Miss Edna and Abigail.

Although the people today had come to meet Vivid, they'd also come to sit and visit with their neighbors. Activities were going on all over the yard: children playing hide and seek; adults gathered in small groups and large, talking, pitching horseshoes, gossiping. Everyone to whom Abigail introduced Vivid smiled and asked questions about her schooling, her parents, and how Black folks were treated where she came from. Vivid didn't mind. The more they knew about her, the more inclined they'd be to let her treat them. Abigail's leg began to ache from all the walking, so she and Miss Edna went to sit with the Quilt Ladies while Vivid continued to stroll among the one hundred or so Grove residents. Under a stand of trees she paused to watch the domino players. Men young and old were slapping the spotted squares of bones down onto makeshift tables fashioned from slabs of wood set atop large barrels. They displayed much enthusiasm as they vied for points. The exuberance in their voices and body movements brought up memories of her Spanish uncles and cousins. Dominoes in one form or another were played all over the world, and her Spanish relatives took their games very seriously. Thinking about her cousins made her think about her parents, and how very much she missed them. She'd suffered the same pangs of loneliness during her studies in Philadelphia. However, during that period she'd had the solace of knowing that the time would pass and she'd be going home when her certification was finished. Here the circumstances were different. There would be no return home. She'd chosen this place to do her life's work. She would get back to San Francisco eventually, but she wouldn't be able to make the trip anytime soon. Deep in thought, she paid little attention to where she was going, and as a result she strayed away from the church clearing. Trees surrounded her on every side. She paused a minute to listen for sounds to lead her back to the gathering, but she couldn't accurately determine which way to proceed.

She was lost.

She sat down on a felled tree to contemplate her next move. Common sense told her to stay put, someone would eventually notice her absence and come looking for her. She hoped.

That someone was Nate. He was calling her name and she stood up and yelled, "I'm over here." She could just about imagine what he'd say about her losing her way a second time.

He yelled back for her to keep hollering. She did, and a few moments later he walked into the cove of trees.

"Admiring the scenery again?"

Because of his distant manner earlier, she chose not to respond to their private joke.

"You always sneak off from a gathering in your honor?"

"Not usually."

"Oh, so you're saying you have done it before."

"Once."

He leaned comfortably against a tree, and asked, "Is this another one of your stories?"

Vivid tried not to smile but responded, "I'm afraid so."

Nate wondered just how he was going to tell her there would be no more kisses when he could barely fight off the urge to pull her into his arms. "Well, I'm listening."

Vivid could feel herself warming from his presence. "It happened during the party my mother gave to celebrate my going away to Michigan."

"She was so glad to get you out of her hair she gave a party?"

"No," Vivid responded in mock offense. "You sound like my father. He said much the same thing."

She paused a moment. "As I was explaining, my mother gave me a big fancy outdoor soiree and invited half of San Francisco. No one gives parties like Francesca Sarita Valdez Lancaster."

"That's your mother."

"That's my mother. I put on a fancy dress, greeted all the guests, and smiled until my face hurt. I was scheduled to leave in two days, and since I knew the two days would be spent packing and preparing, I wanted to pay a last visit to my old tree house."

Nate asked, "You had a tree house?"

"Yes, my father built it for me when I was six."

"Majestic's been after me to build her one, but I've been putting her off because I'm afraid she'll fall out and break her neck."

"Build it for her. Every girl should have a place she

can call her own. I spent most of my days in that house, reading, playing, dreaming.''

Nate had only envisioned Magic trying to jump from a tree house or using it for some other derring-do. He'd never considered it a place for the types of activities Lancaster had just mentioned. She had given him something to think on. ''So you slipped away from your party for one last look before you left for Michigan.''

''I did, and I figured that with such a crush no one would notice. I went to the tree, climbed the rope ladder—''

''In a fancy gown?''

''It's tricky, but I'd been doing it most of my life. I'll have you know that by the time I was ten I could even climb without tearing the hems loose,'' she boasted proudly.

Nate shook his head in wondrous amusement.

''What's the matter?'' Vivid asked, seeing the gesture.

''Nothing, go on.''

She wondered what he was thinking. ''Well, after I climbed up and began looking at my old dolls and sketchpads and reading my diaries, I lost track of time. Next thing I knew my mother was on the ground below angrily calling my name.''

''She was not pleased?''

''She was not pleased in two languages. As I climbed down I felt ten years old again. Here I was, a certified doctor being feted by hundreds of people, and my mother had to pull me down out of my tree house.''

''What did your father say?'' Nate asked.

''He told my mother to be thankful she didn't find me behind the house rolling dice in the dirt with the help.''

Nate smiled inwardly. ''I'd like to meet this father of yours. Maybe he can give me some tips on raising Magic.''

''My father is a wonderful man. In fact, that's why I

became lost today. I was thinking about my parents and how much I missed them, and I didn't pay attention to where I was heading."

"Homesick?"

She answered truthfully. "A bit, yes."

Their eyes met and held.

He said, "Well, we should get back. By the way, do you do this often?"

"Do I do what often?"

"Get lost."

Vivid could feel embarrassment burn her brown cheeks. "Not usually."

"Well, stop it," he told her grimly. "Chasing you across the countryside is making me an old man."

"I'm sorry," Vivid replied, trying not to grin.

"No, you're not," he countered as he led the way out of the cove.

Magic came running out to meet them as they emerged from the trees. "Did you get lost, Dr. Lancaster?" she asked, slipping her hand into her father's.

"Yes, I did, Magic, and your father found me."

"Good, because everybody's waiting on you so we can eat ice cream. Are you really going to marry Dr. Lancaster, Pa?"

Vivid didn't dare look at Nate, who'd stopped to stare at his daughter as if she had grown two heads. "Where did you hear that?" he asked.

"Becky Carpenter."

"Ah, Becky Carpenter," Nate echoed.

"Who's Becky Carpenter?" Vivid asked.

"A school friend of Majestic's and probably the next editor of the *Grayson Gazette*. Magic, Dr. Lancaster and I are not getting married."

"Why not, Pa? Don't you think she's pretty?"

Vivid couldn't resist adding fuel to the fire, and so asked, "Well?"

"Stay out of this," he warned.

Vivid grinned.

"There's more to being married than having a pretty wife, Majestic. Now let me see how fast you can run back down the hill to the church."

"I'll be there before you count to ten, Pa."

"Go!" he yelled, grinning, and Magic took off at a run.

"You're pretty good," Vivid mused aloud.

"At what?"

"Distracting your daughter," Vivid said, even as her gaze grazed his mouth. She looked back up to his eyes and found the impassive distance had returned.

He said flatly, "You and I need to talk later."

She felt deflated. She nodded. "Fine."

They walked back down the hill in silence.

When Vivid and Nate rejoined the gathering they were met with a round of applause. Embarrassed, Vivid dropped her eyes to her shoes in response and smiled as Nate said, "I found her over in the trees about three hundred yards away." Then he looked at Vivid and stated with mock seriousness, "I don't know folks, do we really want a doctor who can get lost within earshot of so many of her neighbors?"

A lot of people raised their voices in support while others gave the doctor a good old-fashioned ribbing. In the end they decided she should stay.

Vivid humbly curtsied, saying, "I apologize for getting lost, and if I haven't said so already, I want to thank you all for today." Her voice became more serious as she looked out over their kind faces. "I realize some of you are very skeptical about my abilities, and that's to be expected; I'm young, I'm a stranger, and I am a woman, but I promise you I'm going to be the best doctor I can be, so—where's this ice cream?"

Her short speech was met with cheers. As the crowd lined up at the ice cream churns, Vivid placed a hand on Nate's arm to stay him a moment.

"I want to thank you," she said earnestly.

"For what?"

"For finding me, of course. And for saying these people were my neighbors. People will be more accepting if they believe you already are."

"Don't read more into it than there is. I'm remaining neutral. But, you're welcome."

As he walked away, Vivid sighed.

At the table set up by the Women's Club, Vivid got a dish of ice cream and a wooden spoon. Eating and walking, she smiled at the people she passed, then stopped at the sound of voices arguing at a table nearby. She couldn't see the principals because of the small crowd ringing the space, but the female voice belonged to Abigail Grayson, and the booming male counterpoint sounded familiar.

Vivid excused herself politely as she maneuvered through the people standing around the table. When she reached the front, she smiled. Sure enough, the male voice belonged to Adam Crowley. His black eyes brushed hers and he smiled. "Ah, finally a female with the brain of a man. Dr. Lancaster, tell this 'historian' that Benjamin Rush is no friend to the race."

Vivid looked from Adam Crowley's smiling eyes to Abigail's flashing ones and said, "Mr. Crowley, before we discuss Benjamin Rush, I'd like to address another point first, if I may?"

He nodded.

She leaned in close and fairly shouted, "A female with the brain of a man? Mr. Crowley, you should be ashamed of yourself."

He chuckled. "Ah, little girl, what a wife you'd make. If I were twenty years younger, I'd court you whether you wanted me to or not."

Then he shouted for Nate, who stood a few feet away talking to a group of farmers, to join them. Nate strolled over, looking first at Vivid, then at Crowley. "What's wrong, Adam?" he asked.

"Marry her, Nate, or I swear I'll truss her up and give her to one of my boys."

Vivid stared. "Mr. Crowley!"

"Look at her, son. She's beautiful, smart, and has a spine. A man can't ask for more than that."

Vivid could not resist the playfulness in the big man's manner. She smiled in spite of herself, then said again, "I am not here to be trussed up and given to anyone, Mr. Crowley."

Vivid wouldn't even look at Nate, so she had no idea how he was taking this whole conversation.

Abigail came to the rescue. "We were discussing Benjamin Rush, Adam, not whether my nephew should marry Dr. Lancaster, though I, too, think that would be a marvelous idea."

"Abigail!" Nate and Vivid shouted in unison.

Abigail ignored the outbursts, saying, "I don't often agree with this foolish old man, but, Nathaniel, I think she would make you a perfect wife. And Viveca, you could do a whole lot worse. Now tell us your opinion of Benjamin Rush."

Vivid stood there, stunned. Next to her, Nate removed his spectacles, rubbed his eyes a moment, then said, "I'll see you folks later," and went back to the farmers.

"Now," Abigail went on as if she hadn't shocked Vivid to her toes. "Didn't Rush help raise money for Reverend Allen's Mother Bethel in Philadelphia?"

"Yes, he did," Adam Crowley stated. "And so did Thomas Jefferson. Are slave owners now friends of the race, too?"

"Of course not," Abigail countered. "One only has to look back at Jefferson's writings to know Jefferson was no friend. And that poor Sally Hemings and the children she bore him," Abigail said sadly. "However, Mr. Rush should be judged in a different light."

Adam Crowley glanced over at Vivid and said, "Will
you please talk to this woman who calls herself a historian? Tell her the esteemed Dr. Rush's theory on why
our race has black skin."

Vivid stared at him wonder. "Mr. Crowley, how do
you know that?" Vivid had learned about Rush in medical school.

"Tell her."

Vivid spoke to Abigail but continued to stare at Adam
Crowley, amazed that he knew of Rush's theory. "Dr.
Rush believed we suffer from a form of leprosy, Abigail." Vivid had been taught not to stare but she
couldn't help herself. "Mr. Crowley—"

He seemed intent upon ignoring Vivid's questions as
he asked his opponent, "Did you hear that, Abigail?
Leprosy. What kind of learned 'friend' is that? Leprosy." He then turned to Vivid. "Thank you, Dr. Lancaster, I believe I can handle things from here."

Vivid gave him a measured look for refusing to satisfy
her curiosity, but she made a mental note to pay a visit
to the Crowley home as soon as time allowed. He owed
her some answers.

Leaving the two older people to their historical wranglings, Vivid slid her way back through the crowd and
resumed eating her ice cream. She saw Eli Grayson talking with Jewel Crowley. The young woman was smiling
and appeared to be in much better health.

As it got closer to dusk, folks began to gather up their
belongings for the ride home. Children were called in
from the surrounding fields. Neighbors hugged in parting and the men in the horseshoe pits and those seated
at the domino tables began to wind down their respective
competitions.

"You ready to head back?"

Vivid turned at the sound of Nate's voice. She looked
up into his eyes and felt her senses humming. "Um, yes,
as soon as I find Abigail."

Vivid sought to remain as politely distant as possible. "Abigail has decided to go back into town with Miss Edna," he told her. "She and Magic will be back later tonight. Miss Edna says you're welcome, too, if you care to join them."

"No. I think I'll go on home, I have some journals to read."

"Well I'm going back, so you can ride with me. I'll get the wagon."

Their short ride home started off in silence. Vivid looked at the beautiful surroundings, fascinated by all she saw, while a grim Nate sat fascinated by the beauty at his side.

"Your aunt and Mr. Crowley are quite the pair," Vivid said to break the mounting tension.

"Yes, they are," he replied. "If anyone should be thinking about marrying up, it's those two."

"Why on earth do you think that? Your aunt seemed very angry at Mr. Crowley."

"You're probably right. She and Adam lock horns over just about everything."

"Then why suggest they marry?"

He looked at her and said, "Because Adam's in love with my Aunt Gail. Has been for most of his life."

Vivid's jaw dropped open.

"Close your mouth before something flies inside," Nate teased gently.

Vivid found her voice and asked, "Does Abigail return his feelings?"

"I'm certain she does, but she's as stubborn as a post. I'm afraid she's going to go to her grave denying it, which will be a pity, because I believe Adam can make her happy."

They rode the remainder of the way in silence.

Nate drove the wagon around to the barn and unhitched the horses. Vivid helped him remove the tack.

He showed her the hooks on the walls, then watched as she hung it.

Vivid, very aware of his perusal, glanced around the large barn. There were enough stalls for six animals though only a few were being used. Viewing the aged plows and other old equipment stacked neatly in one corner, she assumed, at one time the Graysons must have farmed. A large stone fireplace encompassed one of the walls. She'd never seen a fireplace in a barn before. She then walked slowly over to some objects hanging on the wall at the barn's far end. "Do you play tennis around here?" she asked Nate.

He chuckled. "Those are snowshoes."

Embarrassment scalded her cheeks as she returned the shoe to its nail in the wall.

"Don't be embarrassed," he offered gently. "You wouldn't have any knowledge of bear claws."

"Why are they called bear claws?"

"They resemble a bear track in the earth."

She took them down again and peered closely at their construction. On closer look, she felt even more foolish. "Why are these turned up at the toe?" she asked. He was standing too close behind her, his heat penetrating her senses.

"The turned-up toe makes it easier to walk in snow where there are a lot of trees. This pair with the flat round toe is for walking in open spaces where there are no trees."

"You just strap them on and walk?"

"Basically, yes, but it takes a bit of practice to move in them comfortably."

Amazed, Vivid rehung the shoes.

"I'll give you lessons when the snow falls, if you're still here," he added.

Vivid turned to him and asked, "If I'm still here?"

"Yes. If."

Vivid thought about the back-breaking work she'd

done all week and found his remark offensive and disappointing. What would it take to make him see how seriously she took her position here?

She showed him her hands and asked calmly, "Do these look like the hands of a dilettante, Mr. Grayson?"

Nate could not hide his shock; her palms and fingers were raw, red, and cracked.

Vivid continued, "As you undoubtedly know, lye does this to human flesh when you scrub for a living. That's what I've been doing all week, scrubbing so I can make my living. But you don't believe I will stay, so fine. Continue to lie and claim to be neutral, just stay out of my way."

Angry, disappointed, and hurt, Vivid walked to the door of the barn. But she had one more thing to say. "And keep your kisses to yourself from now on."

Then she was gone.

Nate sighed. He hadn't meant to set her off, but on one hand he had gotten the result he'd desired. There would be no more kissing according to her, and that suited him just fine. She could go on about her business and he could take care of his without being further tempted to complicate an already explosive situation.

Chapter 10

A man's loud scream woke Vivid from her sleep. In the darkness, she sat up and listened wondering if she had imagined the sound, hoping that it had been just a dream. She heard only the night songs of the crickets at first, and then the scream came again, harsher, and filled with pain and despair. Chills ran over her flesh as the cry echoed across the night. Vivid slid from her bed, hastily donned her robe, grabbed her bag, and went outside.

In her bare feet she crossed the dark yard, looking up at the Grayson house. There were no lights in the upstairs rooms but the tortured cries sounded as if they'd come from inside.

She found Abigail seated at the kitchen table with her hands clasped tightly around a cup of tea. At Vivid's entrance she looked up and said softly, "Hello, Viveca dear."

"Hello, Abigail," Vivid replied just as softly.

"Did Nate wake you?"

Nate? Vivid stared a moment, then nodded.

"Me, too. Magic used to sleep through them, but not anymore. I suppose it's because she's no longer a small child. I just got her back to sleep." Abigail paused a moment, then said, "Have a seat, dear, and let me tell you a story."

Vivid set her bag on the table and took a chair opposite Abigail.

162

"On the east bank of the Mississippi on April 12,
1864, Rebs overran the Union garrison at Fort Pillow.
My nephew and my brother Absalom were part of that
garrison. It was made up of two hundred sixty-two Black
troops and two hundred ninety-five White troops. When
the Union men realized there was no winning the battle,
they threw down their weapons and surrendered. The
Rebs ignored the gesture."

Abigail had her hands laced so tightly around the cup,
Vivid could see the strain on the veins and flesh. "The
Rebs gave no quarter that day," she whispered. "The
Union men tried to run down the bluff and hide in the
trees, but they were hunted down and shot, especially
the Blacks. Even those who stopped and raised their
hands were murdered where they stood. Of the two hundred sixty-two Black men who'd greeted the dawn that
April morning, only fifty-eight were taken prisoner by
the Rebs; the rest were either killed, wounded, or—like
my nephew—buried alive."

Vivid gasped in horror.

"Yes." Abigail nodded, tears in her eyes. "Fortunately, Nate was among those lucky enough to still be
breathing when the Union forces unearthed the bodies.
My brother, his father, was not."

Vivid could not name the emotions that welled within
her upon hearing of such atrocities. Nothing in her life
could even remotely equate to such awful circumstances.
"He's lucky his mind is still whole."

"Yes, he is. These nightmares occur rarely now, but
when he first came back, he was afraid to sleep. He'd
prowl the woods like a wolf most nights, grabbing a
couple hours of sleep here and there. Even now he man-
ages to get by on only a few hours. I don't believe he's
slept a full, restful night since that April."

"Has he ever described the nightmares?"

"No, and I haven't asked."

"You love him very much, don't you?" Vivid asked softly.

"Yes, I do. If he and Eli could settle their differences, I'd go to my grave a happy old woman. Nate deserves some happiness. When he came back, I truly believed we would have lost him had it not been for Majestic. She was such a tiny little thing. She'd been abandoned and she needed him. That kept him living."

"Nate's wife abandoned his child?" Vivid tried to imagine what sort of circumstances would have caused his wife to abandon the baby girl.

"No. Nate and Cecile never had children. Majestic was found on the steps of one of the hospitals where Nate sought help after Fort Pillow."

"Magic isn't Nate's daughter?"

"Not by blood. But I say a prayer for that mother every night because she gave her to us."

Vivid was stunned but also proud of Nate for rescuing the child. "Did the hospital try to locate the mother?"

"According to Nate, they tried at first, but with all the doctors and nurses had to do, they lacked the resources and the time to investigate fully."

Abigail raised her eyes to the ceiling. "He's quieted."

Vivid was pleased the house was silent again. She hoped the rest of his night would pass peacefully. "Do you think it would help if I spoke to him as his doctor?"

"No," Abigail answered. "Leave it be for now. He prefers to deal with his pain alone. We should respect that."

Vivid didn't know if she agreed, however, Abigail had been dealing with Nate's demons for a long time and Vivid didn't feel right to disregard his aunt's advice, at least for now. "Has he seen a physician at all?"

"A few times after he returned home. A doctor down in South Bend assured him the dreams would go away eventually, and suggested laudanum or an opiate to help him sleep. Nate refused to take them though. He'd seen the men in the army hospitals and he didn't want to trade the nightmares for an addiction.''

As a physician, Vivid understood Nate's stance. "You say the nightmares rarely occur now. How rarely?"

"Lately, only three or four episodes a year. Spring-time seems to be particularly hard for him. During the month of April two years ago, he had one every night for weeks.''

Silence filled the kitchen as both women lost themselves in thought.

"He'll sleep for the rest of the night now. You should go on home to bed, Viveca," Abigail suggested softly, breaking the quiet. "Sun'll be up in a few hours."

Vivid agreed, though after learning Nate's story, she doubted the sleep would be a peaceful one.

Nate sat on the edge of the bed, drenched in sweat, still breathing harshly from the aftermath of the nightmare. Tonight it had been particularly intense. It began, as always, with him lying in the dark of the damp, shallow grave, terrified and surrounded by the dead, but this time, the dampness of the earth felt real. The dull thud of the bodies being tossed atop him sounded as loud as drums, the laughing voices of the Rebs lining the pit, like demons. With the addition of each man thrown in, the piled corpses shifted, lifeless limbs moving macabrely across his face and chest, and in the dream, as he had in reality, he'd gasped to breath in the thin, stale air. Panic and fear howled within him, yet he didn't dare move or make a sound lest the Rebs murder him like all the others. So Nate lay there, letting himself be entombed, his mind screaming the silent screams of the damned.

Nate walked across the room to the open window. He pushed the double panes open further. The air came in slowly, ruffling the curtains a bit, soothing his face. He closed his eyes and let the breeze's touch lift away the remnants of the horror. Would he have to endure these recurrences for the rest of his life? Hadn't he suffered enough, sacrificed enough? Had the death of his beloved father, Absalom, meant anything? The questions were ones he'd been flinging at the heavens for over a decade, without an answer.

The intensity and frequency of the Fort Pillow memories had decreased sharply with time and he hadn't screamed out in horror in many years as he had tonight. He was certain he'd woken Magic and Aunt Gail. He'd have to speak with them in the morning.

He noticed the lone light shining in Lancaster's cabin. Had he awakened her, too? Had his screaming frightened her as much as it had Cecile? He sensed not. She impressed him as being cut from stronger cloth. She'd certainly shown her strength in the barn this evening. They had not parted on the best of terms. He remembered how red and cracked her hands had been. For some unexplained reason he was angered by the sight of her injuries. Why hadn't she waited until he found someone to hire? She should not have been elbow-deep in lye scrubbing. Nate realized she had him in knots. On one hand, he had the interest of the Grove to consider, and on the other hand, he found himself more and more captivated by her lush mouth and his eyes straying more and more to those swaying hips. Finding her yesterday when she got lost had been easy because he'd been covertly following her movements all day. He'd seen her greeting the families and kneeling to talk to the children eye to eye. He noted the respect she gave Garret Turner, even though Nate was sure the man had turned down any offers of assistance she may have pledged. He also noticed that not everyone had greeted her with a smile, but she hadn't let it deter her from behaving graciously to the next person.

He readily admitted to being distant with her, but he had her best interest in mind. While in Kalamazoo, he'd decided there could be no more kisses; her soft, virgin mouth was not for him to toy with. The last time he felt so overwhelmed by a woman he'd married her, making the mistake of a lifetime. And had no intention of making any more mistakes by marrying Lancaster or anyone else. Yet the fortress guarding his heart, sealed shut a decade ago, seemed to be slowly opening its rusted and creaking gates in direct opposition to his will. Viveca Lancaster, with her billiard stick, her rifle, and her lovely black eyes seemed to be turning his world upside down.

Neither Nate nor his daughter made an appearance at breakfast the next morning. When Vivid asked after them, Abigail explained they'd left at first light to go fishing for a couple of days.

After breakfast, Vivid helped Abigail with the dishes. Once they were done, Vivid said, "Abigail, I don't believe your nephew appreciated your teasing yesterday."

Abigail's mahogany face took on a look of absolute innocence. "What teasing?"

"The Nate-and-Viveca-should-marry teasing."

"Oh, that. I wasn't teasing." Abigail poured herself a cup of tea and sat at the kitchen table.

"That's absurd. He and I don't even like each other. Why just yesterday we—never mind." Vivid didn't want to reveal her anger or her bruised feelings.

Abigail peered at her suspiciously. "Viveca, my grandfather put great faith in the spirits. I believe that is why he and the People got along so well."

"The People?"

"The native people."

Vivid nodded in understanding.

"The day my nephew turned one week old, my grandfather took him out to the woods for three days to see if the spirits would reveal Nate's future. Throughout his life, my grandfather kept true to the traditions he learned before his capture. He'd performed this same ritual quest with my father and my brother, Absalom. During the

three days in the woods with Nate, Grandfather saw no
signs from the trees or animals, nor did he hear anything
on the wind. He knew the spirits would often keep the
child's fate to themselves if the future was too bright or
too tragic. Such a thing happened on my brother Absalom's quest, and all the adults assumed a brilliant future
lay ahead. Who among them could have envisioned an
event as horrible as Fort Pillow?'' she said softly.

Vivid felt her sadness. ''So did your grandfather see
a sign for your nephew?''

''Yes, he did. That last night as he lay sleeping he
had a dream. There were two pillars, one aflame, the
other frozen like ice. The ice pillar grew first, filling
the dream like a glacier, then behind it stood the
flame, small at first, then it, too, began to rise. The ice
tried to stand but as the little flame grew larger and
roared red-hot, the ice began to melt. It melted slowly,
he told us, forming the shape of a woman before finally fading away.''

''What became of the flame?''

''The flame turned into a slowly revolving circle of
smaller flames, each of which turned into women from
the village of his youth. They were smiling and dancing
the traditional dance to celebrate a long and happy marriage.''

''So what did it all mean?'' Vivid asked.

''It meant that Nate would have two women in his
life with the ability to wield great power. I am certain
the icy pillar was his first wife, Cecile.''

''Did she die?''

''No, they dissolved their marriage a few months after
the end of the war.''

''I see,'' Vivid said softly, but the knowledge only
raised more questions.

''I believe you are the fiery pillar, Viveca.''

''Abigail, I'm not denying your grandfather may have
had a dream, but I doubt it had anything to do with me.''

"I understand."

"Abigail, you can't possibly believe that."

"Of course I do. I've been waiting for you for ten years."

Vivid looked across the table at her, stunned by this revelation. "Abigail—"

"Viveca, I am not asking you to believe anything I have told you. That is not important. Do you want to have babies, my dear?"

At the abrupt question, Vivid stared into those dark gray eyes that were so reminiscent of Nate's and stammered. "If I marry someone, I'd like to have some daughters, yes."

Abigail smiled. "Just daughters?"

"Well, maybe a son or two. Why do you ask?"

"Because the Graysons have only sons, always have."

Vivid smiled, "Well that's another reason your nephew and I will never marry."

"Scoff while you may, young lady. Just remember I warned you."

"I most certainly will," Vivid said, smiling. "I'm going home now." And with that Vivid departed with a wave and a smile.

That afternoon, Vernon brought over a mule.

"My uncle says she's in good health," he told Vivid as she slowly walked around the animal. She checked the bone structure of its legs and the feel of its spine. The dark eyes appeared clear and surprisingly intelligent. Vivid had never owned a mule, but she knew from her schooling and the summers spent in Mexico that these hard-working animals were born from a male ass and a mare. "Does it have a name?"

"My uncle said the original owner just called it Mule. I suppose you could name it anything you'd like, Dr. Lancaster."

Vivid completed her appraisal. "How much does your uncle want me to pay him?"

"Says it's free, on account of Nate."

"Nate?" Vivid asked, turning to face Vernon. She had to look up as she did with all the men around here. "How does he figure in this?"

"Nate beat my uncle in the horseshoe pits yesterday at the church. The mule was the bet."

"I see," Vivid replied.

"It was all fair and square, Doctor. Everything above board."

"I believe you, Vernon. I wasn't questioning anyone's integrity. I'm just a bit surprised is all. Are you sure your uncle doesn't expect payment?"

"He says it's yours. He also said if you ever need his help with anything to please let him know."

Vivid smiled. "Tell your uncle I said thank you, Vernon."

"And Dr. Lancaster?" Vernon's eyes were very serious. "Welcome to the Grove."

He looked so sincere. Vivid smiled with all the warmth she felt and, holding his hand, thanked him.

Vernon, shy suddenly, walked to his wagon. "Well, I need to get to town and open my shop. You take care of yourself now, Dr. Lancaster. I'll see you soon."

Vernon drove his team down the road and left Vivid in the yard with her new mule.

She named the mule Michigan. Later that same afternoon a very large, fair-skinned man with a full cinnamon-red beard knocked at her door. He introduced himself as Bertram Winslow and the young boy at his side as his son, Caleb. Vivid had never seen the man before in her life.

"I met you yesterday at the church," he explained. "Though I doubt you remember me with so many folks about."

"I'm sorry to say I really don't remember meeting you."

"That's fine, Dr. Lancaster, it isn't important. Nate said you need a wagon."

Vivid nodded at this man who was as big as one of the Crowleys.

"Well, that wagon there wasn't doing me much good sitting out in my pasture, so I thought maybe you could use it. She's still in pretty fair condition. Come on, I'll show you."

As Vivid looked over the relatively small flatbed conveyance, he began to lecture on the fine points of axles, under carriages, and wheel mounts. Vivid had to stop him. "Mr. Winslow, the wagon looks fine. How much do you want for it?"

"Nothing."

"Nothing?"

"Adam Crowley says you're a part of the Grove now. And if Nate says you need a wagon, we find you a wagon. Simple as that."

"Did Nate tell you I'd planned on paying for any wagon he found for me?"

"Can't remember him saying that, but it's no matter."

Vivid looked up at him and wanted to argue but realized that he probably still wouldn't accept her money. "All right, Mr. Winslow, you win, and thank you."

"Any time. You keep yourself well now."

After the man and his son left, Vivid walked around her new wagon and experienced the same sense of amazement she'd experienced when Vernon brought the mule. Free of charge? Had her experience with Adam Crowley really changed folks' attitudes? She wasn't naive enough to believe the sailing would be smooth from here on out, but she did see it as a signal of a good beginning. Nate Grayson's hand in this left her puzzled, however.

She didn't have an opportunity to question him until late evening of the next day.

She was sitting out on her back porch reading a few of the medical journals she'd unearthed in her packing, a paper submitted by Theodor Billroth of the University of Vienna. He was a pioneer in surgical techniques, and in bacterial infections, especially as they pertained to wound fever. The paper, "Investigations of the Vegetal Forms of Cocobacteria Septica," had been published nearly two years ago.

Because of the breakthrough work done by physicians like Billroth and Mr. Lister, over in England, Vivid felt confident that the antiseptic medical practices they advocated, which she embraced wholeheartedly, would soon find favor in the United States. Right now, the techniques were being hotly debated in some medical corners and soundly denounced in others. Many of America's established physicians were still clinging to the theories advocated by Benjamin Rush, the subject of Abigail and Adam Crowley's debate, and one of the original signers of the Declaration of Independence. Some called him the Hippocrates of American medicine. Rush believed infections and disease were the results of noxious miasmas building up in the body. He advocated bleeding, puking, and the blistering of patients to rid the body of these accumulated poisons. He died in 1813, but his sometimes misguided therapies and theories were still practiced by many physicians, especially those who had received their training before 1850.

Vivid had been anxiously anticipating reading the Billroth paper but as she began, the rhythmic ringing of an axe jarred the silence. She tried to ignore it at first but the more she tried, the more distracting the sound became. She'd been inside her office all day, helping the Crowley sons lay her floor, and she didn't want to go in now and miss the last of the daylight. She stepped off the porch, paper in hand, and walked across the grass to the back of the Grayson house.

Nate Grayson was splitting wood, his sleeves rolled up to reveal his muscular arms. He stopped at her approach.

"May I ask how much longer you plan on chopping wood?"

"Why?" he replied, resuming the task.

"I was reading and the sound was distracting me."

He brought the axe down on the large cord again. "I'll be done in about a quarter of an hour. I promised the Widow Moss I'd do this for her . She doesn't have a man, so the Crowleys and I chop her wood."

"That's very neighborly."

He studied her face. "Are you being sarcastic, Lancaster?"

So he'd reverted to calling her Lancaster again. "No, I'm not."

He stopped chopping wood again and looked her in the eye. "Let me see your hands."

Vivid stared, confused, "Why?"

"I want to see if they've healed."

"They're not as red as they were, but they're still chapped."

"Let me see."

She sighed and held up one palm. Her paper under one arm, she then showed him her other palm.

"You should've waited for me to hire someone."

"Why? So you could deride me for not doing my own scrubbing? You believe me to be helpless enough as it is."

He said nothing.

Feeling herself on the edge of another argument, Vivid took a calming breath and said, "Thank you for finding the mule and buggy."

"You're welcome."

Then he began chopping wood again.

"Vernon said you won it in a horseshoe bet."

"Vernon talks too much."

"Why would you get me a free mule if you're so set on my leaving?"

"It's how we do things around here is all."

"You didn't answer my question, Mr. Grayson. It's you I'm asking about."

He lifted his eyes to her and said, "It's not because of that kiss, if that's what you're fishing for."

At that moment Vivid wished she was the fiery pillar of the dream Abigail described so she could reduce him to a handsome mound of ash. "I'm not fishing for anything, least of all your kisses."

He set the axe down. "Something wrong with my kisses?"

The double-edged question would cut her no matter how she answered. By the set of his too-pleased face, he knew it also. "It was a kiss, nothing more."

"Nothing more," he stated, settling his gaze on her lips just long enough to make her heart pound. In spite of his heated perusal, she repeated confidently, "Nothing more."

"I see. You've had better, maybe?"

"Whether I have or not is not open for debate."

"In other words, you haven't."

"You and I are not going to have this talk."

"Didn't you say you were a physician and therefore a simple discussion of the physical realm would not send you running to the hills?"

She had said that. "Yes."

"So a simple kiss, a simple discussion."

"I'm leaving now, Mr. Grayson."

And as she walked away Nate filled his eyes with her swaying skirt and chuckled. "Coward."

Vivid stopped and turned. She surveyed him a moment, then calmly walked back to where he stood with his arms crossed, and looking entirely too handsome for his own good. She said evenly, "Never, ever call anyone raised west of the Rockies a coward unless you have all the aces in the deck, Nathaniel Grayson. I'm going to call your bluff."

"Meaning?"

Despite Vivid's initial bravado, she could not look in his eyes as she spoke. "I melted like wax when you kissed me. I've never been so moved by a man in my life."

"Now, it's your turn," she said.

He gazed at her beautiful face and knew the gates of his heart were opening wider even as he breathed. He had no business wanting this woman, yet he did. He admired the way she stood up for herself, the confidence she exuded. But there was more to her than that. His kiss had melted her, she'd said. He'd been caught off-guard once again by her frankness. The effect of her words could be measured by the hardness of his manhood.

Slowly he reached out and ran a finger over one dark silk cheek. He watched her eyes close, felt the virgin trembling of her skin. When he gently traced the outline of her jaw, then her currant-ripe mouth, the lips parted passionately. He leaned down and kissed her—his answer to her challenge.

Deepening the kiss, his sweetness filling her, he eased her closer, and Vivid responded instinctively. She slid her hands up his rib cage and around to the hard muscles in his back. This was no way to settle a dispute, but she didn't care.

Nate husked against her ear, "Aces around . . ."

He reclaimed her lips and Vivid shuddered in response. His big hands roamed slowly over her back. His fiery, masterful kisses filled her with such new and novel sensations, she could only tremble as he passionately nibbled her bottom lip then teased it captivatingly with his tongue. Her legs seemed to have lost all strength.

Were it not for his hold upon her, Vivid swore she would have pooled into a puddle of water. His kisses on her arched neck made her moan, made her tingle.

When he finally turned her loose, she swayed unsteadily, her senses pulsing.

Nate thought she looked like a woman who'd been thoroughly kissed, but he wanted more. He wanted to bare her body to his caresses and discover if the rest of her was as delectable as her sweet chocolate lips. He'd let her go, however, to keep himself from transforming the fantasy into blazing reality. "So does that meet your definition of a simple kiss?" he asked, his smile entirely too masculine for her liking.

"You're enjoying this, aren't you?"

He nodded. He did enjoy seeing her thrown off-balance. He savored the sight almost as much as he had her lips. "You've been running through my life like a tornado for the last two weeks. I'm simply pleased to have discovered the cure for slowing you down."

"That was your last kiss, Nate Grayson."

"Uh-huh."

"I'm serious."

"If I asked for another, you would say no?"

In response to the heat in his tone and manner, Vivid swallowed. What game was he playing now? "Yes."

"Why?"

And she replied truthfully, "Because I didn't travel all these miles to have my heart trifled with, not even by you." She added softly, "So good evening, Mr. Grayson."

Chapter 11

The next morning, Vivid hitched up Michigan and drove her new wagon into town with plans to stop at Miss Edna's first. She wanted to see if any of the items she'd ordered had arrived.

Miss Edna looked up at her entrance and said, "Oh, good, you're here. I was just about to send someone out after you. Betty Jane Carpenter's baby is overdue. I wanted to see if you'd go with me to check on her."

"Is there a midwife in the Grove?"

"Yes, I'm the midwife. Will you drive?"

Vivid nodded and they hastened out.

"Oh, wait," said Miss Edna in a rush, "I forgot the sign."

While Vivid waited out on the walk, Miss Edna went into the store and came out with a large square of wood. GONE MIDWIFING had been painted on it in large black letters, along with KEY IS AT THE MILL.

Miss Edna set the sign in front of the store's closed door and explained. "While I'm gone, folks can still use the store if the need arises. They simply go and get the extra key. Then they get what they need, lock the door again, and leave the payment and key back at the mill. I pick up the receipts when I return."

The women made a quick stop at Vernon's barbershop. Vivid asked Vernon if he would tell the Graysons where she had gone and he readily agreed. Vivid didn't want Nate searching the woods for her again.

177

With Vivid at the reins the two women passed the time on the road getting to know each other better. Vivid liked Edna. Beneath the battered old hat she wore, she had a keen mind and a ready smile. They talked about San Francisco and Vivid's family. Then Edna told her about her daughter in South Bend. Vivid remembered Jewel Crowley saying that Edna's daughter had fallen in love with Nate. How many other women had fallen prey to his fatal handsomness? she wondered. She put Nate out of her mind and asked Edna, "Did you say you've lived here in the Grove since the fifties?"

"Yes, I have. Came here from Virginia. Of course, there were fewer people here then. Life was a lot harder, too."

"Tell me about Virginia. Is it green like this?"

"Nothing is as green as Michigan, and I've seen a good portion of the country east of the Mississippi. After being in the slave pens at Alexandria I could not believe the beauty here."

"You were in the pens in Alexandria?" Vivid had heard about the pens from her father, who'd been a slave in Kentucky.

"Yes, for nearly three months. It was a horrible, horrible place full of sick, desperate, and dying members of the race. Whole families were jailed in the Bruin and Hill pen in Alexandria when I was there—babies, grandmothers. The only difference between my jail and the big ones Deep South were that folks in Alexandria who were able enough were allowed to write family members in hopes of having their bills paid so they could be freed. Sadly, most wound up being purchased by another master or mistress."

"My father said he'd heard of people who'd died of starvation in the pens. You were lucky."

"Yes, lucky because my brother had a very clever friend who had both French and African blood. He convinced the owners of the pen that he'd been sent by the

New Orleans merchant who'd paid for me. Because of
my fair skin and privileged upbringing, I was headed for
the fancy girl market in New Orleans.''
    Vivid had heard of those places also. The women at
those markets were chosen for their bright skin and cultured ways and were usually purchased as mistresses by
wealthy white planters or businessmen. Some of the
women wound up in pleasure houses, but all were sold
for very high prices.
    "I am a Lee, of the Virginia Lees," Edna continued,
"and if you know anything about the Virginia Lees, you
know that there is a White branch and an African
branch, and all are related. I was the pampered companion of my mistress and half-sister, Charlotte. We were
the same age and had the same father but different mothers."
    "Then how did you wind up in the pens?"
    "When our father died in a hunting accident, the land
and slaves were given over to his brother. His wife took
one look at my face and sent me to the pens less than a
week after she and the new master took possession. I
was her husband's niece, but it didn't matter. She assumed I'd be a threat to the fidelity of her marriage."
    "Couldn't your sister do anything to prevent you
from being sold?"
    "Charlotte did what she did best, she cried. My
mother said being sold was my comeuppance for being
so uppity. I suppose she was right. Charlotte and I had
grown up together; we shared a room, wardrobe, tutors.
I accompanied Charlotte on her grand tour of the continent after her cotillion debut. We both were fluent in
French and read Latin and German."
    Edna intercepted Vivid's stare and said with a wry
smile, "Yes, my dear, I was quite the cultured little Ne-
gress, but I never considered myself a Black, not really.
They were the help, I was not."
    "Edna, I can't believe you felt that way."

"Oh, I did. I was as petulant and as spoiled as a rich
planter's daughter, because in reality I was. My mother
kept cautioning me about forgetting my place and acting
as if I owned slaves instead of being one, but I refused
to listen. I was one of the most beautiful women in the
state of Virginia, Black or White, and no one could tell
me a thing."

"How did the other slaves feel about you?"

"They hated my every step. Looking back, I don't
see as how I blame them. I gave them no respect and
no quarter. I was a mean-spirited and petty young
woman in those days. The pens changed all that."

"Your brother, was he a slave also?"

"No, my two older brothers were freed when they
reached eighteen years of age. Masters did that
sometimes. They freed the sons but rarely the daughters.
That practice alone should have made me pause and
ponder my place in the world, but it did not."

"So you wound up in the pens."

"Yes, and the owners of the pen contracted me sight
unseen to a French businessman for the fine price of
three thousand dollars, in advance."

"That's quite a price."

"I was quite the woman."

Vivid smiled and asked, "So what ever happened to
your brother?"

"He had to leave Virginia, of course. Slave stealing
in parts of the South was a hanging offense. When the
real representative from New Orleans showed up a few
days later and I couldn't be found, my brother and his
friend became wanted slave stealers. Broadsides featur-
ing their likenesses were nailed up all over the county.
Bruin and Hill were very prominent slavers, they had a
reputation to maintain. You can't be in the business of
selling slaves if you can't provide the buyer the goods."

Edna paused a moment as if thinking back. When she
next spoke, her voice was thick with emotion. "My

mother, who'd had no part in the plot, other than to write
my brother and tell him of my plight in the pens, was
sold Deep South. My three sisters who were nine,
eleven, and twelve at that time were immediately taken
overland to the fancy girl markets in New Orleans; the
youngest died on the trip there. Both of my remaining
brothers were taken from their families and jailed. My
freedom came at a heavy, heavy price."

"What became of your brother's friend?"

That question made Edna smile, and Vivid was glad
to see she was no longer so sad. "That man went on to
become the infamous Black Daniel, a thorn in the side
of every slave owner and slave catcher from Georgia to
the Ohio line."

Vivid grinned in confusion, "The Black who?"

"Daniel."

"As in the biblical Daniel?"

"Yes. You should hear the stories folks told about
him. They said he stole hundreds, maybe thousands of
slaves before Appomatox. The slave owners had a
bounty on his head so large, slave catchers and their
dogs were tripping over one another trying to bring him
to ground."

"I've never heard of him. Was he ever appre-
hended?"

"He was far too clever to be caught. He wore dis-
guises quite often. No one really knew what he looked
like for many years until after the war."

"And this was your brother's friend?"

"Yes, and Viveca, he was so handsome, even more
handsome than the Grayson men."

"That's pretty handsome, Miss Edna," Vivid said,
impressed. "Is he still alive?"

"Very much so. He's older now of course, but he
lives outside Detroit and is married to a friend of Abigail's named Hester Montgomery. Oh, stop, turn here,"

Edna said, pointing to a fork in the hard-packed road. "The Carpenter place is just ahead."

The birth of the Carpenter baby spanned three days, but finally the stubborn baby girl consented to being born. After dropping off Miss Edna at her apartments above the store, Vivid returned home so tired that even the simple task of breathing seemed draining. She wearily drove Michigan around to the back of the cabin and unhitched her. In spite of the bone-deep fatigue, Vivid took the time to inspect the mule's hooves for stones and burrs and to fetch her water and oats.

With the mule taken care of, Vivid stepped up onto her back porch. She had only one desire: to go to bed and fall asleep as soon as possible. She put her hand on the door, then stopped and stared at the sight of the swing someone had put up on the far right side of the porch. Fatigue forgotten, she left her medical bag at the door, then walked to the swing. Where on earth had it come from?

It hung suspended from two sturdy lengths of chain and looked as if it had been a church pew in a previous life. It faced out over the countryside and had been bolted into position far enough under the lip of the roof to let occupants enjoy the view even in the rain.

Vivid ran her hand over the smooth, polished dark wood, smiling at the gift as she slowly walked around to the front. She glanced down at the wide seat and halted, stunned. She raised her hand to her mouth, and tears stung her eyes as she stared down in wonder at the beautiful wildflowers. Her hands shook as she picked them up. "Do you like it?"

She spun at the sound of Nate's low-toned voice behind her.

"Did you do this?" she asked softly.

As they stared across the porch at each other she read the answer in his eyes. She wondered what it might be like to come home every evening to find him waiting for her in just this way.

He stood there, arms folded. "You want me to take it down?"

She replied, "No, I don't want you to take it down. It needs to be christened. Come join me."

He sat beside her on the wide seat. To Vivid, the lulling gentle motion felt like heaven, especially after the difficulties of the last three days.

"How did you know I needed this?" she asked, turning her head to look his way.

"Just thought you'd like to have a place to sit outside in the evenings."

Vivid continued to hold his eyes. "And the flowers?" she asked.

"Saw them and thought you'd like them."

"First a mule, then a wagon, and now flowers and a swing. I may put you in charge of my happiness on a permanent basis if you're not careful, Nate Grayson," she whispered.

"If all it takes is a mule and an old church pew, I may take the job."

Vivid stared back at the softly spoken reply.

Whether intentionally or not, he changed the subject by asking, "How'd the Carpenter birthing go?"

"Poorly for the first two days, the baby was breech. Would you really take charge of my happiness?"

He looked over at her and chuckled, "Your people should have called you Curious, not Vivid."

"I'm a physician, it's my nature to be curious." Then she added softly, "You haven't answered my question."

"And I won't."

Vivid didn't press. He'd already told her all she needed to know. "Thank you again for the swing. I couldn't't've asked for a better homecoming present."

Having him seated at her side made for a very good present also, Vivid decided. She'd thought of him often over the past three days, wondering about his nightmares, his first marriage. She especially wanted to talk to him about the nightmares but remembered Abigail's advice, and so kept her silence.

The swing's rhythm was hypnotic. Vivid could feel the weariness in her bones begin to melt away.

Nate turned to ask whether the Carpenter baby had been a boy or girl, but she was asleep.

He carried her into the cabin and laid her gently on the bed. He debated whether to undress her so she could sleep more comfortably, but in the end he simply covered her with a blanket and headed back to his place. He decided that when the time came to undress the lovely Dr. Lancaster in bed, he wanted her wide awake.

The next morning, Nate was out hitching his team to the wagon when he noticed her driving fast down the track that led out to the road. He stepped into her path and waved his arms and she pulled up on the reins and slowed.

"Good morning, Nate," she said, "I apologize for falling asleep on you last night."

He wondered how much longer he would be able to fight off the urge to drag her into his arms again. "No need to apologize. Where are you headed?"

"Over to the Farley place. I'm taking his medical history this morning and I'm late."

"Lancaster, you look dead on your feet. Farley can wait, go on back to bed."

"Nate, I don't have time to discuss this. Mr. Farley is waiting, and I must go."

She slapped the reins down onto Michigan's rump and Nate stepped out of the way to let the wagon pass.

After she and Mr. Farley finished their business, he asked if she would go up the road a piece and look in on a young woman who'd just given birth. Vivid agreed.

By remembering the points on the map he'd drawn for her in the dirt, Vivid took only three-quarters of an hour to find the house he'd mentioned. She'd gotten lost only twice and despaired of ever finding her way around the Grove like the folks who'd lived here most of their lives. People kept telling her to be patient, that she'd learn her way around, but she found it all very frustrating, and it made her feel incompetent.

Vivid hopped down from the wagon, secured the reins to a nearby sapling, then reached in and got her bag. The cabin looked tired. One entire side of the structure sagged, appearing as if it were trying to separate itself from the whole. There were holes in the roof, weeds, mud, and rusting skeletons of wagons in the yard. There was no cleared walkway, so Vivid picked the least muddy path and made her way to the door.

Her knock on the rotting wood door summoned a young, pock-faced dark man who stared at her suspiciously. He slowly looked her up and down, then, as if he didn't like what he saw, spit a stream of tobacco onto the ground beside her feet.

"Who're you?" he finally asked.

"Dr. Lancaster. Mr. Farley sent me to check on the baby."

"Farley needs to mind his own damned business," he said unpleasantly, but to Vivid's surprise he stepped back and let her enter. She almost wished he hadn't when she saw the interior. It was dark, hot, and smelled of rot and sweat. The little bit of light stroking the room came from the holes in the dilapidated roof overhead.

As her eyes worked to adjust to the murky interior, she stepped forward and almost tumbled over something in the dimness. She grabbed out blindly to keep herself erect and came into contact with the warm skin of a small child. "Oh, I'm sorry, sweetheart." She looked down and saw a very dirty, naked little boy of about three years old. He stared up at her with the saddest eyes she'd ever seen, then took off at a toddler's run to a far corner of the room. He huddled down beside a woman lying on a dirty cot. In her arms she cradled a tiny child swaddled in a filthy blanket.

"Are you the doctor?" the woman asked in a reed-thin voice.

Vivid wanted to rail against the poverty and filth of the family's living conditions but she held her tongue. "Yes," she replied softly, "I'm the doctor. What's your name?" Vivid crossed the room and knelt next to the pallet.

The stench coming from the woman made Vivid's stomach churn.

"My name's Sara James. That's my husband, Quentin."

Vivid fought the urge to retch. "How long have you been ill, Sara?"

Vivid glanced at the child in Sara's arms and went stock-still. The baby in the woman's arms looked dead. The stench was coming from the dead child, Vivid realized. She closed her eyes to gather strength, then fought to concentrate on Sara's reply.

"I've been feeling poorly since right after little Willie here was born. He's such a sweet, sweet baby, isn't he?" She kissed his forehead tenderly.

Vivid looked to the husband for some type of explanation, but his surly manner had not changed. He offered no help, so she turned back and asked gently, "How long ago was little Willie born?"

Vivid wanted to take the gray lifeless bundle from Sara's arms but had no idea what she would do or how she would respond.

A concerned Vivid waited as Sara seemed to ponder the question about the birth, but the girl did not offer an answer. Instead, she began to sing a lullaby. The frail voice was hauntingly beautiful. Its purity filled the cabin, banishing the filthy surroundings and fouled air until all that remained was a young woman singing softly to her infant.

Vivid waited until the last clean note faded into the dimness, then said softly, "Sara, I'm going to go outside for a moment and talk to your husband."

Once she and Quentin were outside she stated, "You know the baby is dead."

He nodded, then spit.

"When was the child born?"

"Don't know. She'd already whelped when I got back from fishing a week ago. It was dead then."

Vivid had to take a deep breath to control the trembling that began deep inside her. "The baby needs to be buried. Have you tried to talk to her?"

"Hell, it's dead, let her keep it. Ain't mine no way."

Vivid stared as he added, "Look, in a couple days I'm heading out for the Little Muskegon. They say it's a man's world up there. Do what you want with her."

He walked off toward the small tumbledown shed in back of the place and never said another word.

Back inside the cabin, Sara lay still cuddling the dead child. The naked toddler sat silent in the corner. Vivid had never handled a situation such as this before but knew the truth had to be made clear, no matter how much pain she caused. "Sara?"

Vivid knelt down beside the cot once more.

Sara looked up. Not even the dimness could mask the pain in her brown eyes. "Quentin's leaving, isn't he?"

Vivid solemnly shook her head.

"I didn't mean to go back on my vows. I was lonely. He doesn't understand how lonely it gets out here when he's away months at a time, especially in the winter. My baby's been dead for going on two weeks," she whispered in a tear-thickened voice. "I . . . thought if I pretended to be sick and pretended Willie was still alive, Quentin would claim him as his and wouldn't leave me."

Sara cried then, loud wrenching tears that tore at Vivid's heart. Vivid put an arm around her and held her close until she quieted.

Afterward, Vivid found a shovel in the shack behind the house but saw no sign of Quentin. It took her the better part of an hour to dig a hole deep enough in the hard-packed earth to shelter the baby Willie's remains. When it was done, she reentered the cabin and told Sara it was time. Silently the young woman, still holding the baby, followed Vivid outside.

Sara lovingly placed him in the ground, wrapped in the filthy blanket he'd died in, because she had nothing else. Vivid said a prayer, then with Sara's permission began to gently shovel the dirt back atop the baby's still body. Sara began to sing "Steal Away" in a slow clear voice so filled with grief and mourning, chills ran up and down Vivid's arms as she worked.

At the end of the solemn task, Vivid loaded Sara and the toddler in the wagon, took the reins, and headed the mule toward home.

"I couldn't leave them there," Vivid explained to Abigail once Sara and the toddler Quentin were settled into one of the vacant bedrooms of the Grayson home. Mother and child had been bathed, clothed, and fed.

"You did the right thing, Viveca," Abigail assured her over the pot of tea they were sharing. "Once we get word to Kate Pierce, she'll send for them. Sara's a distant niece if I remember correctly, but family is family to Kate. She wouldn't want Sara and the little one living under those distressing conditions. And the husband said he was going off to the Little Muskegon?"

Vivid nodded in confirmation.

Abigail shook her head with disgust. "Let's hope he never returns."

Just as Abigail predicted, Kate Pierce showed up the next afternoon to retrieve Sara and the toddler. Sara refused to go at first, saying she didn't want to bring her shame into Kate's home, but Kate would hear none of it. Less than an hour after her arrival, Kate's wagon was pulling away from the Grayson home with Sara and her son Quentin atop the seat, waving goodbye to Vivid and Abigail.

Chapter 12

By mid-June, Vivid had been a resident of the Grove for over a month, and because of the high standards she set for herself, she worked from sunup to sundown. She visited families to take medical histories; saw patients in town at her new office; established a clinic at the church so she could see the babies once a week. She traveled from one end of the Grove to the other introducing herself to those she hadn't met and administering to the sick, both young and old. Some nights when she was too far from home to travel back, she slept on whatever accommodations her patients provided.

By the end of June, the residents of the Grove had become accustomed to seeing Vivid and her mule, Michigan, traveling up and down the roads, and everywhere she went they greeted her with neighborly waves and smiles. When she wasn't doctoring she was helping folks plant vegetables or sitting with young ones while the mothers went into town, or giving lectures at the church on every subject from measles to healthier eating.

Nate no longer worried when she was away overnight. Enough people knew her and liked her for him to feel confident that they'd look out for her welfare. She still had a penchant for getting lost, or so he'd been told by some of the townsfolk. But that had to be expected, they all stated in her defense; after all, the Grove covered

quite a bit of territory. They assured him she would soon
know the area as well as anyone.

For the most part, Nate had to admit Dr. Lancaster
had so far proven to be every bit the doctor she'd
claimed. He'd no idea how she'd accomplished it, but
she made a supporter out of the pride-filled Garret
Turner. Turner said he stopped selling off the majority
of his vegetables and milk cream when she explained
the children's health would benefit more from the vegetables and cream being on the table instead of it all
going to market. She'd also made him see the importance of accepting help from his neighbors for the sake
of his children. Nate hoped Turner would now let go of
a bit more pride and take the Men's Association up on
their offer to help him repair his ramshackle cabin and
barn.

Vivid had even gotten Aaron Patterson to let her remove the rotten tooth he'd been so reluctant to have her
examine. The procedure had drawn quite a crowd. Aaron
fainted dead away before she'd barely begun, and so
missed the cheers when she smilingly held up the offending molar for all to see.

However, in spite of all the favorable reports from the
community, and Nate's own burgeoning desire for her,
he continued to harbor reservations. Would she still be
there next year this time? How would his people react
to her leaving if she were tendered another offer for
more money in a larger town at the end of her contract?
In the short time she'd been there, she'd gained trust,
faced down barriers, and held her own against men like
Aaron Patterson, Adam Crowley, and, hell, him. The
people liked her, listened to her, and seemed to be taking
her advice to heart. Once Edna let it be known that Dr.
Lancaster frowned on the so-called benefits of calomel,
many area residents stopped ingesting it, especially after
being made aware of the havoc it played with the teeth
and gums. Nate had been raised by his father to always

put the town's welfare above his own, and so, because of his lingering uncertainties, he had. To provide the Grove an alternative should she indeed decide to move on to greener pastures, he'd posted a cache of letters soliciting another physician, a male this time, just in case. His illogical side, the part of him that could still call up the taste of her kisses, was decidedly unhappy with this decision because she would undoubtedly be hurt and upset by his lack of confidence should the plan ever be revealed. It would also kill any future attempts to explore Viveca Lancaster, the woman. However, his logical side knew that further intimacies with her would only lead to disaster, and he had no qualms about staying the course for the benefit of the Grove. Finding another doctor made sense—just in case.

His logic worked only when Vivid was out of his sight. The trousers she wore most of the time played havoc with his discipline. He'd avoided her as much as possible since the last time he'd kissed her, opting to spend his time with the books in his study, or out in the Grove helping with the spring planting and harvesting, but on the few occasions they had crossed paths, Lancaster and her trousers were all he could see. When she showed up wearing them that first day at his office he'd nearly scalded himself with the coffee he was pouring. It was how he felt every time he saw her: scalded. The sight of her trousered hips as she stepped up into the wagon, the sight of her walking away from him across the field to her cabin, were only two of the more heated memories he had of the vivid Dr. Lancaster. Each and every time he saw her, his whole being centered on one idea—easing the denim down her hips and filling his hands with the lush sweet fullness of her bottom.

When she came walking into the barn as he pitched fresh straw into the stalls, he felt his manhood quicken. He raised his eyes to her face and paused upon seeing the tired circles around her eyes. The urge to soothe her rose and swelled, much in the same way it had the day she'd shown him her red, chapped hands.

He asked, "Do you need something?"

"Just a few moments of your time." Vivid had spent the last few weeks trying to forget her attraction to him. She had a modicum of success as long as she didn't see him. "Abigail and I would like permission to take Magic on a trip to Detroit."

"Why?"

"I thought she might enjoy it."

Vivid strolled over to where the snowshoes were hung on the barn wall and made a point of observing them as she waited for his reply. "And what is this?" she asked, taking down a long pole that had what appeared to be a small snowshoe on the end. "Another kind of snowshoe?"

Nate set the fork in the bale and crossed the barn to where she stood. "No, that is a lacrosse stick."

"Lacrosse?"

He took the stick from her hands and turned it over. "It's a game played originally by the People. They call it Little Brother of War."

"War?" she asked.

"War," he answered.

Judging by the look on his face as he handled the stick, Vivid deduced lacrosse held a very special meaning for Nate Grayson. "How is the game played?" she asked.

"There are two teams. The object is to carry the ball in this cradle at the end of the stick and throw it past the other team's goal."

"The entire stick or simply the ball?"

"The ball."

"Do women play?"

"No."

"You say that with such firmness," Vivid quipped, smiling.

"Because I've learned a few things about you, Lancaster, and I'm telling you now, women do not play lacrosse. We play an annual game in the autumn, and you are not going to be allowed on the field. It's a man's game."

"Men say the same thing about voting," Vivid pointed out saucily.

"I'll bet that mouth of yours has been getting you in trouble since you were born."

"You have learned a few things about me, haven't you, Nate Grayson?"

The air was fairly crackling by now. Devouring her with his eyes, he reached over her shoulder to rehang the lacrosse stick on the nail behind her. His presence spread over her like a thick coat of warm honey.

"Let's see what else I can learn . . ." she heard him whisper, and anticipation rushed over her like the strong winds of a storm. When he lowered his mouth to hers, passion swept her away.

Vivid knew this shouldn't be happening, not again, but she couldn't help herself. She responded with an instinctive parting of her lips, which he brushed with his own before very slowly nibbling each trembling half. He was the only man to ever kiss her this way, the only man to teach her passion, and because she'd always been an avid pupil, and because the man was Nate, Vivid wanted to learn all he desired to teach.

Nate thought her mouth too sweet, her body too soft. Her vividness couldn't possibly have been meant for a mere mortal like himself, but he feasted on her with the hunger of a starving man. Her virgin responses were like spring rain to his parched, long-buried emotions. As he brushed his mouth over her ear, her jaw, and the sweet chocolate expanse of her throat, his desire welled with an intensity he'd never known he possessed. His vows to never touch her again meant little when she was in his arms. He wanted her as he had never wanted a woman before, the consequences be damned.

Vivid trembled when his mouth began to explore the skin beneath her jaw. His kisses against her throat were hot, feverish. She could feel his hands mapping her back and shoulder, then his thumb rubbed softly against the nipple of her breast. She heard herself moan breathlessly as he toyed and teased. This, too, was new, so new that she could only stand on shaking legs and relish the sparkling intensity. He wantonly coaxed the other nipple to a pleading tight point, and when they were prepared to his satisfaction, he dropped his head and bit each bud gently through her shirt. Were it not for his strong arm bracing her back, she was certain she would not have been able to stand.

Vivid was so caught up by the whirlwind of passion, she offered no protest when he slowly began to undo the buttons of her blouse. She offered no protest when he eased aside her chemise. For the first time in her life, she felt the lips of a man teasing her breasts, and all she could do was moan softly and ride the storm.

Her nipples pleaded but he gave no quarter, not with his lips nor with the lightning tip of his tongue. Her whole world seemed centered on the fire charging through her, and when he lifted his head, his eyes held a glittering reflection of her own.

Nate reclaimed her mouth, savoring her response and how perfectly her behind fit his palms. He eased her into his hardness while he languidly and brazenly slid his hands over her hips. The thought of exploring the warmth she treasured between her thighs made him want to undress her fully and take her to the pinnacle of desire, but he would not compromise her so recklessly.

Nor could he stop. He couldn't stop kissing her lips or teasing her dark-tipped breasts. He couldn't resist lingering against the scented hollow of her throat any more than he could resist breathing.

Vivid trembled in response to his bold play. She'd

never experienced such soaring sensations. Her nipples were pebble-hard and damp from his attentions and the brazen hand moving so possessively over her hips and thighs made her moan in the silence of the barn. She sensed herself losing control, could feel herself wanting to succumb to this heat no matter the consequences. She eased her lips from his to halt this sweet torture and her own potential downfall. "Nate . . ."

"Yes . . ." he said in a husky voice as his thumbs rubbed softly over her nipples. Hearing her gasp in response made him place another lingering kiss on her open mouth.

"We . . . must stop, Nate."

Vivid wanted to kiss him forever and fought to remember that they had to end this interlude.

"You're right," he whispered while nibbling her bottom lip. "God, Viveca you could sell these kisses and make a fortune."

"You wouldn't want me selling my kisses . . . would you?"

"You know what I mean . . ."

They finally parted.

Under his hot scrutiny, she took longer than normal to adjust her chemise and redo the buttons with shaking fingers. The heat spiraling through her made her vulnerable still. She had to turn away from him so she could breathe.

Nate chuckled in response to her actions. He ran his eyes over her hips as she worked on her blouse. They'd been lush and yielding in his hands, her thighs soft and firm. He wanted her so badly, he ached.

When she turned to face him again, she appeared to be more in control, but her eyes bore the remnants of passion and her lips were swollen from his kisses. "Well?" he asked her softly.

"Well—they certainly didn't teach me anything about this in medical school."

He grinned. "No?"

"No," she replied, smiling shyly. "I always assumed only the man benefited."

"You have a place on your body that's made only for . . . benefits. Did you know that?"

Avoiding his eyes, because she'd never heard of such a thing, Vivid shook her head no.

"Well, you do," he told her in a quiet voice. He wanted to be the one to show her the true pleasures awaiting a woman as vividly passionate as she, but that service would be rendered by the man she eventually married. The thought of some stranger sharing her kisses made his jaw clench.

"Will you let Magic accompany us?"

He cleared his mind of the visions of another man kissing her as heatedly as he'd done, and said, "I see no real harm in it. And as long as Aunt Gail goes along, I won't have to worry about you getting my daughter lost."

Vivid took mock offense. "I'm getting better at finding my way, you can ask anyone."

Then she added, "Besides, with Eli coming along we'll even have an escort."

"My cousin is going?"

Vivid realized too late she shouldn't have mentioned Eli's involvement. "Uh, yes. Abigail and I thought an escort might be needed."

"And you asked my cousin."

"Abigail asked her son." Vivid sighed with frustration. "Abigail and I assumed you would be too busy to take a mid-week holiday on such little notice."

"I am."

"Well, there you have it."

She peered into his hard-set face and asked softly, "Please, can we not turn this into another battle?"

He wanted to please her, so he acquiesced with an

inclination of his head. "When are you planning to leave?"

"Three days from today. Mary Jane Garrett, the famous lecturer, will be speaking on Friday."

Vivid could tell he was still displeased with the idea of Eli as their escort, but his failure to argue the point eased her mind. "I should head back to my cabin."

Nate didn't want her to leave, but he knew if she stayed, she'd wind up in his arms again. "It's probably best. You had enough trouble fastening your shirt buttons the first time."

The heat of his eyes sent her throbbing senses into another spiral. Vivid realized she wanted him to kiss her again, but outside of brazenly asking, she did not have enough experience with men to know how to bring it about. "Um, thank you for giving your permission for Magic."

"You're welcome," he said, lowering his gaze to her mouth. He was sure those lips would haunt him for the rest of his life if he weren't careful.

A reluctant Vivid left him in the barn.

A reluctant Nate watched her go.

Still reeling from the passionate encounter, Vivid walked back to her cabin and found Eli Grayson seated on her front porch. She slowed her steps, wondering if he'd be able to tell she'd been kissing his cousin a moment ago, but decided that would be impossible.

Eli stood at her approach. "Hello, Viveca. I'm still waiting to do the story you promised for the paper."

Vivid remembered they'd made the date more than a month ago. "Eli, I'm sorry. I've been so busy I forgot. Come on in."

They'd just gotten comfortable when Nate knocked on the door, "Lancaster, you in there?" he called.

"Come on in, Nate," she called back.

He entered, started to speak, but upon seeing his

cousin, said, "Sorry. I'll come back later."

"Hello to you, too, cousin," Eli drawled.

Nate turned to him and said, "I thought you were only going to be around for a few days."

"Changed my mind. Thought I'd avail myself of the scenery for a bit longer," he said, smiling at Vivid.

Nate looked at Vivid, and she felt embarrassment creep into her cheeks. She explained, "I promised Eli a story for his paper."

Nate's expression did not change. Vivid again wondered why the two cousins were so hostile toward each other. She also wanted to know why Nate had come back. Simply looking at him and remembering what they'd shared made her want to be in his arms again.

"I'll be back later," he said and then he left without a backward glance.

After a few silent awkward moments, Vivid and Eli spent an hour or so talking, laughing, and telling stories about their youth.

"Nate and I found an abandoned bear cub once," Eli said, reminiscing. "We must have been about Magic's age. Uncle Absalom always told us, never ever pick up a bear cub, not even if it was dead. Well, this cub was crying and wailing something fierce for its mama."

"Poor little thing."

"Save your sympathy," Eli said with a grin.

"What happened?"

"Well, we'd always wanted a bear cub, and Nate figured Uncle Absalom would let us keep it if it were an orphan, so we picked up the cub and started for home. About a half-mile into the trek the woods got very silent. There were no birds, no wind, nothing. The whole forest seemed to be holding its breath. Then we saw her. The big mama bear came barreling out of the brush like a locomotive. She stood probably six feet and weighed maybe five, six hundred pounds, and she was one angry bear. The only thing that saved us were the trees. If we had been on flat open ground, she probably would have run us down and killed one or both of us, but the trees were pretty dense. To this day I remember us running and screaming and ducking in and out of trees until I thought my lungs would explode. We hopped onto the trunk of that big oak over by the Crowley place and started to climb. The bear climbed up after us.''

"Bears can climb trees?''

"Yes, ma'am, and pretty fast, too.''

"How'd you get away?''

"We kept climbing. She eventually gave up and went back down, but she waited on the ground for us for over two hours. At that point in my life it was the most scared I'd ever been.''

"So did the two of you ever try to rescue another cub?''

"Never.'' He laughed. "Never. But just so you remember, if the woods ever go silent like that, it probably means there's a bear about, and you need to be going in the opposite direction. Fast.''

Vivid vowed to remember.

They talked a bit longer about politics and where each thought the nation might be heading after the upcoming national election. Eli looked over his notes and thought he had enough information on the Grove's new physician to write his story, so he stood to head back to town and his room over the newspaper office.

Vivid walked with him out to the porch.

He smiled at her. "I enjoy your company.''

Vivid looked up into his handsome dark face and saw the Grayson jaw and the smoke-colored eyes. "I enjoy your company also.''

"But you're probably never going to have dinner with me, are you?''

"Never is a long time.''

"If my cousin has his way it will be a long time. Mother told me she believes you're Nate's pillar of fire.''

His words caught her off-guard. "Did she tell you I believe she's mistaken?"

"She did."

"And what do you think?"

"Truthfully?"

She nodded.

"As much as I hate to admit it, she may be right, which means, my dear Viveca, you and I are destined to become no more than friends."

His dark eyes held hers and she said, "Is that so awful?"

"It is when I'd planned on being the one kissing you the way my cousin obviously had been doing when you first walked up."

Vivid blinked at his bluntness.

"No offense intended, but your lips give you away."

She guiltily brought her fingers to her lips.

He chuckled. "Thanks for providing verification."

Vivid's eyes narrowed as she said, "Eli Grayson, you tricked me!"

He grinned. "All part of my charm."

"Well, you turn that charm on someone else," she warned teasingly.

Their eyes held. Vivid thought of how he was going to make some woman very happy one day. He was as handsome as his cousin, and had an infectious, exciting air about him, but Vivid knew that she would not be the woman in Eli's future.

After he left, Vivid went out back and sat on the swing to watch the beautiful sunset. Her reverie was broken by Nate walking up to the porch.

He stopped at the lip of the porch and stood facing the sunset. Vivid ran her eyes over the strong lines of his shoulders and back and once again marveled at his magnificent stature. She then heard him say, "Eli's gone, I see."

"Yes, he is."

Silence.

"He get what he needed for his paper?"

"Yes."

He turned and faced her then, and their eyes held. She realized she had a very serious problem; her attraction to him made her want his kisses whenever he came near. Surely she should be able to exercise more control over her desire.

Their moment was broken by Magic running and yelling, "Pa? Where are you?"

Nate left to see what his daughter wanted and returned with the young girl in tow. "I promised her a story tonight before she went to bed. You'll have to excuse me," he explained.

Magic piped up. "Maybe Dr. Lancaster would like to hear the story, too. My pa is an excellent storyteller."

Nate chuckled. "When did you start using words like 'excellent'?"

"Becky Carpenter said we should all be striving to increase our vocabulary."

"I see," Nate said.

Magic looked at Vivid. "Well, Dr. Lancaster, do you want to hear the story?"

"I don't want to intrude on your and your father's special time."

Magic craned her neck up to her father and asked, "Do you mind, Pa?"

He shook his head that he did not.

Vivid scooted over to make room for Nate on the swing and Magic hopped onto his lap. "What's the story going to be, Pa?"

Nate leaned his head back on the swing as if thinking, then asked, "How about 'How the Bat Got Its Wings'?"

"No, let's save that for lacrosse time. How about a princess story then?" Magic asked eagerly. "You haven't told me a princess story in a long, long time."

She looked at Vivid and said, "Widow Moss said Pa's princess stories were bad for my constitution."

"I see," Vivid replied, though she didn't at all. She was still trying to sort out what a bat story might have to do with the game of lacrosse. She leaned over to ask that question just as Nate started to speak.

"This story is called 'How Mother Africa Got Its Rain.' Once upon a time there was a beautiful dark-skinned princess. Her father was a great African king and her mother a beautiful Spanish queen."

Vivid raised an eyebrow. The princess's ancestral tree sounded a lot like her own, but Vivid kept her peace.

"Did she have a tree house?" Magic interrupted.

Her father looked down at her and asked with a smile, "Majestic, haven't we agreed that you would not interrupt a story when I'm telling it?"

She nodded yes.

"And didn't I promise to build you a tree house when you return from Detroit?"

She nodded yes again.

"Then will you please stop pestering your old pa?"

She nodded yes a third time.

Before Nate could begin his story, Magic whispered loudly to Vivid, "Pa doesn't like me to ask a lot of questions."

Vivid whispered back, "My pa didn't, either."

"Lancaster?" Nate said, leaning over.

"Oh, sorry," she said guiltily. She and Magic shared a silent giggle.

Nate continued. "Anyway, the beautiful princess was loved by her people and she loved them. She was also very brave. When slavers came to their little land, she and her parents led an army and drove the slavers back into the sea."

"She sounds very brave," Magic said softly.

"She was. She had a very big problem, though. There'd been no rain for many years, and all the crops and animals were dying in the heat. Her people were starving.''

"So what did she do?''

"She went to the village shaman, and he told her to go and search for the Thunder God and see if she could barter for some rain.''

The tale continued with the princess's long search for the Thunder God. Nate's descriptions of the tricksters and evil spirits the princess defeated and outsmarted on her quest made Vivid understand why Magic loved her father's princess stories. The princess was smart, brave, and true, and Nate was indeed an excellent storyteller.

The princess searched for so long that at one point in the tale her small sack of food became nearly empty, but even though she was down to her last corn cake, she shared it with a magic raven who was very hungry, too. The raven repaid her for her generosity by revealing the whereabouts of the Thunder God's cave.

"That was nice of him,'' Vivid supplied.

"I think so, too,'' Magic added.

Nate, smiling at yet another interruption, simply shook his head and continued. "The princess found the cave, but the Thunder God took one look at her beauty and told her to go away.''

"But why, Pa?''

He looked down at his daughter and said softly, "He was frightened.''

"He didn't know that the princess wouldn't harm him?''

"No, he didn't.''

"But he was a big strong god, Pa, why was he frightened?''

"Because he really wanted her to stay and visit, and he didn't think she would like someone who lived underground. He'd been alone most of his life and was very, very lonely.''

"He didn't even have a daughter?'' Magic asked.

"No, Majestic, he didn't even have a daughter. He

lived in his dark underground cave all alone, making thunder."

"That's sad, Pa."

"Very sad," Vivid whispered, looking at him.

"Well, the princess thought so, too. So she stayed with him awhile and taught him how to play games and read books and most of all how to smile again. He'd forgotten how to do those things because he'd lived underground for so long.

"After teaching the Thunder God all the things he'd forgotten, the princess then asked about water for her land. By now, the Thunder God was in love with the beautiful princess and he didn't want her to leave."

"Did the princess love him, too, Pa?"

"Yes, and she didn't want to leave him, either, but her people were depending on her for the rain, so she struck a bargain. She agreed to stay underground with him for six months every year and make him smile, and in exchange he promised to give her people all the rain they wanted for those six months. So now in Africa there is a rainy season and a dry season, all thanks to the beautiful brave princess."

Nate glanced down at his daughter's face and smiled. "How was that for a story?"

"I liked it, Pa. Too bad the Thunder God didn't give the people rain all year round, though."

"Well, you know from other stories how gods act sometimes. He probably didn't want the princess to go home at all and pouted the whole time she was away."

Magic nodded, then said, "Well, I liked the story anyway. How about you, Dr. Lancaster, did you like my pa's story?"

He wouldn't look at her but Vivid spoke directly to him anyway, "I liked your pa's story very much."

His gaze brushed over Vivid just long enough to increase the pace of her heartbeat, then he asked his daughter, "Are you ready for bed now?"

She nodded yes. Magic laughed when her pa lifted her to his strong shoulders and carried her home.

The darkness settled in star-studded abandon over the countryside, bringing with it the night's velvet hush and a beautiful moon. Vivid could hear the song of the crickets and the occasional menacing buzz of a mosquito as she sat in the swing. The little biting beasties were an increasing problem now that the nights were warmer. She'd been warned they'd only worsen as the summer progressed, but she sat outside a bit longer anyway, enjoying the night air and mulling over Nate's story of the princess and the Thunder God. Had he purposely chosen this fascinating way to reveal himself and his feelings? She heard a footfall behind her. She turned and heard Nate say, "Thought you'd be inside by now."

Just the sight of him made her senses soar. She hadn't expected he would return. "No, I'm just enjoying sitting here and not having anywhere to be. I love this swing, Nate Grayson. I also loved your story. Magic is lucky to have a storyteller in the family."

He smiled in the dark and said, "I can't believe she's still after me about that tree house."

"She's a persistent little girl."

"That she is," he replied.

Silence settled between them as they each pursued private thoughts.

Nate could feel himself teetering on the edge of an abyss as he gazed at her in the moonlight. His need for her grew stronger with each passing moment. He walked over to where she sat with her trousered legs drawn up onto the seat of the swing. He then stood over her as if coming closer would somehow solve the riddle of his attraction. Being so near only made the need sharpen. Moonbeams streamed over his shoulder, bathing her as she sat looking up at him. His devouring eyes took in the beautiful glory of her coiled hair, the graceful line of her throat, and the soft rise and fall of her breathing from within the loose-fitting shirt as she waited for his next move.

Before he realized what he was about he sat down next to her, moved closer, and with a hand placed gently behind her head, eased her into a kiss. Her mouth was as sweet as he'd remembered, sweeter. He thought kissing her again would cure him of what he knew to be madness, but the dementia spread and flared, making him pull her closer so he could slowly run his hands over her delicate shoulders, the sturdy softness of her spine, and the lush curve of her hip.

"We aren't supposed to be doing this . . ." she whispered, her heart beginning to beat with a familiar sensual rhythm.

He was kissing his way down her throat and up to her ear as his hand cupped her breast. "I know. I'm hoping to find a reason to stop . . . but I haven't yet . . ."

He bent his head to her captured breast and bit her softly through her cotton shirt. Vivid shuddered, and then as he moved to pay tribute to the other side she shuddered once more. His mouth was warm, hot, her nipples aching when he raised his head. "You have a mouth as lush as spring . . ." he whispered just before covering her lips with another long lingering kiss.

Vivid could do nothing but feed on the sensations he evoked. Every brush of his lips across her mouth, the throbbing point of her temple, and the shell of her ear promised passion and gentleness. His touch was like wildfire, his hands like flames as she felt them slowly blazing a trail down her back. There was no sanity here, just a man and a woman caught up in the raw vitality of desire.

Slowly he unbuttoned her shirt and she felt the night breeze sweep her bared skin. He placed kisses against her trembling throat and she moaned softly as his heated palms slid feverishly over her breasts. His touch made her arch, his teasing fingers made her swell. When he eased his hot hand inside her gaping chemise and squeezed her nipple seductively, piercing ripples swept her up and overrode all.

Nate used the teasing friction of his fingers to raise the buds up nice and sweet, then, unable to resist, pulled the chemise down below her breasts and loved her as he'd dreamed. Her breasts were as virgin-ripe as the rest of her firm, lithe body. No man before him had ever explored her until now. No man had ever bared her breasts to the moonlight and his glittering eyes, or tasted her until she moaned his name, as he was doing now. He was the first.

And the only one, he vowed possessively. With renewed determination he pleasured her precious dark jewels until her head dropped back on the swing.

Vivid tingled beneath his large hands boldly tracing her thighs and the roundness of her hip. She could feel him tugging her shirttail free from the waistband of her belted trousers. She arched to give him better access, then sighed as his warm hands slid beneath her chemise and up her bare back. The wanton warmth made her move closer against him so she could seek his lips.

Her boldness made Nate groan and run his hands greedily over the rich curve of her buttocks. As she leaned passionately into his chest, he explored her thighs and legs with savoring hands. Emboldened by her responsiveness and urged on by the throbbing in his manhood, Nate loosened her belt buckle until it opened, then slid the length of leather from around her waist. Next he began freeing the buttons on her pants one by one, until he could slide his fingers over the humid skin of her navel. The thought of what lay beyond drew his hand to circle lower. Suddenly his hand stopped and he looked into her eyes with amused surprise. "Viveca Lancaster, where are your drawers?"

Vivid should have felt a tinge of embarrassment at his discovery, but his hands began moving again, touching

her so gently yet so erotically she almost forgot what
she'd meant to say. "I don't wear . . ."

He pulled her pants down her thighs. "They bunch
up on my legs and . . ." Vivid lost her ability to speak
once he began to explore her.

He eased her across his lap. "Right here . . ." he said,
his hands moving to the core of her soul, "is that lode-
stone I told you about this afternoon. Its only purpose
is to bring you pleasure. I'll show you . . ."

Vivid could feel that part of herself ripening and rising to his touch in much the same way her nipples had.
Yet this pleasure had its own unique heat; it was fuller,
hotter, and more encompassing than any other sensation
she'd ever known. It only took a few more seconds of
his wanton lessons to send the moon crashing into the
stars and for her to feel as if she were at the center of
the explosion. The buffeting aftermath left her panting,
keening, and stunned.

Once the world stopped spinning, she said, "My
goodness. What was that?" His hands were still tutoring
her slowly, letting her feel the remnants of her passion.
She had never ever experienced anything so glorious before.

He grinned down at her knowingly and asked,
"Something else they didn't teach you in medical
school, I take it?"

"Heavens, no. Nate, what did you do to me?"

"I did nothing. Well, I take that back . . ." he said,
sliding his hands boldly over her moonlit breasts. He
smiled, watching her arch to the sensual command. "It's
called a climax, completion. The French call it *le petit
morte.*"

Vivid fought to make her mind do the translation in
spite of him making her nipples rise and ripen once
more. "The little death?"

"The little death," he replied.

"Dying is probably not that pleasurable," Vivid replied, still spiraling because he wouldn't stop touching her. "But I understand why the French call it that . . ."

He kissed her lips. "So do I . . . Now fasten your pants and go on in before I'm tempted to show you another path to the little death . . ."

"Would you really?" Vivid asked, nibbling softly on his tempting bottom lip. "When?"

"Go inside, brazen woman, before your trousers wind up around your ankles and you find yourself sitting on something a bit more lively than this swing."

He could see how perplexed his statement made her and he chuckled at the confusion reflected in her dark eyes. "And you call yourself a doctor," he teased.

Vivid had absolutely no idea what he was intimating but from the sparkle in his gaze, she thought it might be something she would like to try.

In the end, though, Vivid stood and repositioned her clothing all under Nate's blazing scrutiny. As he watched her redo her buttons, he felt his manhood throb painfully not only from being denied but also from knowing that all this time she'd been bare inside those denims. Had he known, he would have carried her off and pleasured her weeks ago.

Vivid said softly, "Thank you for a very . . . enlightening evening, oh mighty Thunder God."

He looked at her and smiled. "You're welcome, brave princess. Now go on in and get some rest. I'll see you in the morning. Give me a kiss first though, Viveca . . ."

Vivid bent to give him a parting kiss and he met it with his own sweet goodbye.

After she went inside Nate sat on the swing taking in the night and waiting for the throbbing in his pants to stop so he could get up and walk home.

It took a while.

Chapter 13

V ivid spent the next two days combing the Grove
for anyone needing her services. She also spread
word that no one could become ill, break a limb, or step
into a bear trap until she returned from Detroit.

On the morning they were scheduled to depart, she,
Magic, and Abigail were joined by Eli after their dawn
breakfast. They were placing their valises into the buggy
they would be taking to the Niles train depot when Nate,
who'd seemed content to watch the proceedings from
the porch, strolled over to where the traveling party had
gathered.

He stood before his cousin. All activity ceased as they
silently confronted each other. Nate then reached into
his pocket and pulled out a coin. "Call it in the air,
cousin," Nate instructed, then tossed the coin high and
let it land in his palm.

Eli grinned. "Heads."

Nate opened his hand and showed it to Eli. "Tails.
Offer your regrets."

Eli looked into his cousin's eyes for a moment, then,
shaking his head, stated, "Ladies, it appears I won't be
able to accompany you to Detroit. My cousin will escort
you instead."

Magic cheered, unmindful of the adults and their intrigue.

Eli asked, "What if it had been tails?"

"Then we would have flipped again."

Eli seemed to assess Nate a moment before asking, "That bad, is it?"

Silence.

Eli chuckled knowingly, "That bad. Well, I've lost the war anyway, you may as well take my place." He then began to remove his things from the buggy.

Abigail shook her head, mumbled something about men and brains, then got into the buggy without another word.

Vivid, having witnessed this amazing encounter, didn't know what to say or think, so she, too, joined Abigail inside the buggy to wait while Nate went back into the house to fetch his traveling gear.

Vivid and the Graysons boarded the Michigan Central Railroad in Niles and took the day-long ride to Detroit. Upon arrival, Nate hailed a hack and the Black driver helped them load their trunks and then they were off.

Abigail had lived in Detroit for many years before and after Mr. Lincoln's war and she proved to be a font of information on the city. She pointed out the sights as the driver headed them east. "That's the famous city hall, dedicated in 1871. We'll visit it tomorrow, but from the top you can see the river and Canada."

The hack rode up the busy avenue and the three adults smiled as Magic gawked at the horse-drawn trolleys. Vivid was impressed by all the buildings and people on the streets. She hadn't known how much she'd missed the hustle and bustle of city life until now. The voices and sounds tugged at her heartstrings.

As they tooled past shops and businesses, they all listened to Abigail tout the city's accomplishments in the manufacturing of soap, paint, and Mr. Vernor's ginger ale. She also told them about the important role Detroit played in shipping and promised they would see the waterfront before they returned home.

They would be staying at Mrs. Fisher's boardinghouse. Mrs. Fisher, a longtime friend of Abigail's, greeted them with hugs and friendly smiles. She showed them to their rooms—one for the women and a separate room down the hall for Nate.

They were too tired from the journey to do any sight-seeing so Nate rented a buggy from Mrs. Fisher's stable and they rode to the home of Abigail's friend, Hester Vale Vachon.

"Is she the woman married to the Black Daniel?" Vivid asked.

Smiling, Abigail asked, "How do you know about that?"

Vivid explained about the story Miss Edna had related.

"Yes, Hester's husband, Caleb, was the Black Daniel. He arranged freedom for many before the war. Hester and Caleb are fine people."

And they were. Caleb Vachon was as handsome as Miss Edna said he would be. He had a complexion as light as churned butter, but despite the age in his face and the gray streaking his hair, he was still a stunningly handsome man. His wife, a beautiful ebony-skinned woman, had prepared a fabulous meal. At the table Vivid watched the Vachons as they teased and smiled at each other. It was easy to see the two were very much in love even after being married over twenty years.

When the evening came to a close, the Vachons walked them out to the rented rig. Abigail lingered over goodbyes with her good friends, while Nate, Vivid, and Magic climbed in. Magic scooted onto the driver's seat near her father while Vivid took a spot in the back.

"Pa, can I ask something?"

Nate looked over at his daughter and said, "Certainly."

"Why does Mrs. Vachon have purple hands?"

Vivid had also noticed the digo hued hands of their hostess.

"She was a slave on an indigo plantation when she

was young. The dye colored her hands that way.'' Nate leaned down and kissed his daughter on the forehead, saying, "Thank you for being polite enough to hold on to that question until now."

Magic beamed with her father's praise.

The next morning after a hearty breakfast at Mrs. Fisher's table, Abigail headed everyone out to tour the city. The first stop was city hall. It was a magnificent structure with turrets and towers and a balcony. On the lawn were six cast-iron deer which Magic found delightful. However, the huge clock centered high on the upper face of the building drew Vivid's attention.

"When the clock was dedicated on July 4 in '71, it was touted as the largest one of its kind in America. The famous clockmaker W. A. Hendrie of Chicago called it his masterpiece," Abigail explained.

Vivid read further information on the clock, courtesy of the printed broadsides provided at the entrance. She read aloud, "The clock's four dials measure eight feet and three inches in diameter. The pendulum weighs one hundred and twenty-five pounds. The bell weighs seven thousand, six hundred seventy pounds."

Nate whistled.

"And the clock cost two thousand, eight hundred and fifty dollars," Vivid stated with amazement. "That's quite a sum."

"Yes, it is," Abigail agreed, "and you should have heard the outraged cries of the taxpayers at the time."

Inside people were milling about in pursuit of whatever business they'd come to conduct.

"Look at all the steps," Magic exclaimed, marveling at the iron staircase. "How many do you think there are, Aunt Gail?"

"I don't know, Majestic. Why don't you count them as you climb to the top? I'll sit here and wait for you all to come back."

Magic went outside to count the stairs to the entrance

and came back declaring there were thirteen in all. Added to Magic's count were the sixty-seven to the stairway, the one hundred forty-three to the clock, and the two hundred thirteen to the top.

Tired and winded, Vivid did not want to climb another stair for at least six months. Fanning herself, she refused to believe the claim that Detroit's oldest citizens made this climb to the top regularly. She didn't think she'd ever lose the burning sensation in her legs.

But the view was magnificent. One could see for miles around. The river stretched like a blue ribbon out before them, dotted with many boats both small and large. Nate pointed out Canada, and Vivid was amazed at how close it appeared. She now understood why the escaped slaves chose to travel here. One could stand on the riverbank and see freedom beckoning on the other side.

Climbers who made it to the top of the Detroit city hall were also given an up-close look at the four iron maidens on the cornices of the tower. Magic read the plaques underneath. "They are Justice, Industry, Art, and Com—" She paused and called, "Pa, what does this last one say?"

Nate came over and peered at the name. "Commerce."

As he explained to Majestic what commerce was, Vivid watched them. He reminded her so much of her own father. Nate cared about the things Majestic cared about, took the time to answer the ten thousand questions she seemed to wake up with every morning, and loved her without restraint. A daughter couldn't ask for a better father.

After leaving city hall they hailed a hack and took in the waterfront where the biggest attraction, as far as Magic was concerned, turned out to be the huge sign advertising Queen Anne Soap. Abigail said the Queen Anne Soap Company had a store downtown where you could redeem their wrappers for merchandise.

They had lunch at a dining room near Mrs. Fisher's place, and Vivid had her first taste of Mr. Vernor's ginger ale. She found the sweet but peppery beverage quite different. Nate, who'd had the drink before and loved its flavor, ordered a large chilled pitcher for himself and Abigail. Magic coughed and set her cup aside. She didn't like it at all.

"Mr. Vernor is a pharmacist, Viveca." Abigail pointed out. "And Detroiters use his ginger ale for everything. They float ice cream in it, use it to baste hams, take it for an upset stomach, and drink it piping hot when the winter sniffles come around."

Vivid stared at the golden-colored liquid in her glass, impressed. "Really?"

"Wait until you taste ice cream floating in it, Lancaster," Nate exclaimed. "There's nothing to compare, especially on a hot day."

"I think it tastes like medicine, Pa."

Nate ordered Magic a glass of the more conventional lemonade and Magic smiled happily.

They spent the rest of the day taking in more sights and shopping. Abigail steered them into a shop to pick up some teas for Miss Edna. While the man behind the counter prepared Abigail's order, Nate, Vivid, and Magic marveled at the bins containing teas from all over the world.

When they returned to the boardinghouse late that evening they were laden down with enough packages and purchases to found their own dry goods store.

The next day was spent at a much slower pace. Nate went to get a haircut and Abigail spent the day visiting with Hester Vachon, which left Vivid and Magic on their own. Abigail had purchased tickets for that evening's speech by Mary Jane Garrett. A reception was to follow and neither Vivid nor Magic wanted to be too tired, so they spent the day relaxing, eating Mrs. Fisher's pound cake, and playing marbles in the dirt behind the house.

When Nate came upon his daughter and Lancaster on their knees, he paused a moment to discreetly feast his eyes on the doctor's upraised hips as she sighted her shot. The flowing black skirt only hinted at the beauty it concealed and Nate swore at himself for letting his imagination linger. He had not come out here to become aroused, though he found it to be a state easily attained when he was around the good doctor. He'd spent most of yesterday trying to find a way to be alone with her. He'd had to settle for a caress with his eyes, a polite hand on the arm as he helped her in and out of the buggy, and the faint trail of her perfume as she passed him by. They'd spent no time alone since the night on the swing and his hands itched to hold her once again.

That evening, Vivid dressed in a beautiful, full-skirted green gown. She placed her grandmother's emeralds in her ears, patted her hair one more time, then went to help Magic with the buttons and sash on her own fancy dress. When all three women were ready they met Nate in Mrs. Fisher's parlor. Vivid had never seen Nate in anything other than the clothes he wore every day back home in the Grove, and she had to admit that formal evening dress made him even more handsome.

On the carriage ride to the Detroit Opera House where Miss Garrett would be speaking, they listened to Abigail reminisce on another Detroit Opera House event that figured very prominently in the city's postwar history.

On April 7, 1870, Blacks and Whites had come to the Detroit Opera House to celebrate the ratification of the Fifteenth Amendment to the Constitution. The day had been declared a civic holiday by the mayor and the state governor, and all the buildings downtown were draped with patriotic flags and bunting. The day began with a cannon salute from the artillerymen of Fort Wayne, one of the oldest forts in the United States. At the sound of the cannon, the troopers from the First Michigan Cavalry, resplendent in Union blue, began the parade up Woodward Avenue, the city's main downtown thoroughfare. Behind them marched the Black Civil War veterans of the Loyal League, followed by more than a thousand Black citizens of Detroit. All along the parade route were banners hailing U.S. Grant, a war hero, then in his first term as president, and banners hailing the Great Emancipator, killed in 1865. Other banners praised Frederick Douglass, William Lloyd Garrison, and John Brown.

The marchers, still heading up Woodward, circled Grand Circus Park, then on to Campus Martius, the spot from which the Phalanx, Detroit's own Black regiment, had marched off to war. The marchers broke ranks to enter the flag-draped opera house. On stage were thirty-two young women dressed in white. From the African Baptist and Methodist churches in the area, they symbolically represented the thirty-two states that had ratified the Fifteenth Amendment, thereby making it the law of the land. In the center of the thirty-two stood two tall young women also clad in white. They represented the goddesses of Truth and Liberty.

After the audience stood at attention to hear the "Star-Spangled Banner," the Reverend W. R. G. Mellen led the opening prayer. He was followed by five hours of speeches given by such dignitaries as Michigan Governor Henry P. Baldwin, who declared that the day of "jubilee" rightfully belonged to Detroit's Black citizens, and by local tailor and Underground Railroad agent William Lambert. Lambert, the chairman of the day's events, introduced some formerly escaped slaves who never would have witnessed jubilee had it not been for the "Road" and its agents. He went on to speak of John Brown and his journey to Detroit before his ill-fated raid at Harper's Ferry, then began praising such men as Detroit hotelier Seymour Finney, whose secret barn loft sheltered hundreds of fugitives as they passed through the city on their way to freedom in Canada and elsewhere. Then as the celebration ended, he introduced well-known caterer John DeBaptiste, who came on stage and promptly resigned as the superintendent and main engineer of the Underground Railroad. "We don't need it anymore," he laughingly told the throng.

The resignation was accepted with ovations and cheers.

In the silence that followed DeBaptiste's resignation, the familiar opening strains of the "Battle Hymn of the Republic" came out of the stillness. The crowd sang quietly at first, but as the chorus swelled and the blended voices gained strength, many sang the final line with tears in their eyes.

Abigail finished the story just as they arrived at the opera house. Vivid and the Graysons joined the hundreds of others who'd come to listen to Mary Jane Garrett speak.

And speak she did. She began by recounting the madness taking place in her home state of Louisiana. Vivid, like everyone else in the country, knew of the horrors being heaped upon the South's duly elected Black Republicans by men proclaiming themselves Redemption Democrats. The nation's Black press had been loudly voicing their anger for years about the country sitting back and doing nothing to protect Black men from being systematically murdered for exercising their dearly won right to vote. Yet hearing Miss Garrett talk about the terrifying massacres occurring in parishes such as Caddo, Catahoula, and Orleans was even more chilling.

To combat this rampage of evil, Garrett and the women of Louisiana were calling for emigration. She eloquently but steadfastly demanded that the husbands and brothers of the race take their women to places out of the South where they could live in security and peace and get homes for themselves and education for their children.

She called upon all those living in the North to lend

their support by informing their Southern relatives about
the call and by signing the petitions she planned to send
to the Congress with the demand that members of the
race be given the rights and privileges that the Constitution guarantees.

Her hour-long talk was met by thunderous applause.
During the reception held in the lobby, Abigail, Nate,
and Vivid penned their signatures to the petitions, and
Abigail and Vivid also added their names to the list of
women who wished to form a local chapter of Garrett's
fledgling organization called the Committee of Five
Hundred Women.

They left the opera house and returned to Mrs. Fisher's boardinghouse. During the ride, Magic vowed to
stay awake all night to ensure the wonderful day would
never end, but she was soon fast asleep in her father's
arms.

Nate, cradling his softly snoring daughter, climbed the
stairs to the women's rented room. He coaxed her out
of her dress and shoes, then covered her with a thin
blanket. With a smile, he bent to press a paternal kiss
upon her brow. "I'd like to take the early train back in
the morning," he said to Vivid and Abigail.

Both women nodded in understanding; tonight would
be their last one here. His eyes touched Vivid's, then he
exited, closing the door softly.

Abigail prepared for bed but Vivid, still feeling the
excitement of the evening, did not want to turn in yet.
"Gail, I think I'm going to go out and get some air.
Will you and Magic be all right?"

"We'll be fine, but you shouldn't stray far."

"I won't," Vivid promised, then picked up her emerald cape and stole out quietly.

The hallway was empty as Vivid made her way to the
stairs. When she passed Nate's door it suddenly opened.
He seemed as surprised as she at the abrupt appearance.

"I was going out for some air," she felt compelled

to explain. She wondered if she would ever become accustomed to his powerful bearing. His shoulders rivaled the width of the door frame.

"I was on my way down to settle our bill," he replied.

It was his eyes, she decided; they were mesmerizing and Vivid had to shake herself free from their spell. "Please ask Mrs. Fisher to separate my portion. I will pay her before we leave in the morning."

"That isn't necessary. I planned on paying her the full amount."

Vivid shook her head. "That's very nice of you, but I'd prefer not to be indebted."

For a moment he said nothing. The two of them simply stood there staring at each other; he fighting the urge to run his finger over the lush set of her lips and she fighting to breathe.

"Come," he said. "I'll walk with you outside. We can discuss it there." He closed his door and escorted her down the hall to the stairs.

It was a beautiful windy night. The full breeze blew across Vivid's face and caught the edges of her cape and dress, whipping the emerald silk softly and rippling the loose tendrils of her hair. She brushed them back, loving the rush of air against her skin.

She and Nate were standing inside a small gazebo centered far out in the field behind the boardinghouse. On the walk down the cleared narrow path, neither spoke a word; she felt awkward and tongue-tied, like a young girl out with a new beau.

His low-toned voice interrupted her thoughts. "You really should let me pay your portion, Lancaster. Look at it as my way of saying thanks for inviting Majestic along."

"I've enjoyed her company immensely."

"Then thank me for having such an adorable daughter by letting me pay your bill. Besides, after all the money you spent yesterday, you could probably use a helping hand.''

"I made reasonable purchases," Vivid countered in mock offense.

"Cuban cigars?"

"Who knew I could find hand-rolled Cuban cigars here? I'll ship them to my father for Christmas."

"The silver baby rattle?"

"My sister in Boston is expecting early next year. It'll be a christening gift. See, all reasonable purchases."

Nate shook his head. "Is your daddy going to eventually pay for all the things you purchased?"

"Heavens no." Vivid laughed. "I have enough money of my own that I can afford to splurge now and again."

"So you're telling me you can afford to pay your portion."

"With the money I have in my accounts, I can probably pay the bills of everyone in the place."

Nate cocked his head sideways and peered at her. "We've never talked about this before, have we?"

"No, we haven't." Vivid wondered if this was going to be another problem between them. Her father had become a wealthy man. Her mother, Francesca, had amassed a sizable portfolio of California land and property over the years, thanks to her shrewd business sense and her friendship with the even shrewder Black businesswoman Biddie Mason. Vivid knew men sometimes resented a woman who didn't need to look to them for financial support.

"Does it bother you that I have a bit of money?"

"No. No, it doesn't." He'd answered without thought, then realized he meant it. He didn't care if she was rich as an ancient Egyptian queen. He just wanted to make love to her.

"Then if it doesn't bother you, I will let you pay my bill."

The awkward silence fell between them again and Vivid turned back to their surroundings, glad for the distraction of the wind and the rustling response of the grasses nearby. Aided by the sliver of the moon above, she could see the shadowy outlines of trees off in the dark distance across the wide open field. The gazebo seemed so isolated, she felt as though she and Nate were the only people in the world.

The temperature had dropped a few degrees, so she pulled the cape closer against the chill. "What are the winters like here?" she asked.

"Fierce, cold. Think a California girl like you can survive?"

"I believe so."

He chuckled.

Vivid was about to take offense; she'd heard that smug chuckle before. "You don't think I'm capable?"

The softness of his reply deflated her temper. "I think you're very capable."

She shivered then, but couldn't be certain whether it originated from the wind or from her attraction to his volatile nearness.

"If you're cold, we can head back inside," he offered.

"I'd like to stay for a few moments more, if we could."

"Then take this," he said as he held out his coat for her.

"What will you wear?" she asked, looking up at him in the darkness.

"Lancaster, for once, no questions, just accept the offer graciously."

Vivid nodded, smiled, and undid the frogs at the neck of her cape. Raising her arms, she held the silk cape behind her head and the night winds lifted it like a sail. Despite the cool temperature, she enjoyed the caress of the air blowing across her shoulders and throat. "I love this Michigan of yours, Nate. The trees, the wind . . ."

She turned and looked over at him. Although shadows masked his eyes, the intensity she sensed made her pause and slowly drop her arms. "Is something wrong?"

In response he moved closer and very slowly traced a finger across her smooth cheek. Vivid went stock-still under his caress, her heart beating fast.

"Why are you doing this to me?" he asked in a soft voice.

Mesmerized, Vivid could only swallow as he continued to speak. "You make me want to take you hunting and fishing . . . berry picking and snowshoeing . . ."

"I'd like to do those things with you . . ."

"I know you would, that's what scares me so . . ."

His thumb moved gently over her lips and he leaned down and kissed her with a heat that branded her as his own. Vivid stepped closer to better feel his lips on hers, and as though it was what he was waiting for, he slid his arm about her waist and eased her against his hard body. The kiss deepened. Vivid ran a hand over the strength of his shoulder. When his tongue slid seductively between her parted lips she began to tremble.

He kissed her neck, making her sigh and melt as he brushed his lips over the scented hollow of her throat. She had no alternative but to let her head drop back and ride the wave of sensations as his hands moved to tease her breasts. The nipples tightened beneath his toying fingers, budding against the emerald satin in anticipation.

Under the night wind, Nate bared her as he slid her dress down below her breasts. With his tongue he boldly circled her trembling nipples. The deep rustling of the trees muffled her gasp as he gently bit each bud, then suckled wantonly. He feasted, teased, filled his hands with her hips and brought her closer. His tongue was lightning and his hands, sliding her gown slowly over her hips, were brewing the storm.

Nate's manhood throbbed with need for her. Her beautiful dark-tipped breasts and the sensual warmth awaiting his exploring hands beneath the luxurious satin gown were driving him to the edge. Her skin was hot and soft; her mouth, as he sought her lips again, a temptation no man could resist. Her kisses could sustain a man for a lifetime, and that was how long Nate wanted to make love to her, for a lifetime.

Vivid thought she could live forever on just his kiss. She didn't care that her dress, now rucked up past her thighs, had probably sustained irreparable harm from being crushed in his large hands. She didn't care because those large hands were warmly cupping the thin material of her drawers, seducing her, stroking her, making her arch.

"Let's take these off . . ."

Vivid offered no protest as he slid her drawers from her legs. She felt wanton, brazen, standing in the wind with her dress held aside, naked but for her stockings and high-heeled shoes; she felt only heat as his strong hands caressed her. She couldn't help herself, she parted her legs to give him more access to all that made her female, and as a reward he slowly sank to his knees and kissed her bared thigh.

"Here's something else they didn't teach you in medical school . . ."

The soft, initial tribute of his love for her made her eyes widen and her legs instinctively close. "Nate, what are you doing?"

Smiling, he looked up at her and said, "Don't you ever stop asking questions?"

Vivid tried to speak but the urge to do so soon vanished under the spell of his hands lazily preparing her for his feast.

"Just relax," he coaxed with both his soft voice and his touch. "Consider this as an extension of your medical education . . ."

When he bent to her again, his devotions were so delicate, his expertise so masterful, she fought to main-

tain her calm but lost the battle very early in the campaign.

Before she knew it, sensations she had never experienced before grabbed her being and left her shattered in
the night. The wind masked the sound of her screaming
his name.

When Vivid finally came back to herself, he was
standing over her chuckling smugly, like a conceited
male.

"Still cold?" he asked.

He'd left her warmer than she could ever remember.
"Where in the world does a man learn something like
that?" she asked.

Nate shook his head and responded playfully,
"Woman, are you still asking questions? I thought I'd
cured you of that just a minute ago."

Vivid's cheeks burned from the memories of his
"cure." "It's because it's all so . . . new."

"I understand."

"Then help me to understand what we're doing, you
and I."

He looked down into her eyes and said softly, "I wish
I knew, Lancaster. I'm still trying to figure out why
you're even here."

Vivid looked out into the night; she didn't know why
she was there, either. Her mother, Francesca, was a
strong believer in fate. Had the fates brought her here
to the wilds of Michigan for the sole purpose of meeting
this one man? "Abigail says I'm the pillar of fire in your
great-grandfather's dream."

She turned to gauge his reaction.

He said nothing in reply. Instead he brought her back
into the circle of his arms and she met his kiss willingly.

A few passionate moments later, he whispered against
her ear, "We should get back. Gail's going to start to
worry."

Vivid knew he was right, but being there with him

was more appealing than seeking her bed. The remnants of this latest encounter still had her senses throbbing. She still wanted to know where men learned to do . . . *that*. She felt swollen everywhere. "I don't want to go in."

"We have to, otherwise . . ." He lowered his mouth to hers and spent a few silent moments nibbling sensually on the sultry treat of her bottom lip.

"Otherwise . . . what?" Vivid asked. She'd learned her lessons of love well and showed him so by licking softly at the edges of his masterful mouth.

"Quit tempting me," he warned in a tone thick with need.

"You should talk . . ."

Several more moments passed, heated with kisses, caresses, and Vivid's soft cries. Her breasts were bared again, her dress lifted, and he once again knelt to make her lush, open, and his. She didn't believe it possible, but she screamed even louder the second time.

Chapter 14

T hey took the train home early the next morning. Nate spent most of his time enjoying the company of his daughter, but every now and then, he'd turn to Vivid with a look that scalded her from the roots of her hair to her toes.

When they arrived in Niles, Vivid was amazed at the amount of goods Nate and the porters unloaded from the boxcar. She couldn't resist teasing him by saying, "And you were critical of the number of purchases I made? Look at all this."

The pile of farm implements, tools, and bolts of cloth were only the tip of the mountain. A good portion of the items were boxed and crated. "Where do you keep the tame animals?" she asked.

He hadn't been able to resist her smile the day he met her at that very station over a month ago, and he certainly wasn't able to resist it now. "Go make yourself useful. See if the livery man brought around our buggy like he was supposed to."

Then he favored her with another one of those heated looks. "I'll take care of the rest of your questions later."

She gave him a sultry little smile, then left to do as he'd asked.

When Nate turned the horses onto the tract that led to the Grove, all the weariness of the journey vanished. Vivid spied the little log cabin she now called home; she drank in the familiar sight of the trees and surrounding flora and realized that she'd become very much attached to this place in the short while she'd been here. She also realized she couldn't imagine living anywhere else.

Nate halted the team beside the Grayson house. Magic immediately hopped down from the wagon and ran straight for the barn to see if queen cat Cleopatra had given birth when they were away, while the adults began unloading the supplies and luggage.

Nate was handing down bags of seed to Vivid, and Gail was leaning on her cane overseeing the process when Eli rode up. Vivid noticed Nate had turned his back on his cousin's arrival, appearing to concentrate instead on maneuvering the items that still needed to be handled.

"Welcome back," Eli called as he strolled up to the wagon. "Need some help?"

Nate and Eli eyed each other, then Nate nodded a terse agreement and they all went to work.

With Eli's help the unloading went swiftly. There were farm implements, dry goods for the store, an anvil for the blacksmith, and numerous other items Nate had promised to bring back for several Grove residents.

When the wagon was nearly empty, Gail headed toward the house, announcing dinner would be ready in less than an hour.

The last crates on the wagon belonged to Vivid. They contained precious new medical books she could hardly wait to read. When they were unearthed she eyed them eagerly. "Eli, those crates on your left are mine. Can you push them this way?"

Eli, standing in the wagon bed, turned to where she pointed and bent to shove the crates to one side.

Nate barked, "Leave them be. I can handle them."

Eli stiffened in response. He turned to his cousin, and for a moment Vivid was sure an argument would ensue. Instead, Eli simply shrugged and said through gritted teeth, "Whatever you say, Nate. How about I take this churn in to Mother?"

Nate nodded. Eli inclined his head respectfully to Vivid, picked up the churn, and headed toward the house.

"Had I known my crates were going to make the two of you fight, I'd've gotten them myself," Vivid said after Eli left. When he didn't respond to her thinly veiled condemnation of his manners, she asked, "The two of you haven't always disliked each other, have you?"

Nate slid her largest crate over to the lip of the wagon bed. "No. We were closer than brothers growing up."

"Then what changed between you?"

He looked at her a moment, then went back to moving her two other crates. "Some things are better left alone, Lancaster." He placed the two smaller crates atop the larger one, picked them all up, and without uttering another word, headed across the meadow to her house.

Once inside, he set the crates down where she directed, then turned to leave. As he reached the door, Vivid said, "Thank you for the holiday."

"You're welcome. Don't forget about dinner."

And he was gone.

About an hour after Nate's departure, Magic came over to announce that dinner was ready. Vivid, in the process of unpacking, had forgotten all about the meal. In truth, she didn't want to go, not now when she could feel the new books calling her. However, she stood and dusted the sawdust from her black skirt. She'd made a promise to Gail, and Vivid always tried to keep her word.

To her pleasure, Eli had stayed to join the meal.

Nate said grace and everyone began eating. Gail asked Magic about Cleopatra and the girl informed all that the much slimmer black feline had been seen in the barn, but the kittens were nowhere to be found. After vowing to continue the search following her evening chores,

Magic then regaled her cousin Eli with all the things she'd witnessed and done on the trip to Detroit. Eli listened raptly and asked all the appropriate questions. Vivid watched the interplay with a smile. It was obvious that Eli loved Magic as much as everyone else. She was glad to see that the feuding cousins had not made the child choose sides.

After she and Magic helped Abigail clean up the kitchen, Vivid prepared to say her goodbyes for the evening. Magic protested Vivid's early leaving. "It isn't dark yet, Dr. Lancaster. I was hoping we could play checkers tonight."

Vivid smiled at the disappointment on Magic's brown face and ran a soothing hand over the dark braided head. "I need to get to sleep. There were a few messages in my box, so I have some patients I need to check on tomorrow. How about we make an appointment for later in the week? Agreed?"

Magic nodded.

Abigail spoke up, "Magic, there's still a bit of light left. Why don't you run over to Jeremiah's and show him your new marbles?"

Delight spread over Magic's features. "Can I Pa?"

"Your chores done?"

She shook her head enthusiastically.

"Then go," her father said. Magic ran to her room to retrieve the marbles, then shot out of the door faster than lightning.

Vivid headed back to her place and sat on her front porch looking through her new books until it became too dark to see the print on the pages. With the night rolling in, the mosquitoes became more voracious and bold. Slapping at one of the little winged beasties feeding nonchalantly on her forearm, she smiled at its demise and went indoors, knowing she'd only lose more blood if she tarried a moment longer.

At about the same time, Nate, having put Magic

to bed, stood at his bedroom window staring down at Lancaster's cabin. She'd been in his thoughts most of the day, helping him relive last night's intimate encounter in the gazebo. The taste of her dark beauty haunted him. Each and every time he had met her eyes that day, he envisioned having her bared and naked to his caresses. Not even Eli's unwanted presence at dinner had dampened his desire. That she could be distracting enough to make him ignore his cousin spoke of her power. He decided that he wanted her, plain and simple.

But to have her he'd have to marry her. She was not a whore in a lumber camp, or one of the accommodating widows up in Kalamazoo. Viveca was cultured, educated, and the town's only doctor. She was also a virgin. Nate had never been a trifling man and he had no plans to begin now. So his choices were either to actively pursue her in front of God and everybody, or to ignore this ache he'd developed for her and get on with his life. He'd considered his life fairly full until now. People in the Grove lived simple lives; he had the love of his daughter, Aunt Gail, friends, and neighbors, and on those ocassions when he needed to let off steam, Eli was always around to lend a hand, but lately he sensed life had not been as complete as he'd believed. Viveca seemed to have relit a spark within him that he'd willingly let go cold. The death of his father, the terrible memories of Fort Pillow, and the dissolution of his marriage had changed him, he readily acknowledged. He'd become less joyous, more serious. Now, over a decade later, he still carried remnants of much pain deep down inside. Yet being with Viveca seemed to be exposing those dark places to light. Even when the two of them were at odds, he found the air around her electrifying, scintillating, vibrant. She made him feel alive, eager to embrace life. The only other person capable of imbuing him with such fullness of spirit had been Majestic.

So what did he want? Logical choice or illogical

choice? The logical choice would be to distance himself;
she made it quite clear where she stood on becoming
involved with a man at this juncture of her life, and the
fate of her position here as doctor still remained unre-
solved. The illogical choice would be to pursue her.

He chose the illogical.

He chose the light.

Inside the cabin, Vivid placed the book she'd been
reading on the shelf with the others in her small library.
Her eyes strayed to her old textbooks standing like sol-
diers on the shelf above. She reached up and took them
down.

The memories associated with the tomes came flood-
ing back as she sat and slowly began to look through
them. Had it really been four years since she'd started
on the road to certification? It seemed like only yesterday that she'd arrived in Philadelphia in 1872 as a member of the twenty-third session of the Women's Medical
College of Pennsylvania. The opening coursework had
spanned twenty-two weeks of intense study. To fulfill
one of the entry requirements, she had practiced for a
year under the watchful eyes of Dr. Duncan and Dr.
Place in her hometown before applying for admission.
They'd made certain to include her when surgical pro-
cedures were undertaken; another prerequisite. Duncan
and Place had worked her hard to get her ready, but the
faculty in Philadelphia worked her even harder. She'd
taken instruction in microscopy under the esteemed Dr.
J. Gibbons Hunt; physiology and hygiene under the college dean, Dean Ann Preston. By the time three years
had passed, she'd been tutored in subjects pertaining to
principles and practices of medicine; surgery; anatomy
and histology; and obstetrics and diseases of women and
children.

Upon graduation she was further required to seek an
internship with an established medical facility. Since her
major studies had been concentrated in the areas of chil-

dren and women's health and her thesis had been the "Treatment and Diagnosis of Children," she and another Black woman in her class, Carrie Still, applied for internships at Boston New England Hospital for Women and Children. The hospital board denied them initially because of their race. When the board subsequently altered its stance a few months later, she and Carrie were allowed to practice.

And now here she sat, in Michigan, looking through the books that made it possible for her to be here. Where did she go from here, though? In the past few weeks she had felt herself being pulled in opposite directions. She loved being a doctor, loved knowing that because of her training and care the children in the Grove would grow up to become healthy adults. She envisioned growing old here, and by then she would probably even know her way around, but where did Nate fit into her future? She never knew she could be so moved by a man. His dark face and spectacled eyes were commanding more and more of her time and thoughts. Last night in the gazebo his soft touches and wanton loving had rendered her absolutely mindless. Every time he looked at her she remembered how brazen he'd been, and how loudly she'd screamed that second time around. How could she fulfill her career goals and yet want nothing more out of life than to have him hold her and love her? The two paths couldn't possibly be compatible, could they? She'd known many women who'd viewed their careers as nothing more than a stepping stone to marriage with a successful man. They'd traded their stethoscopes for wedding rings, baby cribs, and all that being a wife and mother entailed. Few, if any, felt the need to pursue their former goals.

So what did she want? Ideally, she wanted both Nate's love and her doctoring, but she also knew the time would come when she'd have to make a choice.

She decided it might be best to seek some advice, so

she sat at the desk and began writing a letter to her sister Jess.

Vivid loved both her sisters equally but Jess had a tendency to be more frank with her advice. When Vivid needed wisdom or guidance, she wrote to Alicea, but if a man was involved she knew to pen Jess. She looked up from her missive and thought about the passion Nate had brought to her life. The way he kissed, the way his hands brought her nipples to pleading points, came back to her mind with such sensual clarity she could feel her lips tingling. She bent back over her letter and wrote,

Jess, is there a difference between lust and love? If so, please explain. Also, is it proper for a proper woman to experience lust?

She went on to tell her sister what she knew about Nate's past and the feelings she had for him. She filled the last two pages with information about her position as town doctor and a few current events. She began with the scandals plaguing the lame-duck administration of President Grant, then turned to news a bit closer to her heart.

The Democratic governments in the Redemption South have all but gotten rid of their black office holders and continue to laugh at the Fourteenth and Fifteenth Amendments. Washington seems to be laughing with them. Their "let alone policy" has resulted in mass killings and disenfranchisement. The Kluxers and White Leagues feel so free from reprisal, they are now conducting their killings unmasked and in broad daylight. The Chicago Tribune has written, "The long controversy over the black man seems to have reached a finality." The Nation is declaring that The Negro will disappear from the field of national politics. Henceforth, the nation, as a nation, will have nothing more to do with him. Times are harsh everywhere for our race. With all the evil loose in the South, there is talk of a mass migration to Kansas in some of the Black newspapers and broadsides. I will keep you informed of any further discussion on this subject.

Vivid then sent her love to her brother-in-law and hoped he was finding his missionary work fulfilling. She closed by writing,

Much love to you, my dear sister. May the fates bring us together soon.

Vivid signed the letter "La Brat Trabrasera."

She stood up from the chair and stretched. It was late.

She went into her small bedroom and prepared for bed. After donning one of the light, cotton nightgowns she'd purchased in Detroit, she sat on the bed and brushed her thick ebony hair into one long plait. Barefoot, she padded back out to the front to secure the bolt on the door and stopped, stunned, upon seeing Nate Grayson sitting grim-faced at her desk.

"Where'd you come from?" she asked. Surely she hadn't been so engrossed in thought that she hadn't heard him at the door? His sudden appearance reminded her of the day Majestic had mysteriously disappeared. One minute Magic had been in the room and the next moment she was gone. In this case her father seemed to have appeared right out of thin air. "Is something the matter?"

"We need to talk," he stated.

She sat in one of the overstuffed chairs and waited. She'd no idea what he'd come to say, but by his face it appeared to be fairly serious.

He held her gaze. "We've never discussed this attraction that's developed."

Vivid looked away, then quietly replied, "No, we haven't."

He told her softly, "I believe it's time we did."

She nodded.

"It's a foregone conclusion I'm courting you."

His statement surprised her a bit because she'd never considered their encounters in such formal terms. She'd accepted his kisses, yes, and in places that still astounded her, but Nate Grayson courting her? "Is that what this is, courtship?"

"Do you have a better name, or explanation?" he asked.

"I don't know. The . . . encounters . . . everything seemed so . . . spontaneous. I never saw them as being part of a formal courting. I . . . they've just been . . . occurring."

He chuckled at how flustered she became trying to explain their relationship. "Have you ever done this 'occurring' with other men?"

"Of course not," she hissed, slightly outraged.

He smiled. "I knew that, put away your scalpel. I asked because you're not a whore down at Maddie's, Viveca. If this is going to continue, you're going to have to think over some things."

"Such as?"

"Frankly, are you prepared to take on a husband?"

"A husband? When will I need a husband?"

"Probably the very next time you and I are on that swing together."

She went still.

"Or," he continued, looking over at her with a simmering heat in his eyes, "the next time we're alone in the barn—or in the buggy. Take your pick of a thousand places, Viveca."

The burning intensity of his gaze made her feel as if

she'd suddenly caught fire. She drew in a calming breath.

"This is a small community," he went on. "Sooner or later something will be seen, or heard, and then the gossip will begin, and it will undoubtedly be my fault because I can't seem to keep my hands off you . . ."

His tone was so hushed and heated, Vivid shuddered in response.

"I don't want to ruin you or your reputation."

Vivid didn't know what to think or say. He was right; if they continued on this course, sooner or later the fiddler would have to be paid. She'd have not a shred of reputation left if either of the scenarios he described came to pass. "So do you have a suggestion?"

"We could let the situation cool down a bit, and see if it will burn itself out. You've stated your position on marriage."

"Yes, I have. The logical thing to do would be to let things cool down as you said. Who knows, maybe it will simply go away."

"Uh-huh."

She looked over at him and wondered why he was smiling.

"Well, Lancaster," he said, stretching his arms and yawning, "for the first time in, oh, ten years, I'm going to embark upon something totally illogical."

His sudden change of mood made her wary. "Meaning?"

"Meaning I'm not going to let things cool down, because I don't want them to. I'm going to pursue you, Viveca Lancaster, in ways you've never been pursued before."

Vivid blinked. "Why?"

He smiled a knowing smile.

Vivid swallowed. "Nate, I admit I enjoy your kisses, and until I met you I never knew a woman could have so much fun taking off her clothes—" Vivid could not believe the words that had just come out of her mouth. He had her so confused she had to fight to regain her train of thought. "What was I saying?"

"How much fun you had taking off your clothes."

She cut him a look. "No, before that."

"How much you enjoyed my kisses."

"Stop it," she warned, trying to hide her smile.

"Just trying to help," he said reasonably.

"I was saying . . ." She couldn't remember, so instead she asked, "Why in the world do you wish to court me, and don't give me that pleased male smile again."

"Because each and every time I'm around you, Viveca, the only thing I want to do is take you somewhere and make love to you until they hear you screaming in Kalamazoo. Is that frank enough for you?"

She swayed, slightly dizzy from his confession.

"Now you may say you don't want to be courted but your lips say different, so circle your wagons, Princess Hannibal, the battles lines have been drawn."

Part of her was ecstatic at his revelation, but the other part, the part that had studied and spent many nights burning oil in order to become a physician, balked at the idea of her two desires being able to coexist harmoniously.

But even as she stood there, her lips were already anticipating his kisses and her nipples were tightening and raising their shameless little heads. Her body's traitorous reactions were responding to his devilish smile.

Slowly he walked over to her, his eyes devouring her. Her blood began to pound fast.

"I know you didn't come here to be courted," he said. He took her hand and urged her to her feet.

"No, I didn't."

"But fate sometimes changes life around. I vowed to never risk my heart again, but for you . . ."

He reached out and gently traced a crescent on her cheek. "Could it be because of the kisses we've been sharing?'' The velvet finger moved to outline her lips, making her tremble. ''Or maybe it's because of all that screaming you were doing last evening. What do you think?''

Once again memories burned her cheeks. She looked up into his handsome face and asked, ''Have you always been so seductive?''

''Not lately, no, and I'm way out of practice . . .''

Vivid's eyes slid shut from the intensity. *Out of practice?* What would he be like when he regained his former self—more importantly, where in the world would she find the means to resist? ''I need time to think about all this.''

''I'll give you time and I'll go slow. However, I mean to have you, Lancaster, and whenever I find you alone I'm going to do my best to help you make up your mind.''

Nate had already decided she would be worth the chase, and he also knew she would lead him on a merry one. He found the anticipation thrilling.

''What does that mean, exactly?'' Vivid wanted to know.

''Exactly this . . .''

He bent his head and brushed his lips across hers, and Vivid didn't even try to resist. She wanted his kisses.

He kissed her softly at first, the tender flick of his tongue against her parted lips. His palms began sliding up her back, mapping the structure of her shoulders and spine beneath the thin cotton gown. It was selfish, really, this slow tutoring, because it enabled him to savor the tastes, scents, and feel of her at a lazy pace and to show her how very serious he meant to be about this campaign.

He slid his lips up to her ear and nibbled his way down the edge of her throat. ''I mean to have you, Viveca, be it today . . . tomorrow . . . or . . . a year from now. You are mine . . .'' she heard him rasp heatedly.

And she was his, Vivid admitted to herself. Why hadn't her professors told her about this passion? She'd learned nothing about the way her nipples would blossom when his fingers played them gently, or how her senses would bloom. When he dropped his head and brushed his lips across her breasts, she moaned softly, and she caressed the back of his neck. Her medical books claimed women did not enjoy this thick heady heat. The books were wrong.

Nate wanted her in all the ways a man could want a woman, but because he'd pledged to proceed slowly in this, he settled for stealing kisses and undoing the ribbons on the yoke of her gown. Her breasts were beautiful, rich, dark, and so responsive. Filling his hands, he flicked his tongue over one pebbled treasure and then the other. He thrilled hearing the low moan slide from her throat as he suckled her.

Eyes closed, Vivid arched her back, assaulted by dazzling waves of sensations, her dilemmas forgotten. His hand wandered over her, setting off a glowing warmth with a plea all its own. He answered the call by slowly raising her gown and sliding his hands possessively over her bare hips.

He raised his head and stared into her eyes, his slow explorations below her gown continuing, melting her like ice on a summer's day. She keened for him, crooned, and all the while he held her gaze, watching the passion play across her beautiful face.

"Do you still not want to be courted?" he inquired. He was as hard as railroad iron.

"I didn't come here to be courted, no," Vivid whispered through the haze of desire. She could feel the storm gathering in response to his exquisite explorations.

Nate, unable to resist the parted bliss of her mouth, kissed her sweetly, saying, "Such evasive little daisy-eyes . . ."

He increased the intensity of his touch until lightning

flashed behind her eyes and the thunder of the little death echoed through her long and loud.

While she spun in the vortex of the afterglow, he picked her up, carried her back to the bedroom, and seated her gently atop her bed.

Still reeling and throbbing, Vivid looked up into his amused features and remarked, "You don't plan on making this easy for me, do you?"

He smiled. "No."

Chapter 15

O n Monday morning, Miss Edna, who served as the Grove's postmistress, brought the mail to Nate's office. Nate flipped through the small stack and was about to set it aside for reading later when one letter with the word URGENT penned across the bottom caught his eye. He opened it to find a small sheet of paper which said: *Majestic in danger. Miss Satin and I arriving soon. Please prepare accommodations. Holly Rand.* The writing appeared scrawled, as if it had been penned in a haste.

He went still, then read the words again. He turned the penned warning over to see if there might be anything else written that would provide a clue to its meaning or sender. Nothing. He read the words again, but knew no more than he had the first time. What kind of danger? And who were Miss Satin and Holly Rand?

Nate strode into the office of the *Grayson Gazette*. He tossed the mysterious note atop Eli's desk and waited for his cousin to read it. Eli's face went grim. "Is this someone's idea of humor?" Eli asked, turning it over in his hand just as Nate had done.

"I've no idea, but I don't find it funny. It came with the morning post."

"And you've no idea who this Holly person is?"

Nate shook his head.

"Miss Satin sounds like the name of a cathouse queen. The handwriting doesn't look familiar, which

243

means we can just about eliminate anyone local.''

"I have a real bad feeling about this, Eli.''

"So do I. I wish we knew more about Magic's mother.''

"I wish we knew *anything* about her,'' Nate said.

"Well, you and I may have our differences, but we're united on this one. Anyone threatening Majestic will have to deal with us first.''

Nate nodded. "Thanks, cousin. I'm going to let Abigail, the Crowleys, and a few others in on this so they can keep their eyes open. Dammit, I almost forgot about the convention in Indianapolis in three days. I'll have to miss it. I can't leave Majestic here unprotected.''

"That meeting is important, Nate.''

"I know, but Majestic is my life. If anything happens to her while I'm gone—''

"I'll take care of things until you return. Go to Indianapolis.''

They eyed each other.

Eli said softly, "I failed the last time, I know. I'm older now, Nate. This isn't Cecile we're talking about, it's Magic, and I love her very much. Go to the convention. I'll keep her safe, or die trying.''

Nate looked into Eli's eyes and saw, for the first time, not the sixteen-year-old youth who'd committed the ultimate betrayal, but the man Eli had become. When had it happened? When had he grown up? Had Nate's inner pain really been so blinding, he hadn't notice the passing years? Nate observed his cousin a moment longer, then nodded his acceptance of Eli's offer. "You should move back into the house.''

Eli stared. "Are you sure?''

"Yes.''

Nate and Eli spent a few more moments discussing details before Nate crossed the dirt street back to his office. He wondered what kind of threat would Magic be facing. He had no answer, and because he didn't, the father in him was terrified.

After dinner, Nate took Abigail and Vivid into his study and let them see the note. Vivid felt a frisson of fear course through her as she handed the note back to Nate.

Nate asked, "Do you think I should tell her?"

Abigail spoke first, "I believe you should. She's not going to be happy being confined to the house without being told why."

Vivid agreed. "If it were me, I'd want to know. It would probably scare me, but it would make me more careful when I went out."

Nate called Majestic into the study.

"What's the matter, Pa?" Magic looked at Abigail and Vivid, then wanted to know, "Am I in trouble?"

Nate smiled. "No, sweetheart, you're not."

She seemed to relax.

Nate thought it best he get to the heart of the matter. "Majestic, I received a note in the post today, saying you're in danger."

She stared at her father for a long moment, then asked softly, "What type of danger?"

"We don't know."

"That's kind of scary, Pa."

"I know it is, sweetheart, it scared all of us."

Magic swung her head around to Abigail and then to Vivid. Both women nodded.

"So what do we do?" she asked.

"All we can do for now is be especially careful until we find out what the note means."

"Will I have to stay indoors?"

"No, but I do want you to stay out of the woods, and no fishing."

"No fishing?"

"Or rabbit trapping, or frog catching."

"But—"

"Majestic, your safety is the most important thing in the world to us."

"Can't I even play over at Mr. Crowley's or Maddie's? Maddie's dogs wouldn't let anything happen to me, and neither would Mr. Crowley."

Abigail said, "She has a point, Nate."

Vivid had never met Maddie or her dogs, but knew Mr. Crowley and his giant sons would put holy fear in anyone attempting to do Magic harm.

"Pa, I'll be real, real careful. I promise."

Nate looked into her topaz eyes and knew his heart would shatter if anything should happen, but as Abigail pointed out, neither Maddie nor Adam would let her come to harm. "Okay, Majestic, you can go to Adam's and Maddie's *only*. You come home for lunch and never ever leave the house without letting someone in the house know where you will be. Agreed?"

Magic smiled. "Agreed."

Eli moved into the house the next morning, much to everyone's delight.

The day after, Nate very reluctantly left for Indianapolis.

Vivid spent the day at the church overseeing the weekly children's clinic. She missed him already, but the children made the day enjoyable. That evening when she and Michigan turned into the long tree-lined track that separated the Grayson house from her own, she was surprised by all the activity in the yard. Wagons were lined up as if church were being held. Men, many she didn't recognize, were swarming over the place like ants, carrying wood to and from a spot across the yard where a bunch of sawhorses had been erected. Men were on the roof of her cabin while others were on the ground hammering nails into the skeletal wood frame. She tied up Michigan and walked the rest of the way. Many of the men stopped what they were doing as she approached. Those wearing hats tipped them politely in her direction while others nodded their greetings. She met each man's smile with one in return while she wondered why all these men were gathered in the yard.

Finally, Mr. Crowley excused himself from a circle of men and yelled to her over the noise of the hammering and sawing. "Evening, Dr. Lancaster."

"Good evening, Mr. Crowley. What is all this?"

"We're building an addition onto your place."

"What?"

"We're building you an addition onto your place," he repeated.

Vivid shook her head. She'd understood his words the first time. "Why?"

"Because you need one."

A very logical conclusion, Vivid admitted, because the place was dreadfully small, but again, why? "How much do you think it will cost?"

"It's all courtesy of your neighbors, and if you start fussing about wanting to pay them, you're going to risk offending some mighty fine people."

Mr. Farley walked by pushing a wheelbarrow. He must've heard the conversation because as he passed he said, "All we want to hear Doc, is you saying thank you."

She looked into his wise old eyes and realized that he was serious.

Vivid could do nothing but say, "Thank you."

"Smart girl," Mr. Crowley said. "Now, come over here and look at these plans my son Paul drew up. The place won't be fancy, but it'll have a bit more space than you have now."

The plans called for an addition to be built onto the original cabin that would include another bedroom and study, a front room, and a kitchen. The old cabin would have its roof refurbished, walls resealed, and a new plank floor installed. Vivid could then use the additional space for her office and to treat her patients. Mr. Crow-

ley estimated the job would take about a week to ten
days to complete.

"Whose idea was this?" Vivid asked after Mr. Crowley repocketed the hand-drawn plans.

"Nate's."

Vivid could only shake her head. He wasn't even here
and he was still courting. It would serve him right if she
did say yes to his proposal.

She came out of her reverie to find Mr. Crowley
watching her closely. "I'm sorry, Mr. Crowley, did you
say something?"

"You wouldn't happen to have any sisters, would
you?"

"Yes, two."

"They married?"

"Happily."

"Pity," he said.

Vivid laughed and gave him her most sympathetic
look. "Your sons will find wives, Mr. Crowley, I promise. They're all intelligent, handsome men."

"But will these marriages happen before or after they
eat me into the poor house?"

They both laughed.

Vivid left the men and went over to the Grayson
house. In the kitchen she found Abigail staring out the
window. Vivid wondered if Abigail was really that fascinated by the activity in the yard or just the activity of
one particular worker. "Abigail, did you and Mr. Crowley ever settle your differences over Benjamin Rush's
contributions to our race?"

"Yes, we did. We agreed to disagree."

"How long have you and Mr. Crowley known each
other?"

"All of our lives. His wife and I were best friends."

"He told me she passed away some years ago."

"Yes, it's been seven years since we lost Meggie,"
Abigail said softly, her voice tinted with sadness. "Her

given name was Margaret, everyone called her Meggie. I still miss her.''

Abigail turned from the window. "Have you eaten anything today?''

"The Quilt Ladies brought me a basket over at the church around midday.''

Any sadness Abigail may have harbored over her friend Meggie's passing disappeared. "Viveca, it is nearly dark. You need to take the time to eat more often. Who's going to take care of your neighbors if you wither from lack of sustenance? Sit. I'll fix you a plate.''

A knock at the back door saved Vivid from further lecturing. Adam Crowley entered the kitchen.

"We're done for the day, Gail.''

"Good, Adam.''

Vivid watched the two of them. Abigail seemed intent upon ignoring him as she busied herself with fixing Vivid's plate, while he stood observing her with a knowing look in his black eyes.

"Mr. Crowley, if you haven't eaten, why don't you join me?'' Vivid said.

Abigail, who had her back to them, replied, "If he wants to stay, he's welcome.''

"I'm sure he wants to stay, don't you, Mr. Crowley?'' Vivid asked.

He gave Vivid an assessing look, as if trying to ascertain her intent. "Yes, I would like to stay,'' he finally said.

They had a very pleasant repast. Abigail and Mr. Crowley were on their best behavior until the subject of Eli came up. It started out innocently enough. Abigail related Eli's plans to go to Philadelphia when Nate returned to visit the nation's Centennial exhibition. Mr. Crowley lobbed the first shot in the skirmish by saying, "Eli's grown into a fine man, but he should have been *my* son, Gail, our son.''

Vivid was so surprised she dropped her fork, and it clattered on the table.

"Adam Crowley, I am not going to discuss this with you," Abigail replied.

"Not discussing it won't change things," he told her. "He should have been mine, and you damned well know it."

"You have had one too many oaks fall on your head, Adam Crowley. You married Meggie, remember?"

"And why did I marry Meggie, Gail? You didn't want me, you wanted somebody with a bit more polish."

"That isn't true," she snapped.

Her anger seemed to shock Mr. Crowley because he asked quietly, "Why isn't it true?"

Silence.

"Abigail?"

Silence.

He turned to Vivid and said, "See how she is? Talking to her is like trying to converse with a mule."

He stood then and said, "All right, Abigail Grayson, I've had enough of your foolishness. If Nate can court a recalcitrant female, then so can I."

Vivid stared at him in surprise. What had Nate been telling people?

Abigail looked up at him with skeptical eyes and asked, "What are you saying?"

"This is what I'm saying. I'm putting you on notice. Before the snow falls, you and I are going to be man and wife. This has gone on long enough."

"Are you proposing to court me?"

"No, Gail, we're going bear hunting. Yes, woman, I propose to court you."

"You have sawdust where your brain should be."

"With you running me through a sawmill for the last thirty years, it's no wonder. And just so you'll know I'm serious, I'll be making the announcement at church on Sunday."

"You wouldn't dare."

He looked into her eyes and said, "Abigail, you won't believe the things I'm going to dare."

And he left.

Dumbstruck Vivid glanced over at Abigail. In spite of the heated argument, Vivid swore Gail's dark eyes were smiling.

Because of the work on the cabin, Vivid moved into one of the spare rooms in the Grayson house. She spent the night dreaming of Nate.

The next morning she was alerted by one of the men working in the yard that Maddie of Maddie's Emporium needed assistance. He drew her a map in the dirt and Vivid and Michigan were on their way.

When she reached the small whitewashed cabin, she grabbed her bag, and as soon as she was inside the gate, she heard dogs barking angrily. Then she saw five hounds bearing down on her at a very fast pace. Instinct told her to hop back over the fence immediately, but her brain said the dogs would probably jump the fence as well, so Vivid stood absolutely still in hopes of being rescued before she became their lunch.

They circled her, snapping and growling, when a man dressed in buckskin and wearing a large beat-up hat stepped haltingly onto the porch. "Who are you?"

The voice belonged to a woman.

Vivid didn't have time to deal with that surprise, she was too concerned with the intimidating dogs. "Dr. Lancaster."

A sharp whistle pierced the air and the dogs instantly calmed. The woman called, "Now let her pass."

The silent pack parted and, still trembling, Vivid made her way to the porch.

"Come on in. Sorry about the dogs but they know I don't like visitors."

Vivid noticed the woman walking as if her leg was

paining her. "Mr. Avery said you needed my assistance."

"Yes, tried to cut my ankle off with an axe last evening. Want you to take a look at it."

The cabin was plainly furnished and clean. There were no curtains on the windows and no rugs on the shining plank floor. There were, however, books covering every inch of the walls.

"Name's Maddie."

"I'm Viveca."

Maddie tossed off her hat and revealed a beautiful, honey-colored face and a long braid of jet-black hair. She looked to be only a few years older than Vivid. Vivid watched Maddie ease down into a cane-backed chair. Her face was etched with pain as she said, "Let me get my breath here a minute and I'll see if I can get my boot off."

Vivid set her bag on the floor beside the chair and instructed, "You just sit, I'll take the boot off."

Vivid untied the work boot and gently eased it off her foot. A blood-soaked bandage was tied around the ankle. "You must have cut yourself fairly badly. You said you did this last night?"

"Yep, right after supper. I was chopping wood and the damned blade shattered. What was left came down on my ankle."

The bandage, torn from a petticoat, had dried to the wound and Vivid was carefully peeling it away so she could get a look at the cut. "Hold still now, this will hurt."

Maddie cursed a blue streak as Vivid undid the layer of fabric closest to the skin. The cut began to ooze and Vivid peered at it closely, periodically using the bandage to stanch the flow. "The axe blade may have been defective but its sharpness was true. Bit more force and you'd've been cut right down to the bone." The diagonal cut ran from just below her small toe to her ankle on the top side of the foot. Vivid thought stitching it would be best, but it had to be cleaned first.

While Maddie called out directions from her chair in the front room, Vivid found a pot in the small kitchen, then went out to the pump for some water. She brought it back and set it atop the stove to boil.

"I'm going to stitch you up as soon as the water's boiled. Now, you said you were chopping wood. Did you clean it out before you wrapped it?"

"Poured some whiskey on it is all."

Vivid dug around in her bag for her glass magnifier. She held the small oval over the still oozing wound and searched for splinters. The few visible ones she extracted with a pair of tweezers. When the water came to a boil, she poured some into another pot and threaded two large needles with lengths of her sturdiest thread and tossed them in. She put some of the remaining water into a clean china bowl and carried it back to where Maddie sat.

While Maddie grimaced, Vivid methodically dripped the cooling hot water over her foot until the wound ran clear. Careful to keep the blood from filling the wound again, Vivid staunched it lightly and repeatedly. When the area appeared free of debris Vivid went back to the kitchen and retrieved the thread.

"Maddie, if you're a drinking woman, you might want to take a shot of that whiskey right about now because this is going to sting more than a bit."

"I'll be okay, you just go ahead."

"Are you sure?"

Maddie nodded yes.

As Vivid eased the needle into the other woman's skin and began to stitch, Maddie grimaced and winced. She drew in her breath a few times but she didn't flinch. Vivid went about her work as quickly as she could to spare her patient prolonged pain, but the stitches had to be uniform, and as a result it took a bit of time. When it was near done, Vivid smiled and said, "We're almost there."

Vivid tied off the last knot, cut the trailing threads, and looked up at Maddie in triumph but Maddie had fainted.

A whiff of ammonia from the vial in Vivid's bag brought Maddie back to her surroundings. She blinked a few times and coughed, then asked, "Did I faint?"

Vivid nodded yes.

"Guess I'm not as tough as I thought."

Vivid smiled. "Your foot's stitched. You'll have to stay off it as much as you can."

Vivid watched Maddie inspect the stitched wound and heard her say, "It looks real good. Hurts like hell but looks fine."

"It's going to hurt for a few days but it should ease more and more after that. If it just keeps hurting let me know."

"Sure. How much do I owe you?" Maddie asked.

"Nothing. First time visit is always free."

"You'd make a terrible whore, Dr. Lancaster."

Vivid chuckled, saying, "What?"

"Never give anything away, especially a service you can get money for. I was a whore, I know what I'm telling you."

Vivid didn't know what to say to this very beautiful woman dressed in buckskin.

Maddie asked, "You did know you were treating a whore, didn't you, Doctor?"

Vivid shook her head no.

"I'm surprised Avery didn't mention it."

"Why would he?"

"Because most folks, especially Avery's fat wife, believe the words 'whore' and 'Maddie' are synonyms."

She related this without bitterness or rancor; in fact, she'd spoken with a hint of amusement in her tone. "I'm

Grayson Grove's black sheep, or should it be ewe?'' she asked.

Vivid grinned and shrugged.

"Well, ewe or sheep, I'm it. Don't you know about Maddie's Emporium?''

"I've heard of the Emporium, and I heard it bore your name, but that is all I know.''

"Well, I used to own it. Sold it about a year or so ago, though.''

"May I ask why?''

"I was tired of it all. I didn't need the money, and besides, my father died three years ago. That took all the fun out of running a whorehouse.''

Vivid's eyes widened in shock.

"My whoring killed him, which was my intent.''

"Why?'' Vivid had never heard of such a thing.

"Because he killed me, with his piety, his ignorance, and his abuse. You're a doctor, Viveca—ever been beaten for reading books?''

"Of course not.''

"I was, many, many times. My pa believed females didn't need learning. Having babies and waiting on a husband was all I needed to know according to his view of the world.''

"That's horrible.''

"Yes, it is. He took me out of school as soon as I mastered my letters and put me to work at the store. He ran the store before Miss Edna.''

"But didn't anyone try to help you?''

"The Graysons did. When we were young Nate and Eli would meet me every day after school and teach me everything they'd learned that day. Miss Abigail said I was the smartest child she'd ever encountered and she would lend me books on history and literature and I would devour them and hide them in the store's cellar until I could return them. Well, he found my cache one day and . . .'' Maddie paused and her voice softened.

"Dr. Lancaster, he beat me right there in the store. Somebody, I don't remember who now, ran down to the mill and got Nate's father. Mr. Grayson stopped my pa but not before he'd blacked both my eyes and stripped my back with his strap. I can still hear my pa's voice as he laid that strap on me again and again. 'Girls don't need learning,' he said over and over.''

"What did Nate's father do?''

"Wasn't much he could do, my pa was my pa, he was the one raising me. Mr. Absalom did tell him that if it happened again he'd give him a citation and throw him in the Grove jail.''

"So did you give up learning?'' Vivid asked.

"Nope, I had too big of a hunger for it. Still do. The last time he beat me was when I asked him if I could take the examination for Oberlin. I was fifteen. He beat me so hard and long I could barely walk.''

"Did Mr. Grayson put him in jail?''

"Sure did. Didn't matter to me, though, because I packed what little belongings I had and took off up the road.''

"Where'd you go?''

"Fort Wayne, Indiana. Stole the money out of the store's till, had Nate drive me to Niles, and I bought a train ticket.''

"Did you have kin there?''

"Nope, just the address of a drummer who used to sell pa pots. I thought he was handsome in an oily sort of way. He told me once if I was ever up his way to be sure to stop in.''

"Was he a nice man?''

"In my fifteen-year-old naivete I thought he was. He took me to a boardinghouse, paid the landlady a month's rent, and told me not to worry. He bought me clothes and shoes and sometimes even let me accompany him on his drumming. I was in love.''

"It didn't turn out well, I take it?''

"No. He professed to love me, too, and so I let him take my chastity in the back of his wagon on a road outside Chicago. He promised to marry me."

"Did he?"

"No. I look back now and realize how stupid I was—"

"You were fifteen, Maddie."

"Yes, I was, and at fifteen when the man you love tells you we have no money and no place to stay, and would you please let this stranger make love to you just this once for a few dollars so we can eat..." She paused, then shrugged. "You do it. I loved him that much, or so I believed at the time."

"How long did you stay with him?"

"Six, seven months. When he asked me to do it a second time, I refused."

"Did he accept that?"

Maddie chuckled bitterly, "He threatened to kill me if I didn't. Said I owed him, it was the least I could do for all he'd done for me. So rather than have my throat slit, I became his whore. He took me to a hotel in downtown Chicago one night to meet a White gentleman who introduced himself as Mr. Pierce. I must say, the man found me quite fascinating. He'd never met a whore who could conduct an intelligent conversation on world affairs, literature, or history. He asked me if I would consider entering into a contract where I would entertain only him. I asked him if he'd ever hit a woman. He said no and I told him we had a deal."

After that night, Maddie never saw the drummer again. Mr. Pierce leased her a small house in the country and visited her at first only once or twice a week, but as the weeks turned into months and the months into three years, she saw him almost every day. He treated her royally, purchased books for her, fine clothing, jewelry. She had a servant to cook and one to clean. Then all of a sudden the visits stopped.

For a month and a half she heard nothing. The landlady said the lease hadn't been paid for the month and neither had the servants.

To deal with her debts, Maddie used some of her old contacts to sell some of her jewelry. She paid the servants their back wages and a small severance because they had to be let go. She used the rest of the funds to pay the lease, then made tentative arrangements to move and sell her other possessions. She was certain something had happened to her Mr. Pierce and he would not be coming back. Her suspicions were confirmed the next day when a carriage pulled up in front of her house and a beautiful woman stepped out.

"Who was she?" Vivid asked.

"His wife."

"Were you aware he was married?"

"I assumed he was, of course, but part of our agreement had been that I would not inquire about his life away from me, and I never did. He was kind to me. It was all I cared about."

"What did his wife want?"

"It was one of the oddest experiences of my life. She'd come to tell me Mr. Pierce had died in a boating accident. It seemed he'd left me fifteen thousand dollars in his will and she wanted to meet me."

"Fifteen thousand?"

"Yes."

"But isn't it odd for a woman to search out her husband's paramour?"

"I thought so, too, but she wanted to meet me to thank me."

"What on earth for?"

"For giving her husband an outlet for what she termed his 'bestial male urges.' She thanked me, handed me a satchel with the fifteen thousand dollars inside, and told me never to set foot in the state of Illinois again."

"So is that when you came back here?"

"No, did some traveling on the continent for a few months, entertained a few lords and a few crown princes, and then came home to Grayson Grove and opened a whorehouse."

"That must have set a few tongues wagging."

"It certainly did. My father was one of the first people to come pounding on the door, screaming about hell and damnation. I had my doorman escort him out. Made him absolutely furious. The biddies were next."

"The biddies?"

"Yes, the Widow Moss and her ring of busybodies. They were harassing my customers pretty fierce, night after night. So one evening when business was slow I turned my dogs on them. Never seen a bunch of old crones run so fast in all my life."

Vivid couldn't suppress the smile on her face. Maddie then asked, "So how are you and Nate getting along?"

Vivid paused a moment in an effort to figure out where this conversation migh be heading and replied, "Fine."

"Heard about you shooting his hat off his head."

"Seems as if everyone has."

"You know," Maddie said, looking Vivid straight in the eye, "Nate's the only man I've ever really loved."

Vivid didn't know what to say in response to that statement.

Maddie added, "By all rights I should resent you, but you've brought back the smile to his eyes, and that's good. I grew up with Nate and Eli. We hunted frogs together in the spring and built snow forts and played snow snake in the winter. We were so inseparable that during my ninth summer I cried for two days after Miss Abigail explained to me that it would be physically impossible for me to grow up and be a boy."

Vivid chuckled at how disappointed the nine-year-old Maddie must have been upon learning that news.

"But after the mess with Cecile and the war, he

changed. He lost his father, his wife. He'd never had to face that much tragedy and pain before. Glad to hear he's courting you.''

"Seems everyone has heard. Do you mind him courting me?'' Vivid asked.

"Of course I mind. I told you, he's the only man I've ever really loved, weren't you listening?'' Then her voice and face became serious, "But Nate doesn't love me, at least not in the way I'd prefer. He sees me as a sibling or a cousin. I'm glad he's found someone.''

"I haven't really said yes to him though.''

"I am just going to assume that you have a rational explanation.''

"I do.'' And Vivid explained the forces warring inside.

After Maddie heard Vivid's dilemma she said, "I agree, some men would demand you give up medicine. Not Nate. He isn't that way. Trust your heart, Viveca.''

A short while later, Vivid rid Maddie's front room of the clutter that accompanied the stitching and washed up her dishes, much to Maddie's ire.

"Maddie, you need to stay off that foot as much as possible, remember? I'll have the Quilt Ladies bring your meals for the next couple days and check on you.''

Maddie snorted. "The Quilt Ladies? They'd rather walk through town naked than visit the whore's house.''

"Oh, they'll come, and when they do, I want your promise that you won't sic the hounds on them.''

Silence.

Vivid leaned down. "Maddie?''

Vivid waited.

"Oh, all right, Viveca I'll promise, but only because I know they aren't going to come.''

"And the men are putting up an addition to my house. When it's done, and your foot is healed, I expect you to come have dinner.''

Maddie simply stared. "You're inviting me to your house for dinner?"

"Surely former whores eat."

Maddie laughed, then asked, "And if I refuse?"

"Expect to have your hat shot off, because I will come and get you and I will be packing a rifle."

Maddie shook her head and grinned. "No wonder Nate's in such a whirlwind. Are you always this way?"

"I have no idea what you mean."

"Humble also. I like you, Viveca Lancaster. Hate to admit it, but I do."

"I like you, too, Maddie. Shall we agree to be friends?"

Maddie nodded and said softly, "Yes."

Maddie slowly accompanied Vivid out onto the porch, and then whistled for the dogs. "You need to meet them so they won't try and take a plug out of you next time."

The hounds bounded up and met their mistress happily, licking her hands and cavorting until all five of the animals had been stroked. Maddie then held up one finger and they all sat and became watchful and attentive. "This is Dr. Viveca Lancaster," Maddie said.

The dogs turned and looked her over.

Maddie then spoke to Viveca. "Place your hand down by your side and curl your fingers up."

Vivid complied.

"Now, I want you to let each dog sniff the back of your hand. They'll remember you next time."

Vivid walked slowly among the animals and gave each her scent. She rubbed a few backs, stroked a few ears, and scratched a rib here and there. Since none of them snapped or growled she assumed she'd been accepted.

"Very good," Maddie told her pets. "Now go play," she added affectionately. They ran off.

"Well, Maddie, I'm real pleased to know you."

"Pleased to know you, too, Viveca."

"The Quilt Ladies should be by sometime tomorrow."

Maddie snorted.

"You'll see." And with a departing wave she drove away.

Chapter 16

Mr. Crowley was right. The work to finish her new home took exactly seven days.

On the evening it was finished, Vivid walked around her new kitchen and ran her hands over the smooth wood face of the beautiful cabinets Paul Crowley had built and installed. She walked into the bedroom and marveled at the colorful rag rugs the Quilt Ladies had sent as gifts and the emerald-green curtains Abigail had made for the window. The bed taking up most of one side of the room had come as a gift, too, from Mr. Crowley. He'd made the four-poster a few years ago hoping to give it to one of his sons as a wedding gift, but, he told Vivid, as the men moved the bed into her bedroom, that since it didn't appear any of them would be tying the knot anytime soon, she might as well have it.

Because the bed had been built to hold a Crowley, it was large. She took the opportunity to lie atop it for the first time; the comforting cushion of the feather mattress enveloped her. She lay there imagining Nate lying beside her and how it might be to have her babies here. She missed him. Last night she'd dreamed of them making love and she had awakened damp and pulsing. She wished he'd hurry home.

The next morning, Vivid went out to inspect the small box she'd erected down on the road at the end of the drive. She'd installed it so folks could drop off notes and pick up their medicine if she wasn't around. When

263

she found the box empty, she turned back and saw Magic coming her way carrying the chicken-wire cage housing Hector.

Hector was a baby bird Magic had recently found at the base of a tree in the heavily wooded area behind the Crowley place. Vivid remembered how Magic had come to her that day, running and shouting and cradling something in her hands.

"Dr. Lancaster, I found a baby bird!" she'd called with a mixture of elation and concern. "Pa says never take the babies from the nest but this one must've fallen out. I found it on the ground."

The tiny gray form had been just big enough to fill Magic's small palm. It reminded Vivid of Sara's dead child.

"Do you think it's going to live?"

Vivid wanted to express doubt, but Magic's face held such hope, Vivid didn't have the heart. "Do you know anything about raising baby birds?"

Magic shook her head sadly.

"Neither do I."

Nate's voice interrupted the discussion. "What do you have there, Majestic?"

Vivid gave a sigh of relief. As Magic's parent he would be better able to handle such delicate subjects as life and death.

"A baby bird, Pa, and I didn't take it from the nest. It was on the ground. Do you think it'll live if I feed it?"

Nate looked doubtful. "It needs its mother, Majestic."

"But it doesn't have one, Pa. I think I'm going to name it Hector."

"Magic, maybe you ought to wait to see if it will live before you give it a name," Vivid said.

"If I give it a name it will live."

Surprisingly, Hector made it through the first few

days. Vivid donated an old mortar and pestle to the cause and Magic used them to grind up worms and fish scraps. Judging by the size and shape of his beak, Nate determined Hector to be a type of hawk. Magic fed Hector from a small spoon and gave him water with a tiny dropper. Despite the grim expectations of the adults, Hector began to thrive. He had grown fat under Magic's care, and soft ivory and black speckled feathers were now covering the previously gray skin. The bigger he grew, the more demanding he became. Soon the ground worms were no longer sufficient, it seemed. The more Magic fed him the hungrier he seemed to be.

Vivid came back to the present as Magic held up the cage for Vivid to see, "I think he needs real worms, Dr. Lancaster. What do you think?"

Hector was now as fat as a small melon.

"You could be right, Magic. What would you suggest?"

"Well, we could hunt worms tonight after it gets dark. That's what Pa and me do sometimes before we go fishing. You ever hunt worms?"

"No, Magic, can't say as I have. But I'll help if you need me."

"Good," the nine-year-old said, smiling. "Of course, I'll have to check with Aunt Gail to make sure I can stay up late."

"Of course."

Abigail gave her permission, so that evening around dusk, Vivid and Magic began hauling buckets of water from the pump. Then Magic set about teaching Vivid how to hunt worms.

"First thing we have to do is get the ground sopping wet."

Following Magic's lead, Vivid poured the buckets of water into small areas of the vast grass in back of the Grayson house. It hadn't rained in over a week and the ground was very dry. Vivid slapped at the mosquitoes trying to make a meal out of her exposed neck and arms and began to have serious doubts about worm hunting.

When the last bucket had been emptied into the earth, Magic said, "Now we wait until the moon comes up."

The moon came up less than an hour later. Aided by its light and that of the two lanterns, Vivid and Magic returned to their soggy patch of ground.

"We have to be very quiet," Magic explained. "If the worms hear us they won't come out."

Too bad worms don't eat mosquitoes, Vivid thought testily as she swatted herself on the back of the neck.

"Shhh!" Magic cautioned harshly.

A contrite Vivid quieted as Magic whispered "Now watch, Dr. Lancaster."

Magic used her lantern to illuminate a small area of the grass. Any worm not fast enough to slip back into the earth was snatched up by her lightning-quick little brown hands and tossed into her earth-filled bucket. She would then move to a patch of fresh ground and repeat the process. All in all it appeared fairly simple to Vivid. Shine the light, grab a worm, and toss it into the bucket. In practice it proved to be a lot more difficult. Vivid's hands weren't fast enough. She'd see the worm and grab at it but kept coming away with nothing but wet grass and earth. It became very frustrating, especially watching Magic going about the task with such ease.

"It takes practice, Dr. Lancaster. Keep trying, you'll get it."

Vivid kept trying but she didn't get it. She felt as though she'd pulled up every blade of grass in the yard with nothing to show for her efforts. The lack of success coupled with the unrelenting attack of the blood-seeking mosquitoes had her ready to throw in the towel when Nate's voice, dark as the night, caressed her from behind. "Good evening, Lancaster."

She turned and found him standing only a few feet away. The silent forces between them washed over her with such power that for a moment she couldn't find voice to greet him.

"Hi, Pa," Magic said, popping up out of the dark.

Nate picked her up and spun her around until she was giggling with delight. "Hi yourself. Aunt Gail says you're hunting worms for Hector?"

Once again on her feet, Magic replied, "Yep. Pa, you should see how fat he's gotten. The ground-up worms don't fill him up anymore. I thought real worms might be what he needs. Dr. Lancaster's offered to help, but she's having a hard time getting the hang of it."

Vivid confessed truthfully, "I have to admit worm hunting is much more difficult than it looks."

"You ought to let Pa teach you, Dr. Lancaster," Magic suggested. "Pa is a champion worm hunter."

Vivid sought to nip that idea in the bud. "Magic, your father has just returned from a long trip. I'm sure he'd much prefer to go in and relax."

"Oh, I think I have enough strength still to teach you some things before I head off to bed," he remarked easily.

His words rippled through her.

"Good," Magic pronounced and slipped away to resume her hunt.

Vivid still found herself more than a bit tongue-tied. It didn't help matters when he said, "Seven days is a long time to be away from you, Lancaster."

Every inch of her body called out to him in longing.

"I dreamed of you," she confessed before she could catch herself.

"We'd better hunt worms. I'd hate to have my daughter come back and find us rolling in the grass. Follow me."

Under Nate's tutelage, Vivid had a modicum of success. He taught her the importance of patience. "Let the worm think he's in no danger, give him a moment to breathe, then pounce."

The strategy worked. A few minutes later, Vivid caught her first worm. As she crowed with delight, Nate ran to retrieve the bucket from his daughter. When he returned moments later, a very dejected and empty-handed Vivid faced him.

"What happened?" he asked.

"After all that work, I opened my hand and dropped the thing, and it got away."

Nate shook his head and chuckled, "That's a cardinal rule, Lancaster. Never open your hand. You want to try again?"

"Yes. I am not going inside until I get at least one."

And one was all she caught.

All in all, though, it was a successful hunt. Magic and Nate caught enough worms to keep Hector fed for at least a few days, or so they all hoped.

That night, Vivid took a short sponge bath, braided her hair, and slipped into a thin sleeveless gown. As much as she craved Nate's company, she knew not to set her heart on seeing him again until morning. He would probably put Magic to bed, then seek his own bed after the long, tiring drive home.

She walked through the cabin and doused the lights. The night breeze lifted the curtains and cooled the rooms. After the heat and near-stifling humidity of the past few days, the change felt wonderful.

She slipped outside just in time to hear the rumble of thunder far off in the distance. She looked up into the sky and saw fat dark clouds racing across the moon until they devoured it on another booming note. The trees were rustling softly in answer to the far-off storm, caressing the night with their sounds. Vivid could now appreciate Magic's fascination with storms; the air seemed charged, fresh, and vital, making one feel alive with the anticipation of what would come.

Nate's foot step on the porch was such a familiar sound that she didn't even have to turn to verify his presence with her eyes. She stood there, her back to him, and waited silently. The warmth of him singed her as he came behind her and eased his arms around her waist. His lips met the side of her neck as he pulled her back to fit himself more closely against her hips. She shivered in response to his kiss of welcome.

When she turned to greet him with a kiss of her own, he stayed her with a gentle squeeze of his hands on her waist and whispered thickly against her ear, "No, stay just as you are, I want to hold you like this for a little while . . ."

His lips traveled up the side of her throat while his hands slowly roamed her body. She arched in invitation to his hand as it began traveling brazenly over her thighs, her belly, then over the tight buds of her breasts, bringing with it heat, passion, and the sweet opening strains of desire.

Thunder boomed a bit closer and the wind picked up as he turned her and slowly undid the small ribbons on the bodice of her gown. He eased the halves aside, then flicked his tongue across one straining nipple, then the other.

"You're so beautiful . . ." he said softly.

Her head thrown back, Vivid shuddered as he feasted.

It became harder and harder for her to maintain her stance and he took sweet advantage. His hands and lips loved her everywhere. While he continued to pleasure her breasts, he lazily rubbed her loose-fitting gown over the sensitive flesh of her hips, raising it higher, inch by sensual inch until he bared her, thigh to waist. His hand traveled up and down her length, squeezing her possessively, circling her passionately as he gently suckled each nipple in turn. He rubbed gently at the damp warmth anchoring her dark thighs, then slid a caress over the citadel. She arched to the sensations, wanting to experience even more.

Nate gave her more. He leaned down and kissed her

a long moment, then eased away. While their eyes held, he picked her up into his arms and took her over to the swing.

She sat on his lap and he kissed her again, deeply. He teased her nipples until she arched her body. His big hand cupped her behind as he supported her, squeezing the flesh lovingly as he took his time to make sure her breasts would never call for any other man's devotions but his. He feasted as if she were made of chocolate. Her nipples were sweet and ripe as summer blueberries, her hips lush as blooms in May. He wanted her here and now, while the thunder echoed and the wind spoke loudly. He wanted to ease her back and ease himself into paradise.

"Will you come inside with me?" she whispered.

"If we go inside, I'll make love to you . . ."

His hands were so potent and filled her with such bliss, she couldn't speak, she could only brace herself against the strong cradle made by his arm and chest and let him work his magic. His touch on the point from which all her pleasure spread was luxurious, enticing, slow. She eased her legs apart, and he gifted her offering with such magnificence, she moaned and melted from the heat.

The periodic flashes of lightning offered Nate an erotic view of her taking pleasure from his touch. One flash revealed her nipples hard and beautiful as onyx, the next, the arch of her waist with its adorning navel. A particularly brilliant display followed and illuminated her in all her seminude glory as she rose to meet his hand. "You never answered my question, Viveca," he reminded her huskily. "Are you sure?" Nate was harder than he'd ever been before in his life. If she were not a virgin she'd be straddling his straining manhood right there and then.

Vivid, riding the waves of sensation managed to reply, "I'm sure."

"And you know what this means?"

"Yes," she whispered.

Nate's heart soared. "Then let's make you ready . . . Stand for me."

She didn't want to leave his embrace. She didn't want to leave the sweet ache he continued to cultivate so beautifully.

When she didn't comply, seemingly content with her pleasure, he chuckled. "Greedy little Dr. Princess, stand up . . . hold up your gown . . ."

Vivid didn't remember getting to her feet. One moment she'd been spiraling under his hands, and the next she was standing with him kneeling before her. "No screaming now," he whispered amusedly. She had just enough time to brace herself before the first lightning bolt slid across her shrine. Fired by her responsiveness, he eased his big hands up to her thighs to hold her steady, then gently brought her forward.

He pleasured her softly at first, letting the wantonness fill her until she trembled, then he slowly backed away. As she stood before him pulsing in anticipation, his hands returned to the swelling jewel and dabbled softly in concert with the hot, alternating licks of his tongue. The wind swirled around the porch and the lightning momentarily illuminated the intimate tableau against the night. But Vivid neither heard nor cared; his masterful mouth was too knowing, his touch too aware of all that made her woman. When he slid one long finger into her cove, she screamed her release in tandem with the boom of the thunder.

He carried her into the house, kissing her while following her directions to the new bedroom. He set her on the bed as the rains began outside and the wind whipped the curtains furiously. He undressed against the flashes of the storm and Vivid got her first leisurely look at a nude man. He was magnificent. The muscles gleamed darkly, the legs looked powerful, as did the rigid proof of his desire. "You're a well-made man, Nate Grayson . . ."

Nate let her look her fill, then said with a soft chuckle, "Virgins are supposed to cower and cry, princess, not stare greedily."

"Well, I'm new at this," she whispered, her voice sultry. "So while you're furthering my medical education, you'll have to apprise me of all these rules . . ."

Nate's manhood leaped at the saucy, heat-filled invitation. It took all the willpower he possessed not to tumble her back on the bed and apprise her immediately, but she'd never had a man before; he needed to go slow.

He didn't see how he'd ever manage it, however, as he joined her on the bed. Her dark skin was as soft as lilies, her mouth as vibrant as rain. She was born to bloom under his hands, and he was never going to let her go.

"Am I allowed to touch you?" she asked as his lips trailed fire along her throat and then the tempting curve of her shoulder. He cupped her breast then lifted it in offering as he lowered his mouth to feast. He then raised his head and kissed her lushly. "Touch has no rules . . ."

Vivid placed her hand around the object of her curiosity and felt the warmth pulsate against her palm. She slid her small hand up then down the satin shaft while marveling at how something so hard could feel so velvety soft. "Show me . . ." she coaxed quietly against his ear.

Nate covered her hand and intimately showed her the way. He was breathless less than halfway through the lesson, so breathless he had to still her hand and close his eyes to keep from exploding.

"Did I do something wrong?" she asked through the haze of desire. She could feel him throbbing like a heartbeat within the circle of her hand.

"No. Your hot little hands are making it hard to go slow is all."

"Then let's not go slow," she suggested lazily as she lifted her lips to his.

"Brazen woman . . ."

Nate eased her back on the bed, then spread kisses over her skin, paying slow, masterful attention to the two buds on her breasts and the tempting little one between her thighs. When he sensed her to be on the edge of her second release he coaxed open her thighs and partially eased his way into her warmth. She was tight, so tight he had to halt his penetration and let the sensations level for a moment to keep from lustily thrusting his way home. He was a big man; he didn't want to cause her injury, nor did he want this interlude to be something she looked back on with fear or regret. "This may hurt a bit," he confessed, "but only this once . . ."

It did hurt, but just long enough for the pain to register, then it slowly faded into pleasure as he began the age-old dance of man loving woman. Vivid had no idea how she was supposed to respond, so she gave herself up to his tutoring hands and the magic rhythm spreading through her thighs. As the intensity increased, so did his stroking. He teased her intimately, coaxed her brazenly. He gave her the strength of all he had to offer until she could take no more. The release slammed into her with the force of a thunderclap. Every cell in her body caught fire as she rode the wave of the buffeting storm.

Nate could no longer keep himself in check. Watching her arching so deliciously pushed him into his own release. He gripped her hips as the tension climbed, then growled loudly as the world exploded into a brilliant light.

Later, they lay side by side in the darkness listening to the night. The storm had passed on and only faint rumbles of thunder could be heard in the distance. Vivid said softly, "I guess we're doing something more than courting now."

"I think you're right." He chuckled. He turned on his

side and raised himself on an elbow to face her. "Is that so bad?"

"No, Nate, it isn't."

Her reward was a soft kiss.

Nate drew back and asked, "What made you change your mind?" Then, like a self-satisfied male, added, "as if I didn't already know the answer."

"You need to be more humble, Nathaniel Grayson, you really do."

Nate kissed her until the embers of their last encounter slowly glowed to life once again. "Thunder Gods aren't supposed to be humble," he informed her, grazing her nipple with his finger. "Besides, it's hard to be humble when all I have to do is this, to know how much you appreciate me." He lowered his mouth and suckled her until her hips rose and a moan of pleasure slid from her throat.

"See?" he whispered hotly.

He gave her a nibble, then raised his head. "Now, you were saying?"

His attentions had her body in such an uproar, she forgot for a moment what she'd been about to say. "I was saying that your lovemaking played a role, but talking with Maddie made me come to a decision."

"You talked with Maddie? When?"

Vivid explained the circumstances surrounding their meeting.

When she paused in the telling, he asked, "Is she going to be okay? Is she recovered?"

"Yes. The Quilt Ladies helped by bringing her meals and checking on her until she got back on her feet."

He stared, confused. "Why in the world would the Quilt Ladies want to help Maddie after all these years of sniping at her?"

"Because I asked them to."

Nate didn't understand this. The Quilt Ladies had been a thorn in Maddie's side ever since she'd returned.

Even after she sold the Emporium and retired to her books and her beloved dogs, they never let her forget she'd been a whore. To this day the Widow Moss still crossed the street if she encountered Maddie in town. It took the reverend's fiery sermon on forgiveness and being Christian to make the old biddies stop hissing at her whenever Maddie attended church. So he didn't understand their newfound generosity at all. "What did you threaten them with?"

"I told them I'd tell their husbands about the poker games they hold once a week."

"The Quilt Ladies play poker?"

"Every Wednesday night down in Miss Edna's storeroom."

Nate didn't believe this. "How'd you find out?"

"Miss Edna invited me to play, and Nate, if you tell a soul, I will never speak to you again."

"Never is a long time, Dr. Princess. Besides, give me a few moments alone with these dark jewels," he said as he ran his hands over her nipples, "and you'll speak to me. I promise."

Vivid didn't speak at all for the next few moments, she was too busy catching fire.

Nate leaned over and kissed her mouth. "Oh, by the way, so there'll be no misunderstandings, Lancaster, I will be marrying you."

"Oh, really?" she replied, smiling up at him with inner delight.

"Yes, really."

"And suppose I don't care to be Mrs. Nathaniel Grayson?"

"Then I suppose I'll have to spend the rest of the night trying to change your mind."

By the time Nate finished changing Vivid's mind, the sun was rising.

Chapter 17

A̲t church the following Sunday the congregation greeted Nate's announcement of their upcoming marriage with applause and shouts of congratulations. Vivid stood shyly as the reverend gave them both his blessing. She looked over at Magic, who had a grin on her small face the size of Lake Michigan, then Abigail, who had joyous tears in her eyes. Mr. Crowley, not to be upstaged, made his own announcement, an announcement Nate was still chuckling over as they rode home.

He told his aunt sitting beside Vivid, "Aunt Gail, I don't know why you're so mad. It's about time you and Adam had your arguments under the same roof."

"How dare he tell everyone we're courting," Abigail said. "He's one of the most bullheaded, stubborn, and opinionated people on this earth."

"And you're not?" Nate asked.

"That's beside the point. I don't want to be courted by Adam Crowley."

Vivid simply shook her head and smiled as the landscape rolled slowly by.

Vivid spent the month of July trying to escape the miserable humidity, swatting at mosquitoes the size of small birds, and working herself to the bone. Her practice area had widened now that word had gotten around about her skills and good nature, making for many more nights away from home. The Michigan Central Railroad had asked her to doctor their Black porters and cooks

276

and some lumber camps offered her a stipend to treat their injured Black employees.

All in all, she was very busy.

And she didn't see much of Nate, either. He was traveling around the area reporting to the members of the Committee on the meeting he'd attended in Indianapolis. The Committee, or Council as it was called in some places, had been formed by a group of Black veterans after Mr. Lincoln's war. They encouraged Blacks to vote, formed Republican clubs, and ensured that Blacks, especially those newly freed in the South, were not cheated in business transactions or in the courts. However, for the last few years Committee members had been secretly gathering information on the Blacks in the South, and as Nate reported at the Grove's last town meeting, the situation looked hopeless. Many Black men had been killed trying to vote in the South in 1874, and this fall's election promised to be even bloodier. In Mississippi and Louisiana, whole parishes and counties reported no Black men alive over the age of eighteen. Those men fortunate enough to escape the Redemptionist wrath of the White Leagues fled their homes for safer climes, many times leaving their distraught families behind and taking with them nothing more than the clothes on their backs. Because of the rampant violence, some Blacks were calling for migration to Liberia and other parts of Africa. Nate told his neighbors about a man by the name of Henry Adams and a Tennessee man named Benjamin "Pap" Singleton, who were trying to organize a movement out of the South and into the Western territories of Kansas and Nebraska. The so-called representative Negroes like Frederick Douglass were sitting on the fence on the migration issue.

Vivid knew that Nate had to speak with many people before he could come home. But she hoped he would hurry back.

The stove Vivid had ordered through Miss Edna finally arrived. To celebrate, she invited Maddie and Eli to dinner. Nate had been gone two weeks now, and Vivid hoped the company would take her mind off how much she missed him. The dinner went as well as she'd hoped. Vivid loved hearing their stories about how they grew up together.

Eli asked Maddie, "Remember the time Nate and Vincent Red Bird had you convinced you could fly?"

"You would have to bring that up," Maddie replied, but she couldn't suppress her smile. "One of the dumbest things I ever did in my life." Maddie turned to Vivid. "Nate and Vincent claimed to have seen an eagle spirit on the way to school one day and they said the spirit gave them the power of flight."

"And you believed them?"

"I was eight years old, Viveca. The boys were my idols. I believed everything they told me."

Eli laughed. "Nate and Vincent lit a fire and did a ceremonial dance. They fanned smoke on her and told her to start climbing. Nobody really believed she'd be half-brained enough to jump, but she did."

"Broke my arm."

"Oh, no," Vivid cried.

"Oh, yes."

"Don't feel too sorry for her. She got her revenge a few days later," he offered wryly. "When Uncle Absalom found out about Maddie's arm, Nate and I got the worst whipping of our lives for that prank. We couldn't sit for a month."

After the meal, Vivid cleared the table of the dinner dishes and brought out the cobbler she'd made for dessert. At her suggestion they all took their plates out to the back porch where it was much cooler. As they ate, Eli regaled them with what he planned to see on his visit to the Philadelphia Centennial exposition. Ten million people were expected to attend and he would see everything from electric-powered lights, to something called linoleum that was supposed to cover floors. He told them about the wondrous telephone that would be in one of the thousands of displays and the animated wax rendering of Cleopatra. Blacks had been barred from the Centennial's construction gangs and for the most part excluded from the displays. Still, the noted Black painter Edward Bannister won a Centennial prize for his painting *Under the Oaks*, and Mary Lewis Montgomery of the Montgomery family of Davis Bend, Mississippi, won the agricultural award for the world's best cotton, just as she'd done at the St. Louis Fair in 1870.

Vivid walked her guests out to Maddie's wagon at the end of the evening's visit, buoyed by their talk and companionship.

"So," Maddie asked as she picked up the reins, "when's the wedding?"

"I'll know as soon as I receive a letter from my parents letting me know when they can come out. I want them to be here."

"Nate could do a whole lot worse," Maddie said. "I'm happy for you both."

Eli chuckled. "Stop lying, Maddie, you've been in love with Nate since you were nine. You're hoping she gets run over by a train."

Maddie laughed. "He's right, you know. I hate losing, but if I have to lose, I prefer it be to a woman like you, Viveca."

"Thanks, Maddie."

"You're welcome."

She drove off with a wave and left Vivid and Eli standing in the road.

When Vivid awakened the next morning, she and the bed were covered with daisies and black-eyed susans. *Nate!* Jumping from the bed, she washed up, threw on her clothes, and flew out the door.

"Where is he?" Vivid asked breathlessly after entering the Grayson kitchen like a whirlwind.

Abigail laughed. "You're as bad as Majestic. They're out front."

Vivid hurried through the house to the front door. She could see him in the front yard with Magic, but rather than run pell-mell outside, she waited until he was finished talking with his daughter. Magic had missed her pa probably as much as, if not more than, Vivid and she didn't dare interrupt their reunion.

Instead, Vivid feasted her eyes on her husband-to-be. He was as magnificently handsome as ever. The broad shoulders and the trim waist evoked memories of how his muscles felt beneath her hands. He was strong enough to be a gentle man not only in lovemaking but in spirit, too, as evidenced by his relationship with his daughter.

Nate looked up and saw her standing in the doorway, her smile warmed him. He'd gotten back as soon as he could, but it hadn't been quick enough. He missed her with each passing day, wondering what she might be doing and if she was staying out of trouble. There'd be no more wondering now; he was home and her smile beamed only for him.

He spent a few more moments with his daughter, then as Magic went off to show Jeremiah the new slingshot her father had brought back from Kalamazoo, he stepped onto the porch.

"So how are you," he said softly, "besides being in need of a good loving?"

"Nate Grayson!" Vivid replied with a scandalized laugh. She glanced around to make sure he hadn't been overheard by Abigail in the house. "I must find you some humble pills immediately."

"Lancaster, I haven't kissed you in over two weeks. You're as hungry for me as I am for you."

"Very large humble pills," Vivid told him, feeling all

her senses come alive as she looked into his eyes.

"Very large desire," he countered.

Vivid had never played such verbal games with a man before. His frankness sometimes brought heat to her cheeks, but she found the back-and-forth quite stimulating.

He reached out and slowly ran a finger over her mouth, then kissed her with a welcome that made her wish they were in a more secluded place. The reunion was interrupted when Adam Crowley rode up. He greeted them both, then asked if Abigail was home.

Nate and Vivid both nodded, though their eyes were still locked on each other's.

He went in, bellowing Abigail's name.

Nate returned to kissing his wife-to-be, but the argument raging inside the house between Abigail and Adam kept getting louder and louder. "I should probably go in and make sure they aren't killing each other."

Vivid, nibbling his lip, agreed.

He slid his hand over her hips and squeezed her tight, then backed away. "Come on, we'll settle them down, then I'll settle you down . . ."

Inside they found Adam standing in Abigail's study. Abigail had her lips pursed angrily as she sat at her desk with her back to him. The argument involved a book Adam had purchased for Abigail, but he refused to let her see its title or to relinquish it to her hands until Abigail had dinner with him. In the weeks since he'd announced his intentions at the church he'd turned Abigail's usually calm days into spirited chaos. When they weren't arguing over historical questions, he was gifting her with flowers, newspapers, and last week had rendered her speechless by presenting her with a beautifully carved cane. Vivid had been in the kitchen when he'd given her the dark wood stick and listened as he said, "You're going to marry me, Gail. Me, Adam Crowley, like you were supposed to have done thirty-five years ago.''

Today, however, Abigail had not been rendered speechless though Vivid could see her eyes coveting the book in Adam's hand. ''It's a first edition, Abigail,'' he told her. ''You've been wanting to add it to your library for a long time.''

When Nate asked to see the tome, Adam handed it over gladly. Nate looked at the title and said, ''Aunt Gail, I think you'd better tell him yes.''

He showed the title page to Vivid and she smiled; even she knew how valuable Abigail considered this book. On the trip to Detroit she and Abigail had searched high and low for this particular volume but had never found it. ''Nate's right, Abigail.''

In the face of that, Abigail surrendered. ''Okay, Adam Crowley, dinner it will be.''

He handed her the book. They all watched her eyes widen with astonishment as she read the title, then began to slowly turn the pages.

''Yes, Abigail,'' Adam said. ''William Welles Brown's *The Blackman: His Antecedents, His Genius and His Achievements.*''

''Where did you find this, Adam?'' she asked in wonder.

''Boston. I've had a friend there keeping an eye out for it.''

''This is truly a first edition?''

''It says right there, 1863,'' he told her.

From the smile shining in Abigail's eyes, Vivid didn't think it would be long before Mr. Crowley won the Battle of Abigail.

Nate and Vivid slipped away now that the fireworks had been extinguished.

''Where are we going?'' Vivid asked as he pulled her along behind him across the yard.

''Someplace where there's privacy.''

Before Vivid could question him further, a wagon raced up and Sara James jumped down and ran across the yard screaming for Vivid.

Vivid ran to her. "Sara, what's wrong?"

"Oh, Dr. Lancaster, you must come quick. He's trying to kill little Quentin!"

The panic and horror on Sara's face appeared very real. "Who's trying to kill Quentin?" Vivid asked.

"Dr. Hayes! Come with me, please!" Sara begged, then clamped a strong hand on Vivid's wrist and began to pull her toward the wagon.

"Sara, wait, I need to get my bag."

"We don't have time! Oh, God!" She dropped Vivid's hand and ran back to the wagon.

Vivid didn't hesitate, she ran to the cabin to retrieve her bag and heard Nate call, "I'm coming, too, meet me at the wagon."

It took Nate nearly twenty minutes to get them to their destination. On the way, Sara explained that her husband, Quentin, had returned about a week ago. When little Quentin became sick overnight, her husband had fetched the circuit doctor.

Sara did not wait for the horses to stop before she jumped down and ran to the small whitewashed cabin set a ways back from the road. Nate tied up the buggy while Vivid hurried after Sara.

Inside the cabin a bed was positioned in the room's center. Around the bed were two men. Sara's pock-faced husband looked up at their entrance, as did a white-haired man who appeared to be centuries old.

"What the hell you bring her here for?" Quentin asked his wife.

Sara snapped back, "I'm not going to let him kill little Quentin. I want Dr. Lancaster to take a look."

The older man standing beside the bed looked Vivid up and down but said nothing to her. Instead he spoke to Nate. "How are you, Nate?"

"I'm fine. Dr. Hayes, this is Dr. Lancaster. Lancaster, Dr. Wadsworth Hayes."

"Pleased to meet you, Dr. Hayes," Vivid said.

"I'm not so fortunate. I don't like women around when I'm treating a patient," he stated.

Vivid was taken aback by his attack. She gave Nate a questioning look and he shrugged in response.

Vivid tried again. "Dr. Hayes, may I ask what the child is suffering from?"

"No, you may not, little girl. Go away."

Vivid looked at Quentin the elder, who sneered triumphantly, then at Sara, whose fear was still plainly etched across her face. Vivid had had enough of being polite. She walked over to the bed. Leeches were all over the little boy's face and arms. Horrified, she pushed her way to his side and began pulling them off. "Nate! Help me!" she screamed. The angry mouths of the suckers tore away small patches of skin as Vivid flung them away.

The room erupted into chaos, shouts, and curses as Hayes and Sara's husband sought to restrain Vivid, but she fought them angrily, determined to rid the child of the leeches that were certainly killing him.

"Get her out of here, Grayson!" Quentin yelled, trying to stay Vivid's hands. "This is my son, and I don't want her near him!"

"Nooo!" Sara cried. She ran to the bedside and began snatching the leeches from her son's face and arms. Her husband cuffed her sharply with the back of his hand and she recoiled, sobbing.

Wadsworth Hayes fought to hold back the still defiant Vivid and barked breathlessly, "Grayson, remove this woman or I'll have her arrested. Then I'll make damned sure she never practices medicine in this state again!" Nate grabbed Vivid around her small waist and lifted her from the fray. She screamed her outrage, cursing him with every fiber of her being as he carried her outside.

Three days later, Vivid's greatest fear came true. Sara lost her last living child. Hayes had been unable to stop the bleeding once it began. Vivid had seen similar incidents in the wards back in Philadelphia. Sara's little boy had bled to death.

The day of the funeral, Vivid was having a difficult time summoning the strength to attend. She knew Sara would be overwhelmed with grief and might benefit from her presence, but Vivid felt as if she, too, had lost a child, not to death but to ignorance. In the end, though, she did attend and stood in line with all the other people of the Grove who'd come to pay Sara their respects. Her husband Quentin had reportedly left town.

After the burial ceremony, as the carriages and buggies filed sedately out of the graveyard, Vivid found herself unable to leave the gravesite. Unshed tears choked her throat and tightened her breath, but she could not cry. She was too angry, she realized. Angry at Hayes, angry at Nate, angry at the pock-faced Quentin, but most of all angry at herself for not being more forceful in keeping that butcher from the child. She was distracted for a moment by the appearance of the men who'd come to fill in the grave. When she asked if she could assist them, the reverend who'd conducted the service gave her a searching look, then silently handed her a shovel. She dug in beside the men and began to toss gentle shovels of rich Michigan earth down onto the small wooden box resting at the bottom of the hole.

By the time the grave was a quarter filled, Vivid had tears streaming down her face. She saw the reverend glance her way, concern on his face, but Vivid kept up her rhythm, determined to at least help bury the child she'd been unable to help live.

The unchecked tears began to blur her vision, so much so that she didn't notice Nate come up behind her until his hand gently stayed her shovel's movement. Vivid looked into his sad eyes and saw pain as deep as her own. He intimated his desire to bear the burden for her, but she shook him off, saying sadly, ''No, I must do this,'' and went back to her heartbreaking task.

The only sounds in the graveyard were those of the shovels biting into the earth, and the soft flicks of the earth as it landed. When Nate reappeared a moment later, shovel in hand, he took up a position at her side and added another voice to the mournful rhythm.

On the ride home from the graveyard, Nate glanced over at her sitting so silently on the seat beside him. She hadn't spoken a word so far, and it worried him to see the redness in her eyes and the weary slump in her shoulders.

''When was the last time you got a full night's sleep, Lancaster?'' he asked gently.

''Weeks, days ago, I've lost count.''

''You need to rest, you won't be any good to your patients if you're sick.''

''Today proves I'm not any good to my patients, sick or well.''

''There was nothing you could do.''

''I could've done something to keep that boy from being bled to death.''

''Quit blaming yourself. You did everything in your power.''

''Some power—I had the power to curse and scream and that was all. Maybe it wouldn't hurt so much if the child had died of an illness, something I couldn't cure, but he died from ignorance, Nate, pure ignorance.''

''It won't happen again.''

''Yes, it will. Ignorance is the hardest thing to cure.''

''No, it won't. At least not here in the Grove.''

''Why not?''

''Because we have a fancy new city doctor named Viveca Lancaster.''

Vivid turned to him and looked into his eyes. ''What are you saying?'' she asked.

"That I want you to have the position on a permanent basis, starting now."

"Why now, why today?"

"Because you're every bit the doctor you say you are, Lancaster, and I refuse to let Wadsworth Hayes near any of our people again."

His eyes were serious behind the spectacles. She noted that he'd said "our" people as if she was a member of the community, too. Had the last few days not been so filled with tragedy, she might have been more joyous with his decision.

"I'm sorry it took the death of a child to bring this about."

"So am I, Nate," she whispered in reply. "So am I."

They rode the rest of the way in silence. When they reached home, he halted the team in front of her box and waited while she hopped down and searched inside. There were no urgent pleas from sick neighbors, so Vivid climbed back in the buggy and Nate drove them to her door.

"Are you going to be all right alone?" he asked as she turned to leave the seat.

"I believe so. There's still a few hours of daylight left, I think I'll eat and then read a bit. Maybe write my family." The last couple of nights her dreams had been filled with gaping leeches and skeletal old men. She hoped she was tired enough to sleep dreamlessly tonight.

"Come up to the house and eat," he offered. She shook her head no. "I'll be fine here."

He searched her eyes for a long moment, then nodded.

She jumped down and went inside the cabin.

The next morning, Vivid awakened to find Magic tiptoeing around inside the bedroom with a tray of covered dishes in her hands.

"What are you doing, young lady?" Vivid asked sleepily, sitting up.

"Aunt Gail thought you might like something you

didn't have to cook yourself when you woke up.''

Vivid noted for the first time how hot the cabin seemed. There was no breeze this morning, in fact, the heat inside felt like mid-afternoon.

"What time is it?''

"Past noon.''

"What?''

Vivid jumped from bed, ran to her dresser, and picked up her locket timepiece. The small heart-shaped pendant affirmed Magic's words. It was two hours past noon.

"Pa said we were to let you sleep," Magic explained. "He said I'd be in big trouble if me or Hector woke you up. Will you tell him you woke up on your own?''

"Yes, Magic, I will. Where's your father now?''

"Sitting down at the road with a shotgun.''

"Why on earth for?''

"Keep folks from bothering you.''

"People are supposed to bother me, I'm a doctor.''

"Pa says if they're not dying they can come back tomorrow. Says you need to rest.''

Vivid shook her head. She had to speak with that man.

"Are you going to eat now?''

"After I wash up and speak with your father, I will.''

"Well, I'll go tell Aunt Gail you're up and about. Do you need me for any chores?''

"No, dear.''

"Then me and Hector are going hunting over at Mr. Crowley's.''

"Have a good time and be careful," Vivid called as Magic stepped out onto the porch.

Alone again, Vivid pondered the information about Nate and his shotgun as she peeled back the large napkin covering her food. A small stack of flapjacks running with butter tempted her eyes and appetite. She felt as if she hadn't eaten in days. She ran to wash up. Nate would have to wait.

The meal finished, Vivid took the dishes back to the

house and strolled out to the road. Sure enough, there sat Nate, back against a tree, newspaper in hand. The rifle lay across his thighs.

"What is this I hear about you scaring off my patients?" Vivid asked.

Nate looked up at her and gave her a smile that brightened an otherwise overcast day. "Afternoon, Dr. Lazybones."

His voice was a caress.

"Magic told me what you're doing. You really don't need to be out here, you know."

He shook the paper and folded it. "It's my property, I can sit where I want." He stood then and asked, "How do you feel?"

She knew it would be a while before she could rid herself of yesterday's sad event. "I'm rested."

Nate didn't press. He knew he could not bear her pain for her. He also knew she would not be down for long. "Want to go berry picking with me today?"

"Berry picking? Sure."

"You know, I'm still waiting."

"For what?"

"To be greeted properly."

She smiled, remembering that they had been seeking some privacy when Sara James rode up a few days ago.

"Do you want to be properly welcomed while we're berry picking?" she asked with sparkling eyes.

"Maybe."

Vivid's sadness retreated under the effects of his smile and the heat burning in his gaze. "Do I need to bring anything?"

"Nope. Just let me go tell Aunt Gail and we'll be off."

"Is Magic coming along?"

"Not this time. Adam promised to keep an eye on her."

They were off less than an hour later.

When they were a bit up the road, Vivid questioned the pile of items he'd loaded into the back of the wagon: lanterns, bedrolls, tarps, fishing poles. "Do we need all this for berry hunting?"

"Where I like to berry hunt, yes, we do."

"And where might that be?"

"Oh, about a day's drive from here."

Vivid's eyes widened in surprise. "A day's drive?"

"Yep. I told Aunt Gail we'd be back in about three days."

"Nate, I can't possibly be gone for three days."

He simply smiled and said, "By the time I'm done berry picking with you, Lancaster, you're not going to care."

"Such a humble man." She laughed, but the implications had her all a-quiver.

They drove until past dark. He seemed to know where he was headed, however, so Vivid didn't worry. The lantern attached to the wagon's side lit the way for the horses, as did the added light of the glowing moon.

"What happened to Eli's father?" Vivid asked after they'd spent a few moments chuckling over Adam Crowley and the Battle of Abigail.

"Left her before Eli was born. The story goes that he was already married to a woman up in Muskegon at the time."

"That's terrible."

"I know. Aunt Gail thought he really loved her."

"He just up and left?"

"Miss Edna said he was after Aunt Gail's land. At the time she and my pa owned the Grove in equal shares, but according to my grandfather's will, none of the land could be sold without the approval of both."

"And your father wouldn't agree?"

"No. Evidently my father didn't like the man at all. He claimed to be an Oxford-educated scholar. Miss Edna said he was an overbearing windbag who thought the world revolved around his every word.''

"So where did Mr. Crowley fit into the picture?''

"When the good Lord gave out pride, Adam was at the front of the line. The day Abigail married Eli's pa, Adam married Abigail's best friend, Meggie. Abigail moved to Detroit, then came back after the man left her.''

"If Adam loved Abigail so much, why did he let her marry another man?''

"When the so-called Oxford scholar came into Aunt Gail's life, I don't believe Adam seriously considered him a threat. I think Adam just assumed he and Aunt Gail would marry. After all, they'd known each other all their lives. He and my pa were best friends.''

"So now here they are over thirty years later, trying to sort it all out.''

"Yep. A lot of wasted years in between.''

Vivid thought so, too, and was glad she and Nate were on their way to spending the rest of their lives together. She didn't want to squander any of the time they'd been alloted by the fates.

Nate turned the horses off the main road and onto a narrow track that led back into the trees. "Almost there,'' he said.

"There'' turned out to be a small cabin standing alone in the darkness.

Inside, Nate set the lantern on the mantel over the stone fireplace while Vivid looked around. The place was smaller than her cabin back home. It had only one room, but it was clean and dry. A big bed against the wall, a small eating table, and two chairs were the only furnishings.

Vivid went back out into the night to help him bring in the gear from the wagon. Afterward, she dug into the big hamper of food for some dinner, while Nate saw to bedding down the animals. When he returned, they made a meal of smoked salmon and bread and a can of put-up pears.

"What is this place?" Vivid asked.

"Pa and Aunt Gail's old hunting cabin. Eli and I began using it once we became old enough to go hunting by ourselves. He must still be coming up here because the place is clean. I haven't been here in years."

"Are there really berries around here?" she asked, eyeing him skeptically.

Nate shrugged, saying, "Somewhere probably."

"People are going to talk, you know, if they find out we're here together."

"No, they won't, because you're in Kalamazoo attending a lecture and I'm in Battle Creek seeing my lawyer, or that's what Abigail will tell anyone who asks."

"Nate, what if someone needs me?"

"If it's serious enough, Abigail knows to send Adam. Until then the only person needing your care right this minute is me . . ."

Vivid smiled shyly. He had taken care of everything, it seemed, even bringing along changes of clothing. For the first time in weeks she could look forward to a few days of rest and peace. Vivid came over to where he sat on the other side of the small table and eased onto his lap. "I'm all yours . . ." she whispered softly, kissing his lips. "All yours."

She placed her head on his strong chest, closed her eyes, and promptly fell asleep.

As she'd done on the previous morning, Vivid slept into the afternoon. Nate knew she needed the rest, so he let her sleep.

When Vivid awakened, she sat up groggily and peered at her surroundings. The unfamiliarity of the room vanished as she saw Nate standing over the table seasoning a mess of fish. "You're just in time for lunch, madam."

"I fell asleep on you again, didn't I?"

"That's okay, princess. You're here to rest, remember. Besides, that just means I can keep you up till sunrise."

Vivid felt the heat burn her face and smiled.

Nate cooked the fish in a pan over a fire outside. As Vivid ate her lunch of fish and potatoes, she marveled at the beauty around them. They were on the bank of a small, clear-running river. Stately pines grew thickly around the little clearing. The blue sky overhead only added to nature's canvas. "This is a beautiful place," Vivid remarked.

"Yes, it is. It originally belonged to a Napowesipe friend of my grandfather's. When the government forced them off the land, he sold it to my grandfather rather than let the government take it. My grandfather pledged that if any of his friend's family should ever return, the land will revert to them."

"Your grandfather must have been an honorable man."

"My grandfather was taken from the mother continent as a young man. He knew what it meant to have one's life stolen."

After the meal they went berry hunting.

"You actually brought buckets?" Vivid questioned laughingly as he handed her one.

"Yes, I did."

"Well lead the way."

They had a perfect day. Nate pointed out areas that held memories, like the deserted sawmill downstream where he, Eli, and Maddie played when they were young. He also showed her the remnants of a large fire ring once used by the People before their forced removal. "My grandfather would bring Eli and me here at night sometimes. We were very young. He'd build a fire in the ring, then sit us down beside it. He'd remove his clothes and dance the dances he'd done before captivity. For hours he would dance under the moon, singing in a tongue we didn't know. 'Dancing for the ancestors' he called it. He told us that as long as we remembered, and our children remembered, the spirits of all who'd come before would remain alive.''

They continued their walk along the riverbank, holding hands and enjoying the solitude and sunshine. When Nate challenged her to a race, Vivid cheated and ran off early. He caught up to her in just a few strides, swooped her up into his arms, and ran with her screaming and laughing the rest of the way. ''You little cheat,'' he said, grinning, as they reached the tree designated as the goal. He playfully swung her around until she howled for mercy.

Winded and laughing, Nate slid down the base of the tree until he hit the ground with her on his lap. ''Such a cheat . . .''

Their smiling eyes held and the passion they'd both been suppressing for weeks bloomed to life. He leaned over and kissed her gently at first, as if he wanted to reacquaint himself with the softness and shape of her lips. Sweet short kisses made her hungry for a longer, fuller taste of him. Brief whispering kisses set her desire flowing and sent her hands up the strength of his back. In the end he pulled her closer and gave her the long full kiss she desired.

''We're supposed to be looking for berries,'' she told him in a voice made soft by emotion.

''In a moment,'' he replied, savoring the honey of her mouth. He brought his hand up to caress her spine and waist, reveling in the feel of her slim form pressed against him so languidly. He cupped her breast and rubbed his thumb over her nipple until it berried up sweet and ripe. ''Now, let's go,'' he whispered against her lips.

Vivid let him take her hand and pull her to her feet. She pulsed with the haze of desire as he led her deeper into the forest.

They never did find any berries, but Vivid found herself braced against a tree with her shirt open to her waist while Nate lustily picked the variety of berry he enjoyed best. She had her head thrown back as he loved her within the shelter of the pine forest. She could only moan as he slid her skirt to her waist and slowly dragged her drawers down and off. He then knelt to boldly sample a smaller berry he found just as sweet.

The walk back to the cabin took some time because they kept stopping to exchange lingering kisses and caresses. Vivid's body was kiss-swollen everywhere, and Nate was so hard his manhood screamed for release.

Once in the cabin, he laid her on the bed and quickly undressed as she did the same. He set his spectacles on the table and joined her. Neither wanted any more preliminaries, so Nate filled her slowly and completely. The panaroma of pleasure that played across her face as she welcomed him sent his passion higher. He began to coax her with the rhythm of love, watching her arch, listening to her soft intakes of breath. He slid his hands over her hips, then gripped them so she could better receive his stroking, and she took all he had to offer.

Neither of them could take the intensity for long. Nate stiffened first, and was followed into the arms of release by a twisting, breathless Vivid.

As Nate had promised, they made love until dawn.

Rain kept them indoors for the second day, but Nate found a novel way to pass the time. After a late morning meal of coffee, fried ham, and potatoes, he picked up a canvas bag that lay in the corner with the other supplies and placed it atop the table. As he rummaged inside, he told her casually, "I need you to get undressed."

Vivid smiled suggestively.

"Not for that, greedy girl. I want to sketch you."

She gave him a surprised smile. She remembered Abigail mentioning Nate's artistic endeavors, but nude? "You want me nude?"

"Completely." He placed a sketchbook and pencils

and charcoal on the table, then looked over at her. "If it embarrasses you, I won't insist."

"Will anyone see it besides you or me?"

"No."

Vivid began to undress.

"Here, look at these." He handed her another sketch-book.

Vivid took the pad from his hand and sat down. On the pages were sketches of a reclining nude woman. Vivid was so taken by his outstanding talent, she'd looked at four or five of the sketches before she realized she was the subject.

"Nate, these are outstanding, but I never posed for . . ." she said with soft wonder as she continued to look through the drawings. He'd drawn every line, muscle, and sinew to perfection.

"Thank you. I hesitated showing them to you because I didn't want you to be offended."

"Well, some of these are very . . ." Vivid searched for a word that would describe the sensual nature of his sketches.

"Vivid?" he supplied.

A few were very vivid indeed. One in particular had her seated with her back to the artist as she looked over her shoulder at him. The heat rendered in her gaze was all too familiar. The line of her back and the curves of her shoulder and hips were drawn lushly. Another sketch had her lying wantonly nude on the porch swing, her head thrown back in rapture.

Vivid set the pad aside and looked into his eyes. She was speechless.

He broke the silence. "Well, will you pose for me?"

Vivid smiled and finished undressing.

While the rain poured down outside, Nate sketched Vivid as she lay atop the cot.

"When did you first start sketching?" Vivid asked.

"I must've been around ten or eleven. I started because I was jealous of Paul Crowley."

"Really? Why?"

"Because he could draw deer and I couldn't. You probably saw some of his pictures on the walls when you went to treat Jewel."

She did remember seeing them. The walls had held many framed paintings of animals.

"Well, I wanted to draw deer like Paul. Big, lifelike stags with large racks and powerful legs. I told myself if he could do it, so could I. I found I did have a talent for drawing, but only people. I couldn't sketch a buck to save my life." Then he instructed her, "Tilt your head back just a bit."

He posed her in various positions as the morning progressed. At one point he came over to where she lay and very boldly kissed first her mouth, and then the points of her breasts. He stirred her passion until her lips parted and her eyes closed. "Perfect," he whispered, then returned to his sketching. "I want your eyes to be just that way."

Vivid held the pose, still pulsing from his prompting.

By late afternoon, the rain ceased, leaving in its wake a breezy, gray-sky day. Nate put away his sketching materials while Vivid stretched to rid her body of the kinks caused by posing. As she slipped into her clothing, Nate wondered how he'd ever repay her for all she'd done. Because of her he was sketching again, feeling again, loving again. Her smile had coaxed him to bask in its warmth, and after ten long, lonely years, he no longer dwelled below ground. The only way he knew to repay her was to love her with every fiber of his being for the rest of their lives.

"What's the matter?" she asked, seeing him observing her with such seriousness as she recoiled her hair into a knot.

"Just musing on how blessed I am to have you."

Vivid looked into the eyes of the only man she'd ever

loved and replied, "I'm blessed to have you, too, Nate Grayson."

They passed the remnant of the day in idyllic companionship. They took a long walk through the damp countryside and watched hawks soaring against the gray sky. Then they got an up-close view of a big white-tailed doe and her two fawns passing by a few yards away. Over a rise they found a valley blanketed in wildflowers that stretched for as far as they could see. Nate offered to pick as many flowers as she wanted, but she declined. "No, I have plenty back at the cabin. These are too beautiful to die in a vase."

And they were, but Nate thought her more beautiful than a continent of wildflowers.

After they returned to the cabin, they shared a late dinner of the hares caught in the traps Nate had left in the trees, then played a spirited game of checkers. There'd been no sun all day so there was no sunset to cap the evening. It didn't much matter because in every other way their day had been perfect.

In bed that night Vivid asked for a story.

"A bedtime story?" Nate questioned, holding her in the circle of his arms.

"Sure, why not?" Vivid replied, turning to view his face in the shadows cast by the lantern on the table. "Or do you think I'm being silly and young?"

"No, I don't."

"I think I want to hear more adventures of the princess and the Thunder God."

The further adventures of the princess and her Thunder God turned out to be a very erotic, decidedly wanton tale, hardly suitable for children. The brave, dark-skinned princess returned to the god's underground dwelling just as she'd promised, and Vivid's own desire began to unfurl as Nate described the princess's willing seduction. With kisses and soft touches the god coaxed her into his bed. Nate paused a moment to show Vivid just how softly and sweetly the coaxing had been done, then returned to the narration.

As the night lengthened, Nate spun his tale while his hands and lips spun her senses, until a breathless Vivid, like the princess in the story, was begging for release.

"But the Thunder God said, 'Not yet,' " Nate whispered from above her, feeling his manhood throbbing within the tight, warm shelter of her core as his hands gripping her hips fit her movements to his beguiling rhythm. "The god didn't think the princess was ready . . ."

The god gave the princess a few more sultry strokes and watched her face tighten with sensation, then, gifting her with a kiss, slowly withdrew from her treasured warmth.

Both the princess and Vivid groaned with the loss as Nate said, "The god wanted the princess to be heated, and open, and ready to experience *le petit morte*, but he didn't think she was ready. What do you think?"

Vivid thought the princess was very ready. He eased his hand to her center to boldly judge for himself, and her body trembled in response.

"Are you ready, princess?"

His fingers questioned her core with such blazing magnificence, her hips rose from the bed as she answered, "Yes . . ."

So the Thunder God slowly filled his princess with the smoldering iron of his desire. His hands tutored her hips, her straining nipples, the fever-wracked bud at the base of her thighs. The Thunder God loved the princess as he'd never loved anyone else before, and the aching release that followed, filled the cabin with mingled cries of joy.

However, the cries that awakened Vivid later that night had no root in pleasure. Nate was in the throes of a nightmare. Terror-filled moans escaped him as his head moved back and forth upon the pillow. She tried to wake him, but was unable to. She shook his strong shoulder, calling, "Nate!"

But he didn't or couldn't hear her. He was screaming, *"Run, Pa! Run!"* He was flailing around on the bed, throwing his arms about so violently, only grace from above kept Vivid from being inadvertently hit in the face by his powerful fists. "Nate!" she screamed again. "Nate!"

The dream held on, tossing him like flotsam on a violent sea, even as Vivid's pleas filled the night. She had never been so frightened in all her life. She didn't realize she was crying until she tasted the salty wetness on her lips. She flung herself atop him and, holding him as tight as she could, whispered passionately, "Nate, come back to me, please, Nate, I love you, please come back."

Her tears flowed silently against his shoulder, then she stilled as she felt his arm circle her bare back. He pulled her close, then held her tight. She cried quietly but openly in response, basking in his embrace as if it were the breath of life itself.

"I'm sorry, did I scare you?" he asked softly, kissing her brow.

She sniffled, then said, "A bit, yes, but it isn't your fault."

"It was my dream again."

"I know. Abigail told me about it—the last time it happened."

"You heard me that night?"

"Yes."

"And you never mentioned it? Why not?"

"I knew we'd talk about it when the time came."

He looked down at her in the darkness and whispered, "What price will I have to pay for having you in my life?"

Vivid raised herself up and kissed him. "No price. My love for you is always free . . ."

Chapter 18

The last hot days of July slid into the first hot days of August. And Vivid finally received a letter from her parents informing her of their arrival around the end of September. They sent congratulations and love to both their daughter and the prospective groom.

Meanwhile, the Battle of Abigail continued. Down at Miss Edna's store, bets were being placed on how long Abigail would hold out. Mr. Crowley, ever confident, never wavered in his vow to make her his wife and boasted of a wedding soon to come. Abigail, on the other hand, kept to her housework and her books. She continued to deny any plans for a wedding other than the one for Vivid and Nate.

The situation came to a head about mid-month. Maddie had come over to return a few books she'd borrowed from Abigail's library and stayed to visit. Maddie, Abigail, and Vivid were discussing some of the plans for Vivid's wedding when Adam Crowley's loud voice echoed from out in front of the house. "Abigail Grayson, get yourself out here!"

Abigail stiffened as the booming summons took the three women totally by surprise. Vivid and Maddie shared a knowing grin, then went out to the front room and pulled back the curtain to reveal Adam sitting atop his stallion. He looked like a man on a mission.

Abigail had come out of the kitchen behind them and

peered around Maddie and Vivid to the man pledged to be her husband, then moved back.

Vivid turned to her and said, "Abigail, it looks as if you have a caller."

Abigail snorted.

Then Maddie looked back over her shoulder and offered her opinion. "You really should go on out. We all know how muleheaded he can be. He'll be there shouting till nightfall if he takes a mind to it."

Abigail sighed, resigned. With the aid of the beautiful carved cane Adam had given her, she strode regally to the oval mirror hanging above the fireplace and took a moment to check her appearance. She then turned back and said, "How do I look?"

Vivid and Maddie both laughed. Maddie added, "For someone not wanting courting, you're awfully concerned, Miss Gail."

"Watch and learn, young women. Watch and learn."

As she strode away with the air of an African queen, Vivid glanced into Maddie's surprised eyes and both young women howled with laughter.

Maddie slid to the door and Vivid eased back the curtains. Neither was able to resist eavesdropping.

"Adam Crowley, get off my property unless you want buckshot in your backside," Abigail said from the porch.

Inside the house, Vivid shook her head in amusement. A familiar footfall behind her told her it was Nate. He came up and kissed her softly on the neck in greeting. "What's going on out there?"

Maddie answered in a loud whisper, "It's Adam Crowley and Miss Gail."

"What are they arguing over now?" he questioned, bending over Vivid to peek through the curtains.

"We're not really sure," Vivid replied. "Mr. Crowley rode up a moment ago and yelled for Abigail to get herself out there."

The arguing appeared to have ceased. Abigail now stood beside the stallion. Adam dismounted slowly. They were speaking too quietly to be overheard, however, a blink later they were at it again, and in full vocal force.

"No!" Abigail shouted. She emphasized her position by turning her back on him and walking stiffly up the gravel walk leading to the house.

Mr. Crowley vowed aloud, "Gail, you're going to marry me."

"No, I'm not, Adam Crowley. I don't need you playing with my affections."

"It's not your affections I want to play with, woman!"

Abigail came to an abrupt halt. She turned back and stared with a wondrous, yet wary, look.

The eavesdroppers inside anxiously awaited her reply.

Adam Crowley walked up to the woman he loved and Abigail looked up into the lumberjack's eyes. "You are serious, aren't you, Adam?"

"Yes, Gail, I am. Wish I had been this serious thirty years ago."

Then he did something that forever changed Abigail Grayson's life and forever earned him a treasured spot in Vivid's heart. He got down on one knee, took Abigail's hand, and asked, "Abigail Grayson, will you do me the honor of being my wife?"

Before Abigail could reply, Magic came strolling up the walk with Hector perched on her shoulder and a rabbit she'd snared in her hand. "Aunt Gail, can we have this rabbit tonight?"

She stopped then, just as she spied Adam Crowley and said cheerfully, "Oh, I'm sorry, hello, Mr. Crowley. Why are you on your knees, did you lose something? What is it? Hector and I can help."

When Magic began looking around the grass, Nate

hurried out to the porch and in fatherly tones hissed, "Majestic, get in here."

"What did I do, Pa?"

"Nothing, sweet," he said to her. He gave the stunned lovers an apologetic grin, then ushered his daughter inside.

When Nate and Vivid explained to Magic that Mr. Crowley was in the process of proposing marriage, she ran back to the door yelling, "Say yes, Aunt Gail!"

And to the delight of everyone involved, Aunt Gail took her great niece's advice.

The wedding was held a few days later at the church. Proud and beaming, Eli gave his mother away. Once the newlyweds returned from a honeymoon in Detroit, they planned on moving into Nate's home until Adam could build them a new house in the spring.

By August's end, folks were bemoaning the onset of autumn and the inevitable winter to follow, but there were still a few solid weeks of summer left, so everyone made the best of it. There were county fairs to visit, wood to chop, and outbuildings to shore up; corn was harvested, fruits were picked and put up, and Vivid continued making her rounds. She and Michigan tooled up and down the back roads of Cass County dispensing medicines, tending to babies and old folks, and inviting her neighbors to the wedding. Vivid had wanted to keep the ceremony small, but the Grove was having none of that. Abigail, Miss Edna, and Maddie, the coordinators of the grand event, had received nearly one hundred replies from people in the area. Nate had friends all over the state; no one knew how many of them might be planning to attend.

The month of September brought cooler temperatures and brilliant blue skies. The trees had not yet begun to turn but everyone assured Vivid that the magnificent Michigan autumn would be unveiling its colors soon.

The list of the people clamoring for invites to the wedding now numbered close to two hundred. Nate had heard from friends from as far away as Saginaw Bay. Vivid heard from both of her sisters. They'd been told of the wedding in correspondence with their parents. Each sent messages of love and good wishes to their favorite La Brat Trabrasera.

One night Vivid returned home very tired from a four-day trip to a lumber camp near Battle Creek. Three men had gotten into a fight and had tried to hack one another to pieces. She'd sewn one man's ear, and another's leg; for the third, Vivid had stitched his arm the best she could but the axe blade had sliced through so much bone and sinew, only time would tell if he'd be able to keep it or have to undergo amputation.

She wearily led Michigan around to the barn, saw to the mule's care, and then trudged back over to her place. Inside, she found Nate seated at her desk reading a newspaper. He put the paper down at her entrance and said softly, "You look tired, princess."

"I am." She flopped down into the closest chair. "Lord, I don't want to see another lumber beast for at least a year. Talk about being raised in a barn. Between them they had maybe two men who'd even heard of the word 'manners.' "

Nate smiled. He wondered if she would still be doctoring when they were old and gray. He supposed yes, and with each homecoming he would love her even more. "You want me to bring you some water for a bath?"

"Bless you, yes."

"Adam and Abigail won't be back from Indianapolis until tomorrow. Eli's looking at some new presses up in Kalamazoo, and Magic's spending the night over at Maddie's, so . . ." he said, waggling his eyebrows playfully.

"So?" Vivid asked, grinning.

"So I'm spending my night with you."

Standing behind her chair, Nate, using gentle hands, slowly massaged the muscles in her neck and shoulders. After a few silent minutes of his tender care, her fatigue slowly melted away, taking with it the strain in her shoulders and the ache in her spine. She'd missed him in the days she'd been away. She thought how much of a joy it would be, once they married, to come home every evening to him in just this way.

But she'd been living in a lumber camp for the past few days and she dearly needed a bath. "Nate . . ." she whispered, relaxing under the backrub. "You really should let me get that bath . . ."

"I heartily agree. When was the last time you were near some water?"

Vivid's eyes widened and she turned to look up at him. He was grinning, she saw, and in spite of herself, she grinned back. She asked him in regal tones, "Are you implying that I'm not fresh?"

"I'm not implying, Your Majesty, I'm stating fact. You smell like Magic after she's been out playing all day."

Vivid looked up and said huskily, "Then after you bring in the water, you'll have to make sure I get good and clean."

And he did.

He washed her thoroughly and sensually, using both the soapy rag and his hands. She was pulsing from all the attention once he declared her ready to step out of the water. Then he wrapped her in a large flannel drying sheet and laid her on the big bed. He dried her slowly, taking time to trail the flannel over her nipples and the dampness between her thighs, then her back, kissing the line of her spine and running a slow hand over the lushness of her hips while she melted into the softness of the mattress. Vivid had shared many an erotic interlude with Nate and this night would be added to that count.

He made love to her until very late, then they both fell asleep.

As the sun rose in the dawn sky Vivid was awakened by his kiss and his farewell.

She sleepily nodded her understanding and saw him grin at her as he got dressed. "Back to sleep for you, princess. See you later today."

Vivid pulled a sheet around her nudity and slid from the bed to accompany him to the front room. He gave her a parting kiss, then she stared amazed as he kicked aside the rug rag in the center of the floor, and opened a door built into the plank floor.

"My grandfather was a member of the Loyal League and a conductor on the Underground Railroad," he explained.

"So that's how you've been getting in and out without my knowing?"

"Yep, there's a tunnel down here that leads to the barn and a vein that runs to the house."

Vivid walked over and peered down into the dark hole at the base of the ladder. "Does Magic know about this?"

"Yep, has she been popping in and out too?"

Vivid told him about Magic disappearing the day her crates arrived. One moment she'd been there, the next moment she'd disappeared. Finally, an explanation.

"No real reason why I didn't tell you about it before. Guess I just liked the look of surprise on your face when I seemed to appear out of nowhere."

"If I weren't so sleepy, I'd fuss, but I am sleepy, so I'm going back to bed. 'Night, Nate."

She kissed him.

"Night, princess."

After his descent into his grandfather's tunnel, Vivid repositioned the rug and padded back into the bedroom for a few more hours of sleep.

The next morning Vivid came out into the yard to

find Nate, Magic, and Abigail all shading their eyes against the sun and peering up into the sky.

Vivid did the same, but having no idea what she was supposed to be looking for, she gave up and walked over to investigate.

At her approach, Magic said happily, "Look, Viveca, your idea worked. Hector is flying!"

Vivid put her hand up to shield her eyes, and sure enough she spied Hector soaring above the trees. Magic had been at her wit's end trying to coax Hector into trying out his angle-shaped wings. She'd tried tossing him gently off the front porch steps, she'd tried showing him by flapping her own brown arms, all to no avail. Vivid had watched Magic on a couple of occasions flapping her way around the yard while Hector stood silently on the ground, slowly cocking his head this way and that, looking for all the world as if he were trying to determine if his surrogate mama had gone insane.

Vivid's musings were broken as Hector whizzed by just above his audience's heads and everyone ducked.

Magic scolded her pampered pet.

Hector resumed his bullet-fast flight back to the sun. Adam walked up. He sounded astounded as he asked, "Was that Hector?"

"Yes," Magic replied, continuing to view the sky with irritation.

Abigail, viewing the sky with a warning in her eyes, said angrily, "He could hurt someone doing that."

Magic agreed, saying, "Just wait until he gets back here."

"Magic—" Adam began, but the bird whizzed by at eyebrow level again, making everyone crouch defensively as he screamed past.

"Stop it, Hector!" Magic hollered.

"I'm going back inside," Abigail declared. "That bird should be in a cage."

Vivid had to agree and sought safety among the trees

lining the drive. She'd been terrorized enough for one day. Nate and Adam joined her and they all turned their eyes to the sky.

Hector dove and rose, dove and rose. Adam exclaimed, "That's no ordinary hawk she's been raising, folks. Hector's a nighthawk. See that white band on his wings?"

"Are you sure?" Nate asked.

"Sure as I can be until he slows down long enough to get a good look at him."

"Aren't they supposed to hunt at night?"

Adam shook his head. "When they're raised in the nest, yes. Hector doesn't know any better probably."

They could see him circling against the sun.

Vivid asked, "Do they make good pets?"

"Doesn't look like it." Nate chuckled, seeing his daughter duck under Hector's latest pass. Nate had never seen a bird fly so swiftly.

Vivid laughed, watching Magic angrily shaking her small brown fist at the sky, then remarked, "I really pity that bird should she ever get her hands on him."

After a shared laugh, Nate asked Vivid, "How did you get him to fly?"

"I told Magic to drop him off the barn roof. Hector would either fly or break his neck. It was all I could think of."

The focus in the yard shifted to the wagon driving up. Vivid recognized Vernon, but not the older White woman or the small golden-skinned girl seated by her side.

"Who do you think that could be?" Adam asked.

Nate shrugged. He stepped out from the shelter of the trees, took a quick look up at the sky, then walked across the yard to the wagon, Vivid and Adam following.

Vernon was helping the large woman from the wagon.

"Are you Nathaniel Grayson?" she asked in an Irish brogue.

Nate didn't answer for a moment. The little girl sitting so quietly on the seat held his complete attention. She and Majestic favored each other so keenly they could be twins.

The woman's voice brought him back. "My name is Holly Rand, Mr. Grayson. Did you receive my letter?"

"What letter—" he began, then paused. He stared into the woman's black eyes. Holly Rand. "You sent the message about my daughter being in danger?"

She nodded grimly. "I apologize for being so cryptic, but I thought it would be better to explain the situation in person."

Nate looked at the child once more, then at Magic, now walking over to join them with Hector perched atop the leather pad on her shoulder. He thought if not twins they could be sisters.

Holly Rand, seeing Majestic, said, "I didn't know they would favor each other so much."

Nate's head snapped around.

"They're sisters, Mr. Grayson."

"Sisters?"

"Yes. This is Miss Satin. I brought her to you because I didn't know where else to go."

Stunned, Nate scanned the girl's small face. Sisters? He saw that Viveca and Adam appeared just as shocked. Nate realized he didn't want Magic to hear this conversation, at least not until he found out what this visit meant, so when she walked up, he said, "Majestic, go tell Aunt Gail we have guests."

Satin reared back from the sight of Hector, frightened.

"Don't worry," Magic told her, "he only eats rabbits and field mice. Do you want to put him on your shoulder?"

The girl shook her head violently.

Magic looked up at her father and said sagely, "I think she's scared, Pa."

"I think so, too," he said gently. "Now run along and tell Aunt Gail about our guests."

As Magic and Hector departed, Holly Rand said, "She's a lovely child, Mr. Grayson. Somewhere up in heaven her mum is surely smiling."

Later, after Nate and Holly put the girls to bed in Majestic's room, the adults gathered around the kitchen table to hear Holly Rand's story.

"I brought Satin to you because I believe she will be safe here."

"From whom?" Nate asked.

"The girls' distant cousin, Evan Cole. They are standing between him and his late aunt's money."

Nate went still. "How much money are we speaking of?"

"More than I'll ever see in a lifetime, that's for sure," she said. "He's an evil man, Evan Cole. Evil."

Nate looked around the table at the others.

Mrs. Rand said, "Let me start at the beginning. "The girls' mum was a woman named Delia Cole. She was a poor lass with no family when I first met her in Philadelphia. I owned a seamstress shop then and she came to me for a job. She worked for me for over a year. She was a fine seamstress and a fine woman."

She paused a moment as if she was recalling those early memories, then continued. "A man came into the shop one day and you could tell by the cut of his clothes he was wealthy. Delia helped him pick out a shawl as a present for his mother. His name was Garth Cole and he returned every day for the next week to buy gloves, shawls, whatever I had, just so he could see her. Delia was a beautiful woman, and a good girl. She wasn't like some of the shopgirls who went with any man who promised them something pretty. To make a long story short, he courted my Delia and eventually married her. His rich mum carried on something awful when she heard the news. She swore never to speak to him again for marrying so low. Garth and Delia moved away and I lost track of her after that.''

According to Mrs. Rand, in September 1867, Garth was murdered and robbed while coming home from his job as a store clerk. Delia, mother now to a nearly year-old Majestic, stretched their meager savings for as long as she could, but six weeks after her husband's ignoble death, she and her baby were forced out onto the streets. To add to her woes, she learned she was carrying the baby who would be Satin. Out of desperation she went to her husband's family, only to be turned away from the door by Garth's cousin Evan.

Delia went back to the streets. Finding work became increasingly difficult; she had a small child and another on the way, few employers found that combination appealing. Delia tried to find Mrs. Rand, who had since closed her shop and moved away, but in a city as large as Philadelphia, she might as well have been looking for gold in the streets. With winter closing in, she had few options. The charity houses were full. She added her name to the lists with all the others waiting, but she held little hope. She begged on the corners for a while, but the older and more seasoned panhandlers ran her off. She came to a decision. Majestic needed food and warmth or she would surely die. Delia refused to let that happen; Majestic would have a future even if Delia and the unborn child did not. So Delia placed the sleeping baby on the steps of the hospital. Crying silently, she kissed the cold little brow farewell and faded back into the night.

Mrs. Rand paused and looked into Nate's eyes and quietly asked, ''Can you imagine the desperation she must have felt, the anguish of knowing she'd left her dear child with strangers so she wouldn't starve to death? My Lord, I wish I had been there to help her.''

Mrs. Rand then told how Garth Cole's mother went

into decline after learning of her son's death. While Garth and Delia were married, Garth's mother had never once contacted them. She'd never seen Delia, hadn't cared whether there were grandchildren. The prospect of impending death must have changed her mind because she hired a Pinkerton to find Delia, and when he did, Mrs. Cole moved her son's widow into her home.

Vivid asked, "Did she know Delia had come to the house before?"

"No, because Evan didn't tell her."

"Sounds like a real nice fellow," Adam remarked in a voice thick with sarcasm.

Delia was afraid she would be turned back out onto the street should her mother-in-law ever learn Delia had abandoned her elder child, so she never told her of Majestic's birth.

Nate interrupted the narrative to ask, "How long after Majestic's abandonment was Delia found by the Pinkerton?"

"Three weeks later."

Nate shook his head sadly.

Mrs. Cole died a few months before Satin's birth. Her will settled a small pension on Delia and left the bulk of her wealth to the unborn child. Evan Cole was furious. His aunt had bequeathed him a reasonable sum, but he felt entitled to it all.

"After her death the terror began," Mrs. Rand said quietly. "Every day, during Delia's last month of confinement, Evan would come into her room and tell her how easy it would be to dispose of her infant. He talked of strangling and arsenic-laced milk and suffocation."

"Oh, my Lord . . ." Abigail gasped.

"Horrible, horrible things," Mrs. Rand said.

To try and save her child, Delia used some of her funds to hire a Pinkerton to find Mrs. Rand.

"I went to the house and Delia asked me to be her midwife. She knew from working in my shop that I'd

done it occasionally so I said I would. But she wanted
me to say the baby had died in hopes of throwing Evan
off the scent. I did just as she asked. After she gave birth
to Miss Satin, I wrapped the little body completely in a
blanket and announced to Evan the baby was dead. You
should have seen that little toad grin. I hated him for
life at that moment; for life.''

"So where'd you go?''

"Boston. I have a sister there. Miss Satin and I lived
with her until six months ago. Delia sent money for her
care all these years and I kept her safe.''

"Did Delia ever visit?''

"Never. She was too afraid Evan would somehow
find out.''

"So she never saw either of her daughters again,''
Vivid said.

"No.''

A silence settled over the kitchen. Vivid could see
tears in Abigail's eyes.

Nate asked, "So why did you send the note to me?''

"I'm dying, Mr. Grayson, and Evan knows Satin is
alive.''

Nate stilled. "How?''

"When Delia died unexpectedly six months ago, Mrs.
Cole's old butler wrote to tell me of her death. He said
Evan handled the burial and the disposal of her things.
In the process he found her ledgers. Written in them
were the recordings of the payments she'd been sending
all these years. Delia must have taken the butler into her
confidence because he warned me Evan was on his way
to Boston. I packed, and we left the next day.''

"Will he come here?'' Abigail asked.

Mrs. Rand said, "I believe he will. The bulk of her
estate went to charity, but if he can produce Satin for
Mrs. Cole's solicitors, he will be declared guardian until
she comes of age and they will turn the money over to
him.''

"But how will they be sure the Satin he produces isn't a fraud? The baby supposedly died."

Mrs. Rand asked, "Does Majestic have a strawberry birthmark on her left shoulder?"

"Yes, she does."

"So does Satin. All the Cole girls do, according to what Delia said."

Nate found all of this very troubling. "How could he know about Majestic, though?"

"According to the butler, after Evan found the ledgers he began an intense search through her belongings for more clues. He found Majestic's birth paper hidden in the bindings of Delia's Bible. Written below it was your name and the name of this place."

Vivid asked, "Delia knew about Nate?"

"Yes, she told me that a few weeks after she moved into Mrs. Cole's, she went back to the hospital and asked after the baby. She told one of the nurses she'd read about the abandoned baby in the newspaper and was simply curious about what had happened. The nurse told her about a soldier from Michigan who'd taken the baby home. Delia asked if she had the soldier's name and hometown because she wanted to write a note to bless him for being so caring, so the nurse gave her the information."

Mrs. Rand looked to Nate. "Delia said she prayed for you and Majestic every night. She also wanted Satin to be brought here should anything ever happen to me. She said she knew in her heart you would not object."

She was right, Nate realized.

They talked until very late. Finally, they all sought their beds.

When they awakened the next morning, they found Mrs. Rand dead. She'd evidently accomplished her life's mission, and having done so, had slipped into the arms of the Lord. Nate took both girls into his study to explain the situation to them and to tell them they were sisters.

The two girls were having a hard time getting along.

When Nate took Magic aside a few days after Satin's arrival to ask why, Magic said, "She's bossy, Pa, always trying to tell me what to do. She wears those stupid velvet dresses and those dumb little white stockings. She never ever gets dirty and talks like she's got cotton stuffed up her nose."

Vivid, who'd joined them for the conference, smiled at the description. "How are the other children treating her?"

"Like she was some princess in one of Pa's stories. Only she's not brave at all. She's scared to death of Hector, never been fishing, and says girls shouldn't play marbles because of the dust."

"You should try and be friends, Majestic," Nate pointed out.

"I know, Pa, but it's hard to be friends with somebody that doesn't know how to do anything except act pretty."

Vivid had to admit she agreed with Magic on Satin's daily choice of attire. When Vivid drove back from town that afternoon, Satin was dressed in a beautiful blue velvet dress and spotless white stockings. The slippers on her feet looked as if they'd never been worn outside, and Vivid, like Magic, wondered how on earth that could be. Nobody kept herself *that* clean. Even Vivid's older sister, Alicea, who had gone almost her whole life without soiling her clothes or mussing her hair, fell off the wagon now and again. Vivid, dressed in her trousers, boots, and old floppy man's shirt, felt terribly unkempt next to the immaculate youngster.

One day near the end of September, Vivid was in town sweeping off the walk in front of her office. The crisp air flirted with her skirt hem and blew away the bits of debris brought up by the broom. Autumn filled the air. Vivid paused to watch Vernon and his wagon go by. Beside him on the seat sat a strange man dressed as if he were en route to church. He had on a crisp black suit, his white collar starched and the hat on his head proclaimed that he was from the east. Vivid eyed the man, who tipped his hat and she nodded politely in reply. They drove by and Vivid resumed her task. Everyone in town had been alerted to look out for strangers because of the dangers facing Magic and her sister. Vivid didn't think the man on the wagon could be Evan Cole because if he were he would have been riding in the bed of the wagon trussed up. Vernon was Majestic's godfather and was especially incensed that someone would actually want to harm his godchild.

It didn't take long for the word to spread about the identity of the stranger who'd ridden in with Vernon. Vivid got wind of it later that evening and stormed into Nate's study. He wanted to run and hide, but he tried to calm her down instead. "Viveca, I—"

"Don't you Viveca me, Nate Grayson. You sent for another doctor!"

"Let me explain. I—" Nate had forgotten he'd sent those letters.

"You led me on, you—you—if I had my rifle now, I'd shoot you just for the satisfaction of hearing you yell when I extracted the bullets from your hide. You want another doctor, then fine. If you're lucky, he'll marry you, too. I quit!"

And she stormed out.

Nate removed his spectacles and rubbed his weary eyes. He'd really stepped into a bear trap this time.

Vivid was still angry when dressing later that evening for dinner at Mr. Farley's. She knew she'd eventually be calm enough to hear Nate's explanation, but damn him, she hadn't reached that state yet. Supposedly the new doctor had received his degree from the university on the other side of the state. Vivid looked at herself in the glass. She'd opted for one of her fancier dresses, not

to impress Mr. Farley but to keep herself in check. In a
fancy dress and with her hair up she would probably be
less likely to stride across the grass and punch Nate
Grayson in the nose.

She was surprised to see she was not the only person
Mr. Farley had invited that evening. She'd mentioned
her interest in billiards to him one day in passing. To
her delight, he informed her of his own fascination with
the game and invited her to play on the table he kept
under tarps in his barn. They'd played on and off
throughout the summer. Tonight's invitation had been
issued last week and she wondered why the other men
were there.

She'd been in the Grove long enough now to recognize which wagon belonged to whom. From the wealth
of conveyances and teams lining the tract in front of
Hiram's place, most of the Grove's male population was
inside. Vivid eased her mule and wagon into a spot a
short distance from the barn.

She could hear the laughter and voices spilling into
the night as she approached. The entrance glowed with
the lights of lanterns. When she stepped through the
door, the silence made her pause. All the men seemed
frozen in position as they stared.

Eli approached with a glass in his hand and a smile
on his face. He took a quick look over his shoulder at
the men at his back, then asked her, "What are you
doing here?"

"I'm here to play billiards with Hiram."

That brought the men to life with a buzz.

Hiram then walked over to her with a puzzled smile.
"Dr. Lancaster, what are you doing here?"

"We had a date, remember?"

He hit his hand against his forehead. "Oh, that's right.
I'm sorry, Dr. Lancaster. Tonight's Men's Association
meeting night."

She looked around at the men watching so curiously.

She saw Hiram glance at the case she held in her hand, then heard him say, "And you brought your stick, too."

The man whom Vivid had seen in Vernon's wagon strolled up and said, "So you're the little doctor."

Vivid looked him up and down and saw a man entirely too arrogant for his own good. She asked coolly, "And you are?"

"I'm Dr. David Hatcher, University of Michigan."

Hatcher was a handsome brown-skinned man.

Vivid replied, "Dr. Viveca Lancaster."

"And what is that you're carrying?" Hatcher asked.

"It's a billiard cue. I'm not very good, but Mr. Farley has been kind enough to give me some pointers."

Nate, standing in a corner with Adam and Paul Crowley, looked at his companions with a knowing smile. Hatcher had been a royal pain in the rear from the moment he'd arrived. Nate couldn't wait for the man to leave town. Hatcher had spent the day looking down on folks and bragging about the more lucrative offers he'd received from cities like Chicago and Denver. Why he'd not taken advantage of these offers had never been made clear. Adam said, "Two bits says she'll have him bleeding to death in, oh, a quarter of an hour."

Nate shook his head. "I'd be a fool to bet any other way. I've never seen her play, but I've heard her stories."

Meanwhile, over by the door, Vivid asked Hatcher, "Do you play, sir?"

"Oh, most definitely. In fact, I'd be willing to give you a few pointers," he replied, smiling devilishly.

Vivid felt Eli stiffen at her side. To prevent Eli from leaping to her defense Vivid called out to the other men in the barn. "I didn't come to interrupt your evening, gentlemen, but would you mind if Dr. Hatcher and I play a game or two? Then I'll leave."

Over the buzz set off by her request, Adam Crowley's voice boomed out, "Be our guest, Doc."

Nate watched her stride to the table in that beautiful dress. He took great exception to the way Hatcher appeared to be observing the swish of her skirts as she walked, but Nate held himself in check for now. He'd let Viveca get in her shots first.

While the audience took bets, Vivid unsheathed her stick. She saw Hatcher's eyes widen as she firmly screwed the sections together.

Hatcher borrowed one of the sticks Hiram kept for guests, then walked up to the table. Vivid stood emotionlessly while he explained to her that for this competition the winner would be the player able to sink the most balls.

He looked over and said, "I will insist upon dinner when I win, Dr. Lancaster."

Vivid smiled and replied pleasantly, "And I will insist upon your leaving town in the morning when you don't."

Hoots rent the air from the men watching the exchange. Hatcher stared around coolly, then said, "Ladies first."

Vivid took advantage of his graciousness and stepped to the table. She remembered the first real lesson she had ever received in billiards from a fancy Denver gambler when she was ten. He instructed her that before playing she should pick up each ivory ball individually and heft it to determine its weight. Next, look for nicks or cracks. She didn't think that necessary tonight because she knew Hiram kept his balls in good condition. The levelness of the table did cause concern. To test it, she slowly rolled a ball down the table's surface. It pulled to the left as usual but she could compensate. She'd played on worse.

In the end, it didn't take long.

As she sank the last three balls, the crowd cheered with each shot she made. Her very angry opponent never even had a turn at the table.

Vivid silently set her stick against the table. As the bets were paid off among the onlookers, Hatcher insisted the competition be extended to the best two out of three. Vivid didn't quibble. She could best him playing with a spoon. She even let him go first.

It didn't help.

He potted the first three and missed the fourth. Vivid smiled sympathetically at his plight, then took a moment to study the configuration of the remaining balls. Stick in hand, she cozied up to the table's edge and proceeded to sink them all without mussing a hair on her well-coiffed head.

After recasing her stick, Vivid peered into the furious eyes of Dr. David Hatcher, University of Michigan, and said, "Been nice playing with you."

Then she exited with a smile.

Chapter 19

The next morning brought Vivid joy as her parents arrived. Vernon had barely helped her mother down from the hired coach before Vivid came running across the yard to greet her with tears in her eyes. Her mother met the embrace tightly, turning her this way and that as they rejoiced in their reunion. "Oh, Mama . . ."

Vivid got the same intense hug from her tall, handsome father. They were all in tears by the time the greetings were done.

Vivid couldn't help grinning at her parents. She couldn't believe they were actually there. Her mother must have been equally as elated because she pulled Vivid back into her arms and held, and held, and held, tight.

With Adam Crowley's assistance, her parents and their luggage were moved into the Grayson house. Abigail met the visitors with a smile, then showed them to the rooms they would have during their stay.

Lunch consisted of sandwiches made of the leftover ham from last night's dinner and melt-in-your-mouth slices of Abigail's bread and cold, tart lemonade. It was hardly a feast, but the guests thought the hastily prepared repast worthy of kings after the train food they'd been consuming.

Vivid's father asked, "Abigail. what is in this bread? This is magnificent."

"Oats, mealed corn, some honey. I'll write down the

recipe for you before you return home, if you'd like.''

"Please do, and when I serve it back in San Francisco I will call it Abigail Bread.''

Abigail smiled, pleased.

"We need to have a dinner, Joseph, to celebrate Viveca's engagement," Francesca declared. "You can cook—''

Vivid looked down at her plate.

"Viveca, darling, what's wrong?''

"Nate and I have something to settle first, Mama, before you make any plans.'' She still hadn't heard his side.

Vivid looked into her mother's beautiful eyes.

"You haven't called off the wedding, have you?'' Francesca asked her softly.

"Vivid, did you make the boy run off already?'' her father asked.

Everybody at the table chuckled.

"No, Papa," Vivid said, giving him a smiling look. She'd missed his teasing nature in the months she'd been here.

Francesca shook her head at her husband and his wry sense of humor and asked, "Is this something serious?''

"I'm not sure.''

Vivid looked into the face of the woman who'd given her birth and heard her say in Castilian, "Come. Let's take a walk.''

They walked to Vivid's cabin and sat out back on the swing.

Her mother asked, "Do you like this place?''

"I love it here, Mama," Vivid replied with feeling.

Vivid then told her all that had happened since her arrival. She ended by telling her about Nate and David Hatcher.

"How did you ever keep from boxing his ears?'' Francesca asked hotly.

"I put on my best dress to remind myself to be a lady."

"Good idea. Although that hadn't helped a bit at your eighth birthday party. Do you remember?"

Vivid grinned at the memory. She'd had a fight with Dickie Pearson and he'd gotten angry over having to be taken home with a nosebleed after being punched in the nose by a girl.

"You need to talk to him, Viveca."

"I will."

"Where is he now?"

"In town at his office. You'll meet him later."

"And my grandbaby?"

"You now have two."

"Two?"

Vivid explained the intrigue and worry brought on by Satin's arrival, and Francesca listened closely, then asked, "And this Evan Cole is on his way here?"

"Mrs. Rand thought so, yes."

The only thing Mrs. Rand hadn't done was describe Cole. No one had any idea what he looked like, and that brought the most worry.

Nate returned later that afternoon. He'd picked up the girls from school and as they went into the house he crossed the field to Lancaster's cabin. He owed her thanks for sending obnoxious David Hatcher packing. He also hoped she'd listen to his explanation of why he'd sent the letters. He knocked at the cabin door, calling, "Hello, princess, can we talk?"

Vivid walked to the door and let him inside.

"I—" He stopped as his gaze met the coal-black eyes of a small, elegantly attired Black woman seated at Vivid's desk. She had skin the color of rich dark coffee and a face so beautiful it nearly took his breath away. He knew without introduction that she had to be the venerable Francesca he'd heard so much about. "Mrs. Lan-

caster? I'm Nathaniel Grayson. Welcome to Michigan,'
Nate said as he walked over to take her hand.

She smiled up at him and responded in English, "So
pleased to meet you." Then she turned to Vivid and
proclaimed in Castilian, "Viveca, he is so handsome.
He will give me beautiful grandbabies."

"Mama!" Vivid exclaimed.

"What did she say?" Nate questioned, smiling.

Vivid could only laugh at the impressed look on her
mother's face, then told her fiancé, "Nothing, Nate,
she's just being her outrageous self. Behave, Mama."

Nate then made the acquaintance of Vivid's chef father, who to that point had been content to watch. He
looked Nate over slowly, then asked, "How much do
you love my daughter, Nathaniel Grayson?"

The question caught Nate off-guard but he looked at
his skeptical fiancée, filled his eyes with her loveliness,
then turned back to say genuinely, "I love your daughter
as trees love spring rain, sir."

"Good answer, son," Joseph said. "Don't you think
so, Fran?"

"Excellent, excellent," Francesca agreed.

"Let me give you a piece of advice, son. Don't try
and corral this girl's exuberance. Just let her go. You'll
have less gray hair that way." He then pointed to his
own salt-and-pepper hair. "See these? Every one of
these gray hairs belong to that girl over there."

"Papa!"

"Vivid, I have to tell him the truth."

"You're as bad as Mama!"

When the laughs settled down, Vivid asked after David Hatcher.

"Vernon took him to Niles this morning."

And then in front of God, Vivid's parents, and anyone
else who might be around to hear or see, Nate asked
Vivid, "Will you forgive me? I sent those letters soon

after you came to town. I did it because I still had my doubts. I don't anymore.''

Vivid saw the truth in his gaze and nodded.

Francesca applauded softly, then said, "I can see that you love my Trabrasera very much."

Nate smiled at the name, "Yes, ma'am, very much."

She then turned to Vivid, "Viveca, and you love him?"

"Yes, Mama, I do."

"Then we will go ahead with the wedding as soon as your Tia Teresa sends the wedding gown."

Vivid, smiling up at Nate, said, "Yes."

At dinner that evening Magic and Satin joined them, much to Francesca's delight. Magic and, to everyone's surprise, Satin took an instant liking to their soon-to-be grandmother. Francesca was especially interested in Hector.

"I had a falcon when I was young. Her name was Isabella. Does your Hector hunt?"

"No, ma'am. I hunt, he eats."

Francesca shook her head. "Tomorrow, Hector will learn how to begin hunting for himself."

"Really?" Magic responded excitedly.

"Really," Francesca promised.

After Magic and Satin and the other adults had all gone to bed, Vivid sat on the swing nestled in Nate's strong arms. "Magic and my mother seemed to hit it off well."

"Especially when your mother promised to buy her and Satin a circus."

"What?"

"A circus, you know, tame animals, tents?"

"When was this?"

"Sometime after dinner. Majestic said her *abuela* asked her what she wanted more than anything in the world."

"And Magic said a circus."

"Bull's-eye."

"I'll speak to Mama."

"Thank you. It's not that I don't appreciate the gesture, it's just we don't have any room for lions or tigers or bears wearing little skirts."

After a few silent moments Vivid said, "I was very, very angry with you, Nate Grayson."

"I know, princess, but you have to see it from my point of view. I had my doubts, as I said."

"I know you did, but it hurt nonetheless."

"I know and I apologize for that also." He leaned down and kissed her brow. "I'd apologize profusely if I weren't afraid your screaming would awaken your parents."

She playfully elbowed him in the ribs, then lay back and enjoyed the night and the feel of his strength encircling her.

For the next few days, Vivid and Nate squired her parents around the Grove to see the land and to meet the neighbors. Francesca began teaching Hector to hunt, and Magic and Satin to speak Castilian. Nate began to learn that his mother-in-law could be just as vivid as her daughter. He didn't find out how Hector had been training until the Widow Moss stormed into his office in town one morning demanding fifty dollars for the rabbits Hector had killed and devoured. It seemed he'd been hunting in her rabbit hutch. An interrogation of the girls and their *abuela* proved this to be true and Nate paid up. After Nate delivered a stern lecture to the three females, Francesca kissed him on the cheek and swore it wouldn't happen again.

Nate didn't believe it for a minute, but he did go to the mirror and look for gray hairs.

The arm of the injured lumberjack at the camp near Battle Creek had to be amputated. After conducting the surgery, Vivid stayed a few more days to ensure he recovered well, then she and Michigan headed home.

The end of September brought cooler temperatures and days of rain. The gray skies finally broke and the Grove residents went about their business under crisp blue skies and the magnificent turning trees. Vivid had never seen such a riot of colors: brilliant golds, blazing reds, fiery burnt oranges. Vibrant, intense color assaulted the eye from every corner. For these sights alone Vivid vowed to remain in Michigan for the rest of her life.

The end of September also brought the harvest moon—the largest, fattest, most golden moon Vivid and her marveling parents had ever seen.

On the morning of the last day of September, a man Vivid had never seen before strolled up the drive. He walked up to where she sat atop the wagon and said, "Good morning, I am Vincent Red Bird's son, Isaac."

"Good morning, Isaac, I'm Dr. Lancaster, and this is my mother. How may we help you?"

"I'm looking for Nate Grayson."

"Nate's left for town already."

"Well, will you give him this please?"

He handed up a small wooden ball. As she took it and looked at it he added, "I am this year's *skabewis*."

Vivid stared down, confused.

"The word translates as messenger."

She peered again at the ball. "Nate will know what this means?" Vivid handed the ball to her curious mother.

"Of course. It's time for Little Brother of War. Everyone knows that."

"Of course," Vivid echoed.

With the arrival of the *skabewis* the Grove became infected with lacrosse fever. Sticks were taken down and their webbed heads refitted. Nate and Vernon traveled all the way from Battle Creek to St. Joe recruiting players for the Grove team. The game was still more than two weeks away but already tribes were arriving to help the Grove men clear and level the field behind Mr. Farley's place.

The early October days, though crisp, were festive. Because of the recent harvests many fruits and vegetables were given to the doctor in payment for services. Her chef father, who'd taken over the bulk of Abigail's cooking, couldn't have been happier, surrounded by the fresh Michigan bounty.

He discovered apple butter, cornish pasties, popcorn, and paw paws—a potato-sized Michigan tree fruit which, to Vivid, tasted amazingly like bananas. After going hunting with Adam, Joseph treated everyone to beautifully prepared pheasant and grouse, mouth-watering salmon, and a venison dish that brought tears to Adam Crowley's eyes.

More and more people came to set up residence on Farley's field as the days passed. The native people and their supporters took one side of the field and the Grove residents took the other.

The children of both sides cleared the field of stones, sticks, and other bits of natural debris that might cause a player to trip or fall during the contest. Hector stuffed himself royally on the vermin and rabbits flushed out when the children marched down the field banging pots and lids. All rabbit warrens and ground squirrel holes were filled and tamped down; no one wanted the players to suffer broken ankles.

Nate was so busy coordinating events and the movement and placement of people, Vivid rarely saw him until she caught him in town one afternoon in his office.

He looked up at her entrance and smiled. "Well, hello, princess, what can I do for you?"

"I'm on my way home, and I thought I'd stop by to see how you are, I've seen you so rarely lately."

He put away his lists and looked at her from behind his desk. He beckoned her with a long finger.

Vivid came over with a grin. She hopped up on the

desk in front of him. "What?" she asked.

Nate leaned back in his chair and looked at her for a long moment. "Do you know how absolutely beautiful you are?"

"You are obviously in love. Look at me, my hair's a mess, I have on this old man's shirt—two sizes too large—these denims need patching in the knees and in the seat, and . . . mmm . . ."

His kiss silenced her. Seated atop the desk, she was at the perfect height to savor and be savored. "This is nice . . ." she whispered, nibbling his bottom lip, then flicking the point of her tongue against the corners of his mouth. Nate slid his chair closer to her. He effortlessly lifted her slight weight from the desktop and down to the warmth of his lap.

"Will you tell me a bedtime story . . . tonight?"

"Can't," he whispered against the hollow of her throat. He began to undo the buttons of her shirt, kissing as he went.

"Why not?" she questioned heatedly. "Haven't I been a good girl?"

His kisses brushed the tops of her breasts. "Oh, yes, princess. You've been a very good girl . . ."

He'd opened the shirt to her waist and now eased down her thin camisole. He slid his palms over the pebble-hard points and watched her desire spread across her face. "It's against the rules . . . no bedtime stories until after the game."

"Really? Oh, Nate . . ."

His lips were closing over a pleading nipple, while the other received the tender play of his fingers. "Really. Tradition says players must be celibate."

He moved his loving over to the other nipple and left it hard and damp as he lifted up and kissed her on the mouth. He set her back on the desk leaving her to savor her pleasure while he went to draw the office's shades closed.

In the daylight shadows he came back to her. She hadn't moved.

He leaned to kiss her bared breasts again, then slid his hand down to the large leather belt girding her waist. He pushed it away. Vivid helped him ease her trousers down and off. She sat atop the desk in her opened shirt, rucked-down camisole, and drawers.

Fired by her erotic posing, Nate brought his mouth passionately down to her mouth again while he ran his hands over the dark goblets of her breasts. "God, you're beautiful," he proclaimed.

He slid his hands over the dark satin of her bared thighs and heard her moan as he slipped his hand inside her drawers. She moaned again as his caress found her.

Without breaking contact with her warmth, Nate retook his seat. He was as hard as she always made him, but he had to dampen his own passions because he could not have her, not until after the game. Leaning forward, he flicked his tongue against the sweet nook of her navel, and when he moved his kisses lower, she melted in his hand.

Vivid's hips were rising from the desktop in answer to his passionate calls, so he had no trouble ridding her of her drawers. Bare and open, eyes closed, head thrown back, she stiffened as his mouth loved her slowly at first, then with increasing wanton ardor. When his big hands slid beneath her hips to raise her to him more intimately, she couldn't breathe, she couldn't think.

It didn't take long for him to send her soaring into release, and when he did, she yelled his name with a strangled cry.

"Now go home, before I break my vow," he whispered, loving her gently as she came back to earth. "Take this sweetness and go home."

Chapter 20

V ivid took her mother to meet Maddie. The pack of
barking and snapping hounds met them at the gate.
Vivid knew the dogs were familiar with her, but wasn't
sure how they'd react to her mother. She needn't have
worried, because when Francesca began to coo to them
in soft lyrical Castilian, the pack went tame as lambs.
Vivid looked on, astounded. Francesca stepped slowly
into the yard and the hounds began jostling one another
for position in order to receive a petting from her gentle
hands.

Even Maddie, who'd come out on the porch in her
buckskins, stared, amazed, then called, "Who's that with
you, Viveca, a witch?"

"No, Maddie, it's my mother."

"Well, any friend of my dogs is a friend of mine, so
bring her on in."

Maddie and Francesca hit it off famously. Francesca
was awed by all the books she saw when they entered,
and Maddie was impressed by Francesca's way with the
dogs.

"They've never taken to anyone like that before,"
Maddie pointed out as they all sat in her small front
room. "Usually I'm picking folks' skin out of their
teeth."

"I've always liked dogs; maybe they sensed that."

Maddie just shook her head.

They visited for a while, talking about the upcoming

wedding and the lacrosse madness sweeping the countryside, then Vivid asked a question she'd been trying
to have answered for months now. "What happened between Nate and Eli? There's more between them than
politics."

"Nate takes his politics very seriously, but it really
stems from Nate's old wife, Cecile. Cecile committed
adultery with Eli while Nate was away at war, and for
a while after his return."

Vivid stared. "Eli?"

"Yes, Eli. Although she had other lovers, too. Cecile
was a selfish, spoiled little thing. Eli was sixteen, handsome, and so arrogant about his looks, Abigail wanted
to smack him all the time. Made the young women
around here nuts."

"Eli?"

Maddie chuckled, "Eli. He was something when we
were young. Broke hearts from Kalamazoo to the Indiana border. It was a volatile combination. For Eli the
trysts were nothing more than another opportunity to test
his manhood, if you get my meaning, but he grew up
the night Nate found them together."

Maddie paused and looked at Francesca and Vivid.
"Can you imagine Nate's pain? Here people were already whispering about his wife's adulterous behavior,
and then to find out that one of her lovers was his own
cousin, someone Nate had grown to manhood with and
loved all his life. I think Nate went a bit insane. He
dragged Eli out of the bed and beat him nearly to death.
Cecile stood by and watched. The fight spilled out into
the street. Vernon and a few other men managed to separate them, but it was too late. They were never the
same. Nate never forgave Eli. Eli was so ashamed he
wouldn't even fight back. It was awful."

The next morning, Vivid, accompanied by her mother,
Magic, and Satin went over to Mr. Farley's field to see

how the lacrosse preparations were going. The area now resembled a small village. Wagons competed with tents and carriages for spots on the edges of the field, as did the many vendors selling piping hot corn on sticks, lemonade, apple cider, popcorn, and the like. The posts for the goals had been erected, one on each end of the field, standing over the proceedings like silent sentinels.

"What is all this, Magic?" Vivid asked, looking at the stack of goods piled high at one end of the field. She spotted beautiful blankets and quilts, jewelry, guns both ancient and new, boots, moccasins, and even a bicycle.

"These are all the things people are betting," Magic explained as they walked around it. "Pa says back when he was young, the pile would be tall as a man full-grown."

"Do we get to bet anything, Magic?" Satin asked.

"No, we have to be older. Besides, our side always loses, always."

"Really?" Vivid asked with a smile.

"Really. We never win."

The girls asked their grandmother if they might have some of the popped corn and she of course, said, "Of course!"

While her mother went off to spoil her granddaughters, Vivid began a slow weave through the encampments looking at babies and asking to see if anybody needed care. She lanced a few boils, cleaned a few festering wounds, peered into ears and eyes in search of resolutions for various complaints. When any condition seemed serious, she made an appointment to discuss it later at the afflicted person's home or her office.

She saw neighbors and strangers, folks of all races, native women in beautiful beaded dresses, and, a bit later, Magic, the immaculately dressed Satin, and their *abuela* showing off Hector to a knot of impressed youngsters.

In a pasture adjacent to the cleared playing field, Nate

and his team were practicing before a small crowd of Grove supporters. There were about twenty-five men on the field; all had the web-headed sticks in their hands and were running pell-mell down the field, using the sticks to pass the ball to one another as they ran toward the makeshift goal. First one man would carry the ball of wood, then he'd swiftly lob to it another nearby. They kept this up until they were far down the pasture. Adam Crowley, who appeared to be the instructor, stood a few yards away from her, jumping up and down and screaming the whole time. Whether he was offering encouragement or criticism was unclear, but he was certainly loud.

Nate and his team were now running back in her direction at a furious pace, passing the ball just as they'd done before. Adam Crowley was again doing his dance and shouting what sounded like "Opening wings! Opening wings!" but Vivid again had no idea what that meant or even if she was correct.

The men went blazing by, close enough for her to see the sweat pouring down their faces and their bare arms and chests. Vivid had to admit it was quite a treat watching Nate's dark muscles glittering in the sun as he flew past. He must have sensed her thoughts because at that exact moment he looked over at her and grinned, and missed the ball which Vernon passed to him. The ball hit the ground and the game stopped.

Mr. Crowley screamed, snatched his hat off his head, and threw it to the ground. Vivid saw Nate trying to hide his grin at Adam's reaction and she found herself the object of Adam Crowley's pointed gaze. When he beckoned to her, Vivid gulped. Trying to stall, Vivid pointed to herself as if to say, "Me?"

Adam Crowley nodded yes and beckoned to her again.

Vivid heard one of the onlookers say with a chuckle, "You're in trouble now, Doc."

The small crowd laughed and threw teasing comments about her causing Nate's distraction and what Adam was going to do. Vivid tried to take the ribbing with a straight face but could not.

"Yes, Adam," she said.

"Go home."

"Why?"

"Because you are distracting my players, and distracted players do not play well. We are going to win this year but not if my captain is busy staring at a pretty face."

She smiled.

"See, that's what I mean. Go home."

Some of the men in the crowd laughingly agreed with Adam. "Go home, Doc," they cried. "You're gonna make us lose worse than usual. Go home."

Vivid spun on them. "All right, I went to school, I know when I'm not wanted."

She gave Nate a saucy smile before continuing on her way. She took a shortcut through the trees back to the main field, then stopped and stared at the sight of Quentin James standing a few feet away talking to a man Vivid did not know. They were talking intently, then as if sensing her presence, Quentin looked her way. Vivid swore Quentin's eyes grew big with fear for just a moment. The other man, short and squat, stared at her, too. Vivid felt a chilling fear of her own. He tipped his hat and he and Quentin James moved on.

Back at the Grayson house that evening, she told Adam of the strange encounter and he promised to look into it. He came back after the last practice of the day to say that neither Quentin James nor the stranger could be found.

Out on the field the next day, Vivid encountered Abigail and a native woman seated on the benches watching the practices. Vivid looked for Nate and saw him way downfield; these were the only times she could see him.

The teams were sequestered during the final days leading up to the game.

"Viveca, I want you to meet an old friend of mine, Anna Red Bird of the Sturgeon Clan."

"Hello," Vivid said smiling as she placed her bag on the bench and took a seat.

Anna Red Bird glanced at the bag and said, "You are the doctor I've heard so many good things about. I'm glad to finally meet you."

"Pleased to meet you also. Are you related to Isaac Red Bird, the *skabewis*?" Vivid asked.

"Yes, Isaac is my youngest son. He was very excited about being this year's *skabewis*. Remember the year those Kentucky Cherokees came up to play?" Anna Red Bird asked Abigail with a laugh.

"Oh, yes. I thought Adam would strangle that brave to death trying to get that ball. I laughed until I cried. Adam was so furious."

Vivid asked, "Strangling is allowed?"

Mrs. Red Bird laughed. "Only when necessary, and it is sometimes when our clever Cherokee friends play. They love to hide the ball."

"The brave had the ball in his mouth," Abigail explained, chuckling still from the memory. "Back then we would have games with ninety, a hundred men on a side, and in the chaos of all those bodies the players would oftimes lose sight of the ball. On this particular day, the Cherokee brave took advantage of the anarchy and hid the ball in his mouth."

A smiling Anna Red Bird took up the tale, "Adam caught him just as he broke away to dash to the goal, and the next we knew he was strangling him trying to free the ball. That brought the *apisaci* and the drivers out onto the field."

"What are drivers and *apisaci*?" Vivid asked confused.

"The score and foul keepers. They also settle ball

possession disputes so the game keeps moving.''

"So how did they stop Adam from strangling the Cherokee brave?''

"They use long switches to enforce their rules, and after the first couple of blows the Cherokee gave up the ball and Adam gave up his grip, then the game resumed fast and furious as before.''

Vivid shook her head, "Lacrosse sounds like a very novel game.''

Mrs. Red Bird nodded in apparent agreement. "Oh, it is. Back before the French and Americans, the Little Brother of War would sometimes go on for days and hundreds of men would participate. A playing field could be as large as twelve acres.''

She further explained to Vivid that during the old days the games were very intense because they were sometimes used as practices for war. But it was not the only reason the People played. Intertribal ball games were also called to settle land disputes and hunting boundaries. Sometimes a chief called for ball games on his deathbed, and tribes played to honor his life and to ease his passage to the ancestors. The Menominee played ball every spring before the first thunder to cure illness. Each tribe had its own ceremonies and methods of playing.

"Now,'' she said a bit sadly, "there are so few of us left, we have taken customs from all who care to come. The *apisaci* were originally part of the Choctaw game, the drivers are Cherokee and wore turbans on their heads in the old days. We in the Lakes play with a knot from a tree; the Iroquois use a ball of stuffed deer hide.''

Vivid found the information fascinating and asked, "So when did the Grove game begin?''

"Our grandfathers began the tradition back in the early forties,'' Abigail said.

Mrs. Red Bird added, "And in spite of all the government has done and the passage of the years, we continue to honor the families and ancestors of both races, and play.''

The night before the game the Grove hosted the traditional Ball Game Dance. While Vivid and her parents stood with Magic, Satin, Abigail, and the other nonparticipating residents under the flickering light of the torches and ceremonial fires lining the field, the dances commenced on the beat of the traditional groundhog hide–covered drum. Two lines of nearly seventy women of both races, all attired in traditional dresses worked through with beads, needlework, and ribbon appliques, sang and danced slowly in rhythm in the center of the field. Vivid spotted Miss Edna, Maddie, and Adam Crowley's daughter, Jewel, among the Grove women, and the resplendently dressed Anna Red Bird swaying slowly with the women of the People. The blended voices of the women rose in the night with such beauty and power Vivid felt chills course up and down her arms.

Between the lines of women were two shamans, one young, the other old. The two men raised their voices over the singing women, offering prayers and salutations to the ancestors.

While the women continued to dance and chant, and the shamans offered their prayers, the players of both teams, bared to the waist, were dancing at the other end of the torch-lit field. Vivid stared, engrossed, as they gracefully wielded their sticks down by the area of the goal, whirling and turning and striking imaginary goals. Abigail told them that the dance Nate, Eli, and the other Grove men were doing had been added to the ceremony by her father. Some of the movements were similar to the steps of their native competitors. As Vivid watched Nate moving against the oscillating light, she remembered him speaking of his grandfather's dancing the day they'd gone berry hunting. She was certain his grand-

father would be pleased to know his grandsons were
keeping the traditions of their ancestors.

The air was thick with the sounds of drums and singing as Vivid and Abigail headed everyone back to the
house hours later.

Vivid lay in bed surrounded by darkness. Her windows were open and she could hear the faint echoes of
the drum and the sweet voices riding on the night air.
Abigail had told her earlier that back in her youth the
dance would go on all night. Vivid listened for a moment, then as the hour grew late, she drifted into sleep
and dreamed of drums, lacrosse sticks, and the Thunder
God.

The next morning as they ate breakfast before going
to the game, Magic told the story of "How the Bat Got
Its Wings."

According to the Cherokee legend, the land animals
challenged the birds to a ball game. Among the land animals were the bears, because their weight could wear
down the opposition; the deer, because of their swiftness;
and the turtles, because their shells made them impervi-
ous to attack. High up in the trees were their winged
opponents, led by the eagle and the hawk, both known for
their swift, powerful flights. Two little furry creatures
asked the land animals to play but were laughed at because of their small size and turned away. The winged
team took pity on the two creatures and allowed them to
play on their side—but they needed wings.

Magic's voice held everyone rapt as she said, "The
eagle and the hawk thought and thought on how to get
the little ones some wings, then they remembered the
drum they'd used at the Ball Game Dance the night before. There was some groundhog leather left over from
the making of the drum head, so they cut some wings
for one little creature and attached it to his legs. Since
it now had wings the birds changed its name to Tlameha."

"And what does that mean?" Vivid asked.

"Bat," Magic explained. "The birds didn't have any more groundhog leather to make wings for the second little animal, so they decided to make wings out of the animal's own fur."

Francesca chuckled as she asked, "How in the world did they accomplish that?"

"They stretched him," Magic said. "One strong bird got on one side and another strong bird on the other. Then they pulled and pulled until he had wings and they changed its name to Tewa—the flying squirrel."

According to Magic, the ball was tossed up and the flying squirrel who'd gone down to the ground as the bird's representative immediately captured the ball and ran it up the tree to the birds, who kept the ball aloft for some time. The ball dropped from the sky, however, and plunged in the direction of the ground where the land animals waited eagerly.

"But little Tlameha dove out of the sky and grabbed the ball in his teeth, and caught it just before it hit the ground. He did so much fancy flying, not even the deer could catch him. Then he threw the ball into the goal and won the game for the birds."

Vivid and the other adults clapped heartily as she ended the tale, then Anna Red Bird added, "And now, even today, it is traditional for players to interweave a piece of a bat wing into their webbings to aid in their victory."

After the traditional opening ceremonies, the ball was tossed up and the game evolved into a furious-paced contest played against a background of mayhem. Everywhere on the field men were running, shouting, and in some cases slashing at opponents with their stick in an effort to get the ball. The game moved so swiftly, Vivid had a hard time distinguishing the ball carrier from the other players. She watched Eli streak toward the oppo-

nent's goal only to be bowled over by another man. As
he tumbled hard to the ground Eli flipped the ball across
the field, hoping it would land in the webbed stick of
one of his teammates. All the men crashed into one another, slashing and hacking. Finally out of the fray came
a Native man streaking for the Grove's goal. His teammates sprinted after him, swift as the deer in Magic's
story, and once they were near, they spread across the
field like a wing. The ball carrier passed it to one of his
men up the field, but charging toward the wing were the
Crowley sons. The two groups converged like opposing
waves and the center of the field became an eddy of
twisting sticks and turning bodies as players fought for
possession of the ball.

Vivid caught a glimpse of Nate, then lost him in the
revolving fray. She saw Vernon slash at a man and get
hacked across the leg in return for his trouble. As the
game continued Vivid began to see the beauty and grace
of this violent game. The movements of the men were
graceful, powerful. She also began to see why the People
were perennial winners. They were better. They were
faster and much more precise and accurate with their
passes. They seemed to sense without looking when a
teammate was near enough to receive the next forward
pass, while the Grove men were not as skillful. Many
of their passes landed like gifts in the webbing of their
opponents—a fact Adam Crowley kept screaming about
as he yelled instructions.

Two things amazed Vivid as the People scored the
first goal. One, despite the high level of excitement and
drama, those viewing the game were, for the most part,
silent. Not even when the People scored another quick
goal did anyone but the visitors from the cities utter a
cheer.

Secondly, she couldn't understand why tempers
weren't flaring from all the slashing and hacking and
knocking. Men were actually smiling at one another dur-

ing the heated skirmishes. When Eli was bowled over earlier, he'd given his attacker a large grin as the laughing native man helped him to his feet, then they both ran back to join their mates. She leaned over and asked Anna Red Bird, "Why is everyone so silent?"

Anna did not take her eyes from the game as she said, "My people are not as publicly demonstrative as Americans. We enjoy a good contest but we don't see the need to raise our voices or jump up and down like poor Adam over there."

Anna reached over and touched her friend Gail on the arm and said, chuckling, "Gail, maybe you ought to go over there and say something to him before he kills himself."

Abigail Crowley looked over at her husband and said, "You know Adam, he's gotten too old to play and he just doesn't know what to do with himself."

Francesca Lancaster then asked the question Vivid had asked herself earlier. "I would expect more fighting in a game like this."

The Grove scored finally and a few cheers rang out.

"There are few actual fights because you accept the spirit of the Little Brother when you walk out onto the field, otherwise you stand over here and watch as we are doing," Anna Red Bird said with a small smile.

In the end, the People beat the Grove seven goals to two.

After the game, the men dragged themselves back to the field after the traditional wash-off in the small pond on the edge of Mr. Farley's property.

Some of them went to join families while others went over to the crowd circling the pile of goods that had been bet. Most, however, made their way to the makeshift clinic Vivid had set up beside the field.

She treated swollen and bruised ankles, sewed up lacerations on faces and arms, bound up broken ribs and sprained wrists. She splinted a few broken fingers and extracted a few loose teeth. All in all, the players came out of the Little Brother of War relatively unscathed.

Later that evening they celebrated with a big feast. Pigs had been roasting all day in pits tended by Joseph Lancaster and a crew of women from the church. There was a mountain of salmon and a flock of grilled turkeys, along with squash, corn, green beans, and all the cider one could drink. For dessert, there were cakes, pies, and churns and churns of ice cream.

Chapter 21

Vivid awakened to fire. She struggled out of bed coughing from the smoke clogging her lungs and staggered across the room. The thick smoke burned her eyes and throat, blinding and gagging her even as she sought a way out, stumbling through the open bedroom door. The heat and flames in the short hall made her put her arm across her eyes. She hesitated a moment and looked around. The whole house was ablaze; her kitchen, her front room. The flames looked to be fed by winds as it buffeted against the wood logs of the walls. The heat and roar were as intense as the fires of hell. She knew she had to get out or she would die.

She forced herself to brave the flames, moving as quickly as her weakened body would allow, to get to the entrance to the tunnel below the cabin. She took off her gown and used it to wrap her hands as she felt for the small finger hole in the blazing floor. She screamed as hot tongues licked at her hands and arms, but she forced herself to open the small panel and crawl inside. The cool darkness and the sensation of falling were the last things she remembered.

When Vivid opened her eyes again she was in a shadow-filled room. She thought she heard Nate's voice but closed her eyes again and went back to sleep.

The next time Vivid opened her eyes, she drew in a deep breath, only to feel her lungs burn, and she coughed.

"Here, drink this. Slowly, Trabrasera," she heard her mama say in Castilian.

Vivid sipped the cool water, then sank back into the pillows mounded beneath her. As the haze of sleep faded, she turned her head and gazed into the happy, teary eyes of her mother. "Hello, Mama," she croaked, then began to cough again.

She took another sip of water and when the spasm passed heard her mother say, "You need to rest your throat. Don't talk."

"My house?" Vivid rasped.

"Gone, sweetheart, everything gone."

Vivid cried then, silent tears that ran down her face unstaunched.

Francesca said softly, "That is terrible news, I know, but you are alive. Be thankful, my youngest, not sad. What money can buy, money can replace. But your life, that is priceless."

Her mother kissed her softly on the forehead, then laid her cheek there a moment. "Go to sleep now. Everything will be fine, I promise you."

Vivid awakened again after dark. She could see her mother seated near a lamp reading a newspaper. Vivid stared at the lamp's dancing flame and for a moment she felt terror. She closed her eyes and forced away the terrible memory.

Instead she looked around at her surroundings. She had no idea where she was but she assumed she had the Graysons to thank for the bed. The big four-poster seemed even larger than the one Adam Crowley had given her. The canopy over her head was made of quilted emerald silk, trailing sumptuously down to the posts and tied back.

"Where is this, Mama?"

"Nate's room, darling."

Nate's bedroom was large enough for one fireplace in

the wall near where her mother sat reading, and another
in the wall on her side of the room.

She ran her eyes over the cases filled with books and
the armoire and writing desk whose polished dark wood
matched the wood of the bed. Vivid spied a pitcher on
the stand beside the bed and leaned over to pour herself
a cup but stopped in mid-reach upon seeing her bandaged hands and arms. They were as heavily wrapped as
a mummy's. She stared at them a moment, then heard
her mother say, "You burned them fairly badly, my
dear. They'll have to stay that way for a while."

Her mother poured her some water and Vivid drank
slowly. She started coughing immediately afterward. Her
mother, sensing Vivid's confusion about her hands and
arms, asked, "Do you remember going into the tunnel?"

Vivid nodded yes. She remembered the terror and the
pain of the flames cavorting over her hands, then whispered, "But nothing after that."

"Well, the Underground Railroad continues to save
us. Had it not been for that tunnel, we're all certain
you'd not be here. The arsonist must not have known
about it."

Vivid stared.

"Yes, darling, arsonist. Your father said the air was
thick with the smell of kerosene. Someone set that fire
at your front door and at the back. You weren't supposed
to get out."

Vivid was still reeling as she listened to her mother
relate the events that followed Vivid's escape from the
inferno. All the men from the ball game had raced to
help, but the small cabin was already engulfed. In the
end there was nothing anyone could do but stand and
watch it burn. It took five men to restrain Nate so he
wouldn't go run into the flames to find her.

"Viveca, I will go to my grave hearing him scream
your name again and again," she whispered with tears

in her voice. "It was as if his heart were being ripped right from his chest."

Once the flames died the men had gone into the smoldering remains to begin the grim search for her body. The cabin's wood floor had been completely consumed. Beneath the smoking debris littering the ground they found the hole to the tunnel. Nate found her lying on the tunnel floor.

"Your father and I cried like we'd never cried before," her mother said. "He covered you with the shirt from his back and brought you up here to his room. Your papa smeared your arms and hands with the insides of every aloe plant he'd brought with him, and then Abigail and I wrapped your hands, and here you are."

Her father kept aloe because burns were part of his profession. Since he invariably wound up cooking wherever he went, he didn't travel without it. "I want to see Papa and Nate."

"In that order?"

Vivid nodded with a smile.

Her mother left to bring in her father and Vivid thought back to the fire. Who hated her so much that they wanted her to burn alive? The question was still echoing in her mind when her father stuck his gray head in the door.

"Papa!" she rasped happily. He came over to the bed and hugged her as fiercely as her singed skin would allow.

She began to cough from the exertion but he waited patiently until she recovered. He said, "You turned every hair on my head gray with that stunt, girlie. Your papa is getting too old for this."

Then his face and voice turned serious, "Did your mother tell you it was arson?"

She nodded.

"Well, when I get my hands on whoever is responsible they'll know how I feel about someone trying to turn my youngest into a burned Saratoga chip!"

Saratoga chips, or potato chips as some folks called them, had been first introduced by a Black chef up in Saratoga Springs, New York.

"Well, they didn't succeed. But I can't fathom someone wanting me to die such an awful death."

"Everyone feels that way."

She suffered through another coughing fit before asking, "How's Nate, Papa?"

"Doing better now that he knows you're alive. When we thought we'd lost you . . . his grief rivaled mine." Joseph Lancaster paused a moment and gazed lovingly at his youngest daughter. "He's a good man, Vivid. A good, decent man. I'll be proud to call him my son."

"Thank you, Papa. I think he's very special, too."

Joseph bent and kissed her brow. "Rest now, I'll send Nate and your mother up."

When Nate walked through the door moments later, she began to cry silently. Seeing him made her so incredibly happy, she wanted to run to him and have him hold her tight.

Nate asked softly, "Are you crying, Lancaster?"

She answered tearfully, "Yes, Nate, I am."

Nate sat on the bed. He leaned over and brushed his lips against hers softly, "I thought I'd lost you, princess," he whispered. He'd only meant to kiss her lightly, then pull back, but the taste of her, alive and breathing, made him linger and want more. She wanted more, too, because death had almost claimed her and she hungered for the sensations that helped reaffirm her life. "I just want to look at you. Even with no brows and lashes you're as beautiful as the moon rising."

"What?" She immediately brought her hands up to feel her face but it was a useless gesture because she was bandaged. "Nate, get me that hand mirror on the vanity."

"No," he said chuckling softly. "This first . . ."

They shared heated, almost desperate kisses. He instinctively lifted her to his chest, careful not to injure her, but he needed her near. She needed him also and cried sparkling tears of joy as she kissed him in return and ran her bandaged hands up and down his back.

He broke the kiss and just held her tight, tight enough for Vivid to feel the burns on her back sting, but she didn't care. She was in his arms.

A soft knock on the door made them part reluctantly. Nate was standing politely at the bedside when Francesca entered, saying softly, "You should go now, Nate, she needs to sleep."

Nate looked down at her lying so vivid yet so fragile amid the bedding and wanted to climb in and hold her while she slept. "Rest up, princess."

Vivid didn't want him to go. "Will you come back and see me in the morning?"

"If your duenna gives permission."

Nate looked over at Francesca, and she smiled. "We'll see what can be arranged."

Vivid said softly, "Good night, Nate."

"Good night, brave princess."

That night Vivid was awakened by a severe throbbing pain in her hands. Anna Red Bird, who had stayed on to make sure Vivid would recover, brought up some willow bark tea for her to drink. A short time later, the fiery pain began to subside and Vivid went back to sleep.

Nate was allowed to help Vivid with her breakfast each morning. Her hands were still bandaged, though not as heavily.

The first morning he'd come in to assist, the meal had consisted of her favorite, hot oatmeal sweetened with maple syrup, butter, and sweet cream. He'd also brought her toast and tea. Vivid was ravenous and told Nate so, but her mother, seated across the room reading the *Grayson Gazette*, instructed Nate to feed her at a slow pace.

So he did.

Nate slowly teased the tip of the first spoonful across her lips, then whispered, "Open for me, princess . . ."

The words were spoken so heatedly, and conjured up such sensual memories, Vivid felt herself flush with a familar warmth. As he held her captive with his blazing eyes, she opened her mouth and the spoon slid in gently. Her lips closed and he glided the spoon out again.

He spooned up more and repeated each step: first the brush with the spoon, then the heated invitation, then in and—ever so slowly—out.

Her senses were spiraling in response by the time he'd coaxed her to eat a few spoonfuls.

Vivid was certain her mother had not counted on the meal turning into such an erotic exercise, and neither had Vivid.

Just about then, he slowly tore off a small piece of the toast. She watched him dip the bread gently into the sweet cereal and heard him say, "I know you like to dunk your toast . . . so here . . ."

Vivid took the offered morsel, then slid her tongue against his finger before he drew back.

His eyes flared in response to her play, and she whispered sensually, "You started this."

"I'm simply feeding you, nothing more."

For the next few days Nate fed Vivid her breakfast and fed her senses with his eyes and his voice. Were it not for her mama's presence, Vivid was certain she and the Thunder God would have wound up sharing the big canopied bed. With just a simple look he had the power to make her nipples harden and call to him from beneath her gown; make her lips part for the kisses he promised she'd receive once she was well enough. One morning as he fed her the most erotic stack of flapjacks with maple syrup she'd ever consumed, he described in a hushed voice the many ways he planned on loving her when she healed. Every morning when he walked into her room, her breakfast tray in hand, her desire awakened and flowed.

Vivid declared herself well a few days later. She told herself Nate's teasing had not entered into her decision—after all, she had recovered and was especially tired of being in bed—but Nate's eyes burned in her memory as she got up to get dressed.

Her hands no longer needed the dressing, but it would be a while before they were fully healed. Her palms had sustained most of the damage but faithfully, twice a day, she rubbed cocoa butter on them to help speed the process. The cocoa butter had been sent over by Miss Edna. Francesca had purchased every tin in the store.

She couldn't put on her stockings, however, or button her skirt or blouse. That problem was solved by Magic and Satin, who'd been visiting off and on for the past few days. When she asked for their assistance with her buttons and stockings, they helped eagerly, even as Magic asked, "Did they say you could get up today?"

"No, but I'm the doctor, right?"

"Right," Magic agreed.

When they were finished Satin looked up and said, "We're awful glad you didn't burn up, Dr. Lancaster."

She kissed each girl on her brow and said, "Me, too."

The Grayson front parlor was filled with people when she got downstairs, and at her entrance, the room erupted into cheers. She saw Abigail and Adam, Anna and her son Isaac, Nate, Eli, her parents, and Maddie.

Someone moved so Vivid could have a seat on the settee, and when she was settled in she said, "I want to thank everyone for all you've done. If I had to be burned out of my home, I couldn't've had it happen in a better place."

That brought on a few chuckles and many smiles.

Vivid then asked about the search for the arsonist.

"We have nothing but this, so far. We assume it's his."

Nate held up a tattered red flannel shirt. Even after a week it still reeked strongly of kerosene.

"Or hers," Maddie pointed out.

"The shirt is pretty saturated on the front," Joseph said. "Maybe the arsonist accidentally sloshed a good bit of it on himself and then took it off as a precaution before setting the fire."

Everyone else had already agreed that Joseph's conclusion seemed logical and Vivid deemed the theory sound as well.

"But who would do this?" Magic asked. "And why?"

Magic and Satin had been so quiet, no one had even noticed them come in. Nate turned to his daughter and said softly, "Majestic, this is not a conversation for little ears, so why don't you and Satin go outside and play."

"But Pa, we want to help, too."

"I know you do, darling, but I don't want you or Satin poking around. The person that tried to hurt Viveca is very dangerous."

Magic glanced over at Vivid, who said, "Your father is right, Magic. I gave everyone a bad enough scare. We don't want anyone else hurt."

"Okay," she said, obviously against her better judgment.

Nate turned his attention to Satin. "Satin, I want your promise, too, no poking around."

She hesitated just as her sister had done, then gave a weak, "Okay, Uncle Nate," in reply.

He kissed them both and sent them on their way.

"Did anyone believe that performance?" he asked after their departure.

Laughter filled the room.

Vivid spoke up when the humor faded, "I do hope they'll take us seriously though."

Her mother snorted and said, "And this from La Brat Trabrasera herself. May your father and I live long enough to see your hair grayed by a child like you. She lived in a tree house for nearly two years. She'd come home some days looking like she'd been raised by bears."

Nate almost fell off his chair laughing.

Vivid took mock offense. "Mama! Nate Grayson, stop laughing."

Vivid looked over at her father. He said, "Vivid, you know good and well your mother is telling the truth. The day you were born I held you in my arms and looked down into your bright eyes, and you winked up at me big as day. I told your mama then and there, this one is going to be real different from the other two."

More laughter followed that remark and Vivid said, "Papa, new babies can't wink."

"That's what the doctor said at the time, but I know what I saw."

That afternoon, Vivid took a slow walk through her burned-out cabin. The flames had consumed everything from books to instruments. Only a few charred and blackened logs still stood to announce that there had once been walls. All the carefully documented medical histories she'd compiled on her neighbors, months of work, gone because some unknown person wanted to roast her like a piece of corn. In the back she found only the chains from her swing and the burned-out hulk of her brand-new stove. She hunkered down and fished the chains out of the ashes and debris. As she peered at it sadly she sensed Nate standing behind her. She stood and looked over what had been her life.

"I'll put up another swing in the spring," he promised quietly.

She would miss the swing very much, but the question kept echoing in her head, Who would do this? Aloud she asked, "What have I done to make someone hate me this much?"

Nate had no answer.

She turned away from the cabin and let him escort her back to the house.

Anna Red Bird and her son had departed earlier that afternoon. Eli and Maddie took their places at the dinner table.

After the meal, Vivid's parents excused themselves to their rooms. It had been a long day for the recently recovered Vivid so she, too, excused herself.

Alone in Nate's room, Vivid realized she needed help with her buttons. She went to her parents' room and knocked on the door, "Mama?"

She heard scurrying and laughter inside and then silence, then laughter again. Then silence again, followed moments later by her mother calling, "Just a minute, Viveca."

Then she heard her mother say with a laugh, "Viveca, darling, unless the house is on fire, you'll have to come back later. Your father—"

"Go away, girl!" she heard her father shout. "Your mother and I are busy!"

She took the hint and went back to her room wearing a stunned smile.

Inside again, she lay down fully dressed and drifted off to sleep.

Around midnight, Vivid awakened feeling as if she were bound up in a sack. She got up and tried to figure out how to undo her buttons. Her fingertips were still too tender to accomplish such a delicate task and she had to give up. She sighed with frustration and began to look around Nate's room for a razor or a pair of shears. Maybe she could cut herself out. She found nothing.

The house was quiet as Vivid noiselessly made her way down to the kitchen. She knew Abigail kept shears in a drawer there. Surely she'd be able to handle a pair of shears long enough to snip away the buttons of her blouse and skirt. She could always sew them back later.

She made her way through the dark house with the

aid of the moonlight streaming in from the curtains. She paused a moment when she saw the thin line of light beneath the door of Nate's study. Quietly, Vivid placed her ear against the door to make certain she wouldn't be interrupting anything. Silence. She knocked softly.

Nate opened the door, surprised to see her on the other side. He looked behind her, then hustled her in, hastily closing the door again.

"What's wrong?" Vivid laughed.

"Don't want your duenna to find us."

"You'd better put out the lights then."

"Good idea."

His comment drew Vivid's eyes to the lighted lamps and she wondered how long it would be before she stopped shuddering at the sight of a flame. She turned away until all the lamps had been extinguished. In the darkness Vivid relaxed a bit.

He opened the drapes to let in the moonlight. "How's that?" he asked.

"Nice," she whispered.

"Come sit with me then," he offered, gesturing to the small loveseat beneath the big bay window. Nate sat beside her, eased her onto his lap, and pulled her close. "Perfect," he declared.

And to Nate, for this period of time, things were just that: perfect. He never thought he'd hold her again after the terrible fire. The despair he felt when he first saw the cabin ablaze echoed within him still. He hoped it would be the last time he'd experience such wrenching helplessness. She'd survived, however, and because of that he could continue to bask in her smile and watch her stride confidently into a room. He could hear her laugh and see her tears, and rid himself of wondering how he would spend the rest of his life without her love, as he'd done that awful night. The emotions flared again and he gently pulled her close to stop the ache that came with the memories. He whispered against her hair, "What are you doing up so late?"

"I was on my way to the kitchen for Abigail's shears. I can't undo my buttons because my fingertips are too tender to work the holes."

He leaned back to peer down into her face. "Oh, really? Then basically you're at my mercy, is that correct?"

"Basically, correct," she agreed, looking up at him.

"Well, we'll take care of your buttons later. Tell me how you're feeling."

"I'm recovering, I guess. Feels good having you hold me again, though. Very good."

"I've missed you, too."

For a moment they sat in the moonlight, content just being together.

Vivid said, "You and Eli seem to be working out your differences. It's good to see the two of you friends."

He kissed her forehead. "We're making progress."

"It will take weeks, maybe months to restock my medicines and instruments. We can only pray an epidemic or something serious doesn't occur in the meantime."

"I wouldn't worry. The day after we found you, your mama began wiring the doctors over at the college in Ann Arbor about what she needed to buy to get your practice back on its feet. I suppose they wired her back, because she spent that whole next day over in Niles wiring folks in Chicago, Philadelphia, Boston, you name it, placing orders."

"Really? You said she did all this the day after you found me in the tunnel? I don't remember her being gone for a long period of time."

"That's because you were asleep. You slept for a good three days."

He must have felt her shock. "Your father and I sat

with you on the first day while Vernon took her to
Niles."

"Three days?"

"You were drifting in and out, but yes, three days."

"It didn't feel as if that much time passed."

"Well, it did."

"Thanks for finding me."

He whispered in response. "Thanks for being alive."

Then she heard him say, "Now, what do you have to
barter in exchange for this help you need?"

"I have kisses," she stated, her voice a quiet invitation.

He ran a long finger over her succulent mouth and
replied, "As I remember, they are quite sweet, but it's
been such a long time, I may need to sample a few to
see if they are valuable enough to offer as exchange."

"I think you will find them priceless . . ."

He brought his mouth down to hers and found her
welcoming kisses not only priceless but as sweetly fer-
vent as ever. He teased her parted lips with his tongue,
nibbled her with his teeth, and when he'd sampled
enough, he reluctantly drew away.

Nate removed his spectacles and placed them on the
windowsill behind him. In a voice as velvety as the
shadows he requested, "Sit up a moment, princess."

Vivid rose to her knees on the settee between his
spread thighs, and he began to undo the buttons on her
blouse. She kissed his mouth and he paused to enjoy the
treat. It had been such a long time since they'd had the
opportunity to enjoy their passion, each wanted to savor
the other slowly and without haste.

He spread open her blouse, then dropped his head to
flick the tip of his tongue against the hollow of her
throat. Her head dropped back under his fiery advance
across the skin and she placed her slender brown hands
upon his broad shoulders for support. She shivered in
response as his hands cupped her breasts and raised the

camisole-covered tips to his lips, then her body arched as he kissed her breasts until the fabric was damp and a moan slid from her lips. Before she could catch her breath he slid one breast free of the bodice, then boldly suckled the peak. He bared the other and to her delight pleasured it in the same wanton way.

When he released her he smiled smugly at her expression. He then reached behind her, undid the buttons on the waistband of her skirt, and tugged the skirt down until it pooled around her knees. The blouse came off next. She knelt before him scandalously clad in her thin drawers, dark stockings, and ribbon-fronted camisole. It took him only a heartbeat to undo the tiny ribbons, and as the garment gaped open to her waist, his manhood surged as his eyes feasted on her beautiful dark breasts in the moonlight. He ran his palm over one satin bud, then the other. He kissed each one in turn, then raised to kiss her lips. "Remember the morning I promised to take you in a variety of ways?"

He didn't wait for a reply, his hands began roaming sensuously over her behind, squeezing the backs of her thighs and journeying up to tease her breast before sliding down again to her hips. "Do you remember?"

He circled hotly over the shrine between her spread, stockinged thighs and she'd no idea how on earth he expected her to reply. She moaned as he boldly slid his hand inside her drawers.

"You're supposed to answer, not moan . . ." he reminded her softly.

She'd gone without his touch for so long, the initial feel of his hand pleasing her so magnificently had her already tightening on the edges of release. "Yes, I remember . . ."

Release hovered but she didn't want to die the little death so soon. She wanted the sensations to build even higher, wanted to let the pleasure of his hands continue to make her bloom and flow. His dalliance tempted her damp warmth with increased abandon, circling, and tenderly plucking, making her hips rock sensually and her body's desire to gain release harder and harder to stave off.

She was almost beyond control. Through eyes lidded by the haze of passion she saw him watching her, his own gaze diamond-hard. She heard him say huskily, "Don't fight it, princess, let yourself go. I'll give you more, I promise . . ."

And on those words she exploded with such shattering force, she shook as his fingers continued to stroke. She buckled under the soaring impact, then buried her strangled cries into his chest as the little death swept her away.

When she could move again he helped her out of her drawers, then rose to undress. Vivid sat on the settee and marveled at his stature as he stood nude in the moonlight. She wished she had a gift for sketching so she could put on paper the powerful grace in his arms and shoulders, the trim waist, and the sculpted chest. Because he would be her husband, she would even be bold enough to render the beauty of his readiness presenting itself so gloriously.

She reached out and closed her hand around warm hard velvet and felt the familiar throbbing. Holding his power rekindled her own desire, as did seeing the passion on his handsome face as her hand began to move lazily.

Their eyes mated hotly and she heard him say, "You keep that up and you're going to miss out on my adding to your . . . medical training."

His last few words had been uttered in a voice barely above a whisper. She smiled the smile of a woman who had her man in thrall and said, "Well, we wouldn't want that to happen . . . would we?"

She leaned forward and treated him to the same loving he had a habit of lavishing upon her, then as she heard

his soft groans of pleasure, leaned back and reveled in
the sight of his closed eyes and muscle-tensed stance.
"You were saying?" she questioned, then treated him
to one last lingering lick before lifting her eyes.

It took him a moment, but Nate finally managed to
reply, "I was saying you are sometimes too vivid for
your own good."

She smiled.

He sat, saying, "Come let me introduce you to
something I think you'll enjoy."

And she did, immensely. She'd no idea love could be
made while a woman sat astride a man, but the wonder
of it soon passed, replaced by the feel of his desire im-
paling her so magnificently. The positioning made for
an erotic, languid climb back up to pleasure's peak and
they took turns setting the pace every step of the way.

Nate reached the pinnacle first. Gripping her hips, he
poured out his soul and she spiraled over the edge.

Chapter 22

Vivid slept late the next morning. No one minded. Everyone figured she still needed to recover from the fire. Only she and Nate knew her tiredness stemmed from riding a Thunder God until dawn.

Sara James came by to visit one afternoon a few days later, and Vivid was so glad to see her, she hugged her as tightly as she could manage.

Sara looked around the quiet front room and asked, "Is Miss Gail here?"

"No, she and my mother have gone to Kalamazoo for a few days to do some shopping."

"I'm sorry I missed them," Sara said. She had a yellowed handkerchief in her hand and spent a few minutes fidgeting with it while Vivid waited to hear what else Sara might have to say.

"I came by to thank you for all you've done."

Vivid could feel her heart breaking all over again at the remembrance of Sara's double loss. "You've been very strong, Sara."

"It hasn't been easy. That's the other reason I came today, to say goodbye."

"You're going away?"

"Yes, down to Tennessee. I've been staying with Kate, but my uncle's a preacher outside Knoxville and he and his congregation are trying to buy some land in Kansas. They plan on migrating in the spring and I've decided to go with them."

362

"Then I wish you happiness, Sara. Is your husband, Quentin, going along?"

"I haven't seen him since we buried little Quentin. Can't say I miss him any, not anymore. Last I seen him he was cursing you and me both, holding us to blame for little Quentin's death. I don't know where he is and don't much care."

Vivid then told Sara that she had seen Quentin at the lacrosse field.

Sara hadn't seen her husband but when she heard about the fire she expressed her condolences. "Good thing you were able to get out."

"Yes, too bad we haven't been able to find the culprit so far."

"Well, as the reverend always says, the Lord works in mysterious ways. You're a good person, Dr. Lancaster, if you weren't you would have burned up."

Vivid smiled warmly at the genuine tone of Sara's words, then listened as the young woman added, "Wait and see, the person who set that fire will be found out, especially with Mr. Nate on his trail. It won't be long."

"Well, we do have what we believe is the arsonist's shirt. Nate's been showing it around the Grove, but no one recognizes it."

"Can I see it? I probably can't help but it can't hurt to make sure."

Vivid went into the study. Using Nate's hidden key she retrieved the shirt from a locked strongbox in his desk drawer, then carried the shirt back out to show it to Sara.

Sara stared at the material, slightly confused, as Vivid held it out, and asked, "Turn it around so I can see the back."

Vivid complied, pointing out, "Miss Edna has sold hundreds of these flannel shirts over the years. It could belong to anyone."

Then Sara said coldly, "Not anyone. Just Quentin. Hand it here, let me make sure."

Vivid felt the chills race over her body as she passed the shirt to Sara's outstretched hand.

"See," Sara said, pointing to a spot on the shirt's back. "He ripped it on a nail in the barn wall. This is where I stitched the tear."

Vivid saw the stitches. They were fine enough to be overlooked unless one knew they were there. "Is Quentin capable of doing something so awful?"

"Quentin will do anything if someone pays him enough."

Sara took one last look at the shirt and gave it back to Vivid, who asked, "So you haven't seen him?"

"Nope. Like I said, haven't seen him since the day my son died, but that doesn't mean he can't be still around. Have Mr. Nate ask the barkeep over at Miss Maddie's old place. If anyone has seen Quentin, he has; they're old drinking mates."

Sara then offered Vivid a short list of other people and places that might help them discover Quentin's whereabouts. "I want to say I can't believe he would do something so horrible, but I know he would, especially if he was paid to."

Vivid asked, "Sara, do you think someone did?"

She shrugged. "Maybe, maybe not. Like I said, he was mad at both of us. Could be he thought of burning you out on his own, but not likely. He's never been smart enough to plan nothing, at least not since I've known him. What are you going to do, Dr. Lancaster?"

"Wait until Nate and the others return and hear what they think, but in the meantime I'll see what I can learn from these names and places you've given me."

"You be careful," Sara warned.

"Don't worry," Vivid replied. "That last encounter proved a bit close for my tastes. I never want to be in such danger again."

They spoke for a few minutes more, then Sara had to depart. They shared another long, fierce hug of goodbye, and Sara asked, "May I write to you, Dr. Lancaster?"

"Only if you agree to address me as Viveca."

Sara smiled with what looked like shy elation and said, "I'd be pleased to."

"You know, Sara, according to Nate and the Committee men, over the next few years many others of the race may follow you and your uncle's congregation to Kansas to form new towns. So yes, write me so we may gauge their progress and yours."

They parted and Vivid waved until Sara and her wagon disappeared from sight.

Vivid reentered the house and gathered up the cups and other items from the tea. She couldn't help speculating on Sara's startling identification of the red shirt. Could Quentin really be so distraught over the death of his son that he wanted to burn her alive, or had he been paid by someone? Like Sara, Vivid had no way of knowing.

Nate and the men returned late the next day. They were startled by the news of the shirt's owner.

"Do you think he'll be easy to locate?" Vivid asked, looking into Nate's hard eyes.

"The longer it takes me to find him, the angrier I'm going to be. So for his sake, I hope he shows up soon."

Once word got around that the shirt's owner had been identified, the people of the Grove began combing the woods for Quentin James. It took only three days.

Nate found him lying on the Grayson front porch one morning, trussed up in a large burlap seed bag that had been secured at the neck with knotted rope. Only Quentin's head was visible above the bag as he flopped around like a landed fish. The gag on his mouth kept his angry curses from filling the air.

Nate called for everyone to come and look. Vivid

crowded around, as did everyone else. Quentin flopped more intensely as they all stood gawking, the muffled curses rising, but he wasn't going anywhere. They all knew that.

Magic piped up, "Looks like someone pinned a note on him, Pa."

Sure enough, under Quentin's bouncing chin a note had been attached.

Quentin tried to keep Nate from retrieving the piece of brown paper, but Nate planted his big booted foot atop Quentin's waist, only inches away from the most vulnerable portion of his anatomy, and he stilled immediately.

Nate smiled as he leaned down and snatched the note free.

"What's it say?" Joseph Lancaster asked.

"It says, 'I found this varmint in my barn last night trying to run off with Chester. When you're done skinning him, send him back.' It's signed Hiram Farley."

"Hooray for Hiram," Abigail said with a smile.

"Who's Chester?" Francesca asked curiosly.

"Hiram's rooster," Adam explained with a laugh. "Much as Hiram loves that ornery old cock, we might want to look and see if Quentin's been gelded down inside that bag."

Nate looked down at his daughters and said, "Majestic and Satin, isn't it about time you headed off to school?"

Magic dropped her head, then uttered slowly, "Oh, I suppose so." It was plain the girls found the idea of attending school today far less interesting than the man on the porch. However, Vivid went back into the house with her soon-to-be daughters and helped them gather their papers and books. "Think of it this way," she told them, "you'll be able to tell everyone at school Quentin has been found. None of your classmates know."

"You're right, Viveca, but I'd still rather be here today."

"I know, but school's very important."

The sisters reluctantly agreed, then trudged out to the road to await Vernon and the ride to school.

Back on the front porch, Vivid found only her mother and Abigail. The man and the bagged Quentin were gone.

"They took him to the barn," Abigail said.

"To chat," Francesca added.

The chat took only a short while.

Quentin had been hired by Evan Cole. Paid to burn the Grayson home, he had let his grudge against Vivid override his instructions.

Quentin said Cole had been in the area for weeks but that he didn't know the man's present whereabouts. Vernon took Quentin to Niles the next morning, to be jailed there until his trial.

The presidential election intruded upon the search for Cole as the men of the Grove cast their votes. Black men had been given the vote in Michigan in 1867 and had always voted Republican. Like their brethren in the South, they stood solidly behind the party of Mr. Lincoln, even though President Grant's refusal to send troops into the blood-soaked counties of Mississippi had left many Southern Republicans at the mercy of the Redemptionists.

The Centennial year's preelection wranglings had been rife with backroom deals, political scandals, and Republican party infighting. For the first time since 1860 the Republicans began the year with no clear candidate to represent the party as presidential nominee. Former House Speaker James G. Blaine, one of the most popular Republican leaders, seemed almost assured of gaining the nomination until last April, when his name became linked to one of many influence-peddling scandals prevalent in Washington, and within the Grant administration. As Blaine's reputation went up in flames the liberal wing of the party called for a reformer to lead the ticket, thus canceling out the hopes of men such as Roscoe Conkling and Oliver P. Morton. The liberals wanted Secretary of the Treasury Benjamin H. Bristow, but Bristow's investigation of the Whiskey Rings had revealed the involvement of President Grant's personal secretary Orville H. Babcock, and the red-faced party bosses were adamantly opposed.

In the end the Republican name on the ballot turned out to be that of Ohio Governor Rutherford B. Hayes, described as "colorless" by some when compared to Lincoln and Grant, and termed "a third-rate nonentity" by Henry Adams.

Francesca's orders of medical books, supplies, and instruments to replace the ones Vivid had lost in the fire began to arrive the day after the election. Vivid stored some of the boxed goods in the Grayson cellar and the rest at the church. Adam and Nate promised to erect a clinic for her once the weather broke in the spring, but until then she planned on practicing out of the church activity room and from her office in town.

Satin and Magic were now inseparable. Satin had taken to mimicking her older sister's every move. She seldom wore dresses anymore, preferring to romp in the denims Vivid had given her as a gift for her birthday. She could now climb trees, fish, and snare rabbits. She'd even gotten over her fear of Hector and had joined Magic and the big hawk on many of their adventures in the woods behind the Crowley place. The watchful eyes of the family and neighbors were on the children wherever they roamed.

It was Saturday and a beautiful crisp November day when the girls went out early in the morning to see Mr. Crowley's new kittens. By late in the day they had not returned. Vivid could feel ice spreading over her heart. *Where were they?*

Nate immediately went out to look for them, as did Adam Crowley, Eli, and Vivid's father. Vivid, needing to do something besides wait, grabbed her coat and medical bag, hitched up Michigan, and with her mother, went to fetch Maddie and the dogs.

Maddie's yard was eerily quiet as Vivid and Francesca approached the gate.

"Do you think she and the dogs are out for a walk?" asked Francesca.

Vivid had no answer as she glanced around the dark yard. The sense of something being wrong was strong enough for Vivid to touch. Vivid knocked on Maddie's door. When there were no sounds of movement, Vivid knocked again, harder this time, while Francesca peered into the windows.

Vivid raised her fist to pound again but stopped when she heard Francesca gasp. "Viveca, Maddie's on the floor, bleeding. We must get to her!"

Vivid pushed her weight against the door but it was locked from the inside. She frantically glanced around for something to aid her in forcing the door and saw a pile of split wood stacked off to the side. Vivid grabbed a log she hoped would be heavy enough and hurled it into the panes of the big front window.

Vivid and Francesca gingerly climbed through the gaping hole and moved immediately to Maddie's side. Even in the silvery shadows Vivid could see the blood pooled near Maddie's side.

"We need light, Mama." Vivid quickly stripped off her coat, then leaned over her friend's chest in search of a heartbeat, while Francesca hastily lit lamps.

The light showed that she'd been beaten very badly but she was still alive. Her face was a mess of bruises and cuts, her lips split and swollen. Vivid could feel the tears stinging her eyes as she whispered, "Maddie, who did this to you?" Maddie's eyes were both battered shut and there were knife slashes on the sleeves of her buckskins and on the backs of her hands, but Vivid was more concerned with the serious wounds in her side.

Francesca came out of the kitchen carrying a basin of water and a clean cloth. Vivid sent her back for a large knife, which she applied to the seams of Maddie's buckskin shirt. When she peeled the material back she saw that the wound was serious. Maddie began to stir, and Vivid, gently cleaning the wound, said, "Maddie, I'm here. Just lie still."

Maddie moaned and twisted her head slowly. She murmured, "Viveca . . ."

Vivid paused and said, "Lie still, Maddie."

"Nooo," she whispered. Maddie seemed to be fighting off great pain as she struggled to raise herself up so she could look into Vivid's eyes. "Tell Nate . . ."

Her words halted as she grimaced with the effort, "Tell Nate a man has the girls." She stopped again and forced out the word, "Hurry . . ."

Sheer will had fueled Maddie for the past few moments, but in the end her body won the battle. Before she could offer more details, her eyes closed and she slipped back into unconsciousness.

Vivid stitched the wound as precisely as she could, then she and Francesca carried Maddie into her bedroom and gently eased her atop the bed.

Francesca decided she would spend the night with Maddie and Vivid agreed.

"Did Maddie say who did this?" Francesca asked as they covered Maddie with a quilt.

Vivid shook her head, angered at the sight of Maddie's bruised and battered face. "A man. Undoubtedly Cole."

The sounds of knocking at the door and male voices calling her name sent Vivid running to the door.

Nate, Eli, Joseph, and Adam Crowley were with a posse of men on horseback and atop wagons lit with lanterns and torches.

"Have you found the girls?"

"No," Nate said. "What happened to Maddie's window?"

When Vivid described what she and her mother had discovered, the three men hastily followed Vivid back to the bedroom.

"Aw, hell," Nate swore emotionally upon seeing Maddie's state. He went back to the doorway to try and collect himself. "Who did this?" he asked coldly.

"She said a man. She said to tell you a man has the girls. That was all she could manage."

"Well," Nate intoned, "I need some answers."

"Where are the hounds?" Nate asked as they stood in the night air on the front porch.

Vivid replied, "Mama and I asked the same question. We've neither seen them nor heard them."

Vivid stood shivering in the chill while Nate and the men searched the surrounding area. A few moments later, Vivid could hear frantic baying. The hounds sounded fine. Now if only the girls could be found so readily, she mused. Where are they? she asked herself for maybe the hundredth time. She knew Magic could take care of herself out of doors, and Vivid knew Magic would take care of Satin to the best of her nine-year-old's ability, but the weather had turned very cold in the last few days, the nights even colder. She prayed they weren't caught out in the elements. She prayed even harder that they hadn't been harmed.

Nate came around from the back of the house. "Found the hounds down in Maddie's root cellar. What the—" Nate was nearly bowled over by Maddie's hounds bounding up on the porch. One by one they crawled through the small tarp-covered opening cut into the bottom of the door and disappeared inside. Winded, Eli ran up saying, "I tried to pen them up but they wouldn't let me."

Vivid turned and went in after the canines. Dogs had

no business in a sickroom, not even Maddie's dogs. By the time Vivid caught up to them, they were swarming over the bed licking Maddie's bruised face and cut hands and whimpering like children in pain.

"Mama, they can't be in here."

"I know, darling, but they know something is wrong. Look at them. Listen to them."

They were howling mournfully. Some were still atop the bed and others were seated on their haunches on the floor. All were keening.

Nate came up behind Vivid in the doorway, and for a moment neither said a word as the grief continued to flow from the dogs. Eli entered the room, as did Adam Crowley and the men who'd come along on the search. When Maddie stirred, Vivid moved over to the bed. One of the dogs, one Vivid knew to be Maddie's oldest and most beloved, took up a defensive position in front of his mistress, bared his teeth, and growled menacingly at Vivid's approach. Vivid stopped immediately. She heard Nate say, "Settle down, Blue, she's only trying to help. Come here."

The dog eyed Vivid, then Nate.

"Come here, Blue," Nate said firmly.

The dog reluctantly bounded down and sat by Nate, never taking his eyes off the bed.

Vivid moved to her side as Maddie began to move fitfully, calling out, "Run, Magic! Run!"

Nate came quickly to the bedside, and while Vivid poured some of the ground willow bark she'd been given by Anna Red Bird into a cup of water, Nate asked his childhood friend, "Where's Majestic, Maddie?"

"No! Don't hurt them!"

Vivid moved around Nate and lifted Maddie's head so she could drink. Vivid could feel the heat now burning Maddie's skin. She looked over at Nate's stoic face and said softly, "Darling, I don't think you're going to be able to get any answers tonight. She really needs to rest.''

Nate nodded, but Vivid could see the worry and concern haunting his eyes. ''We'll find them,'' she told him.

Vivid and her mother decided to spend the night sitting with Maddie until the fever subsided.

Reluctantly, Nate agreed with Adam and Eli that the darkness prevented any more searching that night. Tomorrow at dawn the search would resume and everyone prayed there would be more answers by then.

Nate held Vivid tightly as they shared a goodbye. She told him, ''Promise me you will go home and try to get some sleep. You'll be no good to anyone if you don't rest.''

Nate smiled through his sadness, ''That sounds a bit like my speeches to you.''

''You're right. So take your own advice.''

''Yes, Doctor.'' He then looked down into her tired eyes and said, ''When this is all settled, will you marry me? Right away?''

''Soon as we find the girls and I take a bath, yes. I will marry you so fast the speed will make your head spin.'' She kissed him lightly. ''Now go home. We'll speak in the morning.''

Chapter 23

M addie spent a fitful night fraught with nightmares
that made her cry out and thrash around, bringing either Vivid or Francesca to the bedside to ease her
back to sleep. Vivid worked on bringing the fever down
with the aid of cold water from Maddie's well. The well
drew on the swift-moving Dowagiac River flowing on
the outer acres of Maddie's land. Nate had explained to
Vivid just the other day that in a few more weeks the
river would begin to freeze, and once it and the other
small lakes and ponds in the area were frozen solid, he'd
promised to teach her to skate on the ice. As Vivid
sponged Maddie down, Nate's promise seemed to have
been made months ago. So much had happened since
the fire, it made Vivid wonder if this place she called
home would ever return to tranquillity.

At dawn, Vivid forced herself out of the chair she'd
slept in and walked bleary-eyed around the sleeping
dogs and over to the bed. The skin on Maddie's forehead
still felt a bit warm beneath Vivid's palm, but not as
heated as before. Vivid was pleased. However, she was
not happy that Blue was lying next to his mistress. She
had spent most of the night getting him off the bed, but
the moment she turned her back or left the room, he'd
go right back to where he wanted to be. Vivid understood the dog's sentiments, but Maddie was ill and Blue
was a dog.

Vivid made her way out to the front room where Francesca slept on the settee under several quilts; the air streaming in through the broken window made the room quite cold. Her snores rose softly on the dawn silence. Vivid smiled wearily and offered up a quiet thanks for her mother's spirit and guidance over the past few weeks. She'd been so unflappable, so gracious, she'd endeared herself to everyone around and had become part of the community. Vivid couldn't imagine having her leave and be thousands of miles away again.

Vivid quietly added more wood to the fire in the grate, then made a quick dash out into the cold morning air for a trip to the privy. She ran back and had almost reached the door when she heard a familiar bird cry. She looked up, searching the trees. The cry pierced the dawn again. Her heart leaped as she finally spotted Hector, soaring against the pearl-gray sky. If he was near, could the girls be far away? She glanced quickly toward the road but saw no one. She did see Hector begin one of his spectacular bullet-swift dives in her direction, and as he neared, Vivid ducked defensively. However, instead of flying by as usual, Hector hit her in the back of the shoulder and nearly knocked her to the ground. She spun to see where the next pass would come from but he was already streaming over her shoulder and again bumped her hard as he went.

Vivid wondered if the bird had finally lost his mind. Hector was nearly full-grown now, and thanks to all the hares and vermin he consumed, was of good size. The talons could rip the flesh from a person's face and Vivid had personally witnessed how efficiently the hooked beak could tear at the flesh of prey. She'd also seen him play this game with the girls before—they called it "Duck!" But Hector didn't seem to be playing. The cries were different, angry-sounding, as if the bird was agitated or upset, and Vivid couldn't remember him attacking anyone this way, ever.

Hector had ceased his assaults and now soared high

above, calling with a skin-chilling cry that, to Vivid's ears, sounded very similar to the keening sent up last night by Maddie's dogs. She thought that if she were a character in one of Nate's myths, she'd conclude that the hawk's strange behavior somehow related to the disappearance of the girls, but in real life there were no magic ravens offering guidance.

Or were there?

Vivid ran into the house and grabbed Maddie's shotgun. She fished out a handful of cartridges from the tin on the edge of a book-filled shelf and fed some into the gun. The rest she stuffed into the pocket of her shirt.

She could hear her mother stirring on the settee behind her. "Trabrasera? What's the matter, have the girls been found?"

In rapid Castilian, Vivid explained the situation.

Francesca moved to the broken window and tried to peer up into the sky. "Hector is here?"

"Yes, and I'm praying he knows where the girls are. Somehow, I don't know how, but you must get word to Nate. I don't know where I'm going, but I'm going."

They spent a precious minute discussing how Vivid could mark her trail, then Vivid ran to get her coat and gloves. She was halfway out the door when her mother called, "Take some of the dogs!"

"Good idea, Mama. I'm going to hitch Michigan and the wagon, you bring the hounds out front."

Vivid had no idea how her mother did it, but by the time Vivid and Michigan were ready, Francesca came out of the house with all but one of the hounds. She even had Blue.

Her mother asked, "Do you have anything in the wagon that belongs to either of the girls? Preferably something they've worn fairly recently?"

Vivid climbed back into the wagon bed to see. She tossed aside tools, tarp-covered blankets, a cot, canteens, and other miscellaneous items, but found nothing. Then

she remembered. Quickly she went back to the bench,
stuck her hand beneath, and groped blindly until she
found Magic's blue bonnet and handed it to her mother.
"It's all I have."

She watched her mother let each of the dogs sniff the
bonnet in turn. Francesca saved Blue for last and let him
get a good smell of the bonnet's wide strings.

Her mother said, "I don't know if this will help them,
but I don't know what else to do."

They were now ready to leave. Hector had been soaring in the sky overhead while Vivid was hitching up the
wagon, but now he stood perched high on a branch of
a nearby leaf-barren tree, observing the proceedings. Her
mother called up to him and then extended her covered
arm. At the command, Hector flew down just as he'd
been trained to do, and landed as gently as his large
curved talons would allow. She kissed him on his golden
curved beak, and speaking in Castilian, told the bird,
"Bring back my granddaughters Magic and Satin and
I'll buy you rabbits for the rest of your life."

She flung him into the sky and the strong wings pro-
pelled him up. Vivid slapped the reins against Michigan's back and they rolled out.

Vivid had many worries as she followed Hector's
flight. Chief among them, could she control the dogs,
would she be able to handle the reins for what might
possibly be a long ride, and had she lost her mind. That
had to be the reason that she was out following a bird.
But at this point, she'd follow an inchworm if she
thought it would lead her to the girls.

High above them, Hector continued to soar. Every so
often, he'd fly a distance ahead, then circle back until
he flew directly overhead again. Vivid swore he was
leading her. She periodically checked his position to
make certain they were proceeding in the direction he
seemed to want her to go, and listened to his impatient-

sounding calls. At one point, she shouted up to the sky, "I'm going as fast as I can."

The dogs, on the other hand, were as silent as assassins. Every few hundred yards, Blue, accompanied by two or three of the others, would peel away from the main party and, with noses down, sniff bases of trees and the leaf covered ground adjacent to the road. They'd investigate for a few moments and then, as if satisfied, head back and join the wagon. The only unconcerned animal in Vivid's party appeared to be Michigan. For the mule, it was just another drive.

Vivid had been stopping periodically to mark their trail by tying pieces of bandages to a roadside tree. If Nate was following he'd be able to find her.

They were traveling west, she thought. Her gloved hands were beginning to hurt from gripping the reins for the past hour. She dearly hoped they'd reach some type of destination soon because she didn't believe she'd be able to drive for much longer. She could now see the river flowing swiftly on her right. She'd only been to this wooded stretch of the Grove once, and at the time she'd been lost, so she had no idea where Hector would lead from here.

About a half-hour later, the bird flew off as had been his pattern. Vivid expected him to circle back as before but he kept going. When he was no longer in sight, she began to worry. The dogs seemed to be agitated by someone or something, too, so she pulled back on the reins and Michigan stopped. She sat a moment to listen. At first she heard only the rush of the river and the wind in the trees. Suddenly, the dogs bounded off into the brush, barking as they disappeared, and paying absolutely no heed to her shouted commands to return.

Filled with frustration, she knew she had to find the dogs, so she drove the wagon to a spot beside the road, tied the mule's reins to a small-trunked tree, and took off with the rifle in one hand and her bag in the other.

She set off walking in the direction the dogs had taken and could hear them barking in the distance somewhere ahead. The path through the thick underbrush had to be no wider than a dinner plate. She pushed aside bramble bushes and stepped over large tree roots, glad she had on her denims. Were she in a skirt, she would have spent the whole time untangling herself from the spiny fingers and thorns.

The path ended at the top of a ridge. Winded and tired, Vivid stopped a moment to gaze down at the rolling meadow below. The beautiful vista set against the wide blue ribbon of the river took her breath away, then her heart stopped at the distant sight of a child running across the meadow as if her life depended on it. Vivid stood too far away to accurately determine if it was Magic or Satin, but she was sure it was one of them. Vivid's elation died as she spotted a man, Cole, running hard to catch the child.

Vivid began to run down the ridge. The barking dogs were bounding swiftly in the child's direction and closing fast. However, Cole was certain to get to the child first.

Vivid stopped and brought the loaded rifle up to her shoulder, sighted, and fired. Although she was still too far away to hit her target, the rifle's crack would let him know the child was no longer alone. Vivid saw him halt immediately and quickly glance around as if trying to determine where the shot came from, but blessedly the child did not stop running. The dogs were almost within striking distance. He seemed to realize this also and ran to a shack among some trees near the riverbank. The door closed just as Maddie's dogs reached it.

The dogs circled the shack, their baying carrying on the wind. Vivid started running, calling to the child still sprinting across the meadow. Vivid watched her stop and look back. Upon seeing Vivid, she turned and ran toward her.

It was Satin. Vivid swept her up and held her tightly as they both cried.

"Are you hurt?" Vivid asked, moving her trained hands lightly over the dirty little face that looked so much like Magic's, and then over her thin shoulders and arms. Vivid was so glad to see her.

Satin shook her head and said excitedly, "He's got Magic tied up inside! We have to rescue her!"

"I know darling, and we will, but I need to know some things first. You said it's a man. Do you know him?"

"No. He said he's our cousin."

"Tell me what happened?"

Satin and Magic had been so intent with their play, they had forgotten about lunch, but Magic, ever the woodswoman, knew Maddie's apple trees still held the last of its fruit, so the girls went there to pick their lunch. While Hector hunted, the girls ate their apples and were about to head the mile and a half back home when they ran across Maddie, who was out gathering wood. Maddie offered to take them home since it would be dark very soon, but she had to unload the wood from the wagon first. Satin, for all her mimicking of her big sister's ways, still had a strong fear of Maddie's dogs, so Satin rode in the wagon with Maddie while Magic walked with the dogs.

When they arrived at Maddie's the girls volunteered to help unload the wood. Because of Satin's fear of the dogs, Maddie penned them up. Hector, seeing the dogs penned, decided it would be a perfect time to introduce the dogs to the game of "Duck!" Hector's lightning-fast dives into the pen made the dogs frantic, and because Magic could not make Hector stop, Maddie took pity on her poor animals and put them in the cellar.

Satin said, "After we put the wood on the porch, we were ready to come home, but I had to go to the privy and Magic did, too, so Maddie told us to go ahead, she

had to fetch a book out of the house for Aunt Gail. When
we came back around to the front of the house, Maddie
wasn't on the wagon, so . . .''

Satin's voice faltered. She looked into Vivid's eyes,
and Vivid saw the fear. Vivid gently pulled Satin into
her lap and held her tight. She kissed her brow and said
softly, "What happened next, Satin?"

There were tears running down Satin's cheeks. "Maddie wasn't on the wagon, like I said, so we went into
the house to find her. The man—he was stabbing at
Maddie with this big old knife and Maddie was screaming and trying to get away."

Satin's tears continued to flow. "We tried to help, but
he was too strong, he threw me and Magic off. Maddie
told us to run, but Magic wouldn't. She kept jumping
on his back. He snatched her around and slapped her
hard. I tried to run out the door but he grabbed me and
pushed me over by Magic. Magic was on the floor—
and she was so still—Aunt Viveca, I thought she was
dead."

She began to sob openly and Vivid whispered through
her own tears, "You girls were very brave, Satin, very
brave. Go on."

"Maddie was lying on the floor and there was all this
blood—then he shook Magic until she woke up and
made us go with him on Maddie's wagon. Hector tried
to help, but the man kept swinging the knife at him until
he flew away."

"How did you get away just now?"

"He was taking me to use the facilities behind the
shack and all of a sudden there was Hector. Aunt Viveca, I've never seen Hector play 'Duck!' so rough before. Hector clawed his shoulder the first time he flew
by and the man grabbed his shoulder and screamed.
When Hector circled the second time, he flew right by
his face and the man started waving his hands trying to
make Hector stop. Magic made me promise that if I

could get away I would. I didn't want to leave her, Aunt Viveca, but I ran. When I saw the dogs, I didn't even think about how scared they make me, I only wanted someone to help my sister.''

''Well, someone is here to help your sister. I'm going down there and I want you to stay here. If anything happens to me, my mule Michigan is back down on the road on the other side of this ridge. You high-tail it back and get your Uncle Nate.''

''But I can't drive, Aunt Viveca, and I wouldn't know which way to go.''

Vivid explained about the bandage ribbons and how, if Satin followed them, they would lead her back to Maddie's. Then Vivid added, ''Satin, you just escaped from a very dangerous man. Driving is very easy compared to that, believe me. Does the man have a gun?''

''All I've seen is that big knife.''

Vivid headed down the meadow. She didn't have a clue as to how she would free Magic, but she would give it a damned good try because at this point she was Magic's only hope.

Vivid approached the shack but halted a good distance away. She could see the dogs. They were no longer barking but were lying in positions around the front of the shack, effectively keeping their prey inside.

Vivid approached the ramshackle dwelling and called out to the man. Vivid searched the sky above for Hector but saw nothing but the gray clouds of late morning.

Then the door opened and Vivid raised the rifle. She could see him standing just inside the shadowy entrance. He was the same short squat man she'd seen with Quentin. Seeing his big arm circling Magic's neck and the big knife he had pointed at the girl's throat, Vivid tightened her jaw. Magic appeared to be maintaining a brave front. There was no evidence of tears in her eyes, just anger.

The dogs rose and began to growl at the sight of the

man. In response he quickly dragged Magic back inside the portal and yelled, "Call the dogs!"

"I think if you let her go, they'll leave you alone."

"Call them off, or I'll slit her throat."

"Then I'll shoot you," she called back easily. "Think about it. You have a knife and I have a gun. I also have the dogs. I possess all the cards. Let her go."

Vivid had no idea what he would do next; any man who'd stabbed Maddie so savagely probably had no qualms about slashing the throat of an innocent child. However, Mrs. Rand had stated that he needed at least one of the girls alive. Vivid could see no way out for Cole. His desperation must be making him act irrationally. Surely he didn't believe she'd simply let him walk away. Vivid and her sisters had been taught to shoot in order to protect themselves and their family. With times being the way they were, a woman of the race had to know how to use a gun and she had to know how to use it well. More importantly, if Magic came to harm it would break Nate's heart, and Vivid could not allow that.

Neither would Hector, it seemed. Hector appeared out of nowhere and he swooped down to rake his talons across Cole's face. Evan Cole screamed and Magic stumbled out of the doorway. She fell to the ground but picked herself up and ran to Vivid at full speed.

Then the dogs attacked.

They became snapping, leaping furies that surrounded him like dervishes. Cole tried to shut the door, but they were steadily herding him out into the open. No matter how much Vivid screamed at them or how many times she fired the rifle, the dogs refused to obey, so she sent Magic up the ridge to join her sister. She didn't want her viewing the awful scene.

While the main pack barked and circled and attacked his neck and arms, Blue sank his fangs into the fleshy part of Cole's calf and shook ferociously. Cole screamed and tried to clutch the injured limb only to have Blue tear into his hands. Out of the sky came Hector, his screech splitting the air. Cole somehow broke free of the dogs and tried to run. However, Blue's bite had crippled him, so all he could do was limp away as fast as his injuries and the dogs would allow.

From behind her Vivid heard the awed voice of Adam Crowley. "They're herding him and bringing him down, like a buck. Nate, look at that!"

Vivid spun and saw not only Adam, but Nate, Eli, her father, and many other men of the Grove spread out over the ridge behind her.

She smiled at Nate as he walked toward her carrying Satin in one arm and Magic in the other.

"Hello, princess," he said.

As some of the men ran down the hill to try and corral the dogs, Vivid looked into his eyes. "Hello yourself."

He bent to kiss her cheek and the movement caused both girls to dip, making them giggle. The happy sounds nearly brought tears to Vivid's eyes. She looked into their dirty little faces and asked. "Are you two sure you're okay?"

They both nodded, and Nate squeezed them until they giggled again. Vivid smiled at the girls who would soon be her daughters.

Eli's voice was filled with concern. "Nate, they're not having much luck calling off Maddie's dogs. Maybe we need to go down there."

The dogs and Hector had backed the severely crippled and bloodied Cole to the banks of the fast-flowing river and were so intent upon tormenting him, they were now lunging and baring their teeth at anyone who came near.

Nate set the girls on the ground and he and the men took off at a run.

They were too late.

"By the time we got down there," Nate later explained, "Hector and the dogs had driven him right over the bank and into the water."

Those who had not been there, including Abigail and Francesca, shook their heads sadly.

Nate continued, "Even if Cole knew how to swim he couldn't, because the muscles in his legs had been torn. Maddie's dogs are hunting dogs and they crippled him just as if he were a buck."

Vivid had checked on Maddie on the way home from the meadow and found her less feverish. While Nate penned and fed the dogs, Vivid evaluated and repacked the wound. The Quilt Ladies were sitting with Maddie for the night.

"How'd you know where to find us, Nate?"

"Hector. Damned bird was playing 'Duck!' when we gathered everybody for the search this morning. It must have been after he led you and the dogs. You said he disappeared for a while?"

Vivid nodded.

"Well, evidently he came to find me. Had us all ducking and crouching, but he kept hitting me and only me square in the back. Had my horse so spooked it was trying to duck with me on its back."

"So you followed him just as I did?"

"It was either that or grab him and stuff him into Aunt Gail's stewing pot. I thought the bird had gone insane."

Everyone laughed.

The discussion turned serious once more as they spent a few moments hashing over the tragic events. Nate was going to have his barrister try to find Cole's solicitors so they could be informed of Cole's death and the girls' whereabouts. Nate's barrister also said that he saw no reason why both girls couldn't become Graysons.

A few days later, Evan Cole's body washed ashore, about three miles downstream from where the animals forced him in.

Chapter 24

⌒ ⌒◯◯⌒ ⌒

They were finally able to hold the wedding on Thanksgiving day. In spite of the two inches of snowfall the night before, most of the Grove showed at the church to witness the ceremony. Because there'd been so much tragedy, folks were pleased to have something to celebrate. Eli and Adam stood up with Nate. Magic and Satin, dressed as beautifully as princesses from one of Nate's stories, stood up with the emerald-gowned Vivid, as did Maddie with the help of a cane.

Vivid looked over at her mother talking to Miss Edna and Adam Crowley's daughter, Jewel, as everyone enjoyed the reception sponsored by the church. In another week or so, her parents would be heading off to Boston to see her sister, Alicea. They'd stayed East longer than planned and so decided to remain on this side of the Rockies until the spring, rather than risk a harrowing train ride home through the snow-filled mountain passes of Colorado and Nevada. They'd spend the winter with Alicea and on the way home to California in the spring, they pledged to include another short visit to the Grove. Near her mother stood her father, talking with a group of men that included Adam Crowley and two of his sons. Vivid was already missing them both.

Vivid set aside her melancholy for the pleasure of watching Nate. He looked so incredibly handsome in his dark vested suit and snow-white shirt. During the ceremony, when he gazed down into her eyes and pledged

386

to love her until the last of his days, her love had known no bounds. In turn she pledged her love to him for all eternity. The resulting kiss had been one she'd been wanting to share for a long time—their first kiss as husband and wife—and it was even more wonderful than she'd dreamed.

Nate looked up from across the room and caught her eye. He excused himself from his cousin and a few friends, while she did the same with the Quilt Ladies.

Amid the crush, Nate leaned down to whisper in her ear, "I'd like to take you out of here."

She smiled up at him. "Well, we don't need Mama Duenna's permission anymore, so lead the way, my husband."

They departed the gathering under a hail of good wishes, congratulations, and applause.

When they got home, Nate led her to his big attic room and scooped her up to carry her across the threshold. He kissed her soundly, then set her gently on her feet.

"Will you tell me a bedtime story?" she asked.

Nate didn't answer at first, preferring to kiss her instead. When he finally released her it took her a moment to open her eyes, but she heard him whisper, "Have you been a good girl?"

Vivid answered with a provocative, "I can be . . ."

Nate felt his manhood come to life and harden. "Will you be this shameless when I'm sixty?"

She gave him a slow sultry smile and whispered, "Only when you make me."

Nate couldn't think of a better way to spend the next thirty years. "Take off that dress."

And when she did, he carried her over to his big bed and told her stories until dawn.

It snowed another four inches that night, and in the morning, Vivid had her first experience with snowshoes. She had quite a bit of trouble moving smoothly in the oversized contraptions, and as a result kept coming to an abrupt halt with one shoe atop the other and falling on her face. Magic and Satin were laughing so hard, Vivid thought the children would harm themselves. Nate, on the other hand, tried to be a bit more tactful and not laugh out loud, but as Vivid quickly toppled over once again, he surrendered and laughed until he cried.

That night, despite the coldness of the weather, Vivid stood outside and gazed up at the sky. The night was so clear, the stars stood out like diamonds on velvet. Who would have thought a skinny little Trabrasera from San Francisco would end up here, surrounded by new friends and new family? So much had happened since she first stepped off the train in Niles and met a man named Nate Grayson. She found it hard to believe it had been only six months ago. The peace of this place had seeped into her bones so deeply, it seemed as if she'd been sheltered in this community for years.

She heard the door open and turned to see Nate step out. He came to stand behind her and kiss her on the cheek. "What are you doing out here?" he asked.

"Counting my blessings."

"Do you have many?"

Vivid turned and looked up into his eyes and said lovingly, "More than there are stars in the sky."

"I love you, too," he told her.

She replied, "Well, if you really love me, you'll go inside and tell Mama she won't be naming the baby. I know she'll want to."

Nate went stock-still. "What baby?"

"Our baby." Then she added, "Oh, I forgot to tell you. You're going to be a papa."

"You forgot?"

She smiled. "No, I'm teasing. I wanted to tell you when we were alone."

"Does anyone else know?"

"No, just you. And if my calculations are correct, the baby is a result of all that berry picking we didn't do. She'll probably be born telling stories," Vivid added with a laugh. That night's story had been and still remained very memorable.

Later, as they lay in bed after a slow sweet bout of lovemaking, Nate asked, "What do you want to name our son?"

Vivid turned to peer into his face and said, "Daughter, Nate, daughter."

He chuckled. "Aunt Gail is the first and last female Grayson in four or five generations, so if you want to believe you're going to have a girl, go right ahead. How does Joseph Absalom sound?"

Vivid went very still. She thought the name was a beautiful tribute. "You're a very special man, Nathaniel Grayson."

"A very special man who fathers boys," he said kissing her. "Boys."

In May of 1877, Viveca Lancaster Grayson gave birth to five-pound Jacob Eli Grayson, and four-pound Joseph Absalom Grayson. Both parents were ecstatic with the double blessing.

Author's Note

D r. Viveca Lancaster is a fictional character created to highlight the remarkable achievements of nineteenth-century Black women like Maria W. Stewart and Mary Shadd who uplifted not only the race but the nation as well. Many of the Black women practicing medicine were not only the first Black women to practice medicine in some states but the first *female* physicians as well, especially in the South. Women were teachers, businesswomen, lecturers, and entertainers. Maggie Lena Walker was an insurance executive and one of the nation's first female bankers. Flora Batson Berger was known as the Black Jenny Lind.

For more information on these fascinating women, and other aspects of Vivid and Nate's story, the following sources may prove helpful:

Cimprich, John, and Mainfort, Robert C. Jr. "Fort Pillow Revisited: New Evidence about an Old Controversy." *Civil War History* 28 (1982): 292–306.

Fields, Harold B. "Free Negroes in Cass County Before the Civil War." *Michigan History*, 44 (December 1960): 375–383.

Giddings, Paula. *When and Where I Enter*. New York: William Morrow, 1984.

Jerrido, Margaret J. "Early Black Women Physicians." *Women & Health*, 5, no. 3 (Fall 1980).

Katz, William Loren. *The Black West.* New York: Anchor Press/Doubleday, 1973.

Lapp, Rudolph M. "The Negro in Gold Rush California." *Journal of Negro History*, 49, no. 2 (April 1964).

Sterling, Dorothy A. *We Are Your Sisters: Black Women in the Nineteenth Century.* New York: Doubleday, 1986.

Vennum, Thomas, Jr. *American Indian Lacrosse: Little Brother of War.* Washington, D.C.: Smithsonian Institution, 1994.

CPSIA information can be obtained
at www.ICGtesting.com
Printed in the USA
FSOW02n2015021017
39441FS